In Anne Bishop's
"By the Time the Witchblood Blooms,"
a witch plants the seeds of revenge.

William C. Dietz delivers corporate
mayhem in "A Family Affair."

You can't lie, mind to mind. Or can you?
Find out in Irene Radford's "The Divi."

The lords of heaven and hell
make a terrible bet in
Dennis L. McKiernan's "Perfidy."

—and 17 other tales of treacherous tirades
and backstabbing betrayals.

TREACHERY
AND
TREASON

Edited by
Laura Anne Gilman
and Jennifer Heddle

A ROC BOOK

ROC
Published by New American Library, a division of
Penguin Putnam Inc., 375 Hudson Street,
New York, New York 10014, U.S.A.
Penguin Books Ltd, 27 Wrights Lane, London W8 5TZ, England
Penguin Books Australia Ltd, Ringwood, Victoria, Australia
Penguin Books Canada Ltd, 10 Alcorn Avenue,
Toronto, Ontario, Canada M4V 3B2
Penguin Books (N.Z.) Ltd, 182–190 Wairau Road,
Auckland 10, New Zealand
Penguin Books Ltd, Registered Offices:
Harmondsworth, Middlesex, England

First published by Roc, an imprint of New American Library, a division of
Penguin Putnam Inc.

First Printing, March 2000
10 9 8 7 6 5 4 3 2 1

 REGISTERED TRADEMARK—MARCA REGISTRADA

Printed in the United States of America

PUBLISHER'S NOTE
This is a work of fiction. Names, characters, places and incidents either are the
product of the author's imagination or are used fictitiously, and any resemblance to
actual persons, living or dead, business establishments, events, or locales is entirely
coincidental.

Contents

Introduction

by
Laura Anne Gilman and Jennifer Heddle

Oh lord. Another anthology.

But wait. The theme, the ideas, the stories. . . .

Let's face it—we've all been there. Betrayed, stabbed in the back, rejected, done wrong, handed the short end of the stick or the raw end of the deal on a silver platter of disloyalty and lies.

Welcome to the human race. And, quite probably, every other race out there. It's in our nature, be it beastly or divine, to betray or be betrayed, to backstab and be surprised when others backstab us.

And it's also in our nature to feel devilish delight when we hear or read about it happening to others. Don't be ashamed—revel in it! And revel in this collection.

For within these pages, twenty-one of the most devious minds you wouldn't want to meet in a dark alley have spun wicked tales of deceit and betrayal, covering every angle from payback to payoff, from full frontal treason to the most subtle duplicity. So read up, and enjoy. Totally guilt-free.

But read it sitting with your back to the wall. Just in case. . . .

Where the Advantage Lies

by Yvonne Coats

They came for Mirabi in the middle of the year's longest night. No hint of trouble had disturbed her late-night meal, and her slumber had been deep and unbroken until her chamber door shattered and the harsh servant lights came on. The Guardians surrounded her before she could struggle free of the bedclothes, and she froze when one, a tall woman, gestured for her to remain still.

The woman said, "You are Milady Mirabi, daughter of the Lord Haddrax and the Lady Francesca."

There would be no point in denying she was Mirabi, so she nodded and sat up straight on the soft bed. She tried hard not to squint under the unfamiliar overhead lighting the staff used when they cleaned her rooms.

A male Guardian gathered up and tossed to Mirabi the clothing she had discarded on her way to bed. She reached for the pile, as the Guardian said, "You are to come with us, to aid in our investigation of crimes against the world of Stythia."

Mirabi clutched her wrinkled clothing and nodded again despite the fear flooding her rational mind. The Guardian spoke precisely the words her father had assured her they always used before taking enemies of Stythia into custody. She asked, "Why?"

"That will no doubt become clear to you in time."

This response also was exactly as her father had claimed it would be. She recognized the irony of finally employing his counsel only after she had killed him.

Her advocate, Ivar Quattro, came for her early the next morning. Mirabi felt sluggish because of lack of sleep and struggled for clarity of thought.

Quattro told her that she would remain in Remorden Keep during the investigation into her father's death. Other than giving simple directions, the Guardians had not spoken to her during the short flight and groundcar trip the night before.

Mirabi felt rumpled, unclean and hungry. The lack of a morning meal didn't trouble her; she was starved for information. She tugged at the security collar, which chafed her neck.

"Stop fidgeting, Milady," Quattro said. "The Judicar won't care how you look, but it's imperative that you control any nervous gestures."

He walked her briskly into Judgment Hall and sat with her at a huge table facing the Judicar's seat. The Judicar's assistant aimed his recorder at her collar and spoke softly into the device, confirming her arrival and taking control of the collar for the length of the hearing. His upper lip wrinkled in a transient sneer, and Mirabi saw that the assistant, at least, had noticed how she looked.

She turned toward the galleries and caught a glimpse of her mother before the collar compelled her to face the Judicar's seat. Her mother wore a familiar dark gray gown and the dense black veil she had put on in public for the past week.

A sudden flurry of activity swept through the Hall as the Judicar entered. Mirabi knew the Judicar was a noble—all the Judicars were—as she knew Quattro was a common man because he was an advocate.

The Judicar was blunt: "Milady Mirabi, your father was poisoned yestereve, at a meal he shared with you."

Mirabi sat very still and thought about what she should say.

"You killed him—" She started to object but the Judicar raised his hand, palm out, and continued. "Do not bother to deny it. We have evidence that you killed him. The purpose of this hearing is to discover your motives."

"What evidence—" Mirabi began, startled to hear her voice so faint.

"Do not prate about evidence, Milady! We are here to discover your reasons, not to dispute the evidence."

Mirabi looked to her advocate, who made an impatient rolling gesture with his right hand, motioning her to answer the Judicar's question.

"Lord Judicar, my reasons are personal. Must they be heard in open court?" Mirabi waved her hand to indicate the galleries above and the professionals' benches behind her. She didn't want any distractions when she spoke to the Judicar.

The Judicar frowned, then ordered the hall cleared. Mirabi heard her mother's voice, but couldn't make out what she said as the Hall emptied.

"You may begin," the Judicar said in a quiet voice. "Speak your reasons plainly and fully, Milady. Speak as though your life depended on it, because it does."

"Lord Judicar," she said, "I don't remember when I first thought about killing my father. It might have been the thousandth time he asked me, 'Where does the Advantage lie?' Whatever I did, whatever I wanted to do, Father cared only about the Advantage it would give him, or me." She saw a fleeting puzzled look on the Judicar's face before he regained his customary impassivity.

"He used implants to control his servants," she continued. "They had no will and little vitality. Watching Father with them was terrible. Sometimes he threatened me with implants—"

"Surely you knew this was not possible," the Judicar said. "Don't you know that nobles cannot be implanted?"

"I did wonder sometimes because whenever I got upset Father laughed and called me a little fool. 'Little fool, easy to fool,' he often said. He never struck me as he did my mother, but in my father's house I saw a hundred, a thousand cruelties, Lord Judicar."

There was silence while Mirabi drank from a tall glass of cool water, soothing her dry throat.

"Please, sir, ask my mother to witness for me," Mirabi requested. "She knows my father's cruelties far better than I."

"You want your mother here, Milady?" The Judicar's expression of intense, shrewd interest gave Mirabi hope that he understood her.

"With all my heart."

"That's a strange expression," the Judicar said. "What does it mean?"

"It's one of my mother's sayings, sir. Isn't it a common one?"

"When did she say this thing to you?"

Mirabi smiled. "Oh, sir, too often for me to pick out a single instance easily."

"Try."

The coldness of the Judicar's voice froze her smile. "Yes. Well . . . she said it when we talked of men I might marry. 'With all my heart, I hope *your* marriage is a happy one,' I remember her saying. My mother often wishes me well, or wishes me love and happiness, and that sort of thing."

"Love and happiness," the Judicar repeated, then grew silent.

"Mirabi," he finally said, "tell me about your mother's house, about how she lives, how she treats her servants."

"I don't know how to begin, sir." Mirabi organized her thoughts as quickly as she could. "I told you that Father's servants were silent and expressionless. It took me a long time to see how much they feared him. But Mother's servants were happy to belong to her. She gave them good clothes and good food, sometimes even a little money to buy treats. There was always singing in her house, and everyone hugged me when I visited and wanted to know how I felt and what I wanted to do."

"So you . . . liked your mother but not your father," the Judicar said slowly.

"Yes."

"I understand your . . . feelings, Milady." The Judicar appeared to be searching for words Mirabi would understand. "But I have yet to hear why you poisoned your father."

"Lord Judicar, did you see my mother in the gallery? She was wearing a veil."

"I saw her."

"It conceals a deep scar on her right cheek. Father cut her last week, through the muscles and into the cheekbone."

"Did you see the attack?" the Judicar asked.

Mirabi shook her head. "He never touched Mother when I was there, but I remember her having bruises from the time I was a tiny girl. She always cautioned me to beware of Father's temper, and I never gave him a reason to strike me. Mother said that Father might not love her but might learn to love me.

"When I was older she tried to hide the bruises, but I always knew when she was hurt. Many times she winced when I hugged her, and I knew that Father had beaten her again."

When she finished Mirabi thought the Judicar looked sad.

"Quattro," the Judicar said, and her advocate stood. "Take her back to Remorden Keep. Bring her back tomorrow morning, to the earliest session."

Quattro bowed deeply to the Judicar, then waved to the assistant to release Mirabi's security collar to his custody. He responded to none of her questions as they returned to the keep, but when her cell door shut behind them, he asked, "Do you understand what's going on, Milady?"

"Of course," she said. "I'm less than a year away from my majority."

"I beg your pardon, Milady, but please tell me what you understand about the inquiry." Quattro's mouth was firm, but his eyes squinted slightly.

"I'm being held because I poisoned my father," she said, speaking carefully and stating only the obvious. "The Judicar wants to know why I did it so he can determine my punishment. Do you think he feels sorry for me? I think he wants to help me."

Quattro nodded, but she didn't think it meant he agreed with her.

She asked nervously, "Do you think it will help if he understands how awful Father really was? He beat his servants. He set me to spy on Mother, and beat her, too. He only cared about me because he thought I was his possession."

Quattro seemed not to know what to say for a moment. Sighing, he finally said, "Just answer the Judicar's questions. He will know what to do."

"Aren't you my advocate? Aren't you supposed to advise me?"

"I am. I have."

" 'Let the Judicar decide' seems to be all your advice."

"Milady, I admit that this inquiry treads ground unfamiliar to me. We must rely on the Judicar's experience to see us through."

She frowned. She was anxious but feared to reveal too much, even to Quattro. "Do you think he will be fair? Will he see that I had to help my mother?" Quattro didn't seem to understand, so she asked the question another way: "Will he be just?"

"Just," Quattro said faintly, then added more firmly, "If anyone knows how to be fair or just, it is a Lord Judicar." He bowed and left her to pace her cell, trying to figure all that might happen the next morning.

Quattro did not come for her. The Judicar's assistant came instead, and his manner was much changed. Today he was polite and quiet, as if she were an elderly relation placed in his temporary care. Mirabi had to remind him to reset her security collar for the short trip to Judgment Hall—she couldn't have left the keep otherwise—and he thanked her for doing so.

When the assistant opened the door to the Hall, Mirabi heard the Judicar's and Quattro's voices raised in argument. She heard one sentence clearly: "What in the Nine Worlds are we going to do with her?"

She hadn't realized the Judicar and her advocate were going to work out the details of her disposition. Their guilty looks when she entered the Hall made it look as if there had been a breach of protocol. This was better than she'd hoped.

Quattro nodded to the Judicar's assistant and took his place beside Mirabi at the advocate's table.

"What were you arguing about?" she asked.

He waved his hand to dismiss her question. "Pay attention to what I have to tell you, Mira—Milady. Your mother is called to appear before the Judicar this morning."

"That's wonderful, Quattro. How did you get the Judicar to agree?"

"It was his idea," Quattro muttered. "You won't be able to speak to her; they're drawing down the shield silencer now."

Mirabi saw a shimmer cutting across the Hall just in front of their table. "Why?" She hadn't anticipated this but tried not to be alarmed.

"You'll be able to hear the Judicar's questions, and her answers." Quattro was frowning. "I wasn't sure you should be here at all."

"But it's my trial."

"No, it's not; it's an *inquiry*, which is very different from a trial. When the chain of events is clear, as in this case— your father's autorecorder caught you poisoning his wine but wasn't set to alert him—the Judicar makes final, indisputable disposition. In a trial the defendant has the right of appeal."

This frightened Mirabi more than anything else she'd heard in Judgment Hall. If she'd misinterpreted the Judicar's intentions, she would have no way to appeal. "Will it be over today?" she asked nervously.

"Probably." She was sure the look on her advocate's face was pity, a commoner pitying a noble. She felt a shiver of relief.

Before she could ask another question the Judicar's assistant rose, and Mirabi's mother walked to a chair in front of the Judicar. She did not look in Mirabi's direction.

"Lady Francesca," the Judicar began, "you are called to assist in this inquiry."

"Yes." Her mother's voice was quiet and assured.

"Your daughter, Milady Mirabi, placed poison in her father's cup two nights ago. She has not revealed where she got the poison, but otherwise we believe we understand the circumstances governing her deeds."

"I am here to help you, Lord Judicar." Mirabi marveled at her mother's composure. "My daughter doubtless concocted the poison herself; she is an accomplished amateur chemist with a keen interest in off-planet science."

Mirabi knew her mother was aware of her interest in science and the discoveries made on other human-settled worlds. But her mother also knew Mirabi had no way to make poisons.

There had been no need to make any poison, or even to find one, because she had one ready-made in the rare candle essence her mother had given her for her fifteenth birthday. Lady Francesca had cautioned Mirabi a dozen times to be careful with the essence, which was harmless when burned but deadly in liquid form.

Mirabi wished she'd told the Judicar about the candle essence, but the shimmer of the shield reminded her it was too late now.

The Judicar regarded Lady Francesca for a moment, then asked, "Wherein was the Advantage to Milady Mirabi? Why should she kill Lord Haddrax, her father?"

Francesca's answer was quick. "Mirabi was always a strangely emotional child, fascinated by the Nine Worlds and their inferior, sentimental ways. Many times I caught her with offworld romances and other types of questionable literature, but no matter how I punished her, Mirabi was determined to learn more. When still quite young, she conceived a . . . well, a 'passion' for becoming a diplomat. Her father refused to allow her to apply to the diplomatic school. Mirabi was wild to attend, but only commoners go there, of course. In any case, Mirabi was always too volatile a personality to interact freely with others, her peers or even commoners. There was no Advantage to placing her there."

"No Advantage to Lord Haddrax?"

"No Advantage to anyone, not even Mirabi. She disagreed, of course." Francesca turned her head slightly toward Mirabi, then faced the Judicar once more. "I didn't suspect how strongly," she added softly.

"It's not true," Mirabi said as she turned to Quattro. "I didn't do it for myself; I did it for *her*. I didn't want Father to hurt her anymore, so I stopped him. I used the candle essence she gave me, the one she said was poison."

Quattro passed his handkerchief to Mirabi, though her eyes were dry, and pressed one of the inserts on his side of the table. "Did you hear that?" Mirabi realized that the Judicar had been listening after all. Excellent.

The Judicar nodded as he pressed a hand to his right ear, his expression grim.

"Lady Francesca," he said, "please remove your veil."

Without hesitating, she did so.

"Please turn to face the advocate's table."

Quattro gasped when he saw her mother's smooth, unblemished face, so Mirabi frowned and grabbed his arm.

"Where are your scars, Lady Francesca?" the Judicar asked.

"Scars?" Her mother's voice sounded coolly puzzled as she half turned to the Judicar.

"Your daughter told us yesterday you wear the veil to cover facial scars."

Mirabi saw a slight smile on her mother's lush lips. "Lord Judicar, as you see I am not scarred. My daughter always indulged in vivid fantasies as a child, but I had no idea they would take such a disAdvantageous shape as she grew."

The Judicar frowned. "I am curious why you started wearing a veil if you had nothing to hide."

"I hoped to start a little fashion for them, nothing more."

"I see." The Judge signaled for the shield silencer to be dropped. "Milady Mirabi, I ask you once again why you poisoned your father." Her mother took a step toward her. "Remain where you are, Lady Francesca, and *say nothing*!"

The Judicar's assistant aimed his court pistol at Mirabi's mother, ready to stop her if she disobeyed.

"Mirabi," the Judicar said again. "Why did you poison Lord Haddrax?"

Letting her tears flow freely, Mirabi said, "I thought he hated her, and he despised me. But I did it for you, Mother, because he hurt you. You know I did. You know I did."

The Judicar's voice was loud: "Lady Francesca, I arrest you for the offense of suborning a minor for your own sole Advantage. Had your husband died but one year cycle later, Mirabi would have inherited by law. I cede your husband's entire estate to his minor child. Your trial will be set for the earliest possible date and, should you be convicted, your entire estate shall be forfeit to your minor child, for her solace and support."

The great Hall was silent for a breath. Mirabi watched as the Judicar's assistant placed a security collar around her mother's neck.

Meeting the Judicar's eyes squarely, Lady Francesca said, "I am confident I will be found blameless, Lord Judicar." Without even a glance in Mirabi's direction, she left the Hall under guard.

Quattro touched Mirabi's shoulder tentatively, and she grabbed his hand and held it tightly. She was touching a commoner, a free man rather than one of her parents' servants, but holding his hand made her nervousness diminish and his increase. She knew he was firmly on her side now.

"What do I do?" Mirabi touched the security collar she still wore. Quattro caught the assistant's attention and pointed at Mirabi's collar. The assistant focused his recorder and released her. Mirabi held the collar in her hands for a moment, then placed it on the table and stood up.

The Judicar said, "You're no longer part of this inquiry, but I must give some thought to your welfare."

"I'll reach my majority in less than a year." She suggested the simplest solution: giving her the unrestricted freedom of a noble.

"Quattro, take Mirabi to quarters here in the Hall and see if you can make things clear to her."

Mirabi marked uneasily that the Judicar avoided using her title. Quattro shifted from foot to foot as he waited for her to walk with him.

In her new, comfortable suite, they sat like equals. Quattro said, "Mirabi, you don't belong among the nobility. The values your mother taught you—loyalty and duty and love—would be no Advantage to you in Stythic society." Mirabi showed him a confused expression.

"Your father was not cruel," Quattro explained. "At least, no more cruel than Stythic law permits. Commoners who have regular contact with Stythic nobles or with humans from the Nine Worlds always have implants. Servants have strong controls built into their implants, while representatives and traders to the Nine Worlds have light ones—primarily the unbreakable impulse to return to Stythia at regular intervals—but implants are a necessity of doing business with or for the nobility."

"Do *you* have an implant?" She knew the answer but wanted time to think.

"Yes."

"What does it do?"

"It allows any Judicar to immobilize me, in his presence, should it prove necessary."

"Does it bother you?"

"Not as long as I give the Judicars no reason to use it."

Mirabi wanted to question Quattro further but didn't dare show too much interest.

"Mirabi, the only reason you are free is because the Judicar determined your actions were not the result of insanity. Your mother manipulated you very carefully. She taught you concepts such as good and evil, which are not valid on Stythia."

"But what will happen to me now?"

Unwillingly, it seemed, Quattro said, "It remains to be seen how, or if, you might be turned to Advantage. A little sentiment in a commoner is tolerated, but the nobility can afford none."

Mirabi looked out the port by her seat and watched Stythia grow steadily smaller. Her parents' holdings had been sold, and she left Stythia as a very wealthy exile. Pretending regret at leaving her homeworld had been the hardest part of her plan.

She smiled contentedly, finally able to savor her escape from the planet of her birth, the world no born noble was ever allowed to leave.

In her hurry to leave the planet, Mirabi almost missed the news of her mother's execution. On Stythia, suborning a minor noble to act against her own Advantage was a far greater crime than murder. The Judicar had suggested she not attend the trial unless called as a witness—she hadn't been—and he forbade her to visit her mother after sentencing. This suited Mirabi; she and her mother had nothing further to say to one another.

Smiling even more broadly, she reflected that her own growing adult awareness had been the real flaw in her mother's plan to acquire her husband's estate.

Her mother's gift of the rare candle essence had alerted Mirabi to her mother's hidden intentions. Each additional warning about its dangerous nature had revealed her mother's plan more fully. Once she understood it completely, Mirabi—a true Stythic, whatever the Judicar and Quattro believed—considered where her own Advantage lay, and acted accordingly.

Mirabi burned with the need to meet humans from the Nine Worlds, many of whom believed in loyalty, honor, trust, and love. Innocents all, compared to Stythics. She suspected that there would be much out there she could turn to her Advantage.

Miranda's Muse

by Esther M. Friesner

"That lousy, no-good, thoughtless, selfish, son of a *bitch*! What do you mean, do I want to see him again?"

The last survivor of Miranda Ford's porcelain snuffbox collection crashed against the rough-hewn stones of the fireplace adorning her home-away-from-home in the Berkshires. She was one of those handsome, highbred women who wore rage as a particularly flattering accessory. With her ice blond hair yanked tightly into a bun, her facial skin pulled tautly into her third "lift," and her tall body crammed tensely into a spandex ski outfit, she looked ready to rupture in several directions at any minute. The dull glass eyes of a Politically Incorrect deer head gazed down upon the devastation she was wreaking, matched by the slightly less lifelike gaze of her literary agent, Billy Samson. It was the first time he'd ever been asked to spend the weekend at Eagle's Aerie (as Miranda had dubbed her rural retreat), supposedly a social *coup-des-coups*. Now here it was, only Friday evening, and already he was envying that dead deer.

"Last time I ever do anything nice for a client," he muttered into his empty shot glass. "Not for a lousy fifteen percent, anyway."

Through a haze of alcohol, he recalled his naive eagerness to combine a nice, relaxing weekend in the mountains with a *primo* ass-kissing op. Miranda Ford was in the same league as Stephen King, Tom Clancy, and Danielle Steel: a person who had become a Franchise. When it came to something so mundane as an actual job of writing, they could all still hit 'em out of the park, but it no longer really mattered. As far as their readers (and publishers) were concerned, all they had to do was show up at bat and look pretty in the uniform.

Miranda's specialty was Women's Books, four-to-five-hundred-page escape hatches for the modern miss-ms.-or mrs. stuck between a glass ceiling and a soccer car pool. Oh, it had been a happy day indeed at the Monk & Pagan Literary Agency when the divinely profitable Ms. Ford had dropped her old representation and come on board. Billy could still recall how his own vague good-team-player joy had bloated into total ecstasy when senior partner Leola Pagan told him that *he* would be the one handling the Ford account.

So he took the assignment. It looked like a plum; how was he supposed to know it would bite like a piranha? It was only after he brushed the stars from his eyes and began studying Miranda's accounts up close and personal that he realized this: The woman had problems. No, better make that Problems. And now they were *his* Problems, too.

For what felt like the seventeenth time that evening, he attempted to make Miranda understand just what it was he was offering to do for her: "Ms. Ford, we at Monk & Pagan know that things haven't been easy for you since your husband died—"

This time Miranda interrupted him by pitching a paperweight. It was a small *objet d'aggression*, but it was made of bronze, and she chose to fling it through the picture window. Glass exploded outward, followed by a reciprocal draft of bitterly cold mountain air.

"Don't you talk to me about that motherless, gutless, dickless bastard," she shouted. "He knew what he was doing, chapter and verse. How *dared* he! Do you know how damned *embarrassing* it is, always having to explain darling Alan's last little self-indulgent antic to every fucking busybody in the business? First they're *soooo* sorry he's dead, then they get that constipated-collie look in their eyes and whisper, 'I heard how he died, dear.' Well, of *course* you heard how he died, you asshole! It was all over the media. And why all that idiotic *whispering*? It's no secret that that worthless piece of eelshit did himself in. It'd be bad enough if that was where the conversation ended, but it never is. *Then* they have to move in closer, and clutch my hand, and run through the same set of asinine questions: Why do I think he did it? Did I ever suspect it was going to happen? Have I considered the possibility that my success made him doubt his manhood? Do I know how difficult it is for any normal man—especially one as sensitive and highly educated as *poor* Alan—to live with the fact that his wife is not only the chief breadwinner but that she also makes enough to support *three* Ivy League spouses, including the limp-dick Eli she married?"

"Now, Ms. Ford—" Billy began, doing his best to get the words out through chattering teeth. Miranda's wrath was keeping her warm, but he was freezing. He staggered across the room and did his fumbling best to close the drapes over the broken window.

Miranda raised not a finger to aid him. "But *that's* not where they leave it either," she went on. "There's still one final word of 'comfort' they want to dump in my lap, and you know what it is? It's telling me that I shouldn't feel *guilty* about the fact that Alan took one last, long bubble bath with a tub full of blood for a chaser. Slitting his wrists, how classic! With a carving knife, the scum. At least if he'd had the courtesy to use a razor, I might've been able to claim he was shaving his palms and it slipped. Guns go off by accident when you're cleaning them, pill bottles can get mixed up *so* easily when you're in a hurry, electrical appliances are nothing but a bunch of warrantied fatal mishaps waiting to happen, people fall out of high windows all the time without really meaning to, and they can unintentionally stab themselves to death with knives in every other room of the house *except* the bathroom. But not him; not Alan. Well, I'll tell you something, Mr. Samson—"

"Billy, please."

"Shut up. I'm talking. I'll tell you that I *don't* feel guilty. I'm too pissed off to feel guilty. And now you ask me if I'd like to see him alive again? Oh, don't I wish! Only not for the reasons you think: I don't want to tell him I'm sorry I ignored him, or outdid him, or that my career ran roughshod over his, or that most of the English-speaking world thinks his last name was Ford, too. I just want him here so I can kick his skinny ass all the way to New Haven and back. How do you like *that*?" She ended with a triumphant, shark-toothed smile.

"I'm sorry," he told her, "but that's *not* what I asked you."

Miranda was not a woman used to being contradicted. Surprise actually rendered her speechless for a moment, then she recovered, and said, "Look, dickybird, I may have been at Woodstock while you were in didies, but I *didn't* stand too close to the speakers, and I am *not* deaf. You asked me whether I wanted—"

"—to see your husband again. Not to see him *alive* again."

"Well, *yuck!*" Miranda made the appropriate face. "Why the hell would you want to suggest something like that? I'm a novelist, not a fucking poet; I don't get my rocks off staring at dead things."

"We know how you get—*got* your inspiration, Ms. Ford," Billy persevered. "Your publisher made it quite clear in the letter of complaint."

"Complaint?" Miranda echoed. "What do those bloodsuckers have to complain about?"

"Merely the fact that you still haven't turned in the book you owe them, the one that's the first deal *our* agency negotiated for you. It's er, more than a bit overdue."

"Overdue? They *invented* overdue! They can take their reserves against returns policy and shove it up their corporate ass! My books make them more money than the bastards know what to do with!"

"Yes," Billy agreed. "*After* you write them."

Miranda gave him a look fit to turn basalt to butter. "Look, I've been blocked, okay?" she snarled. "I've been going through a very rough time of it, emotionally, ever since Alan died. You people have no hearts."

"But you just said that you didn't feel guilty that—"

"Don't pick on me, goddammit!" Miranda yelled in his face. "I'm a grieving widow! Drop dead!"

Billy sighed and cursed the day he'd made himself unfit for decent employment by majoring in American Studies. Miranda was *not* cooperating; she wasn't even listening, not really. He recalled the old joke about the camel's testicles and the two bricks, the punch line of which was: "First you've got to get their attention." He resolved to apply this wisdom forthwith.

"Lady," he said, "cut the crap."

"*What* did you say to me, you little toad? I can get you fired faster than—"

"No, Ms. Ford, you can *not*." The gin was gone, and it had taken Billy's sense of self-preservation with it for a souvenir. He felt he had nothing more to lose. "I'd quit first, just to cheat you out of the satisfaction."

"Just like Alan," she grumbled. "Don't tell me you went to fucking Yale, too."

"As a matter of fact, I did. However, we're not here to discuss my failings, but yours."

"What failings? Aside from marrying Alan Mountroyal Stewart."

"That was no failing. That was the making of you. Do you know why your books sell, Ms. Ford? It's not because of the beautiful, blond, big-boobed heroines, or their glamours careers, their gorgeous homes, their take-no-prisoners shopping safaris, or their tireless, tiresome lovers. *Those* are all just as readily available in a score of generic romance novels. No, Ms. Ford, what makes *your* books shake off the dust of the herd are their *villains*. Or should I say *villain*, singular? Because there's only one, really, and I think we both know who I mean." Billy's hand shot up just in time to intercept and disarm Miranda's slap. "I wouldn't advise striking me, Ms. Ford. I'll endure your temper tantrums and your hissy fits, but I warn you, I will *not* stand for that."

Miranda jerked her arm free of his grip and glared daggers. "Then get out of here."

"Not until I've had my say. *And* a pot of coffee. I'm not getting myself killed on those roads at this hour with this much gin in me."

"Then make some." She threw herself into one of the green Italian leather armchairs near the hearth, crossed her arms, and buried herself in a sulk.

Billy Samson sucked air in through tightly clenched teeth, and told the stuffed deer head, "I really hoped I wasn't going to have to do it this way." Then he reached into the pocket of his corduroy trousers, took out one of

Leola Pagan's most lovingly crafted dollies, and gave it a short, sharp, upward jerk.

Miranda Ford leaped out of her chair and hit the floor, eyes and mouth wide in astonishment. "How—? What—?" she gasped.

Billy offered her his free hand, which she disdained, so he hooked it under her elbow and hauled her to her feet anyhow. "I'm sorry if that was a little rough," he said. "Poppets aren't my specialty; it's just a loaner. Now if you'll be kind enough to make that coffee for me, I can sober up enough to carry on a rational conversation from which both of us will benefit."

"I do *not* make coffee for *men*," Miranda sniped, brushing off the place on her arm which Billy had had the effrontery to touch.

"It's a free country." Billy shrugged. "Want to see what happens when I throw the doll out the window?"

Shortly thereafter, Billy Samson was downing what was possibly the worst cup of caffeinated consciousness he had ever drunk in his life, and that included the swill they served under the alias of "coffee" at Yale. Miranda sat across the sleek oak farmhouse table from him, eyeing him askance and taking guarded sips from her own cup.

"A necromancer, you say," she repeated. "Is that how you made me fall out of my chair? By using your dark and evil powers?"

"No, I told you that was the doll, which is Leola's—I mean Ms. Pagan's handiwork. She likes to describe herself as an all-purpose witch with a personal fondness for ethnic enchantments such as voodoo. Then there are my two fellow agents, Gaylord and Roswell—fairly adept sorcerers, the pair of them. Mr. Monk is a full-fledged magus with a minor talent for augury, and our secretary is coming along nicely with her alchemical studies, but at present I am the only necromancer on the staff of Monk & Pagan." Seeing her slightly mystified expression, he explained, "I'm the only one who knows how to raise the dead."

"Out," said Miranda. For some reason, she pointed dramatically at the refrigerator. The poor woman was understandably upset.

"Not yet," Billy replied. "I've had to sit in this house and listen to you rail against your late husband for hours. Now it's your turn to listen to me."

"Listen to what?" Miranda challenged. "To you explaining why no one at Monk & Pagan told me that I was signing on with a nest of necromancers?"

"Ms. Ford, please," Billy said softly and slowly. "There are very real, very important differences between practitioners of necromancy, such as myself, and the other staff at—"

"Oh, never mind, I don't need to bother listening to you after all, I know what you want to tell me. You mentioned it before, didn't you? I didn't get it, then, but I do now, and I've got your answer: No. No, sir; no, thank you; no fucking way do I *ever* want to see my husband again, alive *or* dead. Even if you can raise the dead—which you'll forgive me if I doubt *just* a smidge—what the hell use would Alan be to me as a goddamn zombie?"

Billy set down his cup and steepled his fingertips. "I don't *do* zombies," he explained with rapidly dwindling patience. "Ms. Pagan would kill me for poaching on her turf. As to your doubts concerning my abilities, they're easily proved or laid out in lavender just as soon as you can take me to Mr. Stewart's gravesite and—"

"You must be out of your mind," said Miranda.

"I must be out of my mind," said Miranda. It was three days later and as rainy a Monday evening as ever made loyal New Yorkers wish for an ass to kick; no one's ass in particular, just a handy set of buttocks suitably sized to present a decent target. She stood at Alan's graveside holding an umbrella over a very fussy Billy Samson.

The agent pulled up the collar of his London Fog raincoat and curtly told her to stop fidgeting and hold the umbrella *properly* before the rain extinguished the brazier. "Otherwise, we'll have to start all over again, and we can't; that was my last black rooster, and I'm not driving all the way out to Pachogue to get another one in this weather."

"If you don't like how I'm holding it, do it yourself," she snapped. "And hurry up! My feet are soaked."

"It's your own fault; you could've had him laid away in a nice, dry mausoleum. It's not like you couldn't afford it." Billy took something small, brown, and wrinkled out of his raincoat pocket and dropped it into the travel-sized bronze tripod between his feet where incense smoked and glowed fitfully. The brown object sent up a great spurt of sparks and a nasty stench when it hit the embers. Miranda gave an involuntary exclamation of disgust and pinched her nose shut, but she held the umbrella steady.

"This *stinks*," she gritted.

"Unavoidable," Billy replied, adding another fetid morsel to the brazier.

"I don't mean *this*." She nodded at the tripod, the mystic symbols Billy had traced in white sand atop Alan's grave, and the remains of the unlucky rooster. "I mean the fact that you were right: I *do* need him. I thought about it all the way back from the mountains. I told myself that his death is *not* the reason I've been blocked, that there must be *hundreds* of other men in this world who are just as horrible and petty and mean-spirited as Alan was, men I could turn into my next set of villains one-two-three, easy as pie." Her shoulders slumped. "Then I woke up and smelled the formaldehyde. No man alive is a tenth the rat that Alan was. Oh, he was good! I could watch him for hours, the same way some people watch nature films where a python slowly swallows a cute little piglet, whole. My books are his biography in installments. Do you want to know how he treated his mother? Check out Dirk Delano in *Wild Winds*."

"Your first book, wasn't it?" Billy remarked rather absently. He was staring into the smoking depths of the brazier with the intensity of a cat minding a mouse hole.

Miranda nodded. "Dirk was the soul of that book—a black, slimy, ugly soul, but that's why you couldn't keep copies on the shelves. Everyone who read it couldn't wait to see that bastard get what was coming to him. But Dirk was only the first of many. Alan's sister went through a messy divorce, and he was right there for her . . . in public. When it was just *en famille* you should've heard him! Remember the scene in *The Keepsake* where Ramsey Porter tells *his* sister that she's a fool to divorce a millionaire over a teensy thing like a lifetime of abuse?"

"Mmmm." Billy made some bizarre gestures, wiggling his fingers through the smoke. It wreathed itself into the misty outline of a bat with wings outspread before wafting away to be snuffed out entirely by the rain. "Yes, I recall it, but I have to say that what I liked better was the part where Ramsey gave false testimony at the closed custody hearing and had that poor woman declared an unfit mother. You couldn't tell whether he was brown-nosing that wretched brother-in-law of his for fun or profit—very nice touch on your part, quite original."

"Who said it was original?" Miranda spoke without a trace of irony. "Alan transgressed, I transcribed. It was all I ever did or ever *had* to do."

"Oh, surely not."

"Well, once in a while I had to leave out Alan's more atrocious escapades. I never *could* use the incident that happened after his cousin came out—and I don't mean as a debutante. There was darling Alan, telling all our friends about how courageous he thought she was. And *there* was darling Alan cornering her in our bedroom, telling her that she only *thought* she was a lesbian because she'd never had a real man, a lack which he was prepared to supply then and there. I finally burst in and put a stop to it when I realized he wasn't going to take no for an answer from that poor girl. I'd show you the memento he gave me for being a 'damn frigid busybody,' but it's too late now." She touched her cheek tenderly, and with a rueful smile said: "Dr. Kiley is an excellent plastic surgeon."

Billy crossed his arms. "You know, we don't *have* to bring him back. You could find a new source of inspiration, or try writing a different sort of book for a change. He sounds like the biggest world-class shit of all time. There are some things even an agent hesitates to do."

"Oh, go ahead, follow through; it's a shame to waste a good rooster. Besides, I'm too lazy to go genre-hopping at this late date, and I *do* want to keep my career alive."

Billy nodded, uncrossed his arms, and rattled through some more broken Latin before glancing back at her and adding; "Even if it means giving part of *your* life to keep *him* alive—sort of—as well?"

Miranda frowned. "Just what, exactly, do you mean by that, Mr. Sams—?"

The ground beneath her feet lurched, trembled, and belched as a narrow crack snaked open across Alan's grave. She yelped with alarm and stumbled against Billy's shoulder. The umbrella tilted at a crazy angle, and rainwater flooded the brazier, extinguishing the contents in a pathetically small exhalation of smoke.

"Too late for explanations," Billy gasped, seizing Miranda's arm with one hand and materializing a small utilitarian dagger with the other. "I should've given you the details before we started, but you didn't believe I could do this anyway, and my feelings were hurt, and Ms. Pagan said that your comeback could be the biggest thing since V.C. Andrews got trademarked, and—Oh, forget about it. My bad." With that, he slashed downward with the dagger, slitting the fleshy part of her palm just at the base of the thumb, at the same time chanting, "Mound of Venus, hear my prayer: Bring him back from Over There. Gooooo, *undead*!"

Miranda screamed. Blood trickled over the dagger, down the length of the blade, and dripped into the riven grave. The earth groaned and tore itself apart along the dotted line. Fire liberally scented with sulfur roared from the chasm, painting the faces of author and agent scarlet and gold.

And then it was over. Alan was there.

"Yum," he said, licking his lips. There was still a spot or two of Miranda's blood clinging to the corners of his mouth. "Smashing little aperitif. Not an acquired taste at all, and *nothing* like chicken. What's for afters?" He eyed her expectantly.

"Oh, no." Miranda backed off, her index fingers in a shaky, makeshift cross. "No, you don't. Not me, not my blood, no way."

"Why not, love?" Alan Mountroyal Stewart plucked the precisely folded handkerchief from the breast pocket of his Brooks Brothers burial suit and gestured with it languidly. "Turnabout is fair play. You drank *my* blood for years." He smiled, and his fangs glittered. They looked more than natural on him, the perfect accessory. Tall and thin, with raven hair and shockingly blue eyes above cheekbones sharp as a bad review, he was a man who had finally found his proper niche in life. Or death.

"I'm afraid you have no choice, Ms. Ford," Billy murmured. He slipped the bloody dagger back into his raincoat pocket and drew her a little aside from the revenant. "He's already had a taste of it, to set the bond. You'd best cooperate."

"Make me." Miranda glared alternately at her agent and her ex, her index fingers now apparently locked in place. "I know the rules: He can't touch me while I'm protected by the sign of the cross. Better slap one together for yourself, Mr. Samson; the bastard looks hungry."

Billy sighed. "I'm safe enough. The rules you know are worthless. In Alan's case, no crosses, garlic, wolfsbane, direct sunlight, nor all the other folderol of classic vampire lore applies."

"You're kidding." Miranda's eyebrows lifted sharply. "Not even the stuff they show on *Buffy*?"

Billy shook his head. "He is no ordinary undead: He is a literary property."

"What the—?"

"I mean that he can roam the earth at liberty, by day *or* night, just as he did in life. And he will be just as he *was* in life, what's more."

"A consummate shit," Miranda said. Alan blew her a kiss.

"A consummate, immortal, *blood-drinking* shit," Billy corrected her. "That much of the lore holds good: He must have blood to survive. Well, blood and sales figures. When they remainder the last book that contains his likeness, he's pulped, too."

"Good. The sooner he's gone—*again*—the better."

"But Ms. Ford, that could take years. Meanwhile, are you willing to shelve your career just for the sake of destroying him? After all the trouble we at Monk & Pagan took to restore your Muse?" He leaned nearer and, shielding his lips with the back of one hand, whispered privily in her ear. "You'll be wanting inspiration soon enough: We've had a nibble from . . . *Hollywood*."

"A movie deal . . ." Miranda breathed the charmed words as if they were a pilgrim's holy prayer. "Honestly?"

Billy nodded. "But it won't fly if you don't stay hot, and you know as well as I that you'll stay hot if you can keep pumping them ou—providing your devoted fans with new and challenging reads."

"Which I can't do without him." Miranda's tough stance softened perceptibly as she accepted her fate. "All right. Anything else I ought to know that you didn't see fit to tell me? Care-and-feeding instructions? Apart from the let-him-drink-my-blood part, I mean."

"Don't pop the iron supplements *too* fast, my sweet," Alan purred. "I get far better miles-to-the-pint than an MG. That little wake-up sip you gave me will see me through a fortnight. Fill me up and you're off the hook for *weeks*. Unless you'd *like* to try it on a hook?" His impromptu impersonation of a flicker-tongued lizard left her cold.

"No, and I don't want to 'try it' in your stinking coffin either."

"Bah. Fairy-tale fluff. I'll use the guest bed, thank you . . . when I'm not using a friendlier kind of mattress." He grinned. "I suppose I'll have to make a whole new set of acquaintances. Wouldn't do to circulate among our old crowd. If they knew I was back, someone might get the wrong idea, and I don't think I want to find out firsthand whether that part about a stake through the heart works on my breed of bloodsucker."

Her hands became fists. "You're despicable."

"But salable," he reminded her. "What a team we'll be! I'll tell you all about my new exploits, you'll turn them into the most prosaic prose, the idiot females in their millions will suck it up like latté, and *I'll* suck—"

"I hope you choke on it, the way you used to choke on every one of my triumphs!" She was showing a lot of teeth, but it wasn't a smile.

The vampire smirked. "*Used* to," he repeated. "Now, being dead and all that, somehow I no longer feel bothered by your so-called literary conquests. Isn't that the drollest thing you've ever—?"

Miranda did not wait for him to finish. She grabbed Billy by the hand, spun on her heel, and dragged him three graves away from Alan, whose mocking laughter followed them. "This is unbearable," she hissed. "I can't stand it!"

"What's wrong?" Billy was badly confused by his client's ferocity. "You'll be writing again, and cracking Hollywood, and you'll only have to give him a teensy *sip* of your blood every so often, and—"

"—and he's *happy*." Miranda loosed her hold on Billy's hand and shifted it to his neck. "He's *content* with this new setup. I'm no longer the thorn in his Yalie side or the slap in his macho face. My success has lost the power to bust his stones." An awful suspicion laid hold of her, and she demanded, "Did you *know* he was going to come back from the dead *this* changed?"

"Er . . ." Billy wriggled out of her clutches, and in a voice that was pure nerves replied, "Yyyyes. You see"—he began speaking rapidly, as if words alone could put a safe stretch of no-man's-land between himself and his irate client—"it's a pretty standard scrap of occult wisdom that passing through the great Gate gives most people a, hrrh, fresh perspective on the things in life that really matter. Clearly your achievements no longer do matter to him. It might almost be viewed as major spiritual progress on the part of your late husband, which in a cosmic sense is highly commenda—" He stopped talking. Miranda's expression was counseling silence, lots of it, and at once.

"How could you do this to me, Billy?" she asked, calling him by his given name for the first time in memory. "How could you deliberately mislead me not once, not twice, but time after time after time? Even for an agent, that's taking it too far. You didn't tell me you'd bring Alan back as a vampire—"

"Not at first, but—but *you* didn't believe I could bring him back at *all*!" Billy protested.

Miranda did not have the floor open to discussion. She went on, "You didn't tell me I'd have to feed him my own blood. And worst of all—"

"But it doesn't have to be *your* blood! Just as long as you're the one who gives it to him. It's a control issue."

Again she ignored him. "Worst of all," she said again, "you didn't tell me that the sweetest part of my life—the chance to hold it over his head and rub his nose in it at the same time—would be over. Done with. Even deader than he is."

"So *what*? What *is* your problem? You're still going to be writing, and getting published, and earning huge advances, and royalties, and book-club sales, and foreign rights, and—!"

"You might have saved my finances, Billy, but you took away my fun." She shook her head sadly. "Without fun, writing's just another fucking day job."

"Helloooo!" Alan's supercilious voice rang out across the graves. "I may be dead, but I still know enough to come in out of the rain. I'm getting *wet* over here, people." He strolled over to join them, uninvited.

"Do you *mind*?" Miranda stamped her foot. "This is business. I'm talking to my agent about a little matter called a breach of trust."

"So he did you dirt, whoop-de-do." Alan's slender hand described swirls in the air.

"I don't believe you understand, Alan," Miranda said, her voice perilously flat. "He said he was going to help, but he betrayed me. *No one* betrays me."

"My ass. And what did *I* do to you all those years?" he sauntered nearer, cock-of-the-walk, defying her.

"All right, then let's say that no one betrays me and gets away with it," she countered. "Divorcing you would've been easy, killing you would've been fun, but I found a better way to give you what you deserved. I'll do it again, too, if you push me. I'll fix you even if it means learning enough necromancy to send you straight back to hell myself."

"Now, now, Ms. Ford." Billy stepped between vampiric husband and volcanic wife, striving to make peace. "That really wouldn't be advisable. You see, your blood's sealed a bond with your late husband, as well as with the Dark Powers. Even if you did manage to send him back to, er, whence he came, I'm afraid that you'd have to go with him."

Miranda whirled on her agent. "Another of your little surprises? For *this* I pay fifteen percent?"

"Uh, in view of the present circumstances I am willing to reduce my customary charges to a mere teeeee . . . er, *twelve* per cen—"

"I wouldn't hear of it. Billy Samson, you're going to get everything that's coming to you."

He didn't know a woman of Miranda's years could move that fast. One second her hand was at her side, the next it was deep in his raincoat pocket, and the next it had slashed his own ceremonial dagger cleanly across his throat. As the blood gushed out, he dimly saw her grab Alan and shove the vampire's face to the streaming wound. Alan tried to make a witty sally, but all he could manage was "Glub!"

As for Billy, all he could manage was a shower of confetti-colored lights before his eyes, and then the long, graceful tumble into darkness.

He awoke on his back with graveyard earth under his hands. The rain had stopped, and the clouds were moving on. He thought he heard the sound of cats quarreling in the distance, then realized that the shrill, angry sounds assaulting his ears were actually human voices.

"Probably a mugging," he muttered, slowly getting to his feet. "Over that way, from the sound of it, which means I'm going to go over *this* way. Step into the middle of a mugging, and a man could get himself kill—"

Suddenly, he remembered one small, pertinent detail.

The gash under his chin was wide and deep, easy for his questing fingers to find. It was still an open wound, but a dry one. "Oh, merry *shit*," he muttered. "So *that* bit of classic lore applies in this case as well."

A large rock came whizzing through the air, missing his head by inches. He pursed his lips in annoyance and peered into the darkness wherefrom it had flown. "Are you two *still* at it?" he demanded, striding across the intervening graves.

Alan and Miranda looked up from their ongoing altercation. His face expressed the sort of distilled and concentrated *ennui* impossible to find outside of Old Money families. She just looked mad.

"You again? What the hell are you doing back?" she wanted to know.

"That's a fine question, since you're the one responsible for my return," Billy told her.

"Me?" Miranda was genuinely nonplussed.

"Don't play the ewe-lamb, Ms. Ford. If a vampire leeches his victim utterly, that victim becomes a vampire as well; *everybody knows that.*" He recited the rule in a thoroughly obnoxious more-arcanely-knowledgeable-than-thou tone of voice.

"Don't you condescend to me, Billy Samson!" Miranda kicked a gravestone to vent her feelings. "You think I'm stupid because I don't happen to know that much about vampires? Well, I don't. The only reason I had Alan drink you was to kill two slugs with one saltshaker. He'd be well fed enough to keep him the hell off my neck for a while and you—Well, *you* were supposed to be dead and stay that way, only you let me down again. Who does a simple, honest, hardworking writer have to screw to get a little basic cooperation around here?"

"Oooh, and no one here but us corpses. Kinky." Alan leered. "Congratulations, Miranda, you're finally starting to lighten up. I like it."

"Shut *up*, Alan." This time Miranda did not kick the gravestone. Alan let out a yelp more proper to a Shih Tzu than to a creature of the night and jumped backwards, out of range. For the first time in a long, long while, Miranda smiled. "Did that *hurt*?" she asked, as enraptured as Oliver Twist experiencing both barrels of a full-gonzo Victorian Christmas.

"No," Alan replied a tad too quickly.

"Yes," Billy said. He straightened the Windsor knot of his blood soaked necktie and smiled too. "In fact, Alan, considering just how much you've just had to eat, I'm surprised it didn't hurt more."

"I can't be hurt!" Alan challenged him. "I'm dead."

"Which means you can't be *killed*, not that you can't be *hurt*."

"I thought that a wooden stake could—"

Billy sighed. It was always so tedious dealing with the uneducated. "That's *destroyed*, not *killed;* there's a semantic difference. Tch, and you a Yale man. As for feeling pain, you're fairly immune most of the time, except just after you've had a feed, and then . . . Well, fill something *that* full of blood, and it's bound to be more sensitive. Q.E.D." Billy darted forward with superhuman speed and dealt Miranda's former husband a mighty thwick of thumb and forefinger to the tip of his nose. Alan howled like a gutted wolf.

Miranda stole forward and linked her arm through her agent's. "Show me more," she crooned.

"Not so fast." Billy forcibly disengaged himself. "There's a thing or two we've got to settle between us first."

"What? An apology? Okay, I'm sorry I killed you and fed you to Alan and turned you into a vampire."

"And—?" Billy prompted.

"Um . . . and I'll buy you a new necktie?"

The agent clicked his tongue. "*And* the matter of our new business relationship. It's not every writer who gets to claim she's got a real cutthroat agent, Miranda. This is going to give me all sorts of leverage with the publishers."

"This is going to be about your fee, isn't it," Miranda stated.

"Of course it's going to be about money!" Alan put in from the safe distance of two graves off. "When is it *not* about money with these people?"

Billy spared him a disdainful twitch of the left nostril. "Shut up, Alan, before I teach Miranda a handy little cantrip that will *compel* you to shut up."

"You can't do that," Alan objected. "Neither can she. The Constitution guarantees me the right to free speech!"

"The Constitution was created *by* dead white guys, not *for* dead white guys. Try to keep the difference straight in your mind. As to my fee, it will be fifteen percent."

Miranda looked relieved. "Thank God, that's the same as it's always been."

"No," said Billy. "Not quite." He turned to Alan. "This time it's *not* about money."

Alan and Miranda were equally bewildered, but she was the first to say, "But if it's not about money, then fifteen percent . . . of . . . what?"

Billy explained.

"Ohhhh, no." Miranda shook her head. "Nuh-uh, you are not getting fifteen percent of *that*. I'm already supporting *one* bloodsucker! Either you change your concept of a writer-agent dinner, or I'm taking my business elsewhere."

"All right, then: twelve percent. But I'm cutting my own throat."

"Better yours than mine. Make it ten. In installments. You want it, you buy it by the shot glass, not the bottle."

"Fine, but when we sign the movie deal, you make sure to throw a couple of screen writers my way."

"If I scrape up a six-pack of actress-models, too, will you shave a few percentage points off on my account?"

"What are you trying to do, Miranda? Kill me? Again?"

They battled on, tweaking a condition here, a perk there. Alan, still damp from the rain and becoming crankier by the minute, tried to stalk off into the night, only to discover that he could not. "Hey!" he protested to the universe in general.

"Oh, shut up, Alan," Billy said absently. "You've just reached the end of your figurative leash is all. You can't go too far from Miranda unless she allows it. I *said* there was a bond between the two of you now."

For the first time since his return, Alan's blasé attitude slipped. "You mean it's more than a metaphor?"

"Think of it as a spiritual choke chain, whither she goeth, and all that. Now Miranda, darling, actress-models are a nice thought, but there's hardly more than a sip in a truck-load. On the other hand, if we're talking stuntmen—"

"With *their* union? I'd never get away with it."

"I want to go home!" Alan piped up. "I want dry clothes, a hot toddy, and the Playboy Channel, *stat.* Wrap it the hell up and—"

The clouds parted and the moon, cold and beautiful as a six-figure advance, shone full upon the graveyard. By its light Alan saw that despite his strident demands, Billy and Miranda were so enmeshed in business wrangles that for all intents and purposes he'd been rendered immaterial. Never, in this life or the previous, had he been so thoroughly, so *professionally* overlooked. Shock, hurt, and a large dollop of resentment showed plainly on his face. Unfortunately, this happened just as Miranda inadvertently happened to glance his way.

"Why, darling," she breathed, smiling ear to ear, "you *do* still care about my career after all."

Alan Mountroyal Stewart was a dead man.

In Man's Image

by John B. Rosenman

"Rise!" his father shouted. "There's a lion on the plains. Grab your spear!"

Twelve-year-old Aaron Okonkwo awoke instantly and left the tent. Grinning up at his father's dark face, he let his eyes travel off across the meager savannah to the even more meager fringe of rain forest.

"Father," he said in Igbo, "how shall I serve you today?"

"I have business," his father answered in the same language, clipping his tie neatly to his starched white shirt. Checking his image in a mirror attached to a palm tree, he continued in English. "Study your lessons. I expect to return by noon."

"Yes, Father," Aaron said. He had hoped to play with Akueke, his new girlfriend, even if she did kiss him all the time and want to hold hands. But business meant his father was meeting with the people who wanted to close the preserve, and he knew he'd better obey.

His father went back into the tent, emerging a moment later in a suit jacket and sunglasses. He headed for the hovercar, then stopped. "Take Nok out for a walk later," he said. "He's been irritable lately."

"Irritable?"

"He needs a mate, and we just don't have one for him.

Even if we did, she might reject him like the first two did because Nok's too smart."

Aaron nodded, then waved a moment later as his father's car rose into the air and glided off.

After he had eaten breakfast and finished a few chores, Aaron went to the primate center. Dr. Thomas, a white man with a neatly trimmed goatee, greeted him with a smile.

"Come to take Nok for a stroll, Aaron?"

"Yes, Dr. Thomas."

"Fine." Dr. Thomas told an attendant to get Nok, then came closer. As he did, Aaron caught the smell of the mints that Thomas constantly chewed. "Just take it easy with him, today, huh? He's been acting a bit peculiar."

"My father says Nok needs a mate."

"No, son, it's not that. It's . . ." Dr. Thomas popped a mint into his mouth, searching for an explanation. "Nok just seems a mite edgy, son. I may have to fiddle with his diet. So don't tire him out and be sure to press the com if you need help." As a cage door clanged in back, Dr. Thomas slipped a small unit into Aaron's shirt pocket. "All right, son?"

"Yes, sir."

"Good!" Dr. Thomas beamed and patted him on the head. "Ah," he said, turning, "here's Nok now."

Aaron watched as the door opened and a handler appeared with Nok, who was barefoot but wore black trousers and a white shirt open at the collar. *Pan troglodytes verus*, Nok's compfile said. One point five meters in height, Nok had all the usual physical traits of masked chimpanzees: large, outstanding ears, a black coat, and a pale, hairless face. His skull, though, was huge, a scientific shortcut to evolution that Aaron's father described as "circumventing Darwin." As usual, Nok's bulging forehead reminded Aaron of the brain tumor that killed Aaron's mother. Nok's robust, lively air, however, belied any suggestion of sickness, as did the cheerful hoot he gave when he saw Aaron.

"Hi, Nok!" Aaron laughed, looking into Nok's face when he joined him. "You want to go for a walk?"

"Like very much," Nok grunted, his surgically altered tongue and vocal cords struggling with the vowels. "Miss wind and sun."

Aaron grinned. "Well, you're going to get your wish, even though Dr. Thomas says you're not feeling well."

Nok's brown, liquid eyes turned to Dr. Thomas, who popped another mint in his mouth. "Are you feeling better, Nok?" Dr. Thomas asked. "I've been thinking of putting more insects in your diet."

Nok raised a long hairy arm. "Insects, yes. 'Specially termites," he said in deep, gravelly tones. "Feeling much better now."

"Are you sure?" Thomas took an ophthalmometer from his desk and examined Nok's eyes. "Doesn't seem to be any problem with your vision. Guess you've just been feeling out of sorts, eh? Not up to any monkey business."

Nok bared his teeth in a broad grin, wrinkling his masked face comically. "Nok need girlfriend for monkey business. Can you find me pretty one?"

"Well, I'll try," Dr. Thomas laughed. "Though I'm not sure what you would consider 'pretty.'" He patted Nok's head, then winked at Aaron. "All right, son, off you two scamps go. And remember what I told you about using the com."

"Sure, Dr. Thomas." Aaron tugged Nok's arm. "Come on, Nok."

Once outside Nok continued to walk upright, even though Aaron knew he longed to walk on all fours, leaning on his knuckles. But men didn't walk that way, and so Nok, who had been rigorously educated and tested since his operations, moved vertically, his shoulders thrust back. The result was an ungainly, shambling gait that Nok not only found uncomfortable, but almost impossible when he wore shoes.

Aaron thought of his father, who also wore white man's clothing, and frowned. It was odd he had to find out from his father that Nok was "irritable." Since Aaron's early childhood, Nok had been his closest friend, almost a surrogate brother. They had played together, even slept together. Now, as they got older, they seemed to be growing apart somehow.

"Are your legs tired, Arrow?" Nok asked gruffly. "Perhaps need more insects in diet."

Aaron, lagging behind, snorted disdainfully. "Dr. Mints has all the answers, doesn't he?"

Nok, who had developed a knack for mimicry, raised his voice, lightening its deep timbre. "All right, son, off you two scamps go." He hooted scornfully, then twisted his face into a crude but effective semblance of Dr. Thomas's. "Care for some mints, my boy? You been acting a mite peculiar, lately."

Aaron laughed. "Oh, Nok!"

Nok advanced, pretending to examine Aaron's eyes with an ophthalmometer. "Hmm. No problem with vision, Arrow. Feeling out of sorts, eh?" He raised a large, hairy hand and patted Aaron's shoulder. "Well, a shot should clear that right up."

Gradually Aaron stopped laughing, for something about Nok's manner troubled him, something that was not caused by drugs or diet. As he looked around, he realized there was something about this day, too. Something different. He opened his senses as his father had taught him, trying to observe his surroundings with an unbiased spirit, as a hunter would. Still, it eluded him. Whatever it was—

The crickets.

He stiffened. Of course. Was it just yesterday that the crickets had filled the world with their shrill song? Now the savannah and bushes and rain forest were silent, as if stricken by some sickness. He tried to remember when the crickets' sound had started to wane, or if his father had mentioned the problem. He should have been more observant.

Nok grabbed his arm. Aaron looked down, seeing Nok's dark, hairy hand holding it.

"Come," Nok grunted. "Race to well."

Off they went. Nok was nearly as tall as Aaron. But even barefooted, running upright was hard for him, and Aaron beat him easily, just as he always did. Reaching the stone well, he leaned over its side and gazed down into the water. When Nok joined him, there were two reflections. Studying them, Aaron was struck by how truly different they were. His small, dark, regular features contrasted sharply with Nok's rubber-lipped, jug-eared appearance, with the masked, mottled face that always seemed to be half in shadow.

"You always win," Nok said.

A jet cut through the sky above them, heading for the city with what his father called a bellyful of pollution. Aaron ignored it, studying their images in the water below. Some tribes, like their own, the Igbo, had once believed that a newborn child was inhabited by the spirit of someone who'd died. If so, whose spirit lived in his body, and whose in Nok's? Did chimpanzees even have spirits? When his mother was alive, Aaron had asked her this, and was told that only humans, who were created in God's image, had immortal souls and could go to heaven. It had seemed unfair, but then, his mother had been a Christian, which angered his father, who felt that an Igbo wife should share her husband's gods. His mother had told his father that all the tribal gods were pagan myths and that she had named her son Aaron after the first high priest of the Hebrews.

Nok was silent. Feeling his friend's hairy arm against his own, Aaron turned to him. "Do you really need a girlfriend, Nok?"

Nok's head turned. The deep brown pools of his eyes met his own. "Arrow, you have a girl. Why can't I?"

Aaron squirmed, remembering Akueke's bright smile, the way she had surprised him with a kiss. "She's a pest, Nok. Sometimes she won't leave me alone."

"They don't even *want* me," Nok said. He raised a hand to pick something out of Aaron's hair, then stopped.

Aaron patted Nok's arm. "Maybe you haven't found the right one yet," he said. "You've only met two."

Nok's face twisted. "Girls like *you*, but they don't want Nok's touch. The way he moves and sounds."

Sympathy for his friend poured through Aaron. He wanted to hug and comfort him, but sensed that Nok didn't want it. Gazing down into the water, he recalled a legend about a man who had cut off the head of a monstrous snake that lived in a rough stone well like this one. As a reward, a beautiful queen married him. Aaron studied his image in the water. Would he ever have the chance to perform such an heroic deed to win the woman of his dreams? If so, what would she be like, and where would he find her?

Beside him, Nok picked up a small stone and dropped it in the well. Their reflections dissolved.

"Come, the forest," Nok said.

They crossed the strip of savannah, heading toward the trees. The weather was so arid, the grass so dry, that one spark could spread like lightning. Aaron had heard his father say this many times, and he was little comforted by the water jets he saw on poles, or the workers patrolling the high fence around the perimeter. Once Nigeria had had a rainy season. Now, thanks to what his father called the belching wonders of civilization, the climate was mostly dry and hot, with smoke-filled skies rich in carcinogens.

Inside the forest, under a canopy of trees, it was cooler, a soothing, verdant gloom. Halting, Aaron removed his shoes and set them down, remembering what his father told him. To join the land, you must share its simplicity. He moved on, trying to be as silent as possible.

Beside him, Nok struggled to walk upright on the uneven terrain. Occasionally he stumbled, making sounds that would have alerted prey, if there had been any.

When Aaron was younger, he had dreamed of traveling to the stars one day and supervising a game preserve on a distant planet. His father's tales of their heritage, though, had changed all that. Now he pretended it was thousands of years earlier, before the first Europeans had set foot on African soil. This forest he walked was thick and unspoiled and all but limitless. It was the Promised Land his mother had envisioned for him, and he would hunt it forever and savor his birthright. And someday, when he grew up, he would be a great warrior-priest, or even become the king of his tribe.

But this forest was silent and unresponsive. Once it had abounded with leopards and birds and wild boars. Now even the crickets were silent, stilled by some secret blight.

He stopped again, gazing up at the trees as Nok clumsily bumped him. "Nok, do you ever think . . ."

"What?" Nok grunted.

"Of climbing a tree, swinging from its branches."

Nok looked up. Shadows cast bars across his face and body. His lips worked strangely. Breathing rapidly, his chest rising and falling, Nok dropped his eyes and picked at his shirt and trousers.

"You can take 'em off," Aaron said, "like I did my shoes."

A pause. "*You* can, Arrow. I can't."

"Why not?"

Nok started to answer, then pointed over Aaron's shoulder. "What is that?"

Aaron turned. "What?"

"On ground. Near your feet."

Aaron stooped, but didn't see anything. "I—"

A stunning blow struck his head, and he collapsed. Half-conscious, he felt rude hands roll him over on his back, yank something from his pocket.

Opening his eyes, he found everything blurred. Gradually the forest returned to focus. Nok crouched over him, holding the com in his hand.

"Nok . . ." His head splitting with pain, he reached weakly up for the com.

Nok snatched it away with a sly grin. "Noooo, I tell about accident." He flipped the com over his shoulder. "So sad you fall and strike head, but jungle dangerous. No place for little boys."

Then Aaron saw Nok's other hand. It still held a blood-stained rock.

"Why?" he whispered in disbelief. "Why, Nok . . ."

Nok leaned down, his lips shearing back from yellow teeth. "Nok sick of being little pet monkey, dressed like doll for boy to play with."

"But . . ." Aaron stopped, his head pounding, remembering how Nok and he had once shared so much, how they had laughed and played. He *loved* Nok, and Nok loved *him*! This couldn't . . .

"Thought I was s-simple m-monkey, didn't you?" Nok asked stammering and slurring the vowels. His face contorted, and he roared in rage at his clumsy speech. Then he leaned closer and sneered, his breath hot with fury on Aaron's face. "Nok sick of being dumb, fur-sniffin' freak in cage!"

"Nok! I never knew you felt . . ." Pain ripped through Aaron's head, growing worse. This couldn't be happening. He thought of his dream of becoming a great hero, a warrior-chief or king, and felt immeasurably foolish. He was even worse than his father, for he was unable to lead or save anyone, let alone himself. What's more, he was ignorant, never even suspecting his best friend was his worst enemy. And if *that* could happen, then life must be so much more mysterious than he had ever imagined.

Gritting his teeth, Aaron struggled up onto his knees. A wave of nausea rose, and his stomach heaved. He fought it down desperately, and raised his eyes to Nok.

"Nok," he gasped. "You can't do this. I . . . I *love* you!"

Nok blinked, and the rock trembled in his hand. "L-Love. Oh, I loooovvvve you!" He raised his free hand and slapped Aaron's face several times, stunning him. "Can't love *me*, boy. Your science opened my eyes and made me see, but I'm still a dirty ape. Good only for swinging in trees!"

"No, Nok, I . . ."

Nok screamed and brought the rock down again. Jerking his head to the side, Aaron felt it graze his temple. He fell backwards and tried to crawl away.

Nok started laughing, a high, *heek heek heek* sound totally unlike the laugh Aaron knew. It almost sounded as if Nok were in pain.

Aaron drove his heels and elbows against the earth, trying to push himself away from Nok. Back back back. Nok hooted and hopped up and down, mocking him. "*Fly*, little Arrow, but must come to earth sometime. Then Nok will kill you." He leapt closer, towering above Aaron, and raised the rock again.

Aaron drove backwards with his feet, gave himself a mighty push.

Then the world fell away as he dropped over a steep bank. He struck the forest floor with his back, missing a jagged rock by inches and driving the breath from his body. Three meters above him, Nok perched on the edge, then clapped his hands and marched about like a triumphant warrior. Aaron saw him raise his hands to the sky.

"Got you now, little *brother*," Nok taunted.

"Please don't!" Aaron gasped. He struggled to say more but couldn't.

"Yes, human child, *beg*!" Nok roared. He drew his shoulders back and tried to strut, lifting his legs awkwardly. Then, grinning, he turned to leap down to Aaron.

As he did, he caught his foot on a vine, twisting himself sideways. For a moment, he seemed to hang in the air, his masked features frozen in surprise. Then he struck the rocky ground beyond Aaron with a sharp crack.

Dazed, gasping for air, Aaron turned and stared at Nok's still form, then crawled over to him—inch by agonizing inch. When Aaron finally reached Nok, the chimpanzee lay quietly, his eyes closed, his head bleeding.

"Nok."

Nok's eyes struggled open, and he smiled, looking just like the friend Aaron remembered. "Aaron," he said, "want to go to jungle."

Aaron wet his lips, forgetting his own throbbing head as he saw more clearly the extent of Nok's injury. A rock had split his skull half-open, exposing the pink-gray tissue of his bioenhanced brain.

"I know," he said. "We'll go . . . tomorrow."

"Together?"

"Yes."

"Aaron?"

Aaron rose to his knees and took his hand. "Yes, Nok."

A tear rolled down Nok's hairy cheek. He squeezed Aaron's hand and pressed it to his lips. "Sorry. Could never be like you. No matter how hard I tried."

Aaron sobbed and started to say something, only to see that Nok's eyes had grown fixed and dull, as if staring out across some vast savannah into an infinitely remote forest. He remembered his mother saying that only humans were created in God's image and possessed souls. Now he watched as his own image dimmed within the depths of Nok's eyes and faded completely.

Aaron gently withdrew his hand from Nok's, feeling as if something inside him had died, too. He stroked his friend's fur, smelling the coppery scent of blood as it oozed from Nok's head. Then he raised his head and stared into the distance.

By the Time the Witchblood Blooms

by Anne Bishop

It was a perfect place for my line of work. For both of my professions, actually, but I was there for only one of them.

The dining house catered to Blood aristos, so it exuded quality and comfort. The sunken main room had a rough-stoned fountain in the center that looked so natural you would swear they had built the room around it. Tables were scattered around the room with plenty of space between them—a sensible precaution, all things considered. The Blood's social structure is such a complicated dance, juggling caste, social rank, and Jewel rank, that an inadvertent nudge could turn into a violent confrontation in the space of a heartbeat.

Not that I would mind, unless something nasty landed on my plate. I enjoy carnage, especially when it's an aristo male being torn into little pieces. Unfortunately, I'm too much of a professional to indulge in things like that very often.

On either side of the sunken main room were large, comfortable booths, discreetly shielded from the tables below by a wall of ferns and lightly spelled so that conversations remained private.

When I'd arrived that afternoon to look the place over,

I'd chosen one of the booths for tonight's little game. The owner of the dining house graciously closed this section of the room so that I and my companion would have it all to ourselves. That wasn't difficult since this was a late dinner even for the Blood, and the few people left in the main room were lingering over drinks by the time my companion arrived.

We settled into the booth, and the game began.

My companion was a Purple Dusk Jeweled Warlord from an aristo family. That gave him some power. His serving one of the stronger Queens in this Territory gave him more. Enough so that he felt he could do anything to anyone as long as they didn't wear darker Jewels than his, didn't come from an aristo family, and didn't serve in a Queen's court.

Which was true. He *could* do anything to anyone and no one could touch him—unless, of course, they hired someone like me.

According to our most ancient legends, the Blood were given their power, their Craft, in order to be the caretakers of the Realms. The Jewels some of us wore not only acted as a reservoir for our power but also indicated how deep—and dark—that power was.

There are many words that could describe what the Blood have become. "Caretaker" isn't one of them.

Which is why, for me, business is so good.

My companion was a handsome-enough man, if you found pigs erotic. Then again, whores don't choose clients based on how they look.

Neither do assassins.

"So, was I your first?" he said, dipping his fingers into the bowl of stained shrimp.

Idiot. I'm half-breed Hayllian, who are a *long*-lived race. My eyes have too much green in them to be pure Hayllian gold, but the light-brown skin and black hair came from the son of a whoring bitch who had sired me.

I daintily cut one of my stuffed-mushroom appetizers. "Ah, no, sugar. Not *my* first." I laughed, soft and husky, and flashed him a look from beneath my lashes. "Your great-great-grandfather perhaps."

He grunted, ate another stained shrimp, and licked the sauce from his fingers in a way, I'm sure, he thought was erotically suggestive. "Might have been old Jozef. I'm a lot like him, you know."

I didn't doubt that for a moment.

He finished the last stained shrimp. The sweet-hot sauce produced beads of sweat on his forehead. Patting his face with his napkin, he shrugged, and said, "They make it too mild here." His eyes wandered back down to my decolletage. "I like things really hot."

Ah, Warlord, I thought as I smiled at him, *soon enough you'll have all the fire you want.*

While we waited for the next course, I rested my elbows lightly on the table, tucked my chin in my laced fingers, and leaned forward to give him a better look at my breasts, which were barely covered by the silk of my dress. It was good he'd eaten all the stained shrimp. I would have hated for a serving boy to snitch the last one and suffer for it.

He patted his forehead with his napkin again. The look he gave me said the heat wasn't just from the stained shrimp.

"So now you're a tenant at a Red Moon house here?" He tried not to sound too eager, but his eyes wandered to my delicately pointed ears, the only physical evidence of my mother's mysterious race.

My ears make me unique, which means expensive, and I *do* have a reputation for being the best of the best. When I choose to settle at a Red Moon house for a while, appointments are made weeks in advance, which is something no other whore can claim. Only half of what I do in bedrooms has anything to do with sex, but it's such *easy* bait.

"No, I'm not a tenant," I said. "This is a pleasure trip. I'm just passing through." Which I had told him when I invited him to dinner.

He still looked sulky and disappointed—because, of course, he hadn't believed it. His kind never do. Then a sly, calculating look came into his eyes. "But you won't be leaving until morning, will you, Sorrel?"

"Surreal," I said, correcting him. The bastard knew perfectly well what my name was. He was just trying to goad me into thinking I was too insignificant to remember so that I would be willing to prove I'm everything *my* reputation says I am.

That was fine with me. I was willing to let him play out his game since it fit in with my own.

I smiled at the serving boy who brought the prime ribs. He placed my dish in front of me, the sharp blade of the knife carefully tucked beneath the meat. I glanced at the knife to confirm there was a small white enamel spot in the handle. My companion's knife had a small red spot.

Perfect.

Giving the boy a flicker of a warning smile, I picked up the knife and began to eat.

The Warlord grunted. "If the owner's going to have a dining house without rooms upstairs, the least he could do is have serving boys who aren't surly." He gave me a leering grin. "Or serving girls."

I gave him a saucy smile in return. "If you want to fill your belly, you come to a dining house. If you want to fill something else, you go to a Red Moon house. Besides, who wants to play with amateurs?"

A vicious light filled his pale eyes. "Playing with amateurs can be quite entertaining."

I just stared at him. He probably thought the vicious light in my own eyes was due to jealousy.

Fool.

I used Craft to chill the air around me, indicating my displeasure, and ate my dinner.

He chafed at the quiet censure, and his expression changed to thwarted-little-boy-turned-mean before he remembered that, if a man wanted to be accommodated by a whore of my skill and reputation, part of the price was the illusion of courtesy.

Hiding his temper, he picked up his fork and wiggled it against the meat. "Meat's good. You can cut it with a fork."

I made a moue when meat juice splashed on the linen tablecloth. Finally realizing I wasn't impressed by his vigorous wrist action, he picked up the knife.

I flashed him a wanton smile of approval and continued to eat.

His conversation was boring, being centered entirely on himself, but I didn't allow my attention to wander. Who knew what interesting tidbits he might let drop as he bragged about his connections?

I was admiring the blood-red, black-edged flower tucked into the fern pot opposite our booth when my companion noticed my gaze wasn't fastened on him.

"What's that?" he grunted, tearing a roll apart and dunking a piece into the butter bowl.

I looked away from the flower and shrugged. If he didn't know witchblood when he saw it, I wasn't about to tell him.

"Pretty," he said, probably thinking it would please me.

I almost laughed.

The meal, thank the Darkness, finally ended. After the

brandy was served, he returned to his hoped-for agenda. "Listen," he said, leaning forward so he could stroke my wrist with his fingers, "since you say you don't have a room and this place is lacking in the finer points of service, I know a place—"

"Regrettably, Warlord, the hour is late, I'm expected elsewhere tomorrow, and my Coach leaves shortly."

His face immediately changed from leering soft to cruelly hard. Despite my youthful looks, I'm not a girl easily frightened into submission. I'm far more of a witch than he ever was a Warlord, and he was just a prick-ass who enjoyed hurting women, especially young women.

I dropped my right hand into my lap and used Craft to call in my favorite stiletto. It would have been a shame to gut him publicly, particularly after I'd gone to such trouble to do the thing so neatly, but he was going to be dead either way, and that was the point.

"What's this?" he growled. "*You* approached *me*. You think you can get me to spend good marks to fill your belly and then just—"

"As you say, *I* invited *you* for dinner." I leaned forward, looking at him with wide-eyed earnestness. "I wanted to meet you. You've a reputation among the ladies. In fact, one girl was left speechless after a night with you. Can you wonder why I'd want to meet you?"

"Since I changed my plans for this evening in order to come here, I expected something more than just dinner."

Of course he had. And he *was* going to get more than dinner. Just not what he expected.

When he finally believed that I wasn't going to go anywhere with him, he started getting nasty, so I cut off his words. There were plenty of other things I wanted to cut off, but I restrained myself. "Since I invited you, it will be my privilege to pay for the meal in exchange for your com-

pany and conversation. Besides, I told you this was a pleasure trip, and I don't mix business with pleasure."

Making one more try to get what he had come for, he
looked at my mouth and suggested that the booth was private enough for me to give him some small comfort. On
any other night, those words alone would have earned him
a knife in the gut, but tonight I simply declined. Mumbling
something about my reputation having gone to my head to
think I could waste a Warlord's time and not be accommo-
dating, he left to find a Red Moon house with more compli-
ant game.

When I was sure he'd gone, I slid out of the booth,
plucked the flower from the pot, tucked it into my water
glass, and settled back into the booth. While I waited, I
called in a pen and the second of my little black books, and
made careful notations about what I had done. Since the ingredients could be found almost anywhere in the Realm of
Terreille, this would be another of my closely guarded little
recipes for death.

I vanished the book just as the owner of the dining house
approached, a snifter of brandy in each hand. He set one in
front of me before gingerly slipping into the booth.

It was always like this. Before, my clients are eager for
the deed to be accomplished, and I'm treated with the def-
erence due my skill. After. . . . After they begin to wonder if
they might not one day be on the receiving end.

I stroked the witchblood petals and waited.

"It's done?" His voice shook a little.

"It's done." I continued to stroke the petals. "Legend
says that the reason witchblood can't be destroyed once it's
planted is that its roots grow so deep they're nourished in
the Dark Realm."

"A plant from Hell?" He swallowed the brandy. "I want
no ghosts or demons here."

Of course he wouldn't. "How is your daughter?"

"The same," he said, wiping his mouth with the back of his hand. "Always the same since that . . . since he . . ."

"How old is she?"

His mouth quivered with the effort to speak. "A child," he finally replied in a broken whisper. "A girl just beginning to be a woman."

Yes. I was twelve the first time I was thrown on my back, but the man was only strong enough to take my virginity. When he was done, I still had my Craft, still wore the Green Jewel that was my birthright. I came away from that bloody bed still a witch, not just a Blood female. I've been paying men back in their own coin ever since.

The owner pushed a carefully folded napkin across the table. I lifted one edge, quickly counted the gold marks. As a whore, even with the fees I charge, it would take almost a month to earn this much. As a first-rate assassin, it was a pittance of my usual fee. But even I, at times, do charity work.

I vanished half the marks and pushed the napkin back across the table. The owner looked troubled—and a little frightened. I sipped my brandy. "Use the rest for the girl," I said with a gentleness harshened by my own memories. "A Black Widow is the only kind of witch who can heal what's left of your daughter's mind and possibly give her back some semblance of a life. One with that much skill will expect to be paid well for her services."

"That has nothing to do with your fee," he protested.

I studied the witchblood. The plant will grow anywhere a witch's blood has been spilled in violence, or where a witch violently killed has been buried. It's true that once it takes root over such a place, nothing can destroy it.

It's also true that if the petals are properly dried, it's a sweet-tasting, unforgiving poison that slowly blossoms into unrelenting pain. It is virulent and undetectable until it's far, far too late.

At this point, the Warlord would be feeling nothing more than a bit of a bellyache, and if, as I suspected, he was already entangled with a young whore, he wouldn't even notice.

The owner cleared his throat nervously. His son, who had insisted on being the serving boy tonight, placed two more snifters of brandy on the table, then shifted from foot to foot. Glancing from his father to me, he said, "What should I do with the knife?"

"Cleanse it as I showed you," I said, "and then bury it deep."

The youth hurried away.

Actually there'd been nothing on the knife the Warlord had used but a glaze made from roots and herbs that would cause the mild bellyache. But they had wanted to see death being made, and since I wasn't about to tell them about the powdered witchblood I'd slipped into the bowl of stained shrimp, the mess I'd created in the kitchen that afternoon while I concocted the glaze had sufficiently impressed them. The Warlord will associate the bellyache with overindulgence, and then forget it. By the time the witchblood blooms, no one will think of this place . . . or me.

I turned my attention back to the owner. "As for my fee, I'm keeping enough for expenses. I don't want the rest."

"But—"

"Hush," I said, smiling at him as I raised the brandy snifter in a small salute. "I was on a pleasure trip when you approached me, and"—I laughed, truly delighted—"as I told my arrogant dinner companion, I don't mix business with pleasure."

A Family Affair

by William C. Dietz

Sublevel 38 of the Sea Tac Residential-Industrial Urbo-plex is a sprawling maze of corridors, passageways and tunnels, some of which are part of the original design and many of which are not. Maybe that's why some of the walls sweat, bulge, and eventually give away.

Anyway, it helps to know your way around. Partly owing to the somewhat iffy infrastructure but also because of the thieves, jackers, addicts, whores, androids, scammers, pimps, pushers, and corrupt cops who prey on the weak, cater to the weirdos, and screw the few honest citizens we have left.

The slimeballs were everywhere as I made my way along the litter-strewn corridor. Leaning against the cold, clammy urine-drenched walls, gathered in tightly knit groups, screwing in doorways, barfing into garbage cans, dancing to bar music, and, in the case of one poor soul, sitting dead on a plastic chair. The Takers, robots with permanently sad faces, would collect the body during the night and take it to the death train. They say the machine is black, like death it-self, and about fifty cars long. It stops in the smaller plexes, too, and while some people get on, nobody gets off. Not till they arrive in North Dakota, where endless rows of graves take up more than a thousand square miles.

I turned a corner, stepped onto "the vard," short for Norley Boulevard, and headed north. Most of the people I passed could be divided into two groups: predators and prey. The predators watched me the way predators always do, through sleepy half-lidded eyes, and the tension generated by their never-ending hunger. Most of them lose interest. After all, why tackle another predator, when there's plenty of prey?

The prey, which is to say regular citizens, travel in protective groups, avoid eye contact with dangerous beings such as myself, and maintain a brisk purposeful stride. Most but not all of the cits make it home in one whole piece.

It doesn't work for vendors, though; people who, like my friend Bobby Wang, are forced to stay in one place all day. Bobby owns a taco stand, a sort of wagon that he and his wife constructed themselves. Each morning they get up, shoo the kids out of their tiny kitchen, and prepare the necessary ingredients.

Once the cart is loaded Bobby kisses Chris good-bye, rolls the wagon out into the hall, and starts his long grueling day. It begins with a walk through dimly lit, graffiti splashed corridors to the point where Tunnel F intersects the romantically named Passageway 123. That's where Bobby hooks up to an illegal power tap, locks the wheels in place, and opens for business.

The local cops, also known as Zebras, or Zeebs because of the skin tight striped body stockings they wear, arrive first. Two breakfast burritos. That's the price they charge for strolling past the stand once every hour.

Then comes a long uncertain day during which business may be moderate, bad, or just plain crappy, none of which matters to the preds who assume it's good and want a cut. That's where I come in. The trouble with being a seven-foot-two-inch bodyguard is that nobody wants to hire you. Not when there are pretty biosculpted models to choose from. It's a struggle to pay the rent on my crummy apartment and feed my two-hundred-and-fifty-pound body. Still, it's all I have, so that's what I do. All of which explains why I tend to show up in the vicinity of Bobby Wang's taco stand about 5:00 P.M. or so. *He* gets an armed guard, which he definitely needs, and I get four or five tacos, or, if business was slow, a couple of leftover burritos. My personal favorite.

On this particular afternoon I sidestepped the remains of a recently stripped messenger droid, wondered who had been stupid enough to send the poor piece of shit below Level 10, rounded a corner, and noticed that Bobby had company. Not the *good* kind, like old friends, but the *bad* kind, of which there are plenty.

Three men, all dressed in leather and lace, surrounded the stand. The largest had a knife. The kind that comes all gussied up with a custom handle, blood gutters, and fancifully curved blade. He appeared to be explaining the weapon to Bobby, who, judging from his expression, was extremely interested.

Bobby isn't very big, maybe five-foot-eight or so, and looks even smaller. That, plus a light frame, receding hairline, and cheap eyeglasses all scream "victim" in letters ten feet tall. The problem is that appearances can be and often are deceiving. Bobby has the heart of a lion. A wonderful trait—but one that could get him killed.

The alpha thug gave Bobby a shove, and, contrary to good sense and the dictates of the subterranean food chain, Bobby shoved back.

The street thugs were amazed. There was a script, a *good* script, in which they shoved and other people didn't. Except *this* guy hadn't read the script, or didn't want to follow it, which made them angry.

The guy with the knife damned near fell, heard someone laugh, and turned bright red. I winced. It was personal now. Bobby was toast.

The thug growled like an animal, assumed what he believed to be the correct knife-fighting stance, and shuffled forward.

Bobby, brave to the last, grabbed the only weapon available: a pair of tongs.

That's when I reached inside my jacket, grabbed the .38 Super, and waved it over my head. "Alright, break it up, and leave while you still can."

Now, this may *sound* ineffective, but it requires a license to pack heat, and the little bastards are hard to come by. Unless you're a corpie, or work for the corpies, like I had.

The knife fighter stopped where he was, but one of his buddies went pocket diving. Maybe he needed to scratch what itched, or grab a piece of gum, but I didn't wait to find out. The .38 jumped in my hand, the thug jerked as the slugs hammered his chest, and a .9mm disposable clattered to the pavement. Its owner landed on top of it.

The thugs hauled butt, all except for the guy with the knife, who looked to me for permission. I nodded, and he ran like hell.

I looked around. Not a Zeeb in sight. Fine with me. They make you fill out forms when you shoot people. A whole lot of them . . . and that makes my head hurt. Passersby averted their eyes, gave us a wide berth, and walked a little faster. Good idea. I motioned to Bobby. "You ready? Let's get the hell out of here."

It took but a moment to roll the body over, collect the .9mm, and give it to my friend. "Here . . . if the guy with the knife comes back, shoot him. What were you thinking anyway? Pushing the guy like that."

Bobby shrugged. "I was tired of taking shit."

"Yeah? Well, that's real nice except for the fact that you have a family. Chris is gonna kick your skinny butt. Now come on, let's haul."

It took the better part of forty-five minutes to escort Bobby home, tell Chris what an idiot her husband was, and collect my tacos. She was still chewing his ass when I left.

Maybe it was the tacos, which I ate while I walked, or maybe it was the brain damage, or maybe, and this seems most likely, I had gotten lazy. Whatever the reason I forgot one of the most important precepts of personal security: Vary your routine.

That's why I was strolling along, licking the grease off my fingers, when a pair of very burly androids converged from left and right, grabbed my arms, lifted my size thirteens right off the pavement, and carried me away. Plenty of people saw it, and none of them said a word.

The one on the left looked like a zombie that someone had forgotten to bury, and the one on the right wore whiteface and a black grim-reaper outfit. They were supposed to look intimidating and they did.

My first thought was that the thugs had located me and were bent on revenge. That didn't make sense though, since they couldn't afford machines like these, and wouldn't use them if they could.

No, the knife fighter and the rest of his posse would want to get close and personal. They would want to *see* their fists hitting my face, *feel* the way my flesh split beneath their knuckles, and *hear* me beg for mercy.

So, who did that leave? The corpies that's who. The handful of men and women who ran all of the major corporations, enjoyed the perks that went with the guarantee of lifetime employment, and used freelancers to handle the grunt work. Millions, no *billions* of people who eked out whatever living they could working for an hourly wage. Competing with each other, robots, and automated machinery for what little work there was. But which ones? And why?

The machines carried me around a corner and into one of the ubiquitous lift tubes that no one ever seemed to use but were plastered with decals that read FOR OFFICIAL USE ONLY, HIGH VOLTAGE, and DANGER! All of which was bullshit meant to keep subterranean scum such as myself from trying to hijack them. The droids turned me around so I could see my own image in the shiny doors. "How 'bout putting me down?"

The zombie looked at the reaper, I imagined that a high-frequency conversation took place, and they put me down. The zombie had a voice like a gearbox filled with gravel. The same clowns who had dressed the machine in graveyard chic had customized its speech patterns. "You make trouble I rip head off."

I had every intention of offering a snappy rejoinder, but the platform coasted to a stop, and the doors slid open. It was dark topside, but there were plenty of lights, and a limo floated not ten feet from the tube.

A greenie had spotted the vehicle and summoned some of his or her buddies. Call them what you will, "Earth-firsters," "tree-huggers," or just plain nuts, the Greenies oppose the corporations and advocate what they call "demechanization," and a return to the land. Land which the corpies just happen to own.

I considered calling on them for help, realized that they didn't give a shit, and ducked as a bottle crashed against the wall above my rather reflective head. The zombie gave a three-hundred-pound nudge and I took the hint. We stepped out onto the pavement. The air stank of sulfur, ozone, and all the other crap that the corpies continued to pump into it. It made me cough. The robots were unaffected. The reaper pointed a long bony finger toward the limo. "Get in."

There seemed to be very little point in debating the issue, so I did as I was told. Something smashed against the roof. The interior smelled of leather, stale cigar smoke, and the faint scent of a woman's perfume. I didn't know what the stuff was called but I liked it.

The zombie planted his steel-plated ass in the seat next to me, the reaper took his place next to the empty driver's seat, and the limo lifted off. The aircar's onboard computer guided the vehicle upward, demanded a slot commensurate with its owner's status, and was integrated into the carefully managed flow of traffic.

Skyscrapers rose all around. They were more like monuments than office buildings, since the corpies didn't need much space, and those freelancers fortunate to cop a few hours of work did most of it from home. Still, you had to stash your computers *somewhere*, and the high-rise boxes, towers, and cylinders functioned like silicon silos.

The limo banked to the left, skimmed an aluminum-clad pyramid, and headed south. Logos floated past. There was Droidware Inc., better known as "the big D," Elexar Corp, Trans Solar, Seculor, and a half dozen more. Individual pustules within the concrete acne that started in Vancouver and stretched south to Ensenada. An endless sprawl of refineries, tank farms, slums, and haz dumps. All leaking their various toxins into the planet's underground bloodstream.

Something beeped, the limo started to lose altitude, and I scanned the buildings ahead. Which were we headed for? Then, as if to answer my question, a luminescent blue *X* materialized at the center of a flat-topped roof. The name

Alfano Inc. was spelled out in twenty-foot-high red letters
and circled the top of the building like a dog chasing its
tail.

It's weird about my memory, how I have days when I
can't remember where I live, interspersed with moments
when everything is so clear. I knew, don't ask me how, that
Alfano Inc. was the nine-hundred-pound gorilla in the ter-
restrial freight business, and that everyone knew the Alfred
Alfano story, partly because it was interesting, and partly
because the old fart never stopped talking about himself.
"The last self-made billionaire," that's what the audio pops
claimed, and maybe it was true.

The limo kissed the center of the *X*, the door whined
open, and the zombie slid off the seat. I followed. It was
breezy outside, breezy enough to blow the worst of the
stink off toward the Cascade Mountains, and cut through
the fabric of my lightweight jacket. The roof was open, and
with the exception of the boxy elevator lobby, flat as a pan-
cake.

There were heavies standing around, not bodyguards like
me, but paramilitary types complete with chemically as-
sisted bodies, urban camos, assault weapons, a lot of attitude. Just the way I used to be when I was a big, bad
Mishimuto Marine.

One of them, a woman with a light machine gun cradled
in her arms, wore a purple crew cut. She eyed my skull
plate as if wondering where she could get one installed.
"You packin'?"

"Yeah. Under my left arm."

She nodded. Her voice was level, one pro to another.
"No offense . . . but we gotta check."

I assumed the posture, arms out, legs spread. One of her
troops ran a metal detector over my body, confirmed the
.38, and got the predictable beep off my head.

"Okay," the woman said. "I ain't got no instructions about your piece . . . but keep it holstered. Andre handles internal security, and he runs a tight ship."

I gestured toward her team. "What's the deal? You expecting trouble or something?"

She grinned. "Of course I am! That's what I get paid for."

It was a good answer, the kind any pro might give, but I thought I saw something in her eyes. A sort of expectant wariness, as if a shit storm was on the way, and might arrive at any moment.

The reaper escorted me across the roof to what looked like a one-story box. It had been fortified with sandbags. More evidence that something was cooking.

Doors slid open, I entered, and found myself standing in front of a full-length portrait of Alfred Alfano. The family patriarch looked like a man who should've been bald—and would be if he stopped rubbing stuff into his scalp. He had dark penetrating eyes, the kind that look right through you, and that some women find interesting. Alfano's nose looked normal enough, but there was something about his mouth, a quality I couldn't quite put my finger on. What was that expression anyway? A smile? Or a sneer? There was no way to be sure. "Mr. Maxon?"

I turned around. The elevator had arrived. The rather polite use of my name stood in marked contrast to the manner in which I had been abducted. The android *sounded* female but *looked* androgynous. "Yes?"

"Please follow me. Mr. Alfano is waiting."

It was tempting to say "So what?" Or to make some other withdrawal from my vast store of witticisms, but I managed to resist. I was alive, which meant Alfano wanted something. Something for which he would pay. Or so I hoped. "Of course. Lead the way."

The elevator was a luxurious affair complete with walnut paneling and some sort of nondescript music. And there was something else as well, the faint but unmistakable scent of expensive cologne, the *same* perfume I had noticed in the limo. Who was this elusive female? And what would she look like? The guy in me wanted to know.

The platform coasted to a stop, and the robot gestured toward the door. The outer part of Alfano's office was quite imposing. A single individual sat behind a rosewood barricade. She looked up from a computer and frowned. She was far too homely to be a robot—and looked a little bit like the portrait I'd seen. A relative? Probably. Corpies use nepotism like glue. In any case the woman looked more like a guard than a secretary. "Yes?"

"Mr. Maxon here to see Mr. Alfano."

I was surprised when the desk Nazi nodded toward the inner sanctum. "Mr. Alfano is on the com right now . . . but go on in. He'll be free in a moment."

Ever obedient, and curious as to what the whole thing was about, I circled the desk and passed through double doors. The room was mostly the way I had expected it to be. A lot of dark wood, shelves full of books that Alfano probably hadn't read, and a forty-acre desk. There was an old-fashioned hinged picture frame. Ornate silver circled two holo stats, one of a young woman so beautiful that she could have been a model, and a second of a woman who, though well made-up, was handsome rather than pretty. Alfano waved a half-smoked cigar toward one of the guest chairs and continued to talk. "So, what are you telling me? That he doesn't *want* her? Who the hell does the punk think he is?"

I took a chair and tried to disappear. Alfano listened to the other person's answer, said, "Yeah, yeah, yeah," and shook his head in disappointment. "All right, Marty, thanks for trying. I'll see you at the shareowner's meeting."

The com set clattered in its cradle, and Alfano turned his attention to me. I noticed that the patriarch was smaller than he appeared to be in the portrait and a good deal older. The eyes were the same however—and seemed to drill their way into my head. "I'm a busy man Mr. Maxon . . . so I hope you'll forgive me if I get straight to the point. Do you know what a shareowner's meeting is?"

I shrugged. "It's an opportunity for the corporation to provide shareowners with information regarding how the business is doing."

"Exactly," Alfano replied. "I have enemies, lots of 'em, and the meeting would make the perfect place for a hit. Everybody knows I'll be there. That's why we hire some freelancers each year, men and women like yourself, to beef up the team."

"Why?" I asked stupidly. "You have plenty of security."

The eyes looked flat and hard. Alfano wasn't used to questions and didn't much care for them. "Think about it, Mr. Maxon. We have to defend the building even when we aren't in it, *especially* when we aren't in it, and still move enough muscle to handle the gathering."

I nodded. "Hobbletygorp."

He looked the way most people do when I say something like that. Surprised, confused, and a little bit annoyed. Can't say as I blame them. The shrinks can't explain the nonsensical words, and neither can I. Odds are that they have something to do with the headaches and the weird repetitive dreams, the worst of which involves some sort of operation. There are doctors, the harsh smell of antiseptics, and a general sense of disorientation. That's when it starts. The general sense of inflow, a virtual blizzard of words and numbers that seem to bury me alive, and choke off my air.

That's when I escape from my body, hover just under the ceiling, and watch them bring me back. I forced a smile and pretended to clear my throat. "Yes, sir. Thanks for the clarification. Who will I report to? Andre?"

There was a change in Alfano's eyes, as if the mention of his security chief indicated that there was some hope for me. He pointed toward the more homely of the two women. "Yes, where the *big* picture is concerned. But your job is to guard my eldest daughter. That's why I chose to interview you myself."

The words rattled like stones on concrete. They sounded false, but I couldn't say why. I nodded. "Yes, sir. I'll do my best."

"Good. We leave in the morning so you won't be able to go home. Find Andre and draw anything you need. He will introduce you to Pru."

"Pru?"

"Prudence, my daughter."

"Yes, of course."

Alfano nodded, examined the end of his cigar, and stubbed it out. The interview was over.

I showed myself out of Alfano's office, requested directions from the desk Nazi, and proceeded down the hall. Now, left to my own devices, I realized how empty the building was, with lots of dark empty offices, unpopulated work cubes, and sterile common areas. The place felt haunted, as if the ghosts of a million laid-off workers still roamed the corridors, taking meetings, kissing ass, and when things went well, making products that people needed and used.

The security chief was where you might expect him to be, on the same floor with the boss, but comfortably removed. To provide the alpha male with some privacy? Or to escape the blast in case a bomb went off? I put *my* money on number two.

I stepped through the door, and entered a completely different world. Steel, plastic, and vinyl had replaced the brass, wood, and carpeting that typified the rest of the building. Security monitors, literally hundreds of them, tiled three long walls. A rack of radios, lights rippling, murmured to one side, while weapons, at least half a million credits' worth, waited in racks.

Andre, assuming he and the man in front of me were one and the same, was a surprise. Rather than the hulk I had expected to see, he was small, *very* small, standing no more than about four feet tall, not counting the power-assisted stilts. Most people would have assumed that he was the victim of a hereditary birth defect, but I knew better. The Mishimuto Marines included an entire battalion of gene-manipulated men and women, so called "specialists" designed to function as crew for exotic weapons systems. "Normals" tended to look down on them, to refer to them as "freaks," and I was no exception. Not till I became one myself. Maybe that's why I took a liking to him. He had a pretty good build for a little guy, brown hair that was pulled back into a ponytail, and level green eyes. "So, who the hell are you?"

I shrugged. "Max Maxon. Mr. Alfano hired me to protect his daughter."

Andre's eyes narrowed. "Which one?"

"Prudence."

"Hmmm," he said. "Interesting."

"How so?"

The security chief ran his eyes the length of my frame, brought them back, and met mine. "Tell me something . . . How good are you? Compared to the very best?"

I didn't care for the question and decided to stall. "Like what? On a scale of one to ten?"

"Sure," the security chief answered easily. "On a scale of one to ten."

I swallowed. It was tempting to exaggerate, to build myself up, but something held me back. The look in Andre's eyes? The knowledge that I couldn't back it up? It didn't matter. I went with the truth. "Maybe a five."

Something changed deep within his eyes. Something subtle but important. He was silent for a moment. When he spoke there was respect in his voice. "That took courage, Maxon . . . more than most people have."

He looked around as if to verify that the room was empty. His voice was little more than a whisper. "Tell me something, Maxon . . . if your daughter was in danger, and you could afford the very best, would you hire a five?"

"No," I said slowly, "I guess I wouldn't."

"Neither would I," Andre replied softly. "So a word to the wise: Watch your six. Who knows? You might live long enough to get paid."

Pay! Something I should have asked Alfano about but had failed to do so. "So," I said casually, "how much *is* the pay? Assuming I live to collect it?"

"Five hundred credits per day," the security chief replied cheerfully, "plus expenses. Not bad, huh? You need anything?" He gestured to the weapons racked along the wall.

I tend to carry at least two backup mags for the .38, but ammo is damned expensive, so why not? "You got any boxes of .38 super hollow-point express lying around?"

Andre nodded. "Yeah, not much though, most of the team prefer .9mm. Let's take a look." The power-assisted stilts made a whining noise as he crossed the room. The security chief checked the shelves, and, like so many things in life, found the stuff he was looking for on the top shelf.

There were four boxes of fifty. A nice little bonus. I took every single one of them.

"So," Andre inquired. "You ready?"

"Reckon so."

"All right, then. Let's pay a visit to Miss Prudence. We leave at oh-dark thirty . . . so you should get acquainted."

Servos whined as the security officer made his way down the hall. Now, viewed from the back, I saw Andre had stuffed a .9mm down the back of his pants. Tried it once but damned near blew my ass off. Stuck with holsters ever since.

We entered an elevator, dropped two levels, and got off. The first thing I noticed was the change in décor. The almost sterile feel of the floors above had been replaced by a beige sort of beauty replete with thick off-white carpets, beautifully crafted wood trim, carefully chosen brass fixtures and paintings. *Lots* of paintings, abstract things mostly, executed in bright primary colors. I liked the one that fronted the elevators, but hey, part of my brain is missing. Andre must have noticed my interest because he nodded toward the jumble of brightly colored shapes. "Miss Pru likes to paint."

The tone was neutral, and his face was blank, but there was no denying the underlying judgment. Andre considered painting to be a waste of time, and judging from the fact that Alfred Alfano's office boasted bare walls, the old man did, too. The security chief pointed toward the far end of the hall. "Both Miss Pru and Miss Linda have suites at the far end of the hall."

I raised an eyebrow. "What? You're bailing out?"

Andre smiled. "She's all yours, Maxon . . . use the radio if you need reinforcements."

"Will anyone come?"

The little big man laughed. "Maybe, if we're in the

mood." Servos whined, doors closed, and the security chief
was gone.

I grumbled to myself as I trudged the length of the hall,
still finding time to make note of the side doors, exits, windows, and the building across the street. It was a big hum-
mer, equal in size to the one I was in, and just as empty. A
few rectangles of white light showed where some poor
slobs were working late, but most of the offices were dark.

The hall ended in what amounted to a small lobby. There
were two sets of white-enameled doors, one to the left and
one to the right. It might have been confusing except for the
fact that some extremely thoughtful soul had mounted brass
plaques next to both. The one on the left read, "MISS
LINDA," and the one on the right said, "MISS PRU." I rang the
bell and spoke into the intercom. "Max Maxon here to see
Miss Prudence."

The voice sounded tinny. "Come in."

I tried the door, found it was unlocked, and shook my
head in disgust. I mean doors won't stop the poppers, not
the more determined kind, but they do slow 'em down. And
seconds, even a few, are damned nice to have. I entered the
suite, secured the door, and went looking for my client. The
color scheme was very much like that found out in the hall,
complete with more splashy paintings, and Beethoven's
Piano Sonata No. 8 in C minor beckoning me on. How did I
know *that*? Good question. I wish I knew.

I passed through an entry hall, entered a sparsely furnished sitting room, and followed the hardwood flooring. It
led me past a nicely equipped kitchen, some doors that
might have led to bedrooms, and out into a solarium. That's
where Miss Prudence was, sitting behind a baby grand,
eyes out of focus.

She sensed my presence, or I thought she did, but kept
on playing. Her hair was dark, her nose was too large, and

her mouth was small and determined. There was nothing wrong with her body, however, which appeared to be in good shape and featured bumps in all the right places. Her clothes were simple but stylish. A white blouse, some nice jewelry, and black slacks. Finally, after the last note had died away, Miss Pru looked up. She started to smile, gave a start, and turned white as a sheet. "Are *you* the man Father hired to protect me?"

I'm used to some double takes, what with the skull plate and all, but this seemed excessive. "Yes," I replied cautiously, "I am. Is there some sort of problem?"

Slowly, as if afflicted by old age, she stood. "I wanted to be sure that's all . . . I had hoped, well, it hardly matters what I had hoped. It's over now."

My eye was drawn to the building across the street.

I ran toward the piano, launched myself into the air, and yelled, "Dork Nop!" at the top of my lungs.

It was supposed to be "Watch out!" but I don't suppose it made much difference as she heard the shout, saw me hurtling straight at her, and threw herself backwards. Glass shattered a fraction of a second later.

Having established themselves in the building across the street, and gone to the trouble of setting up tripods for their custom-made rifles, the poppers had been presented with an irresistible opportunity. Here was their mark sitting in what amounted to a well-lit bubble. What more could any assassin want?

Popper number one, who was almost certainly an apprentice, had the relatively easy job of breaking the glass. Glass, which, if left intact, might deflect the second shot by the journeyman, thereby giving the victim a second to escape. Now, as I harvested that second by landing on top of my already-supine client, I grabbed and rolled her toward the wall.

Frustrated, and blessed with twenty- or thirty-shot clips, the assassins began to hose the area down. The piano jumped and made strange thrumming sounds as armor-piercing slugs tore through the highly polished wood and buried themselves in the floor.

Prudence, who was understandably frightened, wrapped her arms around my neck and pulled me close. This turned out to be a rather pleasant experience since she was not only well put together but smelled divine. That's when I realized that it had been her perfume that I had detected in the limo and elevator.

My thoughts were interrupted by a muffled explosion. The firing stopped. Five or ten seconds passed. Her tone was dry. "Thank you, Mr. Maxon . . . but you can release me now."

"Yes, well, I suppose I can. I'll check. Please keep your head down."

I sat up, rolled onto my knees, and poked my head up over the sill. Smoke poured out of a rather sizable hole in the building across the street. That's when I remembered the woman up on the roof. She, or one of her camo-clad mercenaries, had detected the attack, prepped a rocket launcher, and nailed the poppers with one shot. Prudence stirred at my side.

"You save my life. How did you know?" she asked.

"No big deal," I said as I stood and offered my hand. "Some idiot turned a light on. They turned it off two seconds later but the damage was done. I saw the tripods, guessed what they were for, and took to the air."

"You're not much of a bird," she said while brushing little beads of safety glass off her clothes.

"No? Well, you make one helluva landing pad."

Prudence laughed. Not a little chuckle, but the sort of gut buster you don't hear very often, but tend to remember. She was still laughing when Andre plus a couple of his security people entered the room. They looked at me, and I shrugged. Women. Who can understand 'em?

The better part of three hours had passed before the window was boarded up, the broken glass was removed, and the two of us were left alone. The first thing I did was to ensure that the steel shutters that Prudence hated to use were extended and locked in place. Once that was accomplished I headed for the entry and a semicomfortable chair. Comfortable chairs are a bad idea since I tend to fall asleep in them. Especially when I'm tired . . . which I was. Prudence intercepted me. "Got a minute? I'd like to talk."

I shrugged. "Okay, but I'm not much of a talker."

"We were talking before the shooting started."

I nodded and followed her into the sitting room. She pointed toward a chair and asked if I wanted a drink. I shook my head no, and waited while she built one for herself. Ice clinked as she sat down. I watched her chose the words. "No offense, Maxon, but in spite of what you did for me earlier, you are what Andre would call second or third rate talent."

This was the second time within the last five or six hours someone had told me how pathetic I was, and I was getting tired of it. She must have seen it in my face because she raised a hand. "No, I haven't forgotten who saved my butt, so put your ego in neutral. I have something to say."

I nodded, wondered why I was holding the short end of the stick again, and tried to look attentive. Pru frowned, summoned up an expression that made her look a lot like her father, and started to talk. It seemed that she and her father had never been close, especially after her mother's death and his subsequent remarriage.

Though brilliant during his youth, Alfano had made some mistakes of late, picked the wrong deals, and lost a substantial amount of money. No, the empire wasn't about to crumble, not yet, but repairs were in order. *Serious* repairs, the kind that require millions of credits, and, depending on where you get them, can result in a loss of control. Something the old man wasn't willing to consider.

That left the other possibility, an alliance, or a merger that left him in control. It seemed that there were numerous ways to structure such a relationship, including the ever-popular arranged marriage, which, given some time, would almost certainly create blood ties. Kind of like European nobility used to do hundreds of years before. Anyway, what with a whole room full of disappointed shareowners to deal with, the old man needed a fix.

Pru sipped her drink and I remembered sitting in her father's study while he discussed what? A potential husband? Who didn't want "her?" Whoever *she* was? Now I thought I knew.

"So," Prudence said flatly, "I think we can assume that my father tried to arrange some sort of marriage, couldn't find anyone who would take me, and made the obvious decision. Kill me, market Linda, and close the deal."

I remembered the picture of Linda, figured there'd be plenty of takers, and wondered how *she* felt about all this. I'm a gentleman though, well sometimes, and tried to soften the blow. "You're being too hard on yourself. It's a business deal, remember? *If* you're correct, and that's a mighty big *if*, chances are that the numbers didn't compute."

Pru shook her head. "Thanks, Maxon, but no thanks. You took your medicine, and I'll take mine. You're a five . . . and so am I. Have you seen my father since the poppers attacked? No? Neither have I. Let's be real. He hired the poppers or had someone do it."

She had me there. "Still," I replied, "why kill *you* when he has your sister?"

"She's pretty," Pru responded, "but *I'm* the one with the stock."

"Stock?"

"Yes, stock in the company given to my mother on their wedding day, and passed to me. He needs my block to negotiate a deal—and I won't give it to him. Not without some sort of insurance policy."

"But not your sister?"

"No, because she has a different mother. Or *had*, since Elaine was killed by a car bomb two years back."

"You could change your beneficiary," I said brightly, "so there's no reason to kill you."

There was pity in her eyes. "You really don't get it, do you, Maxon? There would be no one to protect me if I did that . . . greed makes a pretty good motive."

"So," I said doubtfully, "what's left?"

Pru took a long hard pull on her drink and looked out over the glass. "Beats the hell out of me. Your job is to keep me alive until I find an answer."

"What about the meeting?"

Prudence looked thoughtful. "I think we'd better go. It's dangerous, but no worse than sitting here all by ourselves."

I got to my feet. "Yes, ma'am. I'll be ready."

I napped till dawn, got my hands on enough stuff to make myself presentable, and reported for duty. The entire household mustered on the roof at 0800. There was Alfano, puffing on a cigar, Prudence, with circles under her eyes, Linda, who no one thought to introduce, whining about how early it was, and Andre scanning the skies.

Prudence and her father seemed determined to stay as far away from each other as possible, and not a word passed between them. She looked at him, though, as if hoping for some sort of communication, which I found to be surprising until I realized what it was. In spite of what he'd done, or tried to do, Prudence still loved him. And in her own corpie way, understood his motivations. After all, he had tried to make a match, had tried to make it work, but been unable to do so. It was then and only then that the contract went out. Sweet, huh?

The Alfanos traveled in separate aircars, so one missile couldn't kill them all, and so they wouldn't have to spend any time with each other. Though slow when compared to real aircraft the limos took only three hours to reach SF Urboplex. Prudence produced a com set, dialed a number, and caused a partition to drop between our seats. I tried to think of something useful to do, failed, and took a nap. It ended when the car settled onto the Hilton's roof. The partition had been raised and Prudence stared out the driver's side window. It was a busy place, thick with parked vehicles, and people wearing sunglasses, weapons, and a lot of attitude. Most of the shareowners were corpies—and the meeting was about to begin.

It got a little weird after that as Alfred Alfano, Linda Alfano, and a dozen bodyguards all made for the elevator lobby leaving Prudence and me to fend pretty much for ourselves. Androids handled the luggage. I maintained a sharp lookout as we checked in via the rooftop lobby, made our way down to the twenty-seventh floor, and entered her suite. I searched the place and found three listening devices and two vid cams but no bombs, booby traps, or homicidal robots.

Then, with that out of the way, we keyed the door pad to our fingerprints and made our way down to main level, where the actual meeting was scheduled to take place. The lobby itself was quiet as a tomb, but outside, beyond the heavily armored glass, a mob had gathered. The signs said it all: "Down with Alfano, Inc.!" "Back to the soil!" "Earth first!"

The Greenies seemed to surge forward, an army of Zeebs reinforced by security people pushed them back, and Prudence stopped to watch. She was calm, *very* calm, as if nothing much mattered anymore. Then, as if I were the one who had stopped to look, she nodded toward the far side of the lobby. "Enough standing around, Maxon . . . the auditorium is on the far side of the lobby."

The lobby had been furnished with chairs that people rarely sat in, glass-topped coffee tables, and enormous tropical plants. We made our way between them to emerge on the other side. On the doors Andre had guards on the doors. They damned near growled. I nodded in reply.

The auditorium was large, much larger than it needed to be in order to accommodate the forty-odd shareowners who actually showed up. Smartly dressed waiters dispensed appetizers and drinks. One of them spilled something, received a wicked tongue-lashing, and backed away.

Prudence nodded to some of the shareowners as we made our way down the aisle and were shown to our seats. They had preprinted cards on them. Hers read: "Prudence Alfano" and mine said: "Assistant."

Linda took a seat nearby but didn't look our way. There was no sign of Alfano senior. Pru touched my arm. "Maxon . . ."

"Yes?"

"No matter what happens, no matter how my father reacts, *don't* kill him. He may be a first-class dyed in the wool shit, but he's *still* my father."

I was about to ask her what she was talking about but didn't get the opportunity. Martin Zawicki, the company's chief financial officer, took the podium and called the meeting to order. Once that was out of the way there was a good thirty minutes' worth of holo charts and financial mumbo jumbo before the CFO brought the presentation to a close. That's when Alfred Alfano made his appearance, delivered a surprisingly effective speech, and opened the meeting to questions.

There were a couple of softballs, tossed by friends of the family, but the sharks were waiting their turn. A woman with a nurse at her side sucked oxygen through a mask and removed it so that she could speak. Her voice was high and wheezy. "I join those who laud Mr. Alfano for past achievements—but am forced to look to the future. Why has Alfano Inc. lost 4 percent market share during the last twelve months? And what steps does he plan to take?"

There it was, the moment when Alfano would have announced a deal, had there been one in the making. He forced a smile, hinted a new but unspecified initiatives, and pointed to a man in the fourth row. "You, sir. Did *you* have a question?"

The shareowner's suit looked a little too large, as if he had recently lost some weight, or borrowed it from another man. His eyebrows were bushy and untrimmed. Bright blue eyes peered out from under them. "Why yes," the man replied, "I did. My name is Hoskins, Mark Hoskins, a one-time employee of Alfano Inc., presently serving as regional manager for Green Party. We would like to know when you plan to cut your reliance on fossil fuels, address global warming, and provide benefits to freelancers."

Blood suffused Alfano's face, and his jaw started to tighten. "This meeting is for stockholders, Mr. Hoskins . . . Andre will show you out."

"Oh, but I *am* a shareowner," the Greenie replied tightly, "and a rather important one at that. Isn't that correct, Ms. Alfano?"

Every eye in the place swiveled between Linda and Prudence. I felt something cold trickle into the pit of my stomach and allowed my hand to drift under my jacket. Prudence stood. "Yes," she replied, her voice strong and clear. "I joined this morning, and, to demonstrate how sincere I am, donated all of my shares to the party. From this moment forward the Greens control 14.1 percent of Alfano Inc."

It was an audacious move, one that put the screws to her father, *and* purchased some pretty good protection. They might be looney, but the Greens were well organized, and very well armed. And, thanks to all the press her conversion would generate, the tree-huggers had every reason to protect her, to keep their own rep clean. It was a deal worthy of her father.

The crowd sucked air, Alfano reached inside his coat, and I shot him in the knee. A jet of blood sprayed outward, he crumpled, and all hell broke loose. A bullet whizzed past my head, the waiters produced submachine guns, and fired them into the ceiling. That froze everyone in place. Gun smoke drifted beneath the lights.

Hoskins stood and sidestepped toward the aisle, his movements calm and precise. Once there, he turned to look at the audience. "It isn't too late. Earth *can* be saved. Miss Alfano? Are you ready to leave?"

It was nicely done. Just like he had practiced in front of a mirror. Prudence nodded. She made her way to the aisle, and I followed. The waiters covered our exit. Hoskins led us into a restaurant and through the kitchen. A row of employees, all gagged and bound, lined one of the walls. We followed Hoskins out onto a loading dock where an unmarked delivery van waited with opened doors. We stepped inside, took our seats, and strapped in. The driver knew her stuff, and the corpies never came close.

Prudence gave me three days' pay plus a bonus. Not bad,

all things considered. I never saw her again except on the holo, speaking for the Greenies, or when they ran a piece on her paintings. The critics seem to love them, and she smiles a lot.

Her father sent three different poppers after me, got tired of paying for services he never received, and eventually gave up. As for me, well, the money ran out a couple of months ago, but Bobby's still out there, and the burritos are good.

Suspended

by Michelle R. Gawe

"Pickled bat wings," Esther declared.

The mayor's myopic wife blinked at her uncertainly. "I beg your pardon?"

"Pickled bag wings." Esther took the wide jar from the shelf and blew dust off it. She held the container up to the dim light shed by the low-wattage bulb overhead. If she squinted, she could make out the shriveled black shapes in the murky fluid. "This'll fix him up right quick."

She gestured at her guest to proceed up the stairs. The mayor's wife gave her an uneasy look before mounting the steps. She stumbled a bit on the first one, and Esther grabbed her arm.

"Sorry about that," she said gruffly. "I keep telling Geoffrey to tack down that carpet."

"It's—uh—quite all right," the mayor's myopic wife replied. Her bulbous eyes bounced around the basement, clearly searching for a glimpse of Geoffrey.

"He's out," Esther said curtly.

"Ah . . . Of course."

Once upstairs, Esther closed the basement door and pointed at a chair. "Have a seat."

The mayor's wife obeyed immediately, and started twisting the end of her apron. She stared in awe at the electric light dangling over the kitchen table.

"It doesn't flicker," she ventured meekly. "How do you get the flame inside it? Is it . . . is it a spirit?" she asked in a whisper.

"It's called electricity," Esther informed her, screwing up her face with effort as she tried to get the lid off the jar. "Rrrrruh! Damnation and hell toads."

The mayor's wife clapped a hand to her mouth in shock.

"Hell toads and chicken feathers," Esther continued, rooting through her junk drawer for a nifty tool she'd swiped recently from a house in San Diego. "Don't tell me I have to find another one of those things," she grumbled, as her search proved fruitless. "After all the grief I went through—aha!"

She pulled out the tool in triumph. She clamped it around the lid of the jar and tried to turn it. The metal teeth of the tool skittered along the recalcitrant screwtop lid, screeching and leaving bright marks in the tarnished metal.

She threw the tool back into the drawer in disgust, just as a loud thumping emanated from the basement.

"Oh good," Esther muttered. She hurriedly opened the basement door and put the jar on the first step.

"Geoffrey!" she shouted as she closed the door. "Open this jar!"

A loud rustling and thumping came up the stairs, and she heard Geoffrey pick up the jar. There was silence for a moment, and then a loud **pop**.

"Thanks!" she shouted, as the rustling and thumping went back down the steps.

The mayor's wife was still sitting with her hand to her mouth, her eyes so wide they were in some danger of falling right out of her head.

Esther jerked open the door, swept up the open jar and

the lid, and slammed the door again, before too much of the smell could get into the kitchen.

The mayor's wife sniffed suddenly, and a glassy look came into her protuberant eyes. "Oh . . ."

"Here, let me open this window."

Esther threw open her black shutters, and a brisk fall wind flooded the room with the scent of decaying leaves and wood fires from the town. She yanked the string over the table, and the bulb darkened, eliciting a disappointed sigh from the mayor's wife, who was regaining her senses now that Geoffrey's rather distinct odor was being flushed out by the chill breeze. Or maybe it was due to the jar Esther held in one hand. She waved it at her guest, who wrinkled her nose.

"Yes, indeed," Esther said cheerfully. "Pickled bat wings are definitely the way to go."

She pulled out a loaf of only slightly moldy bread, hacked off two thick slices and spread some mustard on one side of each. A piece of slightly dry ham went on one, a juicy slice of tomato and a leaf of lettuce on the other. Then she stuck two fingers into the jar and fished out a limp bat wing. She carefully arranged it on top of the ham so none of the leathery flaps would hang over the edge, then slapped the two pieces of bread together.

"There," she said with satisfaction. "Hand me that piece of cloth there," she said to the mayor's wife, who obligingly handed her a square of orange-stained cheesecloth. She wrapped the sandwich up and give it to her guest, who stared at it dubiously.

"This will keep him from chasing after that hussy?" the mayor's wife asked.

"Sure will," Esther reassured her with a grin. "And even if it doesn't, at least you'll have the satisfaction of knowing he ate a pickled bat wing."

A gleam came into the woman's eyes, and she dropped the sandwich into her shopping basket.

"Thank you, Esther," she said. "Here's your white and yellow thread, and a square of white cloth, as you asked."

"Just marvelous," Esther said, smiling in satisfaction and showing the mayor's wife to the door. "Now, if that sandwich doesn't do the trick, you just come back here, and I'll give you something to give to that hussy. I guarantee *that* will work. No additional charge, of course."

She waved good-bye as the mayor's wife went merrily down the dirt track into the dark forest. An acorn hit Esther in the head, and she scowled upward.

An angel was sitting on the roof, frowning at her. As she watched, he lobbed another acorn at her, shaking his head in disapproval.

Esther waited until the mayor's wife was out of earshot, then said, "Geoffrey, there's nothing wrong with keeping a man from cheating on his wife. And even if there was, you're unemployed! What do you care if it's wrong or not?"

"Pickled bat wings?" he asked her in distaste, his beautiful voice filling the air like music. Esther scowled again.

"I don't argue with a 90 percent success rate, and neither should you. Now get off the roof, unless you're up there nailing down those shingles like I asked you to."

She stomped inside her little cottage, hearing the rustle of wings as he jumped off the roof and settled gently to the ground. He followed her inside, ducking so his wings wouldn't brush the lintel, and the mesmerizing, unique scent of angel filled the house. Esther had always thought it smelled a bit like cloves, but since she seemed to be the only person immune to it, she had no way of knowing what it smelled like to other people.

She said, "She almost tripped on that bit of carpet down-stairs. I asked you to nail that down, too, if you remember."

"Yeah, I know," the angel grumbled. He brightened when he saw the thread. "You got it! Oh, thank you, Esther!"

"You're welcome," she said, waving a hand irritably and putting the lid back on the jar of bat wings. "Now that you can fix your stockings, do you suppose you might get around to fixing the roof too? It's fall, you know. Winter soon. You don't necessarily notice down there in the base-ment, but—"

"I'll do it tomorrow," Geoffrey promised, smiling in de-light as he clutched the thread to his chest. Even Esther wasn't quite immune to the angel's smile, but she merely scowled at him again and shooed him out of the kitchen.

She stood for a moment with her hands on her hips. What to do, what to do? There were clothes and dishes to wash. There was bread to be baked, and floors to be swept. Her eyes flicked over the door into the library, and she brightened. There was a new sack of goodies from the Other Side to be gone through, too. As she started toward the library she heard Geoffrey pounding nails downstairs.

"Oh, all right," she said testily. "I'll do the dratted house-work." She pulled out the broom and started attacking the floor with it.

"Esther?" came a quavering voice from downstairs. "The light went out."

"Hold on a second," Esther replied, opening the base-ment door to let in some light down there. She saw Geof-frey's relieved face shining in the gloom at the base of the stairs. The angel was sitting on the floor cross-legged, grip-ping a hammer in one immaculate hand while he held the carpet straight with the other. "I'll be right back," she said. "Don't start banging again till the light comes back on."

He had resumed hammering before Esther even made it

out the back door. She was unsurprised to hear a squashy thump just as the angel sent up a wail.

"Can't take orders," Esther muttered. "No wonder he got suspended."

She made her way around to the shed behind the house, and found the gerbils in the wheel fast asleep. "Time to change shifts, eh?" she asked, taking the snoozing bundles of bright orange fur out of the enclosed wheel and placing them in their cage. The two gerbils in the other cage were wide-awake and digging obsessively. When Esther transferred them into the plastic wheel, they started racing with boundless energy, and the little generator in the shed started humming again. Esther made sure the sleeping gerbils had water and food in their cage, and decided she really had to get some gerbil tubes on her next trip to the Other Side. That way the gerbils could change shifts on their own, without her having to come back here and switch them every couple of days.

Geoffrey was pounding away when she went back in.

"The enegerbils got pooped out," she called down the stairs. "Remind me to switch them on Tuesday." The angel grunted agreement, but Esther knew his sense of time was faulty and that he would think it was Tuesday in about a week and a half.

"Well, he'll know it's Tuesday when the light goes out again," she said to herself. "I wonder if all angels are afraid of the dark?"

She picked up the broom again, then noticed someone lurking on the forest path at the edge of the clearing. It looked like a man, but the shadows were too deep where he was standing, and she couldn't see his face. With her luck, it was the mayor wanting a love charm for his hussy or a pot of poison for his chubby wife. He wasn't going to get either.

She opened the front door. "Yeah? What do you want?"

"I want to speak to your tenant."

Uh-oh. The mellifluous voice sent a shiver of apprehension up Esther's spine, but she planted her broom firmly on the porch deck, and said, "I don't have a tenant. You've got the wrong house."

The shadowy person chuckled. "Now, Esther. There's no point in lying to me, of all people."

"You're no people," Esther said sourly. "You're worse than people. Get away from my property and go back where you came from. Scat." She menaced the shadowy figure with her broom.

The voice tsked. "Now is that any way to treat an old friend?"

"You might be old, but you're no friend. Away with you. I've got nothing to say to you."

"That may be so, but I've got something to say to Geoffrey."

"Never heard of him. You've got the wrong house. Go pester someone else. Shoo."

"Do you really think you can stop me?"

Esther waved her broom. "You come into my yard, and I'll give you a tanning with this broom, I will. You're not welcome here. Go away."

"Fine. I'll come back later." The figure vanished in a shower of sparks.

"You won't be welcome then either!" Esther shouted. "Damned showoff."

She stomped back into the house and peered out all her windows before opening the door to the basement. The light was off. She crept cautiously down into the darkness and pulled the string. The bare bulb flickered into life, sending a wan yellow light into the gloom. She looked down all the aisles of jars and pots, and finally found the

angel huddled in the farthest, darkest corner, wedged between a rotting trunk and a spool of wire.

"He's gone, honey, you can come out now."

Geoffrey shuddered and lifted bleak eyes. "He'll be
back."

"Well, we'll just worry about that when it happens.
Come on out of there." She held out a wrinkled hand, and
the angel tentatively took it, allowing her to coax him out
of the corner. He stood in the center of the basement with
his head low, his wings streaked with dirt, and cobwebs
tangled in his hair.

"It's no use. He'll get me eventually."

"No he won't. I've got devil's-bane planted all around
this house, and he isn't strong enough to get past it. You
just stay in the yard and you'll be fine."

The angel sighed. "Yes, Esther."

Geoffrey was still glum after dinner. He brushed the
bread crumbs off his robe and licked the honey off his fingers, then sat staring into the small fire Esther had built to
keep the chill out of the house.

"Well? Aren't you going to fix your stockings?" Esther
asked.

"Yes, I suppose so."

He fetched the cloth and thread from the mantel and settled in front of the fire with his only pair of stockings. He'd
been going barefoot ever since ripping them, and Esther
hadn't been able to find a suitable pair either in the village
or on the Other Side. He was ridiculously fastidious about
his attire. He absently reached up to adjust his halo to give
him a better light, but his hand encountered empty air. He
flinched and sank back in despair.

Esther let him alone. She continued cataloging the items
she'd stolen from a tract house in New Jersey: four light-

bulbs, a wrench, a pair of pliers, six C-size Duracell batteries, a bright pink plastic flashlight, two small pots of Sterno, a large box of matches, two romance novels, and a bottle of rose-scented bubble bath. Not a bad haul, considering she'd unexpectedly gone Through into a utility closet. She'd been aiming for a kitchen, but her spell had been tailored to bring her to the room with the most metal in it, and it'd turned out her hosts had had a lot of camping equipment but no culinary interests.

She double-checked her bookmark in the *Incantation Book, Traveler's Edition*. Page twelve, Teleportation. She wiped a finger across a straight line in the Book, and the word *metal* vanished. She tapped her pencil on the table. What should she write as a focus? She still wanted some kitchen items, but so far she'd come out into almost every room *except* the kitchen. Water? No, she'd wind up in someone's shower stall. Iron? No, with her luck, she'd find herself inside a woodstove. Glass? Hmm. That was an idea. Most people had lots of glass in their kitchen. She'd try that next. She penciled in *glass* on the blank line and touched her finger to the word *home* at the bottom of the page. A slight tingle told her that the Book was charged and ready to go. If she'd been out on a Trip, just touching the word would have brought her back to her front porch. She'd be able to make at least one more Trip out and back before having to recharge the magical energies carried by the Book. She closed it carefully and put it back on its shelf, then busied herself finding homes for her new possessions.

Geoffrey shook back his golden hair, impatient with himself, and bent closer to the flickering firelight so he could thread the needle and get on with repairing his hosiery.

He was surprisingly good at sewing. He saw Esther's raised eyebrows, and said, "I was in the Robes and Hose department for a long time. I liked it. It was better than

Loaves and Fishes, anyway. I hated smelling like sardines all the time." He sighed disconsolately. "If they ever let me back in, I'll probably wind up in Scrubbing and Sweeping."

"Well, you never know," Esther said cheerfully. "They might let you have your old job back."

The angel just shook his head.

The next morning, Esther discovered that the mold, which had barely had a toehold on the bread the day before, had rampaged all across the surface during the night.

"Drat," she said. "So much for making another Trip now." She tossed the rest of the loaf out into the yard for the birds and squirrels to argue over, and put her tiny Incantation Book back onto the shelf. If it had just been her, she'd have taken her Trip to the Other Side and grabbed a loaf of Wonder out of someone's kitchen, but Geoffrey was very particular about his bread. She couldn't complain too much, since it was the only thing he ate. She pulled out all the various ingredients she would need and discovered she was out of nuts.

"Geoffrey! If you want nuts in this bread, you'd better go find me some!" she shouted down the basement stars. "And mind you stay in the yard!"

"Yes, Esther," came the angel's muffled voice. She heard him rustling his way through the outside cellar door.

"Where is he?" she muttered an hour later. The dough was all mixed, she had cleaned the kitchen and swept up the spilled flour, and the angel still hadn't returned. Esther usually kneaded the nuts in before letting the bread rise, but she couldn't knead them in if she didn't have them. She stomped out onto the porch, bellowing, "Geoffrey! You're going to have plain bread if you don't get back here right now! Geoffrey! Drat it, you'd better not be chasing after bugs again!"

There was no answer. Esther went down the porch stairs, calling his name. Nothing.

"Oh, Mother Mary, he didn't leave the yard!" she muttered anxiously. "I told him to stay in the yard. Geoffrey!"

She saw a flutter of white off in the woods, and a melodious voice said, "Here I am, Esther! I found a bunch! Come help me!"

Relief washed through her, immediately followed by anger. She stomped out of the yard and into the woods, yelling, "Drat it all, Geoffrey, can't you take a single order? You are *way* out of the yard! What if that nasty old devil comes 'round here again?"

"Esther? Where are you going?" came the angel's perplexed voice from behind her.

Esther spun and saw the angel standing in the yard, his robe gathered up like an apron to carry the chestnuts he'd gathered from the trees right behind the house. The ring of devil's-bane stood between the two of them.

"But if—" Esther spun again and saw the grinning face of a devil behind her.

"Surprise."

"Of all the stupid, idiotic things for me to have done," Esther said bitterly. "I'm way too old to have fallen for that trick."

"Gimme! Gimme, gimme, gimme!" howled the little demon at her feet. It hopped around on its tiny cloven hooves and grabbed at the basket she was carrying. Twelve others joined it, all of them screaming, "Gimme!"

"Say 'please,' you brats!" Esther snapped.

"Gimme!" One of the demons latched onto her leg and bit it. Esther thwacked it with her broom and sent it rolling across the floor, where it started crying.

A larger demon—a *much* larger demon—came through

the door and glared at her. "You are not to strike the children," it said in a voice like a car crash in progress.

"It bit me!" Esther retorted.

"Just feed the children and don't strike them. There are worse places to work than the nursery," the demon said ominously, giving her one final glare before going back into its office. Esther made a rude face at its back and tossed the basket on the floor. Immediately thirteen tiny demons fell on it like a rugby team and tore it apart. Twelve lucky demons got the moldly biscuits and sausages—Esther didn't even want to think about where the sausages came from—and the thirteenth had to content itself with eating the basket.

"Slop time, you little pigs," Esther muttered.

"You are not to be rude to the children," came the demon's voice from the office. Esther brandished her broom in an empty threat at the office door, then leaned on it while she watched the demons start chewing on each other. Squalls went up all around the room.

"Break it up, you little monsters," Esther said, poking her broom between the combatants to separate them. There was no way she was going to put her hands in the way of those rending teeth and claws. "Break it up, I said."

"Esther! It's nice to see you being so supportive to our next generation of hell-raisers," said an amused voice from the door.

Esther sent a glare at the debonair devil leaning in the doorway. "Go away, Ashtoreth," she said, prying the children apart. "I still have nothing to say to you."

"Ah, you've learned my name," the devil said with a grin, twirling his pointed tail in what he no doubt thought to be a rakish manner. "Well, you might not have anything to say to me, but I thought you might have something to say to Geoffrey."

Esther immediately forgot the children, who promptly started gnawing on each other again. She automatically raised her voice to be heard over the din of their shrieks. "Geoffrey? What do you mean?"

Ashtoreth gestured, and the bedraggled angel shuffled into the doorway. His wings were streaked with red dust where they'd brushed against the stone walls, and his newly repaired stockings slumped dispiritedly around his ankles.

"Hello, Esther," Geoffrey said, trying to smile.

Esther whacked her broom into a wall in fury. Little demons scattered—they'd learned about Esther's broom the hard way. "Damn it! I told you to *stay in the yard!*"

"I couldn't leave you down here, Esther. Not when it's my fault you're here at all."

A chill passed through her. "Geoffrey, you didn't—"

"He did!" Ashtoreth said gleefully. "You for him. You go back to your charming little shack in the woods, and Geoffrey . . ." The devil put a proprietary hand on the angel's shoulder. The angel flinched. "Geoffrey stays with us."

"Geoffrey! You *stupid—*"

"I'm sorry, Esther!" the angel interrupted desperately. "I couldn't think of anything else. I'm not very bright, you know that. That's why I got suspended in the first place."

"Ah yes. You let your charge get run over by a train because you were off looking at ladybugs." Ashtoreth laughed. "If it's any consolation, he would've grown up to be a politician anyway. A senator. He would've gone to jail for tax evasion, so it's just as well he got splattered all over the front of that cow-catcher. You've saved the taxpayers some money, my friend."

Geoffrey stuck his jaw out. "You don't know that. You've only got a 70 percent chance of seeing the future accurately."

The devil patted his shoulder consolingly. "The other future was even worse, Geoffrey. It really wasn't fair for them to give you such a difficult child as your first charge. My goodness, the trouble that boy got into, even when you *were* paying attention! I'm telling you, they expected you to fail. They *meant* for you to fail. And then when you did—" He shrugged elegantly. "They kicked you out of the union and sent you to a backward little world that doesn't even have running water. Heaven really isn't everything it's cracked up to be, is it?"

"I didn't come here to join you," Geoffrey said softly. "I told you that."

"I know!" the devil said gaily. "You came to ransom your friend here. Such a noble youngster, our Geoffrey. Now, off you go, Esther." Ashtoreth waved a manicured hand.

"No!" Geoffrey cried, grabbing hold of the devil's arm. Ashtoreth raised a slim brow, and Geoffrey hurriedly released him. "Please. Just let me hug her once before she goes. I never got to thank her for everything she did for me."

"How touching," Ashtoreth said sardonically, smoothing the wrinkles out of his sleeve. "Very well. Be quick about it, the children are eyeing your wings." Indeed, the small demons were creeping around Esther and angling toward the angel's tattered wings, gluttony gleaming in their piglike eyes.

"Back, you unholy terrors!" Esther snapped, swiping at them with her broom. They retreated hastily.

Geoffrey came up to Esther and clasped her shoulders gently, pulling her close. She felt tears come to her eyes. Poor angel. They'd probably put him in an unlit room, if he ever let them know how he felt about the dark. Look what they'd done to her, who loathed even human children.

"You are a big, stupid—" Esther choked out. She felt

something poking into her bony chest. She put a hand up and found her tiny copy of the Incantation Book sitting snugly in a brand-new pocket in the angel's robe. "—brilliant, beautiful angel," she finished, flipping to page twelve and touching the word *home*, teleporting them the hell out of Hell.

Lights flashed around them, and Esther blinked dizzily. Her porch came into focus around her, and she could hear the night sounds of the forest all around her cabin. She smiled in satisfaction.

Geoffrey abruptly sat on the floor, his wings canted at crazy angles and the feathers catching on the rough planks. "I—I'm dizzy," he said with confusion.

"Teleportation, honey. You'll be all right in a minute." Esther, who'd taken the Trip a thousand times, shook it off faster. She patted the angel's shoulder briskly. "That was a smart move, Geoffrey. Very smart. I'm *very* proud of you."

The angel smiled up at her, wobbly but happy. "I did something right."

"Yes, you did. You were very brave, too. I don't think I could have volunteered to swap myself for someone in Hell, even if she was a witch with an Incantation Book."

"Well, I remembered that you always kept it fully charged, and that you always keep the second setting on *home* in case of an emergency. I figured this counted." The angel grinned. "And I didn't go out of the yard, either. I called and called, and when Ashtoreth showed up I made the bargain from *this* side of the devil's-bane."

Esther laughed. "I bet that old devil is chewing his own tail right now! Well, come on up, Geoffrey. There's still no bread in the house, and I'm going to have to start all over again. I'm sure the loaf I started yesterday is full of bugs."

"It is," the angel said eagerly. "And they're interesting bugs, too."

"You and your bugs," the witch grumbled. She turned to go into the house, and noticed a strange glow around her mailbox, out near the edge of the forest. She didn't get mail very often, and she certainly didn't get mail that glowed. She said slowly, "Geoffrey? You didn't leave a jar of fireflies in the postbox again, did you?"

"No." The angel looked out at the mailbox anxiously. "I swear I didn't, Esther. What do you think it is?"

"I don't know. Let's go see. It's inside the yard, we should be safe." She kept a firm hand on her broom as they cautiously walked down the path to the mailbox, which was glowing away as if someone had put a halogen lamp in it.

"Careful, Esther," Geoffrey said nervously, clutching at the witch's sleeve.

Esther turned her broom upside down and held the bristles as she poked the stick end into the handle of the door. She pulled the door open and jumped back in case something leapt out. Nothing did. She and Geoffrey looked at each other.

"Well, let's see what it is." Esther crept forward and peeked into the box. "Um. I think it's for you," she said in a peculiar voice.

Geoffrey leaned forward, his wings spread backward to keep him balanced, and peered cautiously into the interior. He snapped his wings forward in shock and fell to the ground in front of the box, then quickly knelt and put his hands inside.

He drew out a glowing circlet.

"It's my halo. It's my *halo!*" he cried.

He started to put it on over his head, but Esther said, "There's a tag attached to it."

"Uh-oh." The angel peered at the tag. Esther looked over his shoulder, but she couldn't read the angelic script.

"What's it say?" she asked, when the angel started trembling. "Honey, what's wrong?"

"Nothing's wrong," Geoffrey said tearfully. "It's my new assignment. There's a little girl in Hong Kong who needs a Guardian Angel. Oh, Esther, I've been reinstated! I'm back under His protection!" The angel leapt up and plunked his halo above his head, where it glowed like a beacon eight inches over his hair. "I have to go right now!" He stretched his wings, but then suddenly bent down and swept the witch up into an enthusiastic, whirling embrace. "Oh Esther! Thank you for everything!"

"You're welcome," she gasped. At this distance, his scent was overwhelming even to her. "Anytime."

He put her down and raised his arms to the sky. "Thank You!" he shouted. "I'll do a good job this time, I promise! Oh Esther, I really do have to go."

"Well, go on then," she grumbled. "No point wasting time. You never know, she could be getting into trouble right now."

The angel shot her an utterly horrified look and leapt into the sky without another word.

"Come back for a visit once in a while!" Esther shouted after the white blur winging through the night sky. "Hey! You never fixed my roof!"

Borders

by Nancy Jane Moore

A whitewashed, three-story building filled the holo-
screen as the battle schematics dissolved. With a loud
boom, the structure exploded into a shower of concrete
fragments, and flames began to engulf what remained.
"Courtesy CNN" appeared in small white type at the bottom of the screen.

The on-site robotic data reporter panned down the street
away from the fire. Teresa Marquez felt her stomach turn
somersaults as familiar images paraded across the screen:
Tio Pedro's Cantina, where her stepfather Jorge used to
drink his post-work cerveza; the Tienda Marta, where she'd
bought warm Coca-Cola; the old house with the peeling
yellow paint that was reputedly the busiest whorehouse in
Matamoros. She could almost smell the garlic and comino
frying in grease as a corner restaurant came into view.

The data reporter moved to another area, but Teresa
couldn't stand to watch anymore. She sat at rigid attention
and let her eyes glaze over. It was one thing to know that
you were being sent to put down a riot in your hometown—
for Brownsville, Texas, and Matamoros, Mexico, are one
city divided by a river and a national border—but it was another to see the familiar places. She knew if she actually
looked at the faces of the people on the screen, she would

see someone she knew, someone she'd gone to high school with, maybe even someone she'd once fumbled around with in a rusty gas-eating SUV—nobody in her part of Brownsville got an electric car until ten years after they'd first become common.

The screen faded to black, and the lights came up smoothly.

"Our job is simple, ladies and gentlemen: take back the streets of Matamoros from the demonstrators." Major Sawtell shut down the briefing file and looked at his officers. "Are there any questions?"

Teresa refocused her eyes but kept her face a mask to hide her thoughts. If she had learned anything in ten years in the U.S. Army, it was how and when to keep her mouth shut.

"Sir," said a captain, "why isn't the Mexican Army handling this? All the factories and demonstrators are on their side of the border, aren't they?"

"Yes, but American companies own the plants. And most of the demonstrators are Americans who work in the Mexican factories, the maquiladoras. Seems a lot of our people cross into Mexico from Texas to work these days."

Not just these days, Teresa thought. They've been doing that for twenty-five years. Her face remained professionally blank.

Another officer stood up. "Sir," he said, his voice hesitant, "these are civilians, right?"

Sawtell affected a chummy voice. "Lieutenant, I know it's hard for soldiers to think about firing on civilians. And I want to be perfectly clear that you are only to use deadly force as a last resort. But remember, these people have assault rifles and homemade bombs. They burned GMC's biggest plant to the ground, as well as a number of smaller factories. I'm afraid we can't rule out force."

Somebody asked another question, but Teresa had stopped listening. Without looking around, she tried to remember how many officers in the room were Hispanic. About half, she thought—higher than the twenty-five percent proportion for the whole army. The brass probably wanted Spanish speakers. She wasn't sure why. It was pretty clear that they hadn't brought in crack combat troops from all across the country to talk to the rioters. Probably just another one of those decisions by some high-ranking idiot.

Teresa had noticed the same thing when she commanded a platoon in the Colombian drug wars. Though in Colombia the drug-runners had been too well armed for anyone to question whether it was right to shoot at civilians.

The other lieutenant had been a fool to ask, Teresa thought. Sawtell was the kind of commander who marked weaknesses and never forgot them.

The briefing broke up with orders to report to transport at 1300 hours. Teresa sighed. She and her people had arrived from Fort Myers two hours earlier, and they'd be out of there in two more. It was the first time she'd been in San Antonio in three years, and she wasn't going to see anything but a standard army briefing room.

She met with her troop outside the briefing room, and gave them the orders.

"Lieutenant, we really got to go after these people?" someone asked.

"We've got our orders, Corporal." Her voice brooked no argument, and she got none. "You'll be wearing your kevlars." A couple of groans: The more macho among her people thought it sissy to wear the full-body bulletproof armor. She aimed an icy look at one of them. "We'll get our specific assignments once we're on the ground in Matamoros. I suggest you use this time to check out the mess hall. Your next meal's likely to be an MRE."

Teresa watched as they dispersed, jostling each other and cracking jokes. She heard PFC Garza say, "Too fucking hot for kevlars, man."

Corporal Lacey—half his size—punched him in the shoulder. "How you going to do it with all those chicas of yours if you get your balls shot off?"

Garza wiggled his butt. "None of them chingados gonna even come close to me."

Teresa repressed a smile. Her people. Hope Garza hasn't gotten anybody else pregnant, she thought. Don't expect he's ever going to grow up. Got to get Lacey into that college/OCS program I did. She's got the brains—and the toughness—to be a good officer. Best option for a kid from inner-city D.C.

Her senior sergeant stood next to her, staring after the others. Joe Muñoz was a beefy man about her own age, but he stood almost a head shorter. "Lieutenant, can I talk to you a minute?"

"Sure, Sergeant. What's on your mind?"

"Permission to speak freely, ma'am?"

"Granted."

"I think you know I'm from Laredo."

She nodded.

"My old man works in a maquiladora in Nuevo Laredo." He said it with no emotion, but she heard the plea lying behind the words.

She was honest enough to answer the unasked question. "Sergeant, I was born and raised in Brownsville. My stepfather worked in that factory you just saw explode. And there's not a damn thing either one of us can do except follow orders."

He knew better than to argue with army logic. "Yes,

ma'am," he said, and turned away. She wished she could send him home without bad consequences for both of them.

Teresa didn't take her own advice about food. She'd snatched up a stack of carbocaff and pro-energy bars before they'd shipped out of D.C., and she pulled one out to nibble. By late afternoon they'd be in some kind of firefight, and Teresa knew she'd do the whole thing on adrenaline. Snack bars were all she could handle.

The dry August heat of south Texas blasted her face as she left the air-conditioned building, looking for a place to be alone for half an hour or so. Teresa found an empty lounge in the bachelor officers' quarters, pulled out her pocket comp, and clicked onto the net. She wanted to know what unedited media was saying about the riots.

A face appeared on the two-inch-square video display: a dark-skinned man with several days growth of beard, brandishing an aging assault rifle. "Muerte a los bosses!" he shouted in the Tex-Mex of her childhood. She winced.

The text that scrolled by gave a sociological analysis. "While there are certainly numerous factors leading up to these riots, experts agree that the large number of Americans 'reverse-commuting' to the maquiladoras are the key. Although these employees receive higher wages than their Mexican coworkers, they know that they make much less than they would if the jobs were subject to U.S. wage and hour law. And, of course, they receive none of the benefits or safety protections required in the U.S.

"Further, environmental activists claim that increased cancer in the Rio Grande Valley is caused by water and air pollution from the maquiladoras." Teresa switched the news off abruptly; she didn't need experts telling her why the riots started. She remembered all too well going to bed without supper because the money her stepfather brought in for his long days rarely stretched from payday to payday.

And she remembered even more clearly watching him die, as the cancer ate his lungs.

She switched to her e-mail, and reread for about the twentieth time the official notice she'd received a day before the emergency call-up. "This is to inform you that you are on the short list for promotion to captain. The final promotion list will be announced in two weeks."

Captain Marquez. She liked the sound of that. Just before she'd left Fort Myers, her commanding officer had told her that her chances were very good. "They're high on you, Teresa. Don't fuck up this mission, and you're a shoo-in. And I don't mean you have to be a hero out there, like you were in Barranquilla during the drug wars. You can play this one conservative, careful. Err on the side of caution."

Yeah. Just go in and do a good job shooting up your former friends and neighbors. But as much as Teresa hated the assignment, she did want the promotion. And not just because she was ambitious.

She had burned with patriotic fervor when she'd enlisted right out of high school. And while she had lost the naive idealism of her youth, she hadn't lost her pride in protecting others. The army was her job, and she was good at it. It might have been her only choice, but it hadn't been a bad one.

Just get through this one, she told herself.

"Excuse me, ma'am." The baby-faced private standing in front of her looked nervous. "The transports are loading. You are part of the strike force, aren't you, ma'am?"

Teresa jumped to her feet, shutting the comp down in a fluid motion as she did so. "Thank you, soldier. I lost track of the time." She returned the girl's salute, and took off at a dead run for the loading area.

Choppers set her crew down on the southeastern edge of Matamoras. The air temperature was the same as in San

Antonio, but the humidity was about eighty-five percent. It was a familiar wet heat, and brought back memories of sitting in front of a fan, staring at MTV because it was too damn hot to do anything that required movement. The sweet stink of the petrochemical factories hadn't changed, either. She found herself taking short breaths, trying to breathe without smelling anything, a habit from her childhood.

And then there were things to do, far too many things to do. She sent her four squads in different directions, with orders to work their way to the Combined Computer Companies microprocessor plant three miles away. She stayed with Muñoz's squad.

She set the video display that hung near her left eye to rotate among the squads and the com to link her with all four sergeants. The switch at her belt would allow her to flip to all-call if she needed to issue orders to everyone and incoming headquarters commands would override either setting. Practice taught her to limit what she said out loud to things others needed to hear. Her P-20 hung loosely in her right hand.

They hit the first pocket of resistance about a half mile up the road. About thirty rioters blocked the path of the ten-soldier squad. They waved around an assortment of weapons, ranging from the current incarnation of Saturday night specials—pistols that were as likely to blow up in your hand as to shoot someone—to a couple of assault rifles about three generations out of date. They could probably pierce the kevlars, though.

The rioters postured; Muñoz ordered a round fired above their heads. The squad eyed the tops of buildings to lock the targets for their P-20s and fired; the rioters scattered.

Teresa felt a surge of relief. Chalk up another one for the P-20s, she thought. You can avoid killing as well as kill more easily with a weapon that doesn't require a steady hand and eye to aim.

And Joe was doing his job right. He'd read the situation, given the right order. She watched the radar blips of her other troops, conferred with her sergeants, and followed in the squad's wake.

The second confrontation was trickier. A hastily erected barricade composed primarily of junked gas guzzlers blocked the road. A shot ricocheted off a trash can to Teresa's left, and the squad dove for cover.

Joe looked at her. "Gas?"

"Gas."

The squad pulled gas masks up from their necks and hit the gas switch on their P-20s. So much gas was released behind the car barricade that a red-tinged haze hung in the air. Shots were fired haphazardly as rioters scattered. She gave Joe a thumbs-up—two areas secured without bloodshed. The squad spent a half hour clearing the old wrecks out of the street.

The other squads reported in—a couple of firefights, no significant injuries on their side. Teresa didn't ask about rioter casualties.

They were only a couple of blocks from the CCC building when all hell broke loose. A sniper fired, hit one soldier in the shoulder. He went down in spite of the kevlar. Another barrage of fire made everybody scatter.

Over com came a priority report from the leader of her second squad. They had run into significant resistance about a block away on the other side of CCC; should they hold there or move in?

"Move in," Teresa said. "We'll come up this way, catch 'em in a pincer movement."

Joe was crouched next to her, behind a low concrete wall. He'd heard her order to the other squad.

"No choice here," she said. "We'll have to shoot our way through."

He nodded, but made no move to give the order. Teresa gave it herself.

Some of the soldiers laid down a covering fire as the rest of the troop, Joe among them, spread out in a large V. They moved in and out among the cars and walls they used for cover. She could see fire coming from Joe's P-20, but she couldn't tell where he was aiming.

Her view screen showed a small group of rioters slip in from an alley. Several troopers moved to block them off. Rioters went down. Dead, probably, at least most of them. All her people still showed as mobile. They were gradually herding the rioters who hadn't been shot into the street in front of the plant. The other squad would box them in.

She turned to follow and heard Muñoz's voice in her ear. "Retreat."

She looked at him in horror, but before she could countermand the order, people began moving. Teresa saw Lacey, who'd been walking point, jump up and start firing to cover the retreat.

Had the other squad not been counting on them to make the pincer movement happen, she wouldn't have added to the confusion with another order. But she couldn't leave the others out there on their own. She hit the all-call button on com, heard herself scream into the mike, "Cancel that. Move in, take cover." Maybe half the squad followed; the others were still trying to retreat. In the midst of all the choas she saw Lacey take a direct hit and collapse.

"Forward, goddamn you," she screamed, and this time everybody got the message. Everybody but Joe. She grabbed his shoulder and said, "Move your ass." He met her eyes, shook his head.

And there was no time to worry about what he would or

would not do. She had to move, had to lead, and she did, shouting orders by com to the other squad leader and firing as she went. She heard screams, knew people were being hit, were dying. Not my people, please God, she prayed to herself as she ran. More gas grenades were launched, and as the haze cleared, she and her soldiers fired at the rioters, who were retreating toward the approach of the other squad.

She turned a corner. Her other squad was a block away; there were maybe fifty rioters sandwiched between the twenty-odd soldiers. Most of them looked to be armed with halfway-decent rifles, but the gas and steady firing had taken their toll. The rioters looked confused. Several were huddled over downed comrades. Just a few minutes more, and they'd have them without much of a fight.

And then a man jumped on a car, and began to exhort the crowd. "Hermanos y hermanas, we are more than they. Don't let these imperialistas push you back. Fight them. If we die here, we die gloriously."

His words broke the spell. The rioters began to move, began to fire.

"Come on, hermanos y hermanas," the man shouted again.

If he kept that up, more people would die. Teresa pushed the projectile weapon targeting switch on the P-20, looked at him to lock on target, and pressed the trigger. The force blew him off the top of the car. Half the rioters turned in horror to stare at the dead man; a few of the others tried to continue the attack, but the confusion gave the trained soldiers a decided edge. Another five minutes, and most of the rioters were in custody.

Three troopers were attending to Lacey. "Her legs are a mess, Lieutenant," a private reported. Both medevac and prisoner transport had already been called.

Teresa put her hand on Lacey's shoulder, said, "Hang in there, girl." Lacey was on the edge of passing out; Teresa hoped she would. Someone was packing up her legs. Experience told Teresa there wasn't enough left to reattach. The army would give her artificial ones, but they wouldn't be good enough to keep her in the service. And a disability check wouldn't buy your way out of anything but starvation.

Joe Muñoz still stood where she had left him. She placed herself in front of him, and said in a voice shaking with the effort of self-control, "What the fuck possessed you back there?"

He shrugged.

"You nearly got us all killed, ordering that retreat."

He could contain himself no longer. "What we're doing is wrong, Lieutenant. These people, they have good reason to be out here. It isn't right, us killing them."

"It's our job, mister."

"It's wrong, Goddammit. It's fucking wrong."

"You're relieved of duty, Sergeant. I'm calling in the MPs."

He reverted back to military. "Yes, ma'am."

"There's going to be a court-martial. You know that, don't you? Know I have no choice."

"Yes, ma'am."

"Jesus, Joe, you've ruined your career."

He gave her a sardonic grin. "Yeah, well, at least I didn't shoot that guy, Lieutenant."

She wanted to hit him, wanted to scream in his face. If Joe had been doing his job she could have been a good officer and ordered someone else to shoot the leader. Then the blood wouldn't be on her hands. Or at least, then she could tell herself it wasn't on her hands.

She put on her coldest face, tried not to let him see how

much she hurt. "Yeah, I shot the enemy, Sergeant. But you brought down one of your own." It gave her satisfaction to see him wince. She turned on her heel and walked away. There was one more thing she had to do.

She walked over to where the leader's body lay sprawled on the pavement, a bloody mass where most of his torso had been. He didn't look like anyone she actually knew. But he looked like everyone she'd grown up with: a neighbor, someone's older brother, a girlfriend's father.

She felt her stomach heave. Teresa Marquez hadn't thrown up after killing someone since her first battle ten years ago, in a peacekeeping operation in Liberia. She didn't now, but only because of the iron self-control that had let her get this far.

"Lieutenant," a voice said.

She turned toward one of her sergeants.

"We got a report. Most of the city is under control. We're supposed to set up camp, patrol this area."

She nodded. "Take care of it, Sergeant."

He gave her a salute. She returned it halfheartedly. Switching com channels, she managed to check in with the hospital unit. The medic on duty told her Lacey had been on the first chopper to San Antonio. His voice sounded sad. Teresa knew he'd confirm her opinion about the legs if she asked. She didn't.

"Goddamn you, Joe Muñoz," she muttered to herself.

Two hours later, patrols organized, Marquez's people busied themselves setting up camp in the cheap motel they'd commandeered for lodging. Teresa sat in a battered aluminum desk chair alongside the tiny swimming pool and began the steady consumption of a bottle of tequila she'd come across in the chaos. Cheap tequila, barely fermented. But functional.

She had never gotten drunk on duty before. She could

see the soldiers tiptoeing around her, whispering in the corners. She didn't care. She knew there was no way she'd be able to sleep sober.

One of her sergeants came over. "Lieutenant," she tried.

"Have a drink?" Teresa said.

The woman shook her head. "Don't you think you should get some sleep?"

"Oh, come on. Have a drink. Help me drink to the memory of Jorge Izquierda. A good man, mi padrasto Jorge. He played by the rules all his life, and it killed him."

The sergeant gave up. The bottle still had a few ounces in it when Teresa finally passed out.

She'd barely crawled out of bed the next morning, her head ringing, and her stomach protesting, when one of soldiers brought word: Major Sawtell wanted to see her.

She ran fingers through her hair, tried to smooth out the wrinkles in her fatigues that had come from sleeping in them. She knew she looked like hell when she crawled into an open SUV for the short trip to Sawtell's temporary headquarters at another commandeered hotel.

He kept her waiting thirty minutes. Her hangover did not improve while she waited.

Sawtell did not look like a happy man when she walked into his makeshift office. She stood at attention, gave him a salute.

"You look like shit, Lieutenant," he said.

"Yes, sir."

"I heard a report that you got drunk while you were supposed to be supervising perimeter patrols last night. That true?"

"Yes, sir."

"I'm sure you know that's a serious offense."

"Yes, sir."

"You care to give me an explanation?"

"No excuse, sir." It was the right formula answer. And even if the major wanted a real explanation, Teresa wasn't about to give it to him.

He looked at her hard. She stood there, braced, her head throbbing, her stomach roiling.

"You're fucking lucky you did such a good job taking out the chief agitator. It could have gotten very ugly out there, if he hadn't been stopped."

She wanted to scream, wanted to cry. She did neither.

"You look like you have a hell of a hangover, Lieutenant."

"Yes, sir."

"I guess that's punishment enough, given what you pulled off. But I don't ever want to hear you've pulled crap like this again, you hear me."

"Yes, sir."

"I understand Muñoz lost it out there."

"Yes, sir."

"Lucky thing you were with his squad." He said it like he'd guessed she'd been keeping an eye on the sergeant.

"Yes, sir."

He nodded. "Well, get back to work, Lieutenant. This isn't going on your record."

She said, "Thank you, sir," and managed to walk out.

Ten days later, back in Washington, she went to see Lacey at Walter Reed. She watched her totter down the hospital hallway on her artificial legs, angrily waving away offers of help. Back on the ward, the silence between them grew uncomfortable. Teresa hated hospitals; all of them smelled of bleach and antiseptics, an odor of chemicals that overpowered all the other senses. She associated it with death. She wanted to run screaming from the room; she wanted to tell Lacey that everything would be all right. The first response was true, but cowardly; the second was a lie so obvious that it would deceive no one.

Lacey finally spoke. "Lieutenant." She hesitated, took a deep breath. "Lieutenant, do you think you could talk to the doctors about getting me some real legs? You know, like that marathon runner got last year, after he wrecked his car? I heard he's still got a shot at the Olympics, that the new legs work that good."

Her voice speeded up some. "They say I'm the best they ever seen with the artificial ones. I bet I could learn to use real ones in no time, probably be back in the unit in six months, tops. Then," and her voice got quiet, and she sort of mumbled, "then maybe they'd still send me to college."

Teresa patted the girl's hand. "Sure, Lacey. I'll talk to the doctor. If necessary, I'll even take it up with the colonel. That's a promise."

Lacey's eyes looked wet. "Thank you. I'll do you proud. You'll see."

Teresa turned away. She knew Lacey wouldn't want anyone to see her cry.

She caught Lacey's doctor just outside the building as he slipped out to take a break. He shook his head as she explained the situation.

"If it had happened a year ago, maybe we could have gotten her into the experimental program. She's young, otherwise healthy—a perfect guinea pig. But the program's over. Now everyone knows it can be done. And it just costs too damn much." He leaned against the redbrick wall, and looked away. "The army's not going to pay for it. Cheaper to give her artificial legs, and train a replacement."

"Look, can't you just ask?"

He gave a little snort, and looked back at her. "I already did." He pushed himself away from the wall and walked back into the building.

Teresa remembered the doctors her mother had dragged her stepfather to see. They'd had that same sad look of people who could do nothing. She went back to her quarters and composed an official e-mail to the colonel on Lacey's behalf.

Teresa made a special effort for her meeting with the colonel. Her uniform had been so starched and ironed that it practically moved by itself. She'd managed more or less successfully to cover the circles under her eyes with makeup—she hadn't been able to sleep without drinking. A letter resigning her commission rested in her breast pocket. If he didn't agree to help Lacey get new legs, she would quit. She'd served the minimum to pay for her education.

His first words to her were said in a severe tone. "I had an unofficial report from Major Sawtell. Drunk on duty? That doesn't sound like you, Teresa."

"Sorry to let you down, sir." Fuck Sawtell, she thought. She might have known he'd tell the colonel, even if he didn't file an official report.

He let a smile shine through. "Well, hell. You did a nasty job, and we're all human. Besides, Sawtell also told me you shot one of the key agitators, turned things around. It's not going on your record."

She said, "Thank you, sir" automatically.

"But don't let it happen again."

"No, sir."

He grinned at her to let her know he wasn't really displeased. "And now, let me be the first to congratulate you, Captain Marquez."

Teresa tried unsuccessfully to control her surprise. "Sir?"

"The promotion came through, Teresa. And, may I add, it's well deserved." He stood up, and took a pair of captain's bars out of his pocket.

Teresa stood up in a daze. A part of her mind watched from far away as he came over, pinned the bars on her uniform, and stepped back. Her hand came up and saluted automatically.

The colonel returned her salute, and then reached out and shook her hand.

"Thank you sir," she said, still in shock. She took a deep breath. "Sir, about Corporal Lacey."

"Oh, yes. The one who lost her legs. Nothing we can do about that, I'm afraid. Army policy. You understand."

"But sir, the doctors think . . ."

"Captain." The word sounded harsh. He let out a breath. In a softer tone, he said, "I'm glad you're the kind of officer that cares about your troops. That's important. But work on learning when no means no."

"Yes, sir." Her hand came up, almost went to the letter in her pocket, and then relaxed again. What good would it do to quit? It wouldn't get Lacey any legs. And she'd just be destroying herself.

The colonel motioned her back to the chair, and began to tell her about her new assignment.

Captain Marquez. It did sound good. And it meant so many other things. The army might be persuaded to send her on for a graduate degree—she'd made good grades in college. Likely she could transfer out of combat eventually, maybe build a technical career in the service or get the skills to do something else as a civilian. Become somebody. Jorge and her mother had always told her to become somebody.

Become somebody other than killer of those who couldn't get out.

Teresa didn't really hear what the colonel was saying, but it didn't matter. The full orders would come by official e-mail. Tomorrow or the next day she could deal with it.

She struggled to keep her mind blank, to smile and say, "Yes, sir" at the appropriate moments. He finally stopped. They shook hands, saluted, and Teresa made her escape.

She walked back through the main headquarters, where administrative personnel worked at computer stations in a maze of cubicles. No one paid any attention to her as she walked into the copy room, which also housed printers, recycling bins, and the piece of equipment she sought.

Corporal Lacey would haunt her dreams in the days to come, but it was her stepfather she thought of as she fed the resignation letter to the shredder. "Perdoneme, Papa Jorge," she whispered.

Kiss Me, You Fool

by Del Stone Jr.

When Linda answered the knock at the door, she thought it might be her boyfriend, Robert, or what's-her-name from next door, wanting a Diet Coke and a few minutes of conversation, or . . .

Anybody but a monster.

She knew it was a monster right away, because when she opened the door it gave her that single-minded, ferocious monster smile, and its gaze fixed hungrily on her mouth. Her heart performed a little somersault. She hadn't seen many monsters—at least as far as she knew—and always there had been a man nearby to kill it for her. And never had a monster come knocking at her door.

The monster said, "I am selling home-cleaning products. Would you care to see my samples?"

She stuck her tongue out at it.

The monster opened its mouth, unfolding rows of teeth that resembled hypodermic needles.

She closed her mouth.

The monster's mouth snapped shut like a trapdoor.

So then. It was a dumb one, only a third- or fourth-generation monster that had not learned the guile of the eighth or ninth generations, or the altruism of the good monsters that sometimes evolved from the newest generations. It was going door to door, expecting to luck upon a victim as stupid and docile as itself.

She cracked the storm door and looked up and down the street. Why hadn't somebody killed it? Usually the neighborhood kids got a kick out of tormenting the dumb ones, or the teenage boys who wanted to show off for their girlfriends.

But the kids were in school this morning, she remembered. And most people worked nine to five, something she constantly had to remind herself as she worked a two-to-midnight shift.

"I'm offering a special today," the monster droned. "A one-liter container of laundry detergent that removes soil, grass, blood, rust, and oil stains." It hefted a cardboard box that was marked DIET COKE. "It usually sells for $12.95, but today the cost is only $29.99."

Linda rolled her eyes. God, what an imbecile. Still, she couldn't leave it roaming the streets, where it might attack a child. And if she called the Containment Division, it might be all day before they got there. Better just to bring it inside and let Robert take care of it when he arrived. Robert liked doing that, which was one of the reasons she wasn't too crazy about Robert.

So she said, "Yes," and pushed the door open with one hand. "I'd like to buy everything you have!"

It renewed its sharklike smile and stepped inside, carrying the box. Linda directed it to the couch and commanded it to sit, which it did with doggish enthusiasm. The television muttered in the background. She had it tuned to CNN. The reporter was delivering a story about some new alloy or something, reverse-engineered from the thing that had gone down in Mr. Parker's Wheat Field in Manitoba, the thing that had brought the monsters here. She momentarily wondered if it would recognize anything from the footage.

It didn't. It was watching her mouth—it was watching her tongue. It wanted her tongue. Like a coquette, Linda kept her tongue hidden behind her teeth. She knew a third- or fourth-generation monster wouldn't attack her unless a very specific set of circumstances arose. For instance, if she were to kiss it. . . .

"I have many samples to show you," the monster said, aping some filament of memory passed on to it by its host.

The thought of its host brought a brief pang of regret to Linda. She thought he must have been a looker, because the monster was extremely attractive, and monsters were nearly identical in appearance to their last host.

The monster said, "I am selling home-cleaning products. Would you care to see my samples?"

She ignored the question. It wasn't just attractive; it was gorgeous. Well muscled, square-jawed, blond—with delicate, fluttery eyelashes that a man would have hated. The showstoppers were its eyes. They were a deep, glacial blue, and though they reflected no intelligence, she could see in them the potential for a sensitive and caring man. Unlike Robert. Sometimes Robert could be a jerk.

What a waste, she thought, sitting down on the couch beside the monster. She would like to have met this man before he was bitten. A salesman—he had been a salesman, and she guessed that was how he'd come to grief. He must've been wet-brained when it happened—eight beers or unbelievably desperate. Now that the world knew about monsters, nobody was ever bitten by the early generations, unless they were drunk and didn't know what they were doing.

CNN was showing video of a water-collection facility the good monsters had built on their reservation in the Libyan desert. The reporter said the New People—that's what they were called in polite conversation—had designed and built it without any outside help. Linda glanced at the monster beside her. It didn't seem capable of tying its own shoelaces, much less designing a water-condensation plant.

"I'm offering a special today," the monster said, and launched into its sales pitch about laundry detergent.

It really would be a shame to kill it, she told herself. And as she listened to it prattle on, she found herself staring at its crotch. She'd read somewhere, maybe the *National Enquirer*, that monsters with men for hosts went around with permanent erections. Or did she see that in one of Robert's girlie magazines? Maybe the sexual-advice column? She didn't believe those answers anyway. Her sex life had never been so interesting . . . at least since she'd been dating Robert.

Robert. She glanced at her wristwatch. It had only been ten minutes since the monster had knocked at her door. Robert wouldn't be here for at least another forty-five minutes—if he was on time, which usually he wasn't.

By then CNN was doing a story on a monster attack in New York City. Apparently, several eighth- and ninth-generation monsters had disabled a subway and attacked the passengers. A close-up showed a corpse being devoured by maggots—"larvae," the reporter called them. In another shot, the body had been devoured completely, and the maggots were eating each other. In several instances, the life cycles had gone nearly full circle, where a maggot had consumed its competitors and was pupating into a genetic near-duplicate of its human host. Teams of CD Rangers and good-monster volunteers from the reservation were destroying the offspring and scouring nearby boroughs for stragglers.

Linda wrinkled her nose. Eighth- and ninth-generation monsters were dangerous. They were smart and could hide their teeth. And they liked to bite people. Biting people was the monster equivalent of sex.

She turned back to the monster on the couch, which said, "I have many samples to show you."

She found herself wanting to look at its penis. Everything else about it seemed human. Surely its penis would be no different—possibly it would be bigger than Robert's. In fact, that was likely.

Robert again. She glanced at her watch. If he walked in and caught her ogling a monster's cock, well, he always carried a 9mm—an old Argentinian Browning—and things could get messy. It could be a toss-up as to which one of them he shot first. Robert was the suspicious type. He might even think she was . . . she didn't want him thinking that, for God's sake. People who had sex with monsters were perverts. Or thrill seekers. And she was no thrill seeker.

Still, it couldn't hurt to take a peek.

CNN was airing their morning business report. A bio-engineering firm that had learned a trick or two from the monsters about organ regeneration was going public, and Wall Street was in a tizzy.

She ordered the monster to stand. It stood. She went around it and peered out the window. Nobody peered back. She returned to the monster and began to undo its pants. It started to raise its arms to her shoulders, but she barked out a sharp, "No!" and its arms dropped by its side. The first few generations of monsters lacked human intelligence and tended to do what you told them to do. If people had known that from the beginning, none of the slaughters that followed the monsters' arrival would have happened.

She got its pants undone. She slid down the zipper. It wasn't wearing undershorts, and she felt a warm thrill surge through her. She loved it when guys didn't wear undershorts. She'd been trying to make Robert give up his boxer shorts, but convincing Robert to change his ways was like convincing the sun to rise in the west.

She tugged its pants down to its knees, but its shirttails concealed all.

The monster said, "I have many samples to show you."

Linda replied, "I'll bet you do, Sonny."

She grabbed the shirttails and yanked them apart. Buttons popped and flew across the room. Linda's eyelids flew up like window shades, and a little gasp of delight squeaked past her lips.

A monster, all right.

"Oh," she exclaimed, her breath coming in sawed-off, superheated gusts. "Oh, my God."

The monster's penis was enormous, bigger than any she'd ever seen—or imagined, for that matter. It hung between the monster's legs like a club. As she stared, the scrotum began to unpeel from the base, and the testicles sagged down, swaying slightly, and they, too, were enormous.

"I'm offering a special today," the monster began.

"I can see that," Linda whispered hoarsely as the monster rambled on about $29.95 laundry detergent. She circled it, admiring its lean, firm buttocks, and a quick mental picture flickered into her thoughts, a picture of those buttocks flexing and unflexing between her thighs. She was seized by another tremor of desire. She reached out to touch its flanks, then snatched her hand away as if it had been scorched.

Pervert, the word sprang to mind. And then, Robert.

She sighed and looked at her watch again. Twenty minutes until Robert was supposed to be there. But then he was always late, she thought disgustedly. She could be dying, and Robert would be late getting to her deathbed. She'd

fallen into the habit of telling him to be somewhere half an
hour before necessary so they'd only arrive a few minutes
late.

What time had she told him to be here this morning?

Her stomach cramped in panic as she struggled to recall
her telephone conversation with Robert. "Tenish," was
what she'd told him, she suddenly remembered, and she
sighed mightily with relief. That meant he wouldn't be here
for almost an hour.

CNN had paused for a "Hollywood Minute." Variety was
reporting record box-office receipts for *In With The New*, a
buddy-cop movie about a CD Ranger and a good-monster
volunteer investigating an organization of monster drug
smugglers in San Diego.

An hour. It would be an hour before Robert got here.
What could she do in an hour?

"I am selling home-cleaning products," the monster said.

She circled to face it again. Its penis seemed larger, ex-
ceeding its previous impressive and tantalizing hugeness.

She wanted to touch it. What could be the harm in touching it? Would that make her a pervert, or simply curious?

Curious, she decided.

She took its penis in her hand. It felt warm and pliant and
vaguely sticky, like every other penis she'd ever touched.
And was it her imagination, or was it growing again and
stiffening and beginning to stand away from the monster's
thighs? She cupped her hand and began to stroke it, and
yes, it was responding. She stroked faster, and it enlarged to
an immensity that truly made her head spin.

She couldn't breathe. The warmth in her had become an
ache. She went to the window and peeked outside. A police
car cruised down the street, its roof-mounted .50 calibers
swaying gently with the car's movement. Otherwise, nobody was about. She drew the curtains.

God, am I really going to do this? She kicked off her shoes and shimmied out of her jeans. She glanced at the monster's penis and told herself yes, maybe never again, but this time yes. She wriggled her ass to get her panties off, stretched the elastic waistband over her index finger and shot them across the room, rubber-band style.

She ordered the monster to lie down on the couch. It sat, but apparently that was the extent of its understanding, and she had to show it how to recline. "Don't worry, Linda," she murmured. "Into each life a little unsafe sex must fall."

She climbed on top of it. She took its penis and, guiding it with her hand, sank down. It slid into her, and as she descended the pleasure built upon itself, doubling and tripling until something at the back of her skull seemed to burst, and a warm gush of divine, muscular satisfaction flowed down her spine and out across her body, tingling along the nerve paths to the tips of her fingers and toes and nipples.

The monster said, "I have many samples to show you."

She sucked in huge lungfuls of air. A bead of sweat collected at the tip of her nose and fell, splashing against the monster's chest. She couldn't believe she'd gotten off so quickly, but before she could give it much thought that warm feeling returned, and she found herself rocking back and forth, trying to increase the friction. She wished the monster knew what to do, but as she looked into its eyes all she saw was its instinctual longing for her tongue. She clenched her teeth, but it continued to watch.

Then it occurred to her that if she were on the bottom, things might go easier . . . and better. The mental picture of its buttocks between her thighs re-formed, and the thought of all that weight on top of her, the pressure of its chest against her breasts, sent another shudder of desire running through her. She'd have to be careful, though—damned careful. She could become overwrought in her passion and try to kiss it.

She dismounted and got the monster off the couch. Then she lay back and drew it down, on top of her. That proved to be more difficult than she'd anticipated, but after a few moments' effort she got it in a reasonable approximation of a missionary position and once again steered its huge penis inside her. She forced its face to the side, against her shoulder, and felt a brief gust of fear blow through her when it tried to raise its lips to hers. "No!" she ordered, a tremor of unease creeping into her voice. But it obediently laid its head down. God, but she would be in a world of hurt if the monster were a generation or two older. You couldn't tell those monsters what to do. They took what they wanted.

She began to raise her hips against its weight, and the sensation awakened in her an animal reflex of passion. She raised her legs and wrapped them around its legs, using them as leverage to elevate her pelvis ever higher. Her fingernails dug savagely into its back. A man might have protested, but the monster merely said, "Would you care to see my samples?"

She wished it were Robert who aroused this sexual heat in her and she wished it would never end and she wished she could never do anything but this for all eternity. A dynamo was winding up inside her and she could hear it singing in her blood and in her rapid-fire breathing and the staccato rhythm of her heart.

The monster's arms encircled her and squeezed. It began to thrust into her.

She rode with it a moment, the sudden shift in workload a welcome change. Then it raised its face to hers and grinned down at her, and asked, "Having fun?"

The blood seemed to freeze in her veins.

It parted its lips and she saw only human teeth, and a

confused babble of questions arose in her mind all at once, until she saw the rows of monster teeth slide out of their sheaths in the roof of its mouth. Perversely, she tried to remember where she'd heard the interview with the good monster, the one who explained that monsters had been slaves to whatever had built the thing that crashed in Mr. Parker's Wheat Field in Manitoba, that at first, they bit people because they were trying to hide from their former masters. It was simple fear, the good monster had said, that drove them to attack people. Fear, and ignorance of what people really were. But later, when they were smarter and understood the damage they were causing, most of them became good monsters and stopped the attacks, while others went on doing it because they were mentally unbalanced, just like the mentally unbalanced human beings who prey on coeds or wipe out fast-food restaurants filled with customers. And then the good monster had asked that people not judge all monsters for the acts of a few. Linda had almost giggled at that absurdity.

"Your neighbor next door—the one who likes Diet Cokes—she's got a big mouth," the monster said. "She said you'd be here . . . alone. I think she said that so I'd let her go." The monster sighed with affected weariness. "I don't think she's your friend. Not anymore, at least."

The monster continued to thrust into her, but now it felt like rape. "And you—you're very foolish," it smirked. "Falling for that idiot routine. I hope you don't pass that trait to my offspring. They might not let it into the reservation."

Linda clamped her jaw shut. Through gritted teeth, she said, "Why don't you go there now? They'll give you amnesty, and they say they don't need people to reproduce anymore. They say they can do it with each other—"

"And miss all this?" The monster leered. "The fun of it all? Not for the world—this or any other."

She clenched her lips and the monster laughed. "Oh no you don't. You've had your fun. Now I'm going to have mine." Its jaws gaped open to reveal a thicket of thornlike teeth. She turned her head and screamed at the back of her throat, the sound coming out like a muffled, frustrated growl. The monster grabbed her chin and jerked her head forward. It prematurely jetted a squirt of maggots from its teeth, and they writhed helplessly on her chest, seeking and not finding the soft, moist undertissue of her tongue. Her eyes bulged when she saw the maggots, and she screamed again.

The front door banged open.

"Hey, babe, I thought I'd show up early for a ch—"

The monster whirled, and Linda wedged the palm of her hand against its chest and pushed, knocking the monster to the floor.

Robert's mouth was a shocked O. His tongue was clicking. His eyes were full moons.

"Kill it!" Linda screamed. "It's a monster—it was trying to bite me!"

Robert whipped out the .9mm and pulled back the slide. A bullet ratcheted into the chamber.

"Kill it, for God's sake!" she screamed. "Kill it!"

The monster held up its hands, and in a tremulous, almost contrite voice, it said, "Now wait a minute, man! I just wanted to use the telephone. She's the one," it accused, hitching a thumb at Linda, "who wanted to hop in the sack with me. I ain't no monster."

"It's lying," Linda hissed, but some small hint of guilt must have shown on her face because Robert didn't pull the trigger. Instead, he stuck out his tongue at the monster. The monster arched its eyebrows bemusedly, then returned the gesture. Robert snarled, "Let me see your teeth, ass-hole!" and the monster opened its mouth.

Human teeth.

"Oh, Christ!" Linda shouted. "It's an eighth or ninth! It can hide its teeth!"

Robert's face pinched into a scowl.

The monster shook its head frantically. "No way. No! I mean, think about it." It was still holding up its hand. "If I were a monster, why would I be humping this"—it gave her an evil glare—"this chick?"

Robert's scowl deepened. His gaze settled on Linda. "Yeah," he said. "Yeah, Linda. What you got to say about that?"

"He attacked me—"

"He, Linda?"

"IT!" she screamed. "IT attacked me. It broke in here—"

"No," the monster interrupted. "She let me in—"

"It's lying, Robert!" And she began to sob. Always, she'd cried to have her way with Robert—he was a softy for tears. But now they came without pretense.

"—and she ripped off my clothes," the monster continued. It held up the tattered shirt that was missing its buttons.

Robert's face hardened into a kind of stoniness. His eyes narrowed to slits. He fingered the pistol grip as if it were a piece of warm taffy that threatened to melt onto his hands. "Well. This is a fine fucking situation," he said to Linda, his voice an ominous rumble. She snuffled loudly. "You're either a two-timing slut or some kind of sick pervert. Either way, I think you deserve what you got coming to you."

The monster said, "Hey, man. I'm sorry. I didn't know. I mean, she's a fine-looking lady—"

"Shut your trap, you," Robert snapped, and the monster

shut up. "Now. The only way we're gonna find out which one you are is to do a test."

Linda hugged her knees and began to rock back and forth on the couch. She could not stop crying.

"Yeah," Robert went on with a kind of forced serenity. "I think we ought to have ourselves a little test."

Linda shook her head. "Robert. Just kill it, and we can talk about things later. OK?" The words came out in a squeaky whisper.

"No, Linda. Not yet." And he laughed. "We got to have our test first, and here's what I want you to do." He paused, as if savoring the idea. The TV muttered in the background. Finally, he said, "I want you to kiss him."

All the muscles in her face went slack. She uttered a garbled, "No!" If she kissed the monster it would bite her, whether it wanted to or not. Biting was reflexive; monsters could no more control the act than people could stop themselves from having an orgasm.

"Come on, Linda!" Robert brayed. "You already fucked him. Give him a little thank-you kiss. Show him you care."

"No." She shook her head wildly.

Robert leaned into her face until his nose was nearly touching hers. "Kiss him, you bitch. Because if you don't, I swear to God I'll blow your goddamned head off."

She began to weep loudly.

"Kiss him, Linda! Kiss him!"

She groped along the edge of the couch cushion and came up with a maggot. It still squirmed feebly. "This!" she screamed at him. "What do you think this is?"

He glanced at the maggot, and his expression curdled into disgust. He straightened. He looked around the room, and rubbed the back of his neck wearily. Then he looked at her and said mildly, "I didn't see anything."

She threw the maggot at him, and screeched, "Bastard! Murderer—"

"Kiss it!" Robert bellowed.

"IT! That's right, Robert! IT!"

"Kiss it!" he thundered. "Kiss the fucking thing, Linda! KISS IT." His face was the color of boiled lobster. A vein in his neck pulsed. His eyes burned like two rivets drawn from a furnace.

Linda said quietly. "I'd rather you just shoot me. I don't want to die that way."

Robert aimed the gun at her face and held it there, the muscles in his arms standing out and trembling, the pistol's snout quivering. Linda closed her eyes and waited . . . and after a few moments, when nothing happened, she opened them again.

Robert had lowered the gun. Huge tears were running down his cheeks and splashing into the fabric of his shirt, leaving wet blotches. He looked up at her, and in a pleading voice, he said, "How could you—" His voice cracked. "How could you do this—"

"I'm sorry," she blurted. Now, it seemed, only the truth was worth saying. She would tell him the truth. Somehow, she would make him understand. "I lied. I'm sorry. I did let it in—at first because I didn't want it running loose. But then my curiosity got the best of me—and I made a mistake. That's all. Haven't you ever done something you regretted later?"

"Yes," he whispered.

She swung her feet off the couch and started to get up and go to him and put her arms around him, but he planted a palm in her chest and shoved her back down. Her head thumped hard against the armrest, but her confusion was so profound that she barely felt it.

He holstered the pistol and wiped his face with his shirt-sleeve. He snorted and spit, and said, "Yeah, I regret ever hooking up with you." And then he glanced at the monster, and said, "She's all yours, pal."

Linda's breath lodged in her throat. Any shame she might have been feeling came apart as she realized he had not been crying for her but only for himself. She struggled to get off the couch, but Robert was already out the door. A hand closed on her ankle, and she fell. She grabbed for the doorknob, but couldn't reach it.

"Now," the monster said, dragging her back. She began to kick and writhe and scream, but the monster was stronger, impossibly stronger. It flipped her onto her back and threw itself on top of her. All that weight, which had felt so deliriously sensual only a few minutes before, served now to compress her revulsion into something that exceeded terror. Her skin shrank from the monster's touch.

It grinned down at her. "That was nice of him, wasn't it?" it said. Its fangs slid out. It said, "You heard the man, Linda. Kiss me, you fool."

She turned her head to face the TV. The CNN broadcast had cycled over to news again, past the report on the new alloy, past the story about the water plant, to the scene of carnage in the New York subway. Maggots were stripping the bones of a corpse.

As the monster's hand slid around her jaw, she wished it were Robert's corpse there, on the TV screen.

It wasn't Linda anymore, but it looked a lot like her.
And it knew where Robert lived.

Round Dragon, Angry Tiger

by Steven Piziks

Tora crept quietly down the dim corridor. Her slippers made tiny rustling noises on the smooth wooden floor and her heart pounded hard enough to make her kimono shake. Kanzen na Ryu's chambers were just ahead. Tora clutched at the small quartz tiger on its thong around her neck but found no reassurance there.

Enter the room, steal the necklace, she thought. *Enter the room, steal the necklace. But why, Teacher? Why?*

A spark of frustration flared within her but she pinched it out almost without thinking. No anger. Tora's teacher, Kanzen na Ryu, had her reasons.

Control your anger, Tora, she told herself. *Control your anger or you will never find your focus.*

The corridor made a sharp turn ahead and Tora peeped cautiously around the corner. Two husky men clad in red stood on either side of the paper *shoji* screen, hands on their sword hilts. Tora blinked. Guards? Kanzen na Ryu never had guards outside her chamber before.

Tora squinted into the dim light, then bit her lip to keep from crying out. The younger of the two men had broad cheekbones and large, dark eyes that gave him a boyish, even mischievous look despite the serious expression of his face.

Why did it have to be Namio?

The warm evenings he and Tora had sat watching the ocean waves that were his namesake dropped into her memory with excruciating clarity, filling her mind with cool salty breezes and soft, warm sand. They were both anticipating the day when she would become a full sorceress and they could marry. Though Okamoto Namio, as a *samurai*, could marry any woman not of common birth, Tora had kept the idea at arm's length, not wanting to enter into an unequal partnership.

Now Tora was going to force him to commit suicide.

For a moment she was torn between her love for Namio and the duty she had sworn to Kanzen na Ryu ten years ago. It was a painfully short moment; hard duty and inflexible honor had to win out. Namio would have felt the same way.

Tora firmly wiped all expression from her face, then slipped a talisman from its place on her belt and ran shaking fingers over the round porcelain surface, checking for imperfections out of long habit. There were always imperfections, though most of the time only Kanzen na Ryu could see them. Only this morning, Tora had shown Kanzen na Ryu her best talisman to date—a black pearl inlaid with gold sigils. It would change the person who swallowed it into a giant cat. That is, Tora had thought it would until Kanzen na Ryu had decreed it inexcusably flawed and taken it away to destroy later. It had taken several minutes of breathing exercises for Tora to calm herself.

But she is teacher and you are student, Tora reminded herself. *That means she is right. Now go.*

She took a deep breath and rounded the corner. Instantly Namio and the other guard tightened their stances, then Namio relaxed.

"Good evening, Okamoto-san," Tora said, careful to use

Namio's formal name in public. She nodded a brief greet-
ing to the other guard. "I must see the Lady."

"She is sleeping, Lady Tora," Namio said with a shy
smile and bow. He had a low, pleasant voice. "Perhaps you
can return later."

"That I cannot do." Tora paused and looked away. She
pushed deep inside herself, looking for her focus to power
the talisman. But, as usual, she only found the impenetrable
wall of her temper. Nothing but a small flicker of power answered her call. "Can you forgive me, Okamoto-san?"

Namio furrowed his brow. "For what?"

"This." And Tora dropped her talisman. The delicate
porcelain shattered almost silently and a cloud of white,
sweet-smelling mist burst from the shards. Namio and the
other guard had time to give her a surprised look before
they dropped unconscious to the floor. Tora, immune to her
own spell, was thankful that the swirling smoke hid
Namio's face—she didn't know if she could bear to look at
him now.

Perhaps it is not so bad that I cannot focus properly, she
thought in an attempt to concentrate on something else.
Otherwise, the entire palace would be sleeping.

Tora squared her shoulders and slid open the screen to
Kanzen na Ryu's sleeping chamber. Now that she was past
the guards, she had no more need for quiet. The paper walls
of Kanzen na Ryu's palace did little to muffle sound, and
the sorceress certainly knew Tora had arrived.

Moonlight flowed into the room through the garden window opposite Tora and a fresh breeze had already swept
away the last of her sleeping mist. In the far corner, Kanzen
na Ryu's round form lay faceup on her sleeping mat. The
sorceress snored hard enough to rattle the paper walls, but
even a child could tell she wasn't really asleep. Beside
the sleeping mat lay a wooden tray which, judging from the

crumbs and empty cups, had once been piled high with sweetmeats and *sake* jars. Open boxes spilled jewels and coins over the floor, some in neat piles, most in disarray. A low worktable occupied the exact center of the room and Tora padded quickly toward it, wrinkling her nose at the mess. She had never seen Kanzen na Ryu like this. What was happening here?

In the center of the worktable lay the necklace, an ugly thing constructed from jade and onyx stones bound by silver links. Even in the dim moonlight Tora could see symbols etched into the gems.

Tora hesitated. The necklace seemed to be waiting for her to pick it up, a snake hungry for the approach of prey. It had belonged to Kashiwara Toshi, a rival sorcerer, until Kanzen na Ryu had defeated him in battle three days ago and made him her vassal. Kanzen na Ryu had taken the necklace—along with the rest of Toshi's treasure—as tribute.

And now she wants me to steal it from her. But why? Tora shook her head. *No—do not ask questions. Just obey.*

She stretched out a shaky hand and picked up the necklace. It was oddly cold. The moment her fingers touched the stones, a tiny flicker of light licked the sigils, then faded.

Kanzen na Ryu's snoring abruptly ended and she sat up. Talismans on her belt and bracelets tinkled and clattered as she moved; not even a sorceress as powerful as Kanzen na Ryu removed her arsenal, not even to sleep.

"Wonderful!" she exclaimed, and Tora realized with a start how much weight Kanzen na Ryu had gained of late. The name Round Dragon suited her. "Well? What are you waiting for, thief?"

Anger flared. Tora was no thief—her teacher had ordered this. But Tora stuffed the necklace into her sleeve and bowed. "Teacher, please forgive a question from this ignorant student," she said, knowing it was hopeless, but still having to ask. "What will become of—of the two guards outside your door?"

"They shall ask to commit suicide and I shall let them." Kanzen na Ryu leveled a hard gaze at Tora. "They were, after all, lax in their duties, letting you in."

Tora blinked back angry tears. It was the answer she had expected, but Kanzen na Ryu was being unreasonable. The formality of asking to commit *seppuku* would cleanse Namio's honor. Any other master would refuse permission and everything would go on as before.

But Kanzen na Ryu does not like Namio, Tora thought savagely. *She has been making his life miserable since she learned he and I plan to marry. She put him on guard duty on purpose.*

The injustice made Tora want to scream but she firmly clamped her lips together. Perhaps she could persuade Kanzen na Ryu to change her mind, but not if Tora showed distress.

"Leave now," Kanzen na Ryu continued, toying with a lock of long, straight hair. "And do not return. I will not have a cursed student in my service."

Tora clutched at the quartz tiger, the namesake her mother had given her. "Cursed, Teacher?" Her fingers felt suddenly chilly.

"'Cursed?'" Kanzen na Ryu echoed mockingly. "Yes, cursed. The only way to get rid of that *thing*—" Kanzen na Ryu gestured at the necklace and spat on the floor "—is for someone to steal it, something which you have done most admirably. Now get out of my castle before you taint someone else."

"But Teacher, you cannot dismiss me—"

"—without good reason, true. And I have several."

Kanzen na Ryu shot Tora a sideways glance. "You are cursed. You are a thief. And you are the worst student I have ever had. I became your teacher ten years ago only because my sister begged me. Yet you *still* have not found your focus. A flea has more power than you and a monkey has more discipline. I wasted my time and I regret granting my idiot sister's last wish. Now get out."

Tora stared at Kanzen na Ryu in thunderstruck astonishment. How *dared* she? Kanzen na Ryu had orchestrated Namio's death and now she told lies about Mother? Mother had not begged—she had *ordered* Kanzen na Ryu to take Tora as a student. Mother had been eight times more powerful than this bloated bag of fat! Tora's fingers automatically flew to the quartz tiger at her neck, feeling the familiar contours. *Oh, Mother*, she thought, *why did you have to die?*

"Are you deaf girl?" Kanzen na Ryu snapped. "I told you to get out."

The sorceress flicked her hand in curt dismissal and a tiny object came loose from one bracelet. The object flew across the room, bounced twice on the matted floor, and stopped at Tora's feet. Automatically she picked it up, then gasped and looked across the room at Kanzen na Ryu. The object was a black pearl inlaid with familiar gold symbols, symbols Tora had taken hours to create. The anger gathered again as she held up the tiny black talisman. "Teacher?"

Kanzen na Ryu's eyes glittered. "I have had no time to dispose of that yet. Such a flawed talisman is hardly worth my immediate attention."

"But Teacher," Tora said, careful to sound puzzled, "you always stressed the importance of immediately destroying unworthy work before it injured someone."

Kanzen na Ryu got to her feet like a mountain gathering

itself to shed an avalanche. Talismans jangled ominously. "Are you challenging my word, student?"

"I am not longer your student." Tora bowed with a trace of mockery. "You have dismissed me. Is that what gives you leave to steal my work?"

Kanzen na Ryu's face went red as a blowfish. "We shall fight, then. Is that what you want?" Eyes flashing, Kanzen na Ryu plucked a bit of coiled wire from her belt. "I challenge you now."

Tora gasped, but not in fear. Her lip curled in anger. *You would steal my work, call it your own, and challenge me as a thief? You are worse than the daughter of a dog!* Her temper rose, pulsing with her heartbeat. One hand flashed down to her own belt of talismans.

Kanzen na Ryu's eyes went wide, then her face hardened. "Thief!" she shrieked. "I have been robbed! Guards! Where are my guards?"

Tora froze, anger forgotten. Beyond the paper walls of Kanzen na Ryu's room she could hear shouts of alarm.

"Stop thief!" Kanzen na Ryu yelled. "That belongs to me!"

Dropping the pearl into her other sleeve pocket, Tora turned and fled the chamber. She sprinted down the corridor, past Namio's sleeping form, around the corner—and came almost face-to-face with three other *samurai*. Tora didn't even pause to think.

"Quickly!" she said, pointing back down the hallway. "The thief escaped through the garden window!"

The men shoved past her and Tora hurried in the opposite direction, talismans jangling, stolen necklace bouncing heavily in her sleeve pocket. Screams of outrage rose behind her as the warriors charged into Kanzen na Ryu's bedchamber only to find an angry sorceress. Tora pounded through the twists and turns of the castle until she found a side door. She slid it open and darted into the gardens beyond.

"There she is!" "Halt, filthy thief!"

Tora dodged frantically between manicured bushes and shrubs, then stopped dead at the high stone wall surrounding the gardens. She snatched a glance behind her. A half dozen *samurai* were crashing toward her through the bushes. The first, a swarthy man clad only in a loincloth, had almost reached sword range. Tora quickly felt at her talismans and, finding a frog bone, reached inward for her tiny spark of power.

"Die, thief!" the swarthy man shouted, drawing back his arm to swing.

The anger flared again. "I am no thief," she cried, and snapped the frog bone in two just as he swung at her. Tora gathered herself and *leaped.* The magic propelled her high over the gleaming sword, high over the wall, high over the trees surrounding it.

What is happening? she thought dizzily as the air rushed and whistled past her ears. *I should have been lucky to clear the wall.*

She landed safely on the other side, recovered her balance, and dashed for the forests surrounding Kanzen na Ryu's castle without pausing to consider the mystery further. Branches smacked her face and thorns ripped at her hands as she stumbled through the darkness. Eventually she came to a clearing and stopped to lean heavily against a tree for several moments, heart pounding, breath coming in ragged gasps. Crickets chirped in an invisible chorus. No one seemed to be following her. Eventually her breathing slowed. She had done it—escaped!

Then Tora sobered. What did it matter? Namio would be dead by sunrise, and it was her doing. Namio-chan—her ocean wave. She reached savagely into her right sleeve pocket and yanked out the necklace. Smooth, hard stones clacked faintly beneath her fingertips.

And I am cursed. She frowned and peered at each stone, trying to make out the sigils in the dim moonlight. *This is a strange curse—I feel no different.*

Bright light slammed Tora's eyes. Blinded, she yelped in fear and surprise as shouts erupted from the bushes all around her. The necklace fell from her hand.

"Kill her!" a harsh voice ordered. "Before she escapes again."

A whistling sound came at her head. Tora threw herself blindly sideways, then cried out as the blow meant for her neck slashed her shoulder. Fiery pain gushed down her back and hard fingers seized her by the arm, digging in with an iron grip. Instinctively she groped at her talisman belt and located a bit of silk by touch. She ripped it free, flinging it wildly into the breeze.

"Look out!" "She summoned a demon!" "Formation! *Now!*"

The grip on Tora's arm instantly vanished. She fell to her knees, blinking madly as her vision began to return. Not four paces away three *samurai* were facing off uncertainly against a grinning creature that looked like it had been spun from a shadow. The monster was twice the height of a man and possessed sharp teeth and claws. It glided toward the *samurai*, silent and reaching. One of the warriors suddenly shouted a battle cry and charged forward, swinging his blade at the creature's chest. The monster vanished like smoke at the sword's touch. A tattered wisp of silk fluttered to the ground.

"A trick!" the leader snarled. "Get the woman!"

But Tora had already scrambled into the undergrowth. Two trees formed a hollow hidden by a bush and she hurriedly pushed her way inside. Her shoulder roared with pain every time she moved and she could feel warm blood trickling down her back, but she forced herself to remain quiet.

"She fled, Kaminaga-san," one of the other guards was saying. "And we cannot track her in the dark."

In the clearing, Kaminaga, the leader, reached into his pocket and pulled out a length of string. Fastened to the end was a severed human finger. A chill went through Tora, mingling with the hot pain throbbing in her shoulder as Kaminaga let the finger swing freely on the end of the string.

My teacher gave them a talisman, she realized. *Two! One to track me and one to blind me.* Automatically she reached for her belt—and her pocket clinked. Startled, Tora felt in her sleeve and found the necklace.

In the clearing, the finger slowly rotated on its string until it pointed directly at Tora's hiding place. Kaminaga drew his sword. "She went that way," he grunted. "Move."

"This is all Namio's fault," another swordsman grumbled, stepping forward. "If he and Michio had been guarding Kanzen na Ryu-san like true *samurai*, this never would have happened."

"The Round Dragon is being too generous in letting them commit suicide," Kaminaga agreed. "Especially if they let an inept student get past them."

A searing anger bubbled behind Tora's eyes and she clenched her hand around the necklace until the stones bit into her palm. They would dishonor Namio's name like this—these whining children? How *dared* they?

A drop of blood trickled down her fingers and she angrily let the necklace fall to the ground.

Following Kanzen na Ryu's talisman, the *samurai* moved steadily toward Tora's hiding place. Her anger grew, feeding on itself, growing and pulsing, and Tora realized she was shaking. Her wounded shoulder had stopped hurting. She only felt the all-consuming rage. Tora yanked a talisman from her belt and rushed from the hollow.

"Here is your inept student, dishonorable dog," she snarled, and hurled the talisman into Kaminaga's face before he could react. With a grunt of surprise, he threw up his hand to ward it off, but the stone struck his cheek and puffed into red dust. Kaminaga fell screaming to the ground, clawing at his face.

The two remaining swordsmen continued their charge. The first swung at Tora's head, but she managed to duck away. Laughing, she plucked from her belt a wooden fish and tossed it at him. Reflexively he parried it with his sword, but the talisman flared into brilliance the moment it touched the blade. When the light faded, the *samurai* had vanished. Where he had stood, a man-sized carp flopped and gasped frantically on the forest floor. A few paces behind the dying fish, Kaminaga's convulsions had ended. His corpse, twisted into a tortured rictus, stared blankly up at the sky. Tora swallowed. The carp talisman was only supposed to transform the sword. And the other should have cramped Kaminaga's muscles just enough to stop him. She hadn't meant to kill these men—they were only obeying Kanzen na Ryu's orders. Was it the curse? But why would a curse grant her power?

The third man stopped in his tracks, regarding Tora cautiously over the edge of his sword. "You will not catch me, girl," he said. "I know the secret. Your talismans cannot affect me unless I let them touch me, and that I will not do."

Tora wrenched her eyes away from the thrashing fish and turned her attention to him. Her anger began to fade and she felt light-headed.

"Come girl," the *samurai* mocked. "Try again."

Tora pulled a tiny net from her belt and threw it at the man. He smoothly dodged aside. The net flew across the clearing, burst into full size, and wrapped itself around a tree. Tora panted, and black flecks suffused her vision.

"You have few talismans left, girl," the *samurai* said. "And you are growing weaker. I only need to wait for you to bleed to death."

A flicker of helpless frustration rose in Tora's mind and suddenly blew into anger again. The pain receded.

"I cannot imagine," the *samurai* continued, "why Namio would choose someone like you. He must be a greater fool than I thought."

The anger exploded. "Never mention his name!" Tora shrieked. "You are not worthy of it!" She yanked a cracked ball of clay from her waist and threw it at the man. Again he dodged. The talisman hit the ground and dissolved into the earth beneath the grass.

"You are killing yourself," the *samurai* mocked. "The more you act, the worse your wound becomes. You cannot hit me."

"Can I not?" Tora hissed.

The ground behind the warrior moved. Glancing over his shoulder, he saw the earth bubble and roil. A wave of molten rock suddenly roared up, higher and higher. Tora threw back her head, feeling the power of the earth merge with the power of her rage, relishing in the release of years of pent-up emotion. Recklessly she threw the power into the talisman, into the searing liquid, neither knowing nor caring where the energy came from. A high, thin wail pierced the booming wave as it crashed down on the *samurai*.

A fitting death for one who dishonored my Namio's name, she thought exultantly. *The wave of fire honors the wave of water.*

A flying speck of lava landed on Tora's skin and she cried out. The anger vanished and the molten rock abruptly solidified, leaving a small mottled hill of stone. The clearing was completely silent. Nothing moved. Tora stared at the rock, the dead carp, and the twisted corpse of Kaminaga, then sank weakly to her knees with darkness in her eyes. Her skin burned where the lava speck had landed.

It was not the curse, she thought. *It was me. I lost control of my anger and now these men are dead. Oh, Mother—I am sorry.*

The lava had made the air stifling, and she found it hard to breathe. Hot blood flowed in an endless stream down her back. Then Tora noticed a hard lump in her sleeve pocket. Slowly, she reached inside and pulled out the necklace. Tora stared at it stupidly until the blackness claimed her.

Someone shook Tora's shoulder. She tried to push the hand away, but her body was too heavy.

"Wake up, sorceress. You should not sleep any longer." Something crackled in front of her face and a sharp, acrid smell jerked her awake. Tora's eyes flew open and she sat up. She was on a sleeping mat in a small, bare room lit by several paper lanterns. A middle-aged man was kneeling beside her holding a dry leaf under her nose and she automatically pushed his hand—and the awful smell—away. Her torn, bloody kimono had been replaced with a soft green robe, but her tiger amulet still hung in its place around her neck.

"What—?" she began.

"You are well, girl," the man said, laying a calming hand on her shoulder. "Your wound is healed and you are safe."

Tora looked at him. "Who are you?"

"I am Kashiwara Toshi."

The man who had fought Kanzen na Ryu.

Kashiwara Toshi dropped the pungent, crumbled leaf onto a tray next to the sleeping mat. "I felt ripples of magic, ripples that turned into a crashing wave. As one who has taken a vow of healing, I hurried to the site, hoping my meager skill might be of use, and I found you near death."

"Where am I now?" Tora stretched cautiously. Her injured shoulder showed nothing more than a trace of stiffness.

"In my house. The sun has not yet risen, but I felt you should waken." Toshi paused thoughtfully. A large birthmark mottled the cheek under his right eye. "You were close to Kanzen na Ryu's castle. Might one ask what the battle was about?"

"That is none of your concern," Tora said shortly, then she bit her lip and felt for her mother's tiger amulet at her throat. Why was her temper always so difficult to control? Especially today?

"I did not mean that," she said aloud. "Please accept my humble apology, Kashiwara-san. I am unworthy of your help. My temper is forever getting the best of me."

Kashiwara Toshi smiled. "If the battle site is any indication of your temper, I am glad to see it so mildly expressed here."

Tora said nothing.

"You are Tora, correct?" he continued. "Kanzen na Ryu's student?"

Tora hesitated, then decided she had nothing to lose. "I am no longer her student. I am a thief. Dishonored."

"A thief? What did you steal?"

Automatically Tora touched the sleeves of her robe. One pocket clinked, but Tora no longer felt surprise. "I took this at Kanzen na Ryu's command." She pulled the necklace from her pocket. "It used to be yours, correct?"

Toshi's eyes widened. "It did." He shook his head. "If I had thought Kanzen na Ryu would be able to give it away, I never would have given it to her."

"You *gave* this to her?" Anger flared and Tora clenched the necklace that lay cold in her hand. "*You* started this? My love will commit *seppuku* at sunrise and I have killed three other men because of you?" Blindly she felt for her talismans and noticed for the first time they were gone.

"Apologies," Toshi said politely. "I removed your arsenal, sorceress, so you would not harm anyone by accident. Including me."

"You—you—" Tora looked away and forced herself to breathe deeply. Her temper bucked and twisted, but she grimly forced it down.

"Since it is ultimately my fault the necklace fell into your hands," Toshi went on, "I will take it back if you like."

Tora snapped her head around. "What?"

"Give it to me if you do not want it." Toshi held out his hand.

Tora stared. "But Kanzen na Ryu said it can only be stolen. She ordered me to sneak into her bedchamber and steal it from her."

Toshi gave her a puzzled look. "But that—no. Please start from the beginning."

And Tora did, though she had to turn her face away for most of it—she didn't want Toshi to see the tears on her face when she talked about Namio. Toshi listened carefully until she finished.

"Child," he said, "it is obvious you have not thought this through." He held up a forestalling hand when Tora's face darkened. "Please hear me out. It was not completely your fault. There is the necklace."

"You mean the curse?"

"A very bad one." Toshi stared out the room's single open window. The moon had set, leaving dark summer sky behind. "It finds the parts of you that you hate the most—and gives them power."

Tora swallowed. "My temper," she whispered, looking down at the necklace. "I gave in to my temper."

"So it would seem." Toshi got up to pace the *tatami* mats lining the floor. "What I do not understand is why Kanzen na Ryu gave the necklace to you."

"I had to steal it," Tora reminded him.

"You did not. The necklace may be given away, and the receiver must accept it, however unwittingly. It may not be sold or stolen. Kanzen na Ryu lied."

"But—"

"Consider. Kanzen na Ryu fought me and made me her vassal before she took the necklace. How could she, who now owns even my very life, steal from me? Further, Kanzen na Ryu *told* you to take the necklace, and she knew you were in her room from the very first. Is that true theft?"

"No," Tora said slowly. "I suppose it is not."

"I know Kanzen na Ryu." Toshi stopped pacing and sat down by Tora's sleeping mat. "We studied many years together under the same master. She is greedy—and she is afraid. Round Dragon was bullied as a child and fears if she ever appears weak, it will happen again."

Tora nodded with sudden understanding. "Ah. That is why her behavior has changed. The necklace increased her fear and her greed. But Kashiwara-san, Kanzen na Ryu is very powerful. Why did she not simply destroy the necklace?"

"Quite impossible. The necklace strengthens one's weaknesses. Anyone possessing the necklace automatically loses the power to destroy it; the harder one tries, the weaker one gets. Even Kanzen na Ryu." Toshi tapped his chin thoughtfully. "Round Dragon challenged me to battle because she knows my gifts are for healing, not fighting, and she wanted more vassals. After I lost, I gave her the necklace in tribute partly in the hope it would weaken or destroy her and partly to rid myself of it. I possessed it for many years because my healing vows would not allow me to give it to any but a deserving recipient."

"I believe Kanzen na Ryu is quite deserving," Tora put in.

"I believe you are correct," Toshi replied with an ironic little bow. "I was also certain Round Dragon's greed would never let her give it away. But she managed to justify it to herself—an arranged theft that gave her an excuse to rid herself of someone. Her hate for you was stronger than her greed's love for the necklace. Still, I am not sure why. You must be one of her best and most powerful students."

"That is not true," Tora replied quietly. "I am one of her worst."

Toshi blinked. "Her worst?"

"Even after many years, I have been unable to find my inner focus." Tora hung her head. "My talismans are weak and puny. I am no sorceress."

"What you did in that clearing tells me otherwise."

The anger welled up again at Toshi's contradiction. The fact that Tora knew the necklace was causing it did nothing to help. "How can I be a sorceress," she snapped, "if my anger stops me from finding my focus?"

"Has it not occurred to you that anger may *be* your focus?"

The anger abruptly vanished. Tora stared at Toshi, open-mouthed, while her mind raced in little circles.

"I told you Kanzen na Ryu is fearful. Perhaps Kanzen na Ryu even knows of your focus—and that is why she trained you to suppress your anger." Toshi scratched his birthmark. "I doubt it occurred to Kanzen na Ryu that you hate your anger most. I would wager she thought you hated your lack of magical skill, and that the curse would make you lack it even more. Kanzen na Ryu gave the necklace to you so you would no longer be a threat, and she lied so you would not try to give it away."

"And then she decided to be completely safe by ordering my death," Tora said bitterly.

"I believe so." Toshi paused. "What will you do now? I have drawn sigils on the walls of my house that will stop a talisman from detecting people within, but Kanzen na Ryu will doubtless hear of your whereabouts soon from some other source. Servants love to chatter, and mine know you are here."

"I have no idea what to do," Tora confessed helplessly. "I have committed no dishonor if what you say about theft is true, but my fiancé will still kill himself at sunrise and a powerful sorceress still wants me dead."

Toshi stared at the ceiling. "Kanzen na Ryu formally challenged you to battle, correct?"

"Yes, but she shouted for her warriors when I reached for my talismans." A thought struck her. "Kanzen na Ryu was afraid of me—even though *I* had the necklace."

"Even so. Perhaps this is why she taught you to suppress your anger, so you would not one day use it against her," Toshi said. "And I would guess her challenge was a bluff. If you reached for your magic, you accepted it. You are still at battle."

Tora swallowed. "I had not considered this."

Toshi got up and restlessly paced the floor. "Have you considered that if you defeat—or kill—Kanzen na Ryu, all her vassals would become yours, including your fiancé?"

Sudden hope rose in Tora's chest. "Namio would have to ask *me* for permission to commit suicide—and I could refuse. Then I could release him from his vow of service and we could marry Oh, Kashiwara-san—how can I thank you?"

Kashiwara Toshi shrugged. "My advice is poor."

"I believe you are incorrect." Tora rose from the mat with a feeling of purpose, but Toshi held up a hand.

"Wait." He took a deep breath. "Before you go, you should give me the necklace. Fighting simple samurai is very different from fighting a powerful sorceress like Kanzen na Ryu. Your temper would overwhelm your concentration and you would lose."

Tora looked down at the cold jade and onyx in her hand and suddenly felt an irrational urge to refuse. Kashiwara Toshi had done so much for her, and the necklace had given her so much power. But then the faces of the men she had killed sprang into her mind. Was that the sort of power she wanted?

Oh, this is an evil thing, she thought. *I do not wish for a kind man like Kashiwara-san to take it, but he is correct. Kanzen na Ryu would win because—*

Tora gasped and almost staggered as a sudden idea rose in her mind. Afraid she would fall, Toshi hurried forward to steady her.

"Are you well, sorceress?" he asked.

"Thank you, I am fine," Tora reassured him distractedly. She paused, letting her thoughts coalesce.

"Sorceress?" Toshi said, still hovering at her side.

Tora blinked at the man, as if surprised to see him standing there, then bowed. "Thank you for your help, Kashiwara-san. I must go. There is a battle to finish."

"But the necklace—"

"That will not be a problem," Tora said with growing confidence. "I will fight Round Dragon and I will win." She put on the necklace and held out her hand. "But first I need my talismans back. Please, Kashiwara-san. I know what I am doing."

Toshi stared at her for a long moment, then nodded and

pulled Tora's belt from the recesses of his robe. Only four talismans remained. He also produced the black pearl.

"This was in your sleeve pocket," he said, handing it to her. "And now, Lady Sorceress, will you return to this humble vassal's home after your victory?"

"Of course, Kashiwara-san. And as part of my gratitude, I will free you from your vow."

A servant showed Tora out and pointed her toward the road that would take her to Kanzen na Ryu's castle. Tora gazed upward at the dark summer sky, then removed the necklace and put one hand on her tiger amulet.

The necklace focuses the owner's weaknesses, she thought. *But my weakness is what gives me strength.*

The tiger amulet grew warm in her grip and Tora remembered her mother—her soft hands, her low voice, her smiling, lively face. So different from the face she had worn in death, pale and wasted from a disease that had slowly consumed her from the inside despite the healer's touch. Tora remembered holding her mother's hand as it spasmed one last time and went limp. Eventually it went cold.

Why did you abandon me, Mother? You died and left me all alone, alone with Kanzen na Ryu. I hate Round Dragon, Mother. I hate her!

Familiar pain and anger welled up again, but rather than fight it, Tora dived into the emotion with relish. For years she had forced herself to control her temper, but this time she used her hard-won skills not to dampen the anger, but to channel it.

Into the necklace.

I hate her, Mother. I hate her for keeping me ignorant. I hate her for stealing my work. I hate her for deceiving me.

The necklace twisted in her hands, sending the rage back fourfold. Grimly Tora fought to return every scrap. Onyx and jade glowed like green and black coals, but the stones

were icy cold. A *tsunami* of sheer outrage thundered over
Tora and she cried out under the unexpected pressure. Her
plan had been to force the necklace to take more anger,
more power, than it could hold, but the necklace met the
challenge with ease. It hissed and spat as if it were alive,
took Tora's anger, and gave back rage. Tora fell gasping to
her knees and consciousness began to slip away. She wasn't
strong enough. The necklace was winning.

*Kanzen na Ryu is a monster, Mother, and you left me
alone with her. Why did you make her take me as a student?
Why?* The pressure increased and Tora's vision blurred. She
reached inside herself, looking for more anger, more hatred
to feed the necklace. And even as she sought it, it appeared.
More anger than she had ever dreamed possible crashed
over her, filling body, mind, and soul with searing white
heat. Tora raised her head and roared to the skies.

"I hate you, Mother!" she bellowed. "You betrayed me,
and *I hate you!*"

The necklace abruptly sprang from Tora's grasp. Silver
links flew in every direction and a dozen earsplitting *cracks*
assailed her ears as every stone detonated. Tora threw up
her hands to protect her face from flying shards until the
noise ended. When she finally uncovered her eyes, the
necklace was nowhere to be seen.

Tora sat down shakily on the hard, dusty road. She
should be dead. The necklace should have killed her. Instead, it was gone, and so was the curse. Tora's rage had
been too strong for it to contain.

But only because I admitted to another hate, she thought.
How can I hate my own mother?

A small tear trickled from Tora's eye. After a moment,
she wiped it away, took a deep breath, and turned her attention inward. The anger was still there, but now that she
knew its source, its power swelled at her command. Only at

her command. She then surveyed her talismans with grim satisfaction. Just five left, counting the black pearl.

More than enough, she thought, grinning a catlike grin. *I am very angry with Kanzen na Ryu.*

In one smooth motion Tora swallowed the black pearl and called on her temper. Muscles flowed, bones expanded, teeth became sharp, and a moment later standing on the starlit road was the largest tiger the world had ever seen.

Round Dragon, prepare for Angry Tiger.

Tora spread her whiskers against the warm night air, then twitched her tail and padded ominously toward Kanzen na Ryu's paper palace.

The Judas Lesson

by Jerry Oltion

The aroma of fresh-baked cookies was nearly irresistible. The buttery, sugar-and-cinnamon smell had drawn Chris all the way from his upstairs bedroom, through the living room, where his mother was decorating the tree, to the kitchen. He stopped in the doorway and inhaled deeply. Snickerdoodles. Still warm on the baking pan, and nobody around to see him take one.

Yeah, right. This close to Judasmas, it was bound to be a setup. No doubt Tina, his older sister, had baked them and left them out just to tempt him. She was probably waiting around the corner to nab him the moment he took his first bite.

He stepped closer. The refrigerator switched off just then, and in the sudden silence Chris heard the high-pitched mosquito whine of a camera flash charging up. But Tina didn't have a camera. That could only mean—

Chris whirled around to put his back to the cookies, and shouted, "Mom! Tina's got your camera!"

Behind him, Tina said, "Damn!"

"And she swore, too!"

Their mother came into the kitchen, a faint smile on her face. She held a bright red glass ornament in one hand. "Tina?" she asked.

Tina slunk into the kitchen from the dining room, the 35mm camera dangling by its strap. "Okay, I swore, but I asked to borrow the camera. You remember that."

"That's true, dear. But do watch your mouth. Just because you lost a chance to set up your brother isn't reason enough to swear."

Excited at turning the tables on his sister, Chris cried out, "I get snitch points, I get snitch points!"

His mother's smile faded. "Well, I don't know. I'm afraid Santa Jude won't be very impressed with just ratting on someone for swearing. You'll have to do more than that." Chris slumped his shoulders disappointedly, and his mother tousled his hair. "Don't worry. There's still plenty of time before Judasmas to weasel your way onto Santa's fink list."

"I hope so," Chris muttered. "I want him to bring me a bicycle." He was old enough to suspect that Santa Jude was actually his father, and he had never actually seen anyone tallying points on a list, but Chris knew that his record was terrible this year, and somehow word got around. Whether Santa was real or just Dad, if Chris didn't set someone up and do it soon, he would be walking for another year.

His mother smiled patiently. "Now remember, presents aren't the main reason for betraying your loved ones. You do it for *them*."

Yeah, right, Chris thought. *And Tina's a saint.* But he held his tongue.

At school the next day, he made his move. It was the last day before vacation, and this close to Judasmas the kids were being especially wary of setups, but Chris had come up with something even more tempting than snickerdoodles. He had left his locker door ajar and carefully placed his brand-new SuperSleuth evidence-gathering kit so one corner stuck out in plain sight. He'd hidden the mousetrap, of course, balanced precariously so it would fall out at the first jostle. Then he hid in the boys' bathroom until he heard a scream.

He stopped with the door partway open when he saw who he'd caught. Tom Douglas, the class bully. But it was too late to back out now. This was obviously a setup, and Tom knew whose locker it was. Besides, Miss Pembley had already come to the door of her English classroom, and two girls were coming down the hallway. *Somebody* was going to take credit for this, and it might as well be Chris.

Since he was in school, he had to use the formal declaration. So he stepped out of the bathroom and said loudly, "In the name of Judas the Savior, I betray you." His voice echoed in the tile-and-brick hallway.

Julie Jones and Patty Metzger, Chris's secret love, were just walking by. Julie giggled and said, "You're supposed to kiss him."

Chris blushed. Technically she was right. That was how Saint Judas had betrayed the messiah and thus saved the world from two thousand years of war and strife. And Miss Pembley was a stickler for the rules. But before Chris could even pucker up, Tom flung the mousetrap to the floor and sneered at him. "If ya try it, twerp, you'll regret it."

Julie giggled again, but Patty saw her opportunity to score. She leaned up close to Tom and kissed him on the cheek, then announced, "The betrayal is mine. And I get double points, because in addition to attempted theft, Tom is resisting his martyrdom."

Chris burned with embarrassment. Not only had he lost the sting, but Patty should be kissing *him*, not Tom. Of course she knew nothing of his infatuation with her, but still . . .

Miss Pembley said, "Very good, Patty. Judas himself would be proud." She turned to Chris and shook her head sadly. "Sorry, Chris, but she scooped your sting fair and square. Now you kids run along. Shouldn't you all be in class?"

"Yes, ma'am," said Julie. She and Patty walked away, whispering and giggling.

Tom waited to see if Miss Pembley would leave him alone with Chris, but when it became obvious that she wouldn't, he slouched away too, his eyes saying everything that needed to be said. There would be trouble later.

Chris closed his locker tight this time and made sure it was locked. He left his evidence kit inside. Tom would no doubt love to take it away from him after he beat him up.

He should have brought it with him. Someone had broken the pencil sharpener in the social studies room before class, and Chris had to stand by and watch while Bob Wyman used *his* kit to lift off the culprit's fingerprints. Then of course, Bob had to test all the kids in class until he found a match. Chris waited, bored, but his boredom suddenly ended when Bob leaned close and gave him a quick, dry kiss on the cheek.

"What?" Chris said, startled. The whole class laughed, including Mr. Dixon.

"You broke the pencil sharpener," Bob told him.

"No I didn't."

"Yours were the last fingerprints on it."

Chris couldn't understand it. He hadn't touched the sharpener. But then he remembered who Bob hung out with: Tom Douglas. He'd been framed! Bob had probably lifted the damning fingerprint from Chris's locker, then broken the pencil sharpener himself and pretended to remove Chris's print from the handle.

But how could Chris prove that? He had no witnesses.

Unless Patty and Julie had seen something. Chris turned toward Patty and said, "You know I was framed. Tell them."

Patty looked at him with cold, compassionless eyes. "I don't know anything about this," she said.

"But . . . but . . . you scooped my sting this morning! Of course you know about it."

"What sting?" Patty asked.

The class began to buzz with whispers as the kids realized what she was doing, but Chris ignored them.

"The sting when I lured Tom into stealing my evidence kit from my locker. You took the credit for catching him."

Patty shook her head. "I was never near your locker."

The class burst into applause. Mr. Dixon said, "Excellent, Patty. Three denials in a row. You're well on your way to sainthood yourself. As for you, young man," he said to Chris, "I'm afraid you're on your way to the principal's office."

There was no use fighting it. Patty might grandstand a resisted martyrdom charge if he did, but right after a denial she might not, and Chris had no intention of giving a freebie to anyone else. So he squared his shoulders and walked out of the room, pausing only to say, "Merry Judasmas" to Patty as he passed.

She narrowed her eyes, clearly expecting some kind of trick, but when Chris merely walked out of the room he heard her whisper, "Wow." He smiled, but an instant later he felt the knife slide into his heart when she completed her thought: "What a messiah."

I'm not either, he thought, blinking back tears. *I'm just as sneaky and selfish as anyone.*

But he just couldn't seem to prove it. He followed his sister, Tina, around the house all evening, but he couldn't get any dirt on her at all. He caught his mother taking

Judas's name in vain when she burned the dinner rolls, but when he tried to betray her to Dad, he simply told Chris to stop annoying people over insignificant transgressions.

And so it went for the next three days. School was out for the holidays, so most of his easy targets were unavailable. And every scheme, every scam that Chris tried at home ultimately failed. The trip wire in front of the refrigerator only caught his mom when she got up to make breakfast. The chocolate bar that he bought with his own money and left in plain sight on his desk stayed put. Even the ball of Mom's angora wool yarn that he nudged under the couch failed to lure the cat.

Judasmas morning dawned bright and clear, but Chris felt only hollow dread. His snitch list was practically nonexistent. He knew without looking that Santa Jude had left no bicycle for him.

But Dad came into his room all smiles and made him get up anyway. He held out a brand-new white bathrobe and said, "Here, put this on. You're our special boy this morning."

"Really?" With mounting excitement, Chris put on the robe and let his dad lead him downstairs. He'd always thought bad things happened to little boys who couldn't betray a loved one for Judasmas. But that was evidently all make-believe, like the tooth fairy and the rotten-egg rat.

Then he saw the cross where the tree had been last night. Mom and Tina stood beneath its arms, spear and sour wine at the ready. Dad had propped a ladder up against the post, and now he nudged Chris toward it. "Climb up," he said. "Don't worry about falling. We'll tie you in place."

Chris felt his stomach constrict. He heard a sound like the ocean in his ears. "I—" he said, but his mom interrupted him.

"Oh, I'm so proud!" she exclaimed as she held out a

crown of thorns and set it gently on his head. "It's been ages since we've had a genuine martyr in the family. This will be the best Judasmas ever!"

"But—"

"Get up there, sissy," Tina said impatiently. "I want to open my presents."

He wanted to run. This was all wrong. He wasn't a good person; he'd just had a string of bad luck. But that, he supposed, was how someone became a martyr. And his luck could get even worse if he resisted. Tina gripped her spear like she meant business.

So Chris climbed the ladder and let Dad tie his arms and feet to the cross. Then he hung there while Mom and Dad and Tina opened all the presents that Santa Jude had brought, including the thirty pieces of silver for Tina for being the best snitch in the family. When he tired they gave him sour wine in a sponge, and though it tasted terrible, it revived him enough to manage a weak smile when people started coming to see the splendid pageant he made. And when Patty Metzger actually kissed his feet, he thought he had died and gone to Heaven.

But that, it seemed, was still a few moments away. So he worked up enough breath to whisper one last time, "Merry Judasmas, Patty." He wished he had a gift for her, some token of his admiration to let her know how much she meant to him, but he had nothing left to give. Then he looked out over the living room full of upturned faces and surprisingly, perhaps miraculously, he recalled the words of the prophet. Yes, he was already on the cross; he might as well do it right. He wet his lips, lifted his head, and with his last breath recited the Messiah's Mistake: "Father, forgive them; for they know not what they do."

The Fine Art of Betrayal

by Karen Haber

When Vida Lindskog spied the painting hanging in the front casement of Gallery Kruzick, she knew right away who had done it. The hand of the master was apparent in every brushstroke, every nuance. She stared, balled her fists, and thought: *Maurie, you're dead and still you're betraying me.*

It was her late husband's work, unmistakable—the exuberant colors, the masterful composition, every characteristic smear, every nuance. The great Maurice Lindskog, the "man who put expression back into Expressionism"—and hadn't she coined that phrase for him, among her many other acts of unstinting devotion?—might have returned from the dead and painted that picture yesterday.

If not yesterday then last week. *Let's face it,* Vida thought, *channeling dead artists is hot, hot, hot, and Maurie is now available.*

Who? she wondered, stricken to her soul. What bitch had beaten her to her very own dead husband? She, Vida, the grieving widow who had put her own promising painting career aside years ago so that Maurie could have the support he deserved and needed. She who, right this very minute, could have been in the studio channeling Maurie's skills-from-beyond-the-grave onto canvas herself if she hadn't first had to bring soup to her cousin Nancy who was sick at home with an abscess—don't ask where—from her recent surgery, and then pick up her Kenneth Cole pumps from the shoe repair, and then, of course, there was the bill to be renegotiated for the restoration of that sixteenth-century Chinese bronze she had bought at Sotheby's, not to mention food shopping, although to be honest she didn't have much appetite, and later there was the checkbook to balance and more bills to pay.

She stared in the gallery window, fuming.

Who, she would like to know, was better qualified to channel Maurie Lindskog than his own widow? And yet here she stood on some filthy sidewalk in Tribeca, screwed again because some *arriviste* had stampeded past her as she fulfilled her family and personal responsibilities. Some pisher who probably didn't even have a checkbook to balance. It really wasn't fair. She would have stamped her foot but she was wearing her favorite pair of Manolo Blahnik mules, the ones with the pink Lucite heels.

Dammit, it should have been her work hanging in that window. Hadn't she been trying—trying!—to channel Maurie, night after night, without the least little smidgen of success? How could he do this to her?

Who had suffered through Maurie's infidelities and infantile needs, his depressions and enthusiasms, his voracious ego and nagging insecurities? Hadn't she, Vida Ruben Lindskog, once-promising art student anointed and married by the master, learned to ride out the manic highs and ninth-circle-of-hell lows?

She had rocked him through his night fears, avoided the word "crux" and the letter "Q" on Wednesdays, sworn by the carrot diet then tossed two bushels of the damned things down the incinerator and rushed out to Dean and DeLuca when Maurie's famished inner beast roared for pastrami.

All the while, also, obeying all his *meshuggeneh* commandments about thrift—straining her eyes under impossibly dim lightbulbs, recycling paper clips, and keeping stubby pencils whose erasers were not allowed to give out before the lead. And she didn't even want to think about the string.

But now, now—when all had been said, done, and cremated—did Maurie finally give her her due? Now that he was dead did he send even a smidgen of his prodigious talents her way? Now, when she was stepping out of his shadow, finally free, in the prime of life and ready for the spotlight—she had even found a good hairdresser, for God's sake—where was he? As usual, Maurie had screwed her over for another painter. In death as in life. *Well,* she thought, *not this time, you son of a bitch.*

Vida stared at the signature on the painting. If only she had brought her bifocals, but she hated the frames. Squinting, she moved her head slowly from side to side, trying to make out the name. An M and an A swam into focus. The name on the canvas appeared to be Matthew Conant. A man.

Maurie could still surprise her.

She swung open the gallery door, her black Prada tote nearly decapitating a passing Chinese grandmother yoked to nine bulging plastic bags. Sweeping past the wide-eyed receptionist, Vida sailed into the burnished wood-lined office of the director. It was like walking into a very large humidor.

Vida and Marjorie Kruzick were old and amiable enemies, and had been ever since Marge had tried to gouge Maurie on a commission for a sale to a French dealer. Vida had caught her, and, of course, Marge had claimed that it was all a misunderstanding, confusion over currency conversion. Of course.

Marge was intent on her computer screen, her back to the

door. Vida peripherally noted the grey roots lurking under the brassy dye job and thought: *Poor dear.* She would really have to give her Philippe's phone number. He could work wonders, especially with grey hair.

"I'm sorry," Marge snapped. "I'm busy." She looked up. "Oh." Her lips tightened, managing a prim smile. "Vida. To what do I owe the pleasure?"

Vida allowed herself a small ripple of amusement. Now that Maurie had finally "left the museum," no gallery owner, dealer, or museum official would dare to treat the Widow Lindskog badly, not when she might be hoarding unseen masterpieces. Well, let them grovel. They didn't need to find out just yet that she had already emptied her cupboards—and, thanks to her lawyer, those of Maurie's former mistresses as well—of every Lindskog canvas worth selling. She tossed back her mane of caramel curls, and said, "Marge, that painting out front? Who is that?"

Marge's smile sharpened as though she detected the blood spoor of a sale. "Isn't he marvelous? Matt Conant. A big, big new talent. *Brushnews* is interested, even talking about doing a feature on him. I can get you a price list—"

"No thank you." Vida bared her own teeth in a mirthless grin. "Better put *Brushnews* on hold, Margie. I'd call his style a trifle derivative, wouldn't you? In fact, I'd call it outright plagiarism. Lindskog regurgitated."

"Vida, be reasonable. *Of course* he's channeling Maurie. There's nothing illegal about it."

"Reasonable, my right foot. Where does this Matt Conant live? I want to confront the scheming little *goniff* directly."

"I'm sorry, I can't tell you."

"Yes, you can."

"Look, Vida, it's time to let go. I know that Maurie was a big personality and cast a big shadow—"

"Spare me the amateur psychology, please. Just give me this Conant's address."

"Artist-channeling is no crime. Everybody's doing it. Surely you remember all the excitement when we heard that late de Kooning was *really* late-late Pollock."

"It's not the concept I have a problem with," Vida said. "It's the execution—or executor, to be more precise."

"What do you mean?"

"It's my turn, dammit. Mine. *I* want to channel Maurie. It's my right, not some pipsqueak art student's. But somehow I can't get him to help me."

The ice cracked in Marge's expression, and Vida thought she saw actual sympathy, perhaps even pity, rising toward the surface. Pity, from Marjorie Kruzick. It was unendurable.

"Vida, you can't compel great talent," Marge said softly. "Not before death and certainly not after. Why don't you try to do your own work now? You've got the time and the space."

"My own work? Get real, Marge. It's too late. I gave it all away—all of my own juice—to him. It's Maurie or nothing. And I've been to some of the best facilitators. All my receptors are wide-open. But something keeps going wrong."

"Vida—"

Her voice rose. "If I can't have Maurie, then nobody else can. Now give me that address, Marge, or I'll go to court and get it. You know that I will."

Marge shrugged and hit a few buttons on her keyboard. A second later the printer spat out a sheet of paper. "Here. He's usually at home. I shall, of course, notify him that you're coming."

"Fine. Good to see you, darling. Kiss-kiss." Vida flounced out of the gallery.

Once she was back on the sidewalk she paused to make certain that nobody she knew was passing by. Then she held the paper with Matthew Conant's address right under her nose, squinting. Park Slope, for God's sake. Not even Manhattan. A dreary place, Brooklyn, and an expensive taxi ride. Not the kind of safari one embarked upon lightly.

She would have to put it off. Luckily, she had a lunch date: that charming young man from the Jefferson Mint, what was his name? Andrew. Yes. She was meeting Andrew at the Harem at noon. After that she would confront this Conant and explain her rights.

A bundle of rags stirred on the sidewalk and, like an exercise in morphing, out of that seeming pile of garbage came a hand, an arm, a shoulder leading to a face. Vida saw that what she had mistaken for just another pile of New York garbage was in fact an old dilapidated woman. Hunched into herself, face grey, gaze unfocused, she nevertheless seemed to retain the strength of mind to hold out her palm to every passerby. A crude sign sat on the pavement next to her. "Starving Widow of Starved Artist."

Vida couldn't help herself. From her jacket pocket she pulled out a dime, two nickels, and five pennies. Then she reminded herself that Maurie could no longer complain about her impulsive charity, and doubled the amount. She placed it gently in the withered palm. As a rule she didn't believe in giving street people money, but here was her sister, another widow, another victim of the art game. "Good luck," Vida whispered, and strode on feeling better and stronger.

The Harem was packed with artists, their agents, their publicists, their stylists, and their stylists' publicists. Flashes of light danced off their gold Rolex watches and off the cubic yards of their dyed-weaved-permed-highlighted hair. Fitful blats of recorded bebop occasionally penetrated the loud rumble of nonstop gossip.

A group of woebegone would-be diners waited near the front desk, wilting. They were out of luck, Vida thought. No reservation, no table.

She pushed her way to the front of the crowd and smiled up at Saleem, the tall, slickly handsome maître d'. She had always taken care to tip him lavishly behind Maurie's back.

"Ah, Madame Lindskog. A pleasure. Table for two." With a courtly bow he waved her into the dining room and settled her at a good—but not great—table a smidgen too close to the kitchen.

"Madame is well?" Saleem didn't wait for her response. "Madame looks fabulous. Jennifer will be your waitress. Enjoy."

A sulky-looking redhead in a droopy harem outfit sidled up to the table and said to the air behind Vida's ear, "Do you want to see a wine list?"

"I always have the Gewurtztraminer," Vida said. "Half bottle, *very* cold. And don't jostle it on the way to the table."

The redhead rolled her eyes. "Of course."

"And I'll have my usual."

"Which is?"

"A crab salad with endive instead of lettuce."

"Sorry, no subs."

"You must be new here," Vida said. "Just tell the chef that Vida wants endive."

"Okay. Endive it is."

"Wonderful. And remind him to cut it into bite-size pieces. And to go easy on the tarragon?"

"Anything else?"

"Oh, please bring me lavash instead of rolls? And a bit of salsa for dipping."

The wine, when it arrived, had an odd resinous taste. Vida felt certain that the waitress hadn't followed her directions or—worse yet—had given her a glass of retsina instead. She was about to complain when a loud discussion at the next table caught her attention.

"So she used the purple candles . . ."

"Purple candles? How gauche."

"Well, that's what I thought, too. I've never heard of a spirit responding to purple before."

Vida forgot her wine. Her heart began to pound. Two women were speaking, a blonde with the skin of an infant and the eyes of a corpse, and her companion, a mousy woman with dark hair, a long nose, and a too-tight face-lift. Both of them were wearing last year's Lagerfelds with matching gold-edged sunglasses.

"But Sanjay told her to do it," said the face-lift.

"And," the dead-eyed blonde prompted, "what Sanjay says, goes. So it worked? Purple candles?"

"Absolutely. It had to be the candles, darling. What else? For four nights running he called her and what did he get? Nothing, not even one miserable shriek or rattling chain. But"—and here the face-lift's voice swelled with triumph—"on the fifth night, when he lit the purple candles, she appeared—a bit misty around the edges, he said, but looking remarkably good, everything considered—and showed him where she had hidden her diamonds." She nodded heavily. "In her tennis socks, of course. It was the one place he hadn't looked."

Vida's eyes widened. Sanjay Chapati, *the* channeling facilitator, had specified purple candles! Chapati was notoriously overbooked. Vida herself had tried to get an appointment and finally had given up after being put on Sanjay's waiting list. Her own facilitator, Nicki Sandor, had insisted on red because Maurie had always hated purple.

But these two women actually knew someone who had managed to hire Sanjay Chapati. And Sanjay had specified purple candles. *Purple* candles. As simple as that. If only she had known.

All thoughts of tracking down Matthew Conant fled from Vida's mind. She just had to find some purple candles right away. And, she told herself, in all fairness she should really give Maurice another chance. After all, how did she know what the afterlife was like? He might be confused, trying to find her, aiming but firing blindly. And here she was hardly helping him, using the wrong color candles, for God's sake! Poor dear lost Maurie. She would help him tonight. It was her duty.

"Mrs. Lindskog? Sorry I'm late." Andrew-from-the-Jefferson-Mint stood over her, his grin sheepish, his hair perfectly windblown. "Traffic was the usual."

Vida gathered her thoughts. "Andy. Sit down, dear. I've already ordered—hope you don't mind. Would you like a sip of wine?"

He had the good grace to wait several minutes before launching into his sales pitch. "I was wondering if you'd had a chance to consider our proposal? We'd very much like to enhance Maurice Lindskog's considerable name by marketing tasteful theme-related items suitable for museum gift shops."

Vida too easily remembered Maurie's rantings against the commodification of great artists by their estates. Picasso the coffee mug. Matisse the T-shirt. Never in a thousand years could she permit the use of Maurie's work or his name by these "marketeers." But she enjoyed having lunch with attractive young men—especially when they were paying—and so she gave Andy a sympathetic smile. "I've been so busy lately," she said. "I'm terribly sorry. Tell me again just what you had in mind."

Thirty minutes later she decided that she had had enough of lunch, enough of Andy, and especially, enough of the Jefferson Mint. Bedsheets. Shower curtains, for God's sake.

She flagged down the waitress. "Please wrap up the rest of that salad—and maybe add a little more crab to refresh it." She ignored the girl's look of amazement. "Andy, angel, I'm so sorry to eat and run, but I've got another appointment."

"But I haven't even gotten to the dog beds—"

"Oh, dear. I'm so sorry. Perhaps next time." She tucked the Jefferson Mint prospectus into her purse next to the crab salad. Good thing she had brought the tote today. "Let's do it again, soon." Trailing air kisses, Vida slipped out of the restaurant and set her course for Bloomingdale's.

Safe within the perfumed walls of the Desideratum department, she found the perfect candles: deep amethyst, subtly tapered, with a marvelous silky texture, and marked down fifteen percent. Vida felt certain that Maurie would love them. Tonight her dreams might finally begin to come true.

As soon as she was safely behind the triple-dead-bolted doors of her new penthouse, Vida set about making herself ready. She drew the blinds on the New York skyline and programmed the CD player for twelve uninterrupted hours of Gregorian chants.

Sonorous cantillations filled the apartment. She bathed in low-fat sheep's milk, then rubbed herself liberally with a pungent cinnamon-and-clove oil mixture. When that dried she donned a silky peignoir in shades of lavender and mint green.

"Dona, nobus . . ." sang the monks.

Hands shaking with excitement, Vida placed the purple candles at each point of the pentagram chalked upon her polished hardwood floor, anointed them in turn with the cinnamon mixture, and lit them. They flared and sputtered for a moment before settling into steady, winking golden flames.

In her excitement she almost forgot the incense. Only when that was ignited and filling the air with sweet snaking smoke did Vida begin to intone Maurie's name. It became a free-form poem, a croon in counterpoint to the monks' chanting. Sprawling across the center of the pentagram, she murmured, "Maurie, Maurie," over and over.

To regulate her breathing she counted slowly, in-out, one-two.

Five hundred breaths had come and gone when she began to notice that her left foot was asleep.

Was it a sign from Maurie? Or, perhaps, the beginning of a heart attack? She loosened the neckline and sleeves of the peignoir to help her circulation.

But she had lost track of her count! There was nothing for it but to begin again.

In-out, in-out. One, two, three, four. The numbness seemed to be spreading. Yes, definitely. It had to be Maurie. His spirit was creeping over her. Would he appear in a blaze of glory or merely possess her body? She closed her eyes and willed herself to do his bidding.

When she opened her eyes the sun was pouring through the venetian blinds, leaving stripes on the wall behind her head. The candles had burned themselves out and their hardened remains were welded to the floor.

The canvas before her was still bare. No Maurie, no nothing. The clock said 7:45. She had slept through the night, undisturbed, while Maurie had, no doubt, been partying somewhere else.

"All right, then," Vida muttered. "This is war."

The cab ride was slow and jolting, and she eventually had to plot the entire route for the bald nearsighted Uzbekistani driver. His command of English was quite poor but he certainly seemed able to count when she attempted to shortchange him.

"You should pay me," she said. "For doing all the work."

He shrugged, pocketed her money, and left her coughing in a cloud of fumes.

Matthew Conant's name was not on the mailbox outside the door, but the address was the one that Marge had given her. *The little rodent must live here,* Vida thought.

The door showed the scars of scratched graffiti that had been incompletely painted over. She rang the bell, and whispered, *"En garde."*

On her third ring a man answered. He was younger than she had expected, with a soft face and guileless blue eyes. His head was close-shaven, and he wore three earrings in his right ear, a diamond stud in his left nostril, and a ring in his lower lip. He was, of course, dressed totally in black.

"I'm Vida Lindskog," she said sharply. "And I assume that you are Matthew Conant."

"Yeah." Conant paused and did a classic double take. "Wife of *the* Lindskog?"

"That's right."

"Cool."

Vida pushed her way past him and began to march up the stairs. "I want to talk to you."

He skipped along behind her like an eager puppy. "Sure. Hey, I hear that you're a painter, too."

"Well, yes, I—" she almost fell for it. He looked so open, sounded so innocent, and seemed so interested. But there was just a trifle too much animation to his face, wasn't there? A bit too much of a polished "good listener" stance to his body, to the tilt of his head. He was putting her on, softening her up. Well, forget it. He was dealing with a master here.

"I didn't come to talk about me, I came to talk about you." She smiled a wide false smile and looked around the place.

It was the usual artist's magpie nest: empty wire spools tipped on their sides, scraps of bright paper glued to the wall with smears of paint, dolls' heads aligned along a dusty fold-down-from-the-wall ironing board, deflating silver balloons, cracked china cups, aluminum pop-top rings strung like talismans on a long wire loop.

Vida selected the only chair—a molded plastic number from the 1950s—brushed off the seat, and settled in. "I hear you're doing some good work these days."

"Rad." Conant perched beside her on a pile of cinder blocks. His Adam's apple made a quick up-and-down motion. "You know my work?"

"Saw it, to be precise. In Marjorie Kruzick's window."

"Yeah. Marge is cool. The best."

"I'm glad to hear it. Young artists deserve support. But I don't see any of your work here."

"It's all at the gallery. Nothing's left."

She struck. "Then you'll have to contact Maurie to churn out the next batch?"

Instead of acting surprised, or even wounded, Conant smiled with an agreeableness that Vida found quite irritating. "Yeah, exactly. It's so cool that you understand."

"Have you been channeling my husband for long?"

"About two months." Conant ducked his head sheepishly. "To be honest, I was hoping for Klee or Miró. But I guess that channelers can't be choosers." He shrugged. "Anyway, it's an honor to provide an outlet for Maurice Lindskog's talents. Before he came through I was ready to chuck it all and move to Seattle to design computer games."

"How lucky for you."

"Can I get you something to drink, Mrs. Lindskog? Like maybe a cup of tea?"

"Tea would be fine. Black. Two sugars. Not too hot."

Beaming, he vanished into the kitchen.

As soon as he was gone Vida stood up, back aching from the chair, and scanned the room for channeling aids.

To her dismay she saw some dusty old candles—surely he hadn't used those?—and some dried, cracked old tubes of what might have been aromatic ointments. Was that scuffed and faded scar in the middle of the living room floor the remains of a chalked pentagram? It could just as easily have been the remains of some ancient pizza, or a bloodstain.

What was this Conant's secret? Why had he been chosen by Maurice over her? Vida swore to herself that if he turned that ingenuousness on her one more time, she would kick him, hard, right in his innocence.

Wait. There, on the table, under a pile of week-old newspapers. Surely under there? She paged through the lot impatiently but found only obsolete copies of *Wired* magazine. Well, what did you expect, she asked herself, a copy of *Channeling Great Artists for Fun & Profit*?

"Teatime." Conant emerged from the kitchen bearing a battered tray with two mugs and a crumpled box of cookies. "I think these Lorna Doones aren't too old."

Vida picked up her cup, took one sip of the dusty-tasting liquid, and put it down. "Lovely. Now, young man, I want you to tell me exactly how you've been managing to reach my husband."

"Oh, okay." He munched a cookie, swallowed, and, with a grave expression, began to explain. "Y'see, I'd heard about these great-artist channelings in art school. And since I wasn't having any luck on my own I figured, why not go for it? But I never expected to have such success—and on the first try!"

"Oh, really?" Vida began to wish that there was something stronger than tea in her cup. "On the first try? Maurie came as soon as you called?"

"Yeah. Radical, isn't it? Well, see, my facilitator, Sanjay Chapati, wrote a book on this."

Vida wondered if she was the only person in New York whom Sanjay Chapati hadn't counseled. "A book, you say? What sort of book?"

"On channeling. Well, it's really still in the galley-proof stages. But I've got a copy in the bathroom. Let me get it for you." He was up like a shot, and back just as quickly, proferring a dog-eared folder. "Here."

Vida hadn't thought about checking the bathroom. She glanced down at the title: *How to Make a Living Channeling Great Dead Artists*. "It looks very interesting."

"Oh, it is. Really. Hey, why don't you try it? The incantations are absolutely the best. Everybody agrees about that."

"I couldn't possibly—"

"No, I insist. Take it with you. What kind of a guy would I be if I didn't help a colleague?"

He was really a very nice boy, Vida decided. Very respectful and understanding. "Well, if you sincerely mean it."

"Cool. Wouldn't it be neat if we both channeled Maurie?"

"Real cool." Vida smiled. "Well, Matt, I've enjoyed our chat, but I'm afraid I'd better run along before traffic becomes even more impossible."

"Oh, not yet. Please. I haven't even had a chance to show you my sketchbooks."

Much later, and only after she had agreed to sign a copy of the Met catalog for Maurice's retrospective, Vida escaped. Matt Conant perched on the staircase behind her. "Good luck," he called. "Just follow the instructions."

Once she was ensconced in the taxi's backseat—with the doors locked and the driver given his directions—she dragged out her silver purse flask and took a long pull of rum to calm her nerves. Feeling better, Vida grabbed up the manuscript.

She read carefully, nodding at certain points. Ah, she thought. There it was. What she had needed all along. Yes, purple candles were fine. But she had to use yellow ones, too. And make a cross on her forehead of lemon balm and parsley. Walk the candle circuit twice, backward, and once forward. Forget the sheep milk. Nix on the Gregorian chants.

"Beware," the text said, "of making yourself too receptive."

Vida laughed at the very notion. *All this time I've been doing it all wrong,* she thought. *Well, now I'll make up for it.* If four purple candles were good, eight would be even better.

The pristine canvases awaited, gessoed and primed.

The paints and brushes were laid out in careful rows. The glass palette and mineral oil sat within arm's reach, ready.

Vida chalked the pentagram with elaborate care, the purple oil pastel crumbling beneath her fingers. The lemon-balm-and-parsley cross felt oddly sticky upon her brow. She lit the incense and as its smoky scent filled the air, anointed and lit each purple candle and each yellow one, moving from left to right, working her way around the pentagram. As each candle flame hissed to life she felt a growing confidence that this, finally, would work. Backward and then forward, she walked the candle circuit, intoning:

"With fire, with herbs, I consecrate this space
Push back the walls, open the way.
Make a path between the worlds, from him to me.
Bring me what is mine, what is owed."

Even before she had finished her chant the ground beneath her feet began to tremble, and her words echoed eerily: "What is owed, owed, owed."

Unearthly silver light filled the pentagram and washed over her into the room. Now the floor shook, and the windows rattled as though an earthquake had struck the very bedrock of Manhattan.

Was that a faint voice she heard at the back of her head, behind her somewhere? She couldn't quite make out the words. Well, Maurie could be that way. She reached for him. With all her formidable strength of will. And this time—this time—he came to her.

Vida felt herself being filled, a spirit moving into her very bones, her marrow. Her hands began to twitch, her heart to pound. With great excitement she reached for her brushes. The paint, she must have the paint! The names on the tubes were themselves an incantation: Viridian, Alizarin, Cerulean.

She went to work, slapping the paint on, practically stabbing the colors into the canvas as she made one bold statement after another. Oh, the confidence, the exhilaration! She'd never known it could be like this. "Yes, Maurie," she cried. "Oh, yes, yes, yes. Don't stop!"

The canvases began to line the walls as she finished one after another. And then, to her surprise, she felt a subtle shifting within.

She turned and went back to the first canvas she had finished, a splendid aria of blues and greens. But now the brush sought out ochre and burnt sienna. A muddy stripe here. A dark note there. What was happening? These minor-key colors had never been in Maurie's repertoire. She was ruining these paintings.

Vida tried to fling the brush from her grasp, but her hand wouldn't unclench. It had become a claw around the brush's wooden handle. Slowly she saw a shape emerge on the canvas. Her fears faded as she began to understand. Death *had* changed Maurie. He had reconsidered representation and was adopting it right before her eyes. How thrilling. Oh, she'd known he had it in him.

She worked tirelessly, filling, refining. The blue and green became a mere background echo. What she had now was a dark and tortured portrait of a skull. A cow skull.

Vida gasped. It couldn't be. But yes, yes, who else? Oh, it was a dream, too much to ask for. She, Vida Lindskog, had been especially blessed, found especially worthy. For now she knew that the spirit which guided her brush was not merely Maurie's but that of another artist as well. One of the great ones. O'Keeffe. She was experiencing a rare double-channeling: Maurie *and* Georgia O'Keeffe. Vida gave her forebears full credit for her a strong constitution— a lesser vessel could never have borne these gifts. "Thank you," she whispered. "Oh, thank you."

And now she painted even more quickly than before, marrying O'Keeffe's arid realism to Maurie's exuberant colorist techniques. Huge suggestive flowers and heroic seashells emerged from her brush. She painted on, and on. The sky began to lighten between the slats of the venetian blinds. Vida painted on.

An odd note, flat and plangent, echoed suddenly in the room. Vida felt a harsh trembling move through her. She was emptied out, purged. The brush fell from her limp fingers.

"Maurie?" Vida cried. "Maurie, what is it? What's happening?"

At first there was silence. It took her a while to make out the nearly inaudible response in the back of her head.

"Not. Maurie."

"Miss O'Keeffe, then," she said. "Please, tell me. What's wrong?"

"Not her, either."

Fear gripped Vida. Who then? What spirit had slipped through the curtain between worlds to nestle within her?

"Who?" She cried. "Who are you? Tell me!"

"Merde," came the answer. "Everything is merde."

Her hand moved of its own volition. As she watched in horrified fascination, it hovered over the palette table, dipping down for a moment as if to clutch a brush or a paint tube. Then it flashed out and seized the turp bucket.

Splash!

The image on canvas began to melt and run.

Vida tried to stop it, gain control of her own hands.

Splash!

The cow's skull painting, ruined, made an ochre puddle on the floor. Vida cried out as if it had been her own flesh that had suffered the violation.

She grabbed up a tube of black, and, weeping, squeezed ribbons of paint down the front of another canvas. Then she plunged both hands into the gooey mess and smeared until the image beneath it was completely obliterated. Next she staggered to a blue-green landscape and, smudging as she went, wrote "This is not art" across the face of it.

She couldn't stop herself. No matter how hard she tried she couldn't pull away from the canvases. Vida moaned like a wounded animal as, piece by piece, she destroyed the splendid work of the past several hours.

When the canvases were all ruined and Vida's face was running with tears the carnage stopped. Her arm went limp.

"Thank God," she whispered.

Now, with a sickening thud in the pit of her belly Vida realized what had happened. For the first time in her life she had been successful. Too successful. Not only had she channeled Maurie, and O'Keeffe, she had also channeled Marcel Duchamp.

Duchamp. The eternal prankster.

Everybody channeled him. Everyone. In life he may have been elusive, but in death he was the great buttinsky. No one wanted his posthumous work—there was too much of it around. Bitterly Vida gazed around the room. These canvases were worthless. She wouldn't be able to give them away.

Again, tears filled her eyes. She should have known. She should have expected it. This was all Maurie's doing. In death as in life. With a heartfelt wail, she cursed her late husband. Only he would have opened a channel to her on a party line.

She could imagine him in the afterlife, partying with Duchamp, O'Keeffe, Pollock, and the rest: *Who's that knocking at the door? Poor little Vida. What's that she's asking for? Silly girl. Let's really give her what she wants. What a giggle.*

She dried her eyes, gathered up the canvases, and stacked them by the incinerator. The paints went directly down the hatch into the flames. Eyes closed, Vida listened to the distant roar, nodding as though she held a seashell to her ear. Next she mopped up the floor as best she could, hoping that her cleaning lady had some technique for dealing with turpentine on hardwood.

That done, she showered, brewed a pot of espresso, and had three cups. As she sipped, her resolve hardened. She would never attempt to channel Maurie again. Never. She was finished with all of that. Finished. Done.

Vida glanced at the clock. Ten in the morning. How had it gotten so late? She felt better now. Much better. She was free. Really and truly free. It was her time. Vida's time, Vida's life. Now she would show everybody what she could really do.

She reached for the telephone and dialed.

"Hello, Andrew? Listen, dear, I've been thinking about your proposal. Yes, and I've decided to grant the Jefferson Mint full access to Maurie's work. Yes, I'm excited too. Especially about the bedsheet- and matching-shower-curtain concepts."

Frozen

Tom Cool

With thanks to BS & Turkey Citizens, LN, DM and SL, M.D.

Frigid winds whipped past Marlena's face. Long black hair streaming, she peered down into the dim valley where the three frozen rivers joined. Marlena imagined the under-ice waters sluicing from the city's sewers carrying botched viral experiments and criminally dumped biochemicals.

City of Pittsburgh, the first American city to industrialize, the first to postindustrialize, oozes new poisons. Without poison, can it be Pittsburgh?

Overhead, the broad path of the Milky Way shone clear, its stars unblinking. The northern night air was clear, dry, and cold, focusing the starlight.

She pushed away from the iron handrail. Abandoning the promenade, she turned down a street of darkened restaurants and headed for the after-hours club. Karl would be there, partying with his new women.

The club, Babylon, had no sign, only a blackened steel door the cognoscenti rapped in code. Across the street stood a row of bricked-up buildings not yet reclaimed from the plague years. Between two such blind buildings ran a deserted alleyway. In its shadows, Marlena stood and watched the black door of Babylon. Here the winds howled. This was perfect: hidden, dark, and cold.

She reached into her pocket and thumbed off her coat's thermostat. She snugged a custom-fit mask to her face, then set the thermostats of her mask, gloves and boots at half body warmth, unsealing her coat and her blouse, baring her chest to the freezing wind, which instantly stripped the warmth from her skin.

As if apprehensive, inside her chest the symbiote stirred. She knew that she should have felt frightened, but the symbiote harvested from her bloodstream and her brain the chemicals of fear.

The wind triggered her verbal imagination:

> Winter winds scour cities void of life
> Sand the skulls clean of dreams

The door of the Babylon banged open, blasting the street with loud music and bright colored lights. Red and yellow lights . . .

Her sister's wedding in the Pitt chapel, a jagged granite monolith dropped from Gothic skies. Inside, the memory of a younger self admired its stained-glass windows, trapped daylight rioting in ruby red, emerald green, diamond blue patchworks of nameless saints, so beautiful it hurt her eyes. A hired woman played the harp angelically. A strange man, a friend of a friend, perhaps, stood in the left pews with the groom's people . . . tall, densely built, dark, with a devil haircut and a sharp goatee. At the reception, they talked and danced.

Karl, leaping from the ruin of the '38 World's Fair Tower, free-falling until experts were hollering, opening his chute so low that it barely filled before he was running toward her, the chute billowing like red-silk wings behind him. Soaring with survivor's euphoria, his body as vibrant

as a superman's, he had hugged her and kissed her for the
first time.

The wind numbed her lips. Deeply she inhaled, filling
her lungs with cold. Her hand twitched toward the thermostat in the coat pocket, but she forced herself not to touch it.
Marlena shrugged off her coat and allowed it to fall to the
icy ground. Now the wind whipped the warmth from her
back. Already cold pinpricks of pain pierced the flesh of
her chest.

Instinctively her head reared back, searching for help,
seeing in the high gap between the blind buildings only the
cold and steady stars. A meteorite streaked, a long green
scratch ending in a tiny explosion, a beautiful flaw in the
heavens . . . The satellite, where everything should have
been perfect . . . Karl handing her the golden gift tickets.
PolarOrbit IX Resort. The sleek hypersonic shuttle had
lifted them smoothly from Dulles, rockets kicking them up
to spin the Earth, once, curvaceously, before rendezvous
and the magnetic kiss of the satellite's dock.

They floated weightless for a week, their brains euphoric
with vertigo suppressants and their muscles vibrating with
electric microshocks minimizing atrophy. They felt like
thrumming angels.

With an orbit about two hundred kilometers high, PolarOrbit IX maintained a consistently spectacular view of
the beautiful and violent Earth. During the south-to-north
passages over the Atlantic, they could see four tropical
storms and hurricanes, a curving line of whirling dervishes
launched from Africa toward the Caribbean. The oligarchs
would bet on the hours that the storms would be upgraded
to hurricanes, where the hurricanes would make landfall.

Karl enjoyed the gaming and drunken hubbub of the
Earth-side observatory, spending every waking hour there,
betting millions and skin-popping rozaleine. Marlena spent

more time alone in the smaller outward observatory, where she had a lonely view of a half-moon no bigger than the Moon seen from the Earth, but clear and backdropped by hard stars. She could see dimly the darkside of the Moon by reflected Earthlight. The terminator marked the halfway point between the new moon and the stone blossom of the full moon . . . man, halfway between the amoebae and the angels . . .

She forced herself to return to the Earth-side observatory, knowing Karl would look for her. The cadre of oligarchs was gaggling, swilling champagne and jabbering about the storms. Swinging up from the blindingly brilliant snows and melting glaciers of the Antarctic, PolarOrbit IX hauled over the horizon of the storms. Men barked and women chittered as money cards changed hands. Hurricane Aleph was striking Jamaica. A bent old man was crowing because he had bet five million on Jamaica. As he hooted, Marlena resisted the urge to tell him that her mother's mother had emigrated from the island.

It was too much. Wordlessly, Marlena retreated to the private cabin. Moments later, the door swung open. Karl emerged, launched himself, snagged Marlena so that they spun and bumped against a bulkhead. He seemed drugged.

"You don't seem to be enjoying yourself," he said accusingly.

Marlena smiled crookedly and shook her head, "Oh no, I'm fine . . . I was just writing."

The suddenness of the attack dazed and confused her. Even during the assault, she couldn't accept its reality. In her peripheral vision, the cold bright half-orb of the Moon spun, then a padded bulkhead slammed into her shoulder. Weightless, she bounced and cartwheeled, the Moon under her feet. Karl's upside-down face, distorted in a leer of rage, loomed suddenly near her. A hard hand pulled at her

arm, whipping her around, the sudden torque popping her
vertebrae, the sound inside of her like twenty knuckles
cracked sequentially. Marlena found herself trying to swim
through the air toward the Moon, as if brilliant airless rock
were a place of refuge. Tears sprang to her eyes, welled and
flowed away from her in salty globules, small satellites, little experiments in the surface tension of misery. Her throat
ached; she dragged her breaths in raspy sobs, begging him
to stop.

Suddenly, the lights brightened, the Moon dimmed, the
door opened. She looked around for Karl; the movement
hurt her neck. His disappearance seemed magical. One of
her tears impacted her forehead. She became aware of rasp-
ing sobs, the voice unrecognizable as her own.

The mere memory of terror, an empty shadow without
affect. The day after the free clinic had turned her away, the
corporate thugs had visited her and threatened to gouge out
her bloody kidneys . . .

". . . sell them at market price—"

"Don't ever try to have the symbiote removed again."

"Not before the contracted date . . ."

Marlena had smiled like a wan angel and thanked them
for their time.

The symbiote . . . was it still warm within her body?

Although it was her living warmth leaving, following the
remorseless laws of thermodynamics, it felt as if the cold
was invading her body, claiming her tissue by tissue. Her
neck and abdomen were stinging, as if thousands of small
needles were prickling her skin. The muscles of her torso
and limbs spasmed. Her thoughts grew jumbled. Her teeth
chattered. To survive, all she had to do was to walk from
this dark alley and enter any building, even the Babylon,
but she refused to surrender.

Deep inside her, she could feel the symbiote begin to

move. In her sinuses, where it mainly lived, yes, but also in
her neck, where its tendrils curled around her pituitary and
adenoids, and deeper, near her heart and liver, even in her
lower abdomen, where it supped from her ovaries. It was
stirring. That was good.

Luci would think her so clever. She could see Luci Stern-
berg's face, round as the full moon, luminescent with ge-
nius. Her poetry as subtle and precious as pearls, but as
obscure as all the century's poems.

In her confusion, Marlena heard her younger voice wondering whether she should hire a personal justice of the
peace.

"Personal justice is oxymoronic," Luci said. "Justice is
either impersonal and universal or it is not justice. Retalia-
tion is not justice, it's just good shooting." Luci's room surrounded her, with its curtains of crushed blue velvet, clung
with hundreds of shed locust exoskeletons; its witchy artifacts of spheres, crystals, incense sticks and guttering candles; its clutter of hand-bound books, antique poetry
journals, and acid-free papers . . .

"I don't think—"

"You have to forget him. Romance with the likes of him
is not love; it's a legal form of bestiality."

Marlena steeled herself to confess the most awful part.

"I still love him."

Luci lifted an eyebrow.

"You're a young girl, and you don't know who you are,"
she said, speaking in a low, simple, and intimate voice, as
if, for once, posterity was not taking notes. "Your poems
have been nothing more than natural talent and natural
beauty. A beautiful girl, when she's young, can't help being
beautiful, any more than an orchid. To be beautiful at fifty,
that takes character. The right choices. Discipline. So tell

me: You love him, but do you love the part of yourself that
loves him?"

Marlena recognized this as one of Luci's big questions.

"No. Yes. I do and I don't. It's wild, natural . . . but it's
stupid. Mindless, really. It's a part of me through which I
feel connected, but I don't particularly like what I'm connected to."

Luci smiled gently. "Would you, in and of yourself, have
chosen this part of you?"

"No."

"Then get rid of it or grow beyond it."

"How?"

"There are those who uninstall their hearts, but—"

Other acolytes entered Luci's room, babbling of Eastern
European design theory. Drifting faces of psychoanalysts,
priests, critics, licensed brujos, psychics . . . she passed
through their hands like a treasure increasingly tarnished.

Cold lights. Her unkempt apartment. Among the fast-
food clutter and unwashed clothes, a sad pile of copper dol-
lars thrown onto the ragged, dirty carpet. Marlena clung to
that that moment, looking at the coins, when she had decided to uninstall her heart. Because she wanted to evolve
past the human condition, where ecstasy turned to agony,
simply because men used women for pleasure. Better to
uninstall her heart, and with it, all the secretions that drove
her as relentlessly as the mating imperative drove insects
and lizards.

Contracts signed, her body no longer her own, now chattel
to the corporation. The surgery had been painless. The corporation's med-techs snaked in fiber-optically guided probes,
investigating her most private tissues, pinching samples that
the surgical robot sucked back into itself, analyzing the
chemistries of her blood, mucous, endocrinal tissues, adenoids. The med-techs smiled. She was pure. The product

would be top-drawer. That day, they began the brewing in their germless cauldrons. Drawn from her own DNA spliced on a computer-crafted egg, the symbiote matured in only a week. When she returned, the doctors covered her eyes and administered local anesthesia. Though they never let her see it, she knew it was a mucousy gelatinous mass. They introduced it to her nostrils. Following its genetic programming, recognizing its host, it crawled into her: a slimy tendril at first, but then more and more, insinuating itself into her head. She could not really feel it, but there was a sensation of congestion that caused her a moment of panic. The attendant nurse stroked her forehead, soothing her.

"It'll just be a minute," the nurse said. "Hush . . ."

Then it branched itself slyly throughout her body. The base of her neck felt full, then she felt an uncomfortable sensation in her chest, then in her pelvic girdle, and finally, in her lower abdomen just below her navel.

They made her rest for fifteen minutes. When she stood, she could feel herself heavier by perhaps two kilograms.

For the first few days, she felt relatively normal. The symbiote was programmed to delay its feedings. After a week, she felt light-headed and forgetful, then, clear, cold, and certain. Her thoughts ran smoothly. It was like the end of menstruation.

The woman with the equipment who would visit her. She would snake a thin, flexible tube up her nose, drawing from her the rich serums that the symbiote harvested: endorphins, neurotransmitters, hormones, adrenaline . . . all the complex chemicals that nature could manufacture with unmatchable fidelity. The basis of so many profitable drugs.

Marlena's arms spasmed. She returned to herself, remembering vaguely why she was standing in a dark alley with the wind whipping past her flesh. She no longer felt the cold. Her hands, face, and feet felt hot; her abdomen felt numb. Her center had grown vague, as if her body were dissolving into another, perhaps better, world.

She fantasized about walking back to a diner down the street. It would be so nice. In the diner, the air would be warm and moist, smelling of roasted coffee beans and baked sugar and cinnamon. She would rest her legs, straddling a stool, leaning her tired arms on the counter and drinking a mug of hot coffee. The waitress would smile softly. Underneath her tired habitualness would be a mother's care.

Without emotions, Marlena discovered that nothing made a difference. Pretty intellectual considerations were not enough. She realized it the night she reread Akhmatova's "Requiem," but didn't feel the emotions behind the words. When she read all her recent poetry, she realized they were sterile mental drills. Worthless. Without emotions, her life was worthless.

From her posthuman pinnacle of intellectual clarity, she believed that she had solved the puzzle . . . quite elegantly . . . but now it was hard to remember the puzzle itself.

> Winter winds . . . what was it? Something . . . life
> Death. Yes, death . . . did something . . . dreams . . .

Following a biologic imperative, the symbiote was abandoning its cooling host. Its slimy mass was filling her mouth, blocking the air passages at the back of the throat. The gag reflex was insistent, but Marlena fought it. Welling into her mouth, the symbiote drew its mass up, oozing smoothly through the small cuts in internal membranes that the robotic surgeon had built for it. Marlena tried to keep her teeth from chattering as the symbiote pressed forward, seeking escape from the cooling body. She opened her mouth slightly; it welled past her lips and the mouth hole of the mask. She could feel it oozing past her chin as its other extremity oozed up her throat. She gagged, propelling the thing forward and outward, though tendrils of its mucousy mass still trailed in her guts.

Across the street, one shadow shifted and stirred and elongated until, in the middle of the street, it took the form of a dark woman with flat black eyes. The woman stumbled up to Marlena and reached out to touch her masked cheek. Beyond the eye slits, frozen tears crusted eyelashes. Bared breasts shimmered a translucent blue. Awkwardly because of the cold, the dark woman flicked a medical sensor at Marlena's neck. Wind whipped the tip of the sensor so it missed Marlena's flesh by a millimeter. The sensor's display glowed rows of zeroes.

Dead, the dark woman thought. I waited like she paid me to, but I must have waited too long. That's all right, though . . . I can keep the rest of the product for myself . . . the good stuff . . .

She cupped her hands below Marlena's face. Slowly, the still-warm symbiote oozed into her palms. Patiently she waited until its limpid mass trusted its weight fully to her. Still, in the end, it took an insistent tug to pull the last trailing from out of the throat. She turned and hustled back across the street, back into a windowless van in the back of the alley. Inside, she extracted the endorphins, hormones, and other precious biochemicals. She flashed them for bacteria and viruses. Fingers trembling, she loaded up a syringe and skin-popped the best for herself.

While the winds howled outside, the woman's eyes teared not with pity, but with scavenged ecstasy. She fixed a second hit, spraying it transcutaneously into her jugular.

Ten minutes later, the fifth hit was not as sweet. She had used up the best of Marlena's biochemicals. Mixing a cocktail of the dregs, she added synthetics to the formula that Marlena had provided.

Exiting the alley, the dark woman glanced across the street. She could not see Marlena's form among the shadows of the alley. With a steel-headed cane, she rapped the knock code on the door of the Babylon.

The club's insides sweltered with music, smoke, moisture, and movement. Deep bass notes shook the clothing, vibrated the sweaty bodies that gyrated and bounced to the rhythms. Neon, laser, and ultraviolet lights strobed.

Karl was collapsed in a corner. His women had abandoned him, their short-term romance having run its course. His amphetamine-accelerated heart was jumping like a hooked trout against his sternum.

By the light of mirror-ball reflections, the woman recognized Karl.

"Hey, man," she said. "What can I fix you with?"

"Nothing," Karl said. "I'm fine."

With the familiarity of a mortician, the dark woman flicked Karl's wrist with a medical sensor.

"Oh that's no good," she breathed. "You got imbalances. Let me fix it up."

Wearily, Karl handed the woman a money card to swipe dry. She verified the swipe more carefully than she had tested Marlena for vital signs. Satisfied, she injected Karl with an imprecise hostility, then she retreated into the darkness, her job done.

Heavy with seratonin antagonists and dopamine inhibitors, depressants eked from Marlena's brain, the biochemicals hit Karl like a black tidal wave cresting on shore, overwhelming him, destroying the flimsy structures of his ego, sucking him down into a primal sunless sea of godless despair. Karl's throat convulsed painfully. His aching eyes leaked with tears, crying for eyes, that for all of his love, might be sightless icy orbs.

In the diner, Marlena straddled a stool, thinking slowly that the place was as warm as a hothouse. She could smell old grease, dish soap, steam, and coffee. The waitress approached her. A young woman who had run three rows of decorative scars across her right cheek.

"You look half-froze."

"It's . . . cold outside."

The waitress bustled and served up a steamy washcloth on a stainless-steel plate.

Marlena wiped her neck. Her flesh stung. "What would you like?"

"Hot tea."

With her hands wrapped around the hot ceramic mug, Marlena felt the first twinge of joy she had felt in many months. While she waited for her order, the lines of poetry turned within her imagination. She scribbled them onto a paper napkin:

> Winter winds scour the city free of life
> Sand my skull clean of dreams
> Yet I witness the stone flower bloom
> A full Moon amid airless stars . . .

The steaming mug of tea sat next to the napkin with its scribbled lines. She would work them until they rocked Luci back on her heels. She wouldn't write for Karl; she had written her farewell to him in a biochemical poem.

To drink the tea this hot would be too much, she knew. Of course she should go to the hospital, but she had had enough of med-techs for now. She would sit and let the warmth seep back into her body. When the tea was merely warm, she would take it into her.

The Traitor

by Lois Tilton

They say human sacrifice has a long history. I suppose there are times when the gods just won't accept anything less. But even when the priests took a bull or a goat to the altar instead of a man, they used to sprinkle its head with water before they brought out the knife, to make it nod its head, to make it consent. That was always the important part: The sacrifice had to go willingly.

Now the gods demand a confession. Am I willing? Do I consent to the knife? I suppose I must be, or else why would I be writing this now?

The first thing: We were all volunteers. A hundred volunteers for every man chosen, even though we all knew we might never be coming back. It was a long way out to where we were going, and no one sure exactly what we might be going to find, even with the probe report to tell us.

What the probe had shown us: a world. Not just a planet, not just a barren chunk of rock like every other possibility we'd seen in all those years of searching, until the whole project was almost abandoned. This time it was a real, living world, with growing things, with an oxygen atmosphere, with clouds and storms to fly through.

And we'd found it first. That was the important thing. The world was empty, unoccupied, unclaimed.

None of us had ever met hostile aliens then, any other form of life. But sometimes a probe—automated, unmanned—would just suddenly vanish. A split second's burst of static, then nothing more ever came back. Hostile aliens, that was one theory. Who didn't want us intruding into their space, didn't want us spying on them. There was no proof, of course. But when the *Aspera* finally set off on its journey, the ship was armed.

Maybe that should have told us something, right then. Or maybe not. We were supposed to be a peaceful expedition, going out to settle a new world, to claim it for humanity. But Terrabeta was ours and we were ready to defend it, if necessary.

My primary assignment was shuttle pilot. On Earth, I'd been a cloud-wrangler, a meteorologist, and I'd be doing that job, too, on Beta. But the shuttles were also capable of being armed as fighter craft, and my qualifications included six years as a reserve AirSpace pilot. While we traveled outward, we trained on sims set to recreate Beta's heavier atmosphere, but the trainers included a lot of combat scenarios.

They crept into my dreams: *Climb! Try to get above him! Lock on target! No! Look out!*

I hadn't signed on to fight, to lock some enemy into my targeting system and open fire. No, my real dream was to fly through Terrabeta's storms, mapping the atmosphere of a new world.

"Are they really anticipating a fight?" I asked the flight captain, who'd been an AirSpace Regular on Earth. Captain Wu was part of the *Aspera* command structure, they might have told him things they kept from the rest of us. "Should we expect to be going into combat?"

But Wu only shrugged, and said, "It's contingency training, that's all. Just in case, you know. None of us know for sure what's out there, Waldek."

None of us knew.

But after years in transit, years of waiting, we finally dropped into the Iota Persei system. Every man on board crowded in front of the viewscreens to stare at the display, to see it for themselves, the image slowly resolving into a disc, a sun, marginally smaller, dimmer, cooler than Sol. And still too faint to make out, but we knew it was there: Iota Persei II, Terrabeta. The world we'd come to claim.

I wonder if anyone on Earth can imagine how we felt during those weeks, those months as we made our approach through the system. It was all men on the ship—a political decision, not one we were happy with. Our job was to lay claim to Beta, survey the world, establish the foundation of a settlement. Then, when it was secured, send back to Earth for the first civilian colonists. For the women and children. Our own families, if they still survived, would have priority. That was the promise driving us all. A home for my boys, my two sons. I'd volunteered for this, but it had been hard, all those years, alone, without them. Now the goal was finally in sight.

Yet already, as we approached the world, it was becoming obvious that something was wrong. *Aliens*—that's what everyone was saying. Rumors—there'd been something on scan. Some kind of contact—hostile contact. Command wasn't saying.

The shuttle pilots were asking, "Are we going to have to fight?" All those combat sims, all that training—was it for this? I think Captain Wu was aware that letting the rumors grow would only make things worse, but he had his orders. Still, he wasn't the kind of man who could easily lie. "We don't know yet. We're not sure. There's a situation, we should be prepared . . . that's all I can say now."

But of course everyone couldn't help wondering what was really going on. Rumors led to quarrels:

—*There was an alien attack on the ship. They're just not telling us.*

—*You don't know anything! Where's your evidence, where's your proof?*

—*You're wrong, it was a message warning us to leave the system.*

—*Some people will believe anything!*

The tension got to everyone. There were two other pilots in my group: Gutierrez and Vikram. I wouldn't say we were friends—Euros weren't popular on the ship, and there weren't that many of us, on account of the quotas. It was Gutierrez who finally came up with the real answer, even before Command admitted it officially. "It's the probe, it's gone missing."

Vikram as always was dubious. "You mean the broadcasts have stopped. That doesn't mean anything, not after so long."

"No! I mean the probe isn't there in orbit anymore! They took it out!"

"*Who* took it out?"

"They did! Aliens, whoever they are."

Vikram was always the reasonable one. "It could have been a malfunction, it could have been hit by a meteor or something . . ."

"If that's all it was, Command would have said so."

Suddenly it all came together in my mind—"They must have known!"

"What do you mean, Waldek?" the other two demanded.

"Back on Earth, they must have known, all along. Before they sent us out. When they decided to arm the ship."

"I don't see what difference it makes," Gutierrez insisted, with an edge in his voice that warned me to back off.

And Vikram said, "It could have happened—whatever happened to the probe—anytime before we came into the system."

"I suppose it could have," I agreed. But the shuttles had been fitted for weapons systems before we left Earth. And those combat sims. And the way Command refused for so long to confirm the probe's loss. It all added up in my mind: *They lied to us.*

Later, when I had more time to think, I wasn't so sure. Maybe Vikram was right, and the Galactics took out the probe after the *Aspera* was already under way. Maybe the weapons systems were just like Captain Wu said: a contingency measure. Wu was never good at lying about things like that. But maybe he never knew the truth. Maybe they lied to him, too.

I remember the expression on his face when he came to tell us: "All shuttle pilots report to the hangar bays."

"Are we going to fight?"

Grimly, "It's possible. There's someone out there. They may not want us here. We need to be ready, in case we need to defend the ship."

But of course we would have had to ready the shuttles at any event, now that we were approaching Beta. Every shuttle pilot had been trained to do the routine maintenance on his own ship, to install and check out the system modules. The weapons system, that I'd hoped I'd never have to use. *Contingencies. Self-defense. That's all.*

Had they lied?

Of course it wasn't long before everyone on the ship knew: It was aliens. Aliens who'd taken out the probe that we'd left in orbit around Beta, hostile aliens occupying the world. *Our* world.

And we all knew we were getting ready to fight, whether Command admitted it or not.

What other alternatives did we have? Turn around and go back? We all knew it would have been political suicide, not just for the men in Command, for their nations. The resources put into *Aspera* meant too much to let them just abandon the project now. Even if they hadn't known, from the beginning, what we were going to find when we arrived.

Negotiate? With aliens? It wasn't a popular option.

—No! They destroyed our probe!

—We found this world first! It's them or us!

Maybe Command was considering it. I don't know. They never told the rest of us much more than they wanted us to hear, and they didn't much listen to our opinions, either. The *Aspera* wasn't a democracy.

But then everything changed. We were summoned, every man on the ship, to assemble in the main hall. It was Hassan who stepped up to speak, the ship's Exec. He told us, "Today, Captain Wu Xian made a survey flight into Terrabeta's atmosphere. Some hostile force has shot him down."

For a few minutes you couldn't hear another word as everyone reacted to the news.

—Who? Why?

—Did he eject? Is there a chance he could still be alive?

But Hassan said no. "The shuttle was hit by an energy beam from the planet's surface that disabled its basic control systems. Captain Wu did not eject. The ship crashed on the surface. We have no grounds for supposing he could have survived. I repeat: He was *attacked*. This was no accident, it was an attack—unprovoked, unwarranted—from a hostile alien force onworld. But you can see for yourselves."

I looked up to see the image appearing on the main

viewscreen: our new world, Terrabeta, spreading out to its horizons. Wu was flying the shuttle over a hilly country, studded with lakes. He followed the rising land, and a large sinuous river came into sight. I knew that river, I recognized it from the charts, from the sims, and all I could think for a moment was: *It could have been me, I could have been the one they sent, instead of Wu.* And I couldn't help myself, I wanted it, even though I knew what I was going to see next.

The shuttle followed the river until it split and spread into a broad estuary, then Wu turned back from the coastline. In the far distance, like a low-lying bank of storm clouds, a mountain range came into view. The shuttle banked, turning sharply, but at just that moment the image broke up into static for an instant. Then the screen went blank.

This time, the only reaction was silence, until Hassan stepped up again. "That was from the shuttle's flight recorder. Now, this is what *Aspera*'s instruments showed us."

Again we saw the same landscape come up on the screen, but it was computer-enhanced, like the imaging system of a weathersat, and this time we could see a bright blue spear of energy leap in an instant from ground to ship just before the signal broke up.

"There you see it," Hassan told us again, "an unwarranted, unprovoked attack."

Men all around me started to curse then, and swear they'd make the aliens pay for Wu's murder. But the urgent question in my mind: *Was it armed? Was the weapons system on Wu's shuttle armed when he took it down?*

Hassan didn't leave anyone wondering what we were going to do about it. "The Command staff has worked out a plan of action. Our scan shows no signs of any other enemy presence downworld—just the single base. We can eliminate it, take out the only obstacle to our possession of Terrabeta." He went on, "Make no mistake, we have *no intention* of surrendering our claim here. Earth has put too much into this project, expended too many resources for us to abandon it now."

So it was already decided. I felt sick inside, listening to all the men around me cheering Hassan, damning the aliens. It had all gone wrong, so tragically wrong, when Terrabeta was supposed to mean such hope. Now Wu Xian was dead, and we were going to do something drastic and terrible, something irrevocable.

When the rest were dismissed, Hassan called all the shuttle pilots for orders: to finish readying the ships now, with all weapons systems installed and armed.

Not everyone agreed. I wasn't the only one. People like Ram Vikram objected, "We don't know what they can do, what kind of firepower they have. What if they retaliate, fire back at the ship?"

"The ship stays out of orbit, out of range," Gutierrez insisted.

"We don't know what their range is!"

I added, "The aliens on that base didn't come here from nowhere, you know. What happens when their people come back looking for them, when they find us on Beta, instead?"

But the argument had caught the attention of others working on their own ships. Mpande stepped up to me with a belligerent sneer. "So what if it was some Euro they shot down, Waldek, would you sit here and do nothing then?"

That was too much. Captain Wu had been one of the nearest I'd had to a friend on this ship, outside the small clan of Euros. But Vikram got between us before either one landed a blow. "Break it up! We've all got work to do!"

And to me, once Mpande had gone back to his own bird, "Don't pay attention to him, he's xeno, everyone knows it. We know how it was with you and the captain."

I tried to explain, "I just think we're going into this too fast. There have to be options. There has to be some other way we could try to work this out with them, first."

Gutierrez shook his head. "It's them or us. We need this world. We claimed it first."

Vikram only shrugged. "You may be right, Waldek. It bothers me, too. But we have our orders. What else can we do?"

It was what they all said, even the ones who agreed with me: "We have our orders. We don't have a choice."

But I couldn't sleep at night, knowing what we were going to do. What I was going to do. Command had decided not to risk the *Aspera,* not to trust the ship's firepower against the unknown alien defenses. They were going to stand back out of orbit while the shuttles did the job of sending a hundred tons of iron-heavy rock down onto the alien base, obliterating it.

I couldn't sleep. But the scene was so clear in my mind when I closed my eyes, the view from Wu's shuttle as he banked sharply to the right, directly above the alien base. Was he armed? I wondered again. And how would it have appeared from the ground, from the alien's point of view? The arrival of a strange ship in orbit, a possibly armed, hostile craft bearing down on them? Did they fire in self-defense? Did they misidentify the shuttle as an enemy? There were so many possibilities, questions we hadn't even asked.

I didn't want trouble, I never meant to cause trouble. But I couldn't stop myself thinking: How many of the aliens on that base were we going to kill? How many people? Did they have women with them? Children? Their families? Is that what they were trying to protect?

They're the enemy. The alien enemy. And they killed Captain Wu, never forget that.

But we don't know why! We haven't really tried to find out why.

And the more I thought about it, the more it seemed to me that it was wrong what we were doing, wrong to start our occupation of Beta with an act of violence, without trying to find an alternative, without at least trying to learn the truth.

So that's why I did it. The only reason, really. Or else I would have had to live the rest of my life knowing I could have tried to stop it, before it was too late.

It was almost too late.

I remember how I climbed into my shuttle's cockpit to test the arming sequence. How I powered up the engine, engaged the life support. I could feel the vibration of the power as I put my hand on the command bar. Sims tried to reproduce that sensation, but it was never quite the same.

Control was talking at me through my helmet comm, confirming my systems were all greenlight. "Engaging arming function," I announced. The bank of lights flashed on the console.

"Arming function engaged, TA-68," Control replied.

"Disengaging arming function." The lights flashed off.

I took a breath.

I knew there was no going back if I did this. On that score, at least, I had no doubt at all.

I hit the emergency override to blow the bay doors. There was a ten-second delay while the alarm blasted, people everywhere running for takeholds, and Control screaming in my ear, "TA-68, what the hell are you doing?"

Then the bay doors opened, I fell through, pulled the command bar back, and accelerated away from *Aspera*, heading for Terrabeta's atmosphere.

Control was still yelling in my head, "Shuttle 68! Waldek! Your flight is unauthorized! Return to the ship!" I ignored it, even when higher authority was invoked and I heard: "Shuttle 68, this is Lieutenant Tsai. This is an order, identify yourself! Waldek, is that you? If you fail to return to the ship immediately, your actions will be considered mutiny and desertion in the face of the enemy! Do you hear me? *Turn that bird around and bring it back to the ship— now!*"

At that point, I switched off the comm. It was hard enough to handle the navigation without Control ranting at me. I had no course preprogrammed in, but I figured if I had to, I could take it by eyeball after all those hours spent with the sims.

First thing, I got a full-range scan going, hoping to pick up some kind of signal or emission from the alien base, the signal I was halfway sure Captain Wu had been homing on when they shot him down. My instruments picked it right up: a clear signal repeated at regular intervals, a beacon reaching out toward space—no way anyone could have missed it. They'd known—all along, they'd known it was there, without telling anyone. Another lie.

But what the scan also showed me was a blip on my tail, coming from the ship. So they were sending somebody after me. And according to the scan, the craft was fully armed. I suppose I hadn't figured on that, but I wasn't really surprised. At least they didn't have anything faster than my own bird, so it was going to come down to the pilot.

For a moment, I wondered who it might be. Vikram? Mpande? Mpande would just love the chance to shoot down another Euro. But he'd have to catch me, first. I set the navcomp to home in on the alien beacon, and concentrated on the flight. After all, it would probably be my last chance to fly, no matter what happened. But this was it, I was finally living my dream, to ride the stormwinds of another world.

I hit the atmosphere, heavier than Earth's. The shuttle's powerful jets kicked on, and it took all my concentration for a while to fight the air masses trying to pull me in. Then I was into the clouds. Weather was thick on Beta today, and I knew that whoever was after me would be just as blind as I was, but he'd have me on scan. I checked my own scan—he was still out of range.

I was just about to think I could see light starting to break through the cover, when suddenly I felt a sharp tingling sensation all through my body, standing my hair on end. It lasted only an instant, but the shuttle was completely dead under my hand—all instruments, all controls. *Lightning!* was my first, instinctive reaction, but I knew better. This was what Captain Wu had felt, just moments before his shuttle crashed to the ground. The alien weapon . . .

For a few more seconds, inertia kept me going, but the shuttle was never designed as a glider, and all my systems were gone, the screens and readouts were black; no response from the command bar, nothing from gyros or rudder. My shuttle was dead, I was thinking. I'd made the worst mistake I could have made, and now I was going to die . . .

Only I didn't.

That was the first shock, waking up, realizing I was still alive.

Then the smell hit me. It was vile, something like formic acid and sulfur, filling my nose and throat. My stomach tried to heave it up, but the effort made me realize I couldn't move! I managed to open my eyes and I saw them. I hadn't imagined . . . I couldn't ever have imagined . . .

They had me immobilized naked on a tilted frame, clamped to it like a specimen for vivisection. I couldn't see what they'd already done to me, couldn't move my head to see, but there were four or five of them hovering over me now, they were probing—

I couldn't fight them, I couldn't resist or do anything but beg them to stop, to wait, to listen to reason. That's what it had all been about, hadn't it, that our two sides should just listen to reason? But none of it had any effect, as if they couldn't understand me, or even hear what I was trying to say.

Then the first needle started to go into my eye, and that's when I started to scream, but they never even hesitated, the probes went into one eye, then the other, and I knew they were going into my brain, and that's when . . .

They were *in* my brain. I don't know how else to explain it. They went into my brain, and I could feel them taking everything they wanted. I never talked, I never told them—but I couldn't stop them taking it: Earth, the *Aspera,* Terrabeta, the missing probe. What Command was planning to do.

Then somehow—I don't understand it—but I was understanding them, what they were saying: **. . . an unwarranted, unprovoked attack on a Galactic base.**

"No!" I said it aloud without thinking, still choking on the bile that burned my throat. "*We* never attacked! You shot first! You shot down Wu's shuttle!"

—The shuttlecraft was armed.

"He never fired! It was only a survey flight. How could we know what your beacon was, what it meant? How could we know? If he was armed, it was in self-defense, because of what you did to our probe. But he never fired! You shot him down! *Unwarranted, unprovoked!*"

I could feel them again in my brain, probing my memories of the event, while I watched on the viewscreen as Captain Wu turned his craft above the enemy base, the blue lance of deadly energy that burned out his guidance systems and killed his engine.

—**The pilot's death was not intended. But he ignored our beacon.**

"You destroyed our probe! *Our* beacon! We left the probe in orbit, but when we finally came here, there was nothing. No beacon, no signals. Not when we found this world." Unless they'd lied to us, all along, back on Earth. The aliens took that from me, too, the doubt.

—**Your beacon had no standing in Galactic law. You were not in occupation of this world. We occupied this world first. You knew this. Why didn't you leave this system when you first detected our presence?**

It was hard to answer. It hurt to talk, with my throat burning and starting to fill with blood. Why was I the one forced to defend policies I had no part in making, decisions I'd opposed? Why wasn't it Hassan here instead, to defend Command's actions? All I could say was, "It was too far, it took too long for us to come here. We couldn't go back."

—**This is no valid excuse. Your ship trespassed into an occupied system, ignored the beacon. We tried to warn you away, but even after your first craft was downed, you launched a second attack—**

"No! That's a lie!"

—**The other ship with you. It attacked. It fired.**

I hadn't known. It must have been Mpande, then, and I knew who his target had been. But I was past being able to talk anymore, I was choking on the blood in my throat, and I felt the alien impatience pushing past my words, into my mind, taking the whole thing: what I was trying to do, to warn them, to stop it somehow before it was too late.

After that, I didn't know anything for a while. Not what happened to the ship, not until the Galactics told me. I'm just glad more people didn't get hurt. I never wanted anyone to be hurt, that was the whole point.

They offered, you know, when it was over, to let me stay. The Galactics did. On Beta. With them. But even then I couldn't stand the sight of them. God, the smell of them.

I mean, I can understand what they did to me. And why. That it was the only way to communicate in the emergency. But every time I caught a whiff of that smell, I was back on the dissection table with the probe drilling into my eye . . .

No, it wasn't really a choice. I couldn't spend the rest of my life with aliens. I couldn't stay.

So I guess I know what's going to happen now. I know what they're saying about me. The ship lost, those men who were killed—somebody's going to have to pay for all that.

The thing is: I thought I was doing the right thing, trying to save lives, even if they were alien lives. But I didn't really know if I was right. They told me—the Galactics told me—that if we'd dropped that rock, they would have destroyed the *Aspera* and everyone on the ship, in self-defense. So I guess I could say I'd saved them all from that, by stopping them. Only I don't expect anyone else is going to agree. The ship is lost, and they've got to have someone to blame.

But I keep going back there in my mind, over and over. Back to the hangar bay when I blew open those doors. What if I'd been wrong?

So I don't know. It's hard. If I had it to do again . . . to decide . . . I just don't know.

What's in a Name?

by Douglas Smith

"I said 'Rah-*TAY*-toe' and he said 'Rah-*TAH*-toe.'" Hari glanced at the steaming pool of melting flesh and bubbling bodily fluids that had moments before been the wizard Sanfalor. A glance was all he could afford as the demon that Sanfalor had summoned, a tad less than perfectly, was lurching toward him.

"Rah-*TAY*-toe is correct," the demon rasped, scuffling splayed feet through the pentagram drawn in yellow powder on the tower-room floor. The demon resembled a six-foot purple parrot, except for the scales and snakelike arms ending in gleaming talons.

"It was that phony nobility-class accent he always affected," Hari said, scanning the room for an escape route.

"Even for a wizard, Sanfalor was a snob." The demon took a nasty swipe at Hari with a dripping green appendage. The little man scooted back. "You're fast," the demon said.

Hari leapt over another slash, landing among broken flasks and scattered scrolls. Rolling to his feet, he scrambled up a wall of dusty shelves toward a high window, throwing down leather-bound books as he went. Ten shelves up, he stopped and looked down, breathless.

"Pretty nimble, too." The demon smiled up at him, then closed its eyes, seeming to concentrate. It exploded.

A spray of green ichor hit Hari in the face and a stench of rotting meat punched him in the stomach. He wiped his eyes on the sleeve of his shirt and looked down again. The parrot-demon was gone, replaced by a creature with the hindquarters of an eagle, front quarters of a lion, and a head reminiscent of a crocodile.

"Where'd your buddy go?" Hari asked, holding his nose.

"It's still me," the demon hissed in a throatier voice. "I just needed some new equipment, given your location." Large black wings unfolded from the creature's broad back.

Hari swore and threw a large volume of *Lycanthropy for Fun and Profit,* scoring a hit on the thing's mottled snout.

"Ouch! Good shot." The demon rubbed his nose with a paw. "Fast, nimble, good with the hands, and in need of a demon." Something that Hari took for a grin curled around rows of pointed teeth. "You're a thief!" The demon's tone was triumphant.

Hari snorted. "A thief! I, oh, malodorous one, am none other than Hari of Trana, purloiner of the Pendant of Peetbro, acquirer of the Amulet of Ankster, stealer of the Spittoon of Sudprie, and famed throughout Taryaryo."

The demon shrugged. "Never heard of you."

In spite of his predicament, Hari felt injured. "Never?"

"Never."

Hari scowled. "Well, I've never heard of you, either, lizard snout. I don't know why I let Sanfalor talk me into a peasant-class demon. I wanted a demon lord. Oh, I remember now." Hari grinned down. "He gave me a discount on you."

"*Discount!* That miserable moth-eaten mage was discounting me? Doesn't he . . . didn't he know who I am?" The wings disappeared again as red flames flickered in yellow eyes.

Hari looked at the still-bubbling pool on the floor. "Apparently not."

"Well, thief, I am . . ." The demon paused to make a series of disgusting noises that Hari interpreted as demon throat-clearing. "I am Lewee-thorbruster-tenfi-makaluster-indockondingy-loinclutcher-prewsatar . . ."

Hari looked up to the tower window above him. Even if he made it, the demon could follow him outside. He sighed and stretched out on the shelf. This would take a while.

". . . tintinganalong-quionverbat-rah-tay-toe-malfeasiator . . ." Hari examined his fingernails as the demon paused for a breath. ". . . do-do-do-dah-dah-dah-dah-helfion-zarf-buket-squidprokwo-hamnjeez-ohnrie-dupplcapa- . . ." The demon took another breath and finished, ". . . joenz."

Hari lay on the shelf, leaning on an elbow. "Yeah, I know. I listened for five days while Sanfalor practiced saying it, and he still blew it." He looked down. "Loinclutcher?"

The demon flashed those pointed teeth again. "A demon trick. Throw a bit of humor in the middle of the name. The wizard starts chuckling halfway through and messes up the rest."

"Do-do-do-dah-dah-dah?"

"Do-do-do-dah-dah-dah-*DAH*. See? Everyone does that. They leave off the last 'dah.' I got that from a music group on this world called Earth. Works really well when someone from there tries to summon me. They start singing the song, and screw up every time. Then, dinner." He looked up at Hari. "Which reminds me . . ." His wings opened again.

Hari sat up. "Wait a minute! Why are you after me?"

The demon shrugged. "You know the rules. If you mess up in the summoning—wrong pattern on the floor, bad hand movements, improper incantation etiquette, mispronounce the demon's name—the summonee, me, is not bound, and the summoner, you, is demon bait." The wings flapped.

"Hey! I'm not the summoner. Sanfalor called you, and Sanfalor messed up. You've already had your revenge on him."

"But I'm hungry," the demon whined, staring at Sanfalor's remains and rubbing his chin. "I get caught up in the moment. Let loose with a blast of demon bolts and 'poof'—there goes my meal." He looked at Hari again. "Fortunately, I have other options. Besides, you hired him." The wings flapped harder.

"I just watched. He did the summoning. Don't you guys have rules?" Hari drew a long dagger from his leather tunic.

Eyeing the dagger, the demon dropped its wings again. "Of course we do! The laws surrounding the summoning of demons are clearly stated in the Demon and Wizard Covenant in the year of Our Darkest One, 666. We got a fancy scribe called a 'lawyer' from Earth to do it. He did a bang-up job, and it didn't cost us a cent, since he'd already sold his soul to the boss."

"And it says that you can kill innocent bystanders?"

"How innocent can a thief be?" The demon eyed the dagger again. "What do you want me for anyway? Or to be more precise, what are you trying to steal that you can't handle?"

"I *can* handle it—probably. I just want things to go smoothly with no, uh, complications." Hari glanced at Sanfalor. "You're my insurance."

The demon threw back its leathery head and emitted a guttural hacking sound, which Hari assumed was a laugh. "Yeah, right. Translation: I take all the risks and do all the dirty work. So, what're you after?" Another explosion cut off Hari's reply. When the smoke cleared, a handsome young man stood in the demon's place, clothed in rich silks and leathers.

"Do you have to keep doing that?" Hari growled, gripping the edge of the shelf.

"Doing what?" The demon's voice was deep and melodious.

"Exploding like that. It's very irritating."

"Really?"

"Yes!"

The demon exploded again. Hari cursed, rubbing smoke from his eyes. Another human male stood below, broader and blond, but also richly attired. The demon looked himself over. "One of my best. Major babe bait! Chick chaser extraordinaire."

"Excuse me?"

"Chicks, babes. Les femmes! Girls. Women. You know?" Rubbing his hands together, the demon ran an inhumanly long tongue over very red lips. "Nothing like a little human poontang to get the ol' demon juices flowing."

"You have sex with our women? That's disgusting."

"Damn right. Especially when I change to demon form halfway through." The demon grinned. "But we all need a hobby. Now, back to the subject. What're you after?"

Hari used the point of the dagger to clean under his nails. "Oh, just a little item called the Orb of the Porcine Prince."

The demon howled with laughter, and Hari tightened his grip on the dagger. The demon kept laughing till tears streamed down his face. "The Pig's Eye. He's after the Pig's Eye," he said to no one in particular. "Oh, this is rich."

"A wild guess but I gather you've heard of it."

The demon stopped laughing, and drew a breath. His

face became solemn. "Five hundred and seventy-two," he said.

"Five hundred and seventy-two what?"

"Dead thieves!" The demon started to howl again, slapping his thigh with a broad tanned hand. "That's how many of your kind have gotten toasted trying for the Pig's Eye." He stopped laughing again and glared at Hari. "Not to mention several of my brethren that got hauled along on the attempts."

Hari shook his head and tried to look confident. "That won't happen to you."

"Damn right. I won't be there." The demon straightened and folded its arms across its chest. "Well, see you around."

Hari sat up on the shelf. "Wait! What do you mean? You're leaving? You're not going to try to eat me?"

The demon shook his head. "Nah. I'll get you next time."

"Next time?"

"Oh sure. I know thieves. You have it in your head to go after the Pig's Eye. You'll try to summon me again. You'll screw up. I'll eat you. Simple."

Hari scowled. "Sanfalor has the necessary materials here, and I have his books. I know the pentagram procedure."

The demon shrugged. "Child's play. Probably still a challenge for you, though." Hari growled and the demon continued. "The hard part starts with the hand manipulations when you begin the incantation. Very tricky."

Hari grinned and raised both his hands before him, moving his fingers through an intricate dance in the air. The demon stared at him. "Hmm, pretty good. Forgot you were a thief. Quick hands. Still, there's the name. You have to get it *just* right. If you don't . . ." He looked at Sanfalor's remains. "Well, be seeing ya!" He exploded.

A pile of dead rats lay where the demon had stood. Hari scrambled down and, avoiding the rats, walked over to stare at the now congealing mass that had been his wizard-for-hire. "Yes, indeed. There is the name." Hari scratched his chin.

"Affected accent, indeed!"

Hari spun around. "Who's there?"

"Moth-eaten mage, am I? Why, that refugee from an offal heap just caught me on an off day!"

Hari stared down in amazement at a small brown toad, hopping about among the broken flasks and spilled powders on the tower room floor.

"Sanfalor?" he said, feeling extremely silly.

"The same. I saw that look on its face when I summoned it, and I knew I had been less than exact in my conjuring. So I was ready when he most wrongfully attacked my person, having prepared this good creature to accept my cons . . . consc . . ."

"Conciousness?" Hari offered.

"Exactly. Thank you, thief. Smaller brain, you know. Has trouble with those poly . . . big words." The toad hopped over to look up at Hari.

Hari cleared a spot among the debris and sat on the floor facing the toad. "Where's my money?"

"Money? What money?" The toad began to hop away. Hari's hand flashed out. He raised it to his face and opened it. The toad quivered on his palm. "I warn you, sir, put me down or the most dire con . . . con . . ."

"Consequences."

"Thank you . . . will befall you."

"What're you going to do? Give me warts?"

"Very well, I did warn you." With that the toad closed his eyes and began to quiver. Hari heard a "poof" behind him, and turned around. A scrawny rooster, looking very dazed, swayed back and forth. It lifted a bedraggled head, offered a tentative "cock-a-doodle-doo?" then fell over.

Hari turned back to the toad. "Very impressive."

The toad lowered its head and placed a front leg over its eyes. "I was trying for a cockatrice. It's this toad brain. I can't fit all of my conc . . . you know, all of me into it."

"You didn't do much better with a whole brain, if you ask me. I want my money back. You didn't deliver me a demon."

"Yes I did."

"A *bound* demon, mage."

The toad trembled on his palm. "I spent it already."

Hari lifted his hand so that the toad was right in front of his face. "What did you say?" The toad shook. Hari felt something warm trickle onto his hand. He dropped the toad to the floor, and it disappeared under the shelves. Swearing to himself and wiping his hand on his trousers, Hari peered under the shelves. "Come out of there."

"I can help you. We can summon him again." Sanfalor's voice came from behind Hari this time. Hari spun around. The rooster was looking at him, head cocked to one side.

Hari squinted at the bird. "Sanfalor?"

"Yes indeed," the rooster replied.

"Please don't kill me," came a voice from under the shelves. The toad hopped out a few inches.

Hari looked from rooster to toad. "Sanfalor?"

"Yes," chorused both creatures. "You see," the toad said, "since I couldn't quite fit all of my consc . . ."

". . . iousness into the toad," piped the rooster, "I decided to split myself into two creatures. So I stand before you, Sanfalor the mighty, once again." The rooster puffed out its chest, and several feathers floated to the floor.

Hari groaned. "I'm doomed. I'll never get the Pig's Eye now. I've no more money for a wizard, and I need a demon."

"You're a thief. Why don't you just steal more money?" the rooster asked.

"Good idea!" the toad piped.

"Thank you," the rooster replied.

Hari glared at both of them. "Because of the curse. Which you couldn't remove. Which is why I need the Pig's Eye. Which is why I need a demon. Which is why I hired you."

"Curse? What . . ." the toad began.

". . . curse?" the rooster finished.

"You don't remember?"

"Remember what?" both creatures chimed together.

Hari growled and pulled his dagger. The rooster squawked. "Wait! It's being split into two . . ."

". . . small brains," the toad said from under the shelves again. "I don't seem to have complete memories."

Hari slumped against the shelves. "On my last job, I heisted this jeweled staff from a wizard in Awtwa. I must have tripped some sort of warding spell. It laid this curse on me." Both the toad and rooster cocked their heads to one side. Hari sighed and went on. "I am now forced to always, and I mean always . . ." Hari groaned. ". . . tell the truth."

"The whole truth?" the toad said.

"And nothing but the truth?" the rooster offered.

"So help me, gods," Hari said.

"That must be very . . ."

". . . restricting, for a thief."

"Restricting!" Hari snapped. "You try thieving when you have to answer every question truthfully. What, Mister Guard? What do I want? Oh, I'm just here to steal the crown jewels. Can I come in?" Hari buried his face in his hands.

"It's coming back . . ." the rooster began.

". . . to me now. Yes, I couldn't lift the curse. Very complex spell. But I found that . . ." the toad said.

". . . it could be broken by one ritual that required a certain magical artifact," the rooster finished.

"The Orb of the Porcine Prince. The Pig's Eye," Hari said. "The most heavily protected little item owned by the vilest dark wizard in all of Taryaryo. And if I don't break the curse by Midsummer's Eve, it becomes permanent."

The rooster drew itself up as tall as it could. "Sir thief, I regret my failure and will endea . . . endeav . . ."

". . . try to make amends," the toad said, hopping over to the rooster. "Together we will summon the demon. Then I will accompany you on your quest of the . . . what was it again?"

"Dog's breakfast?" the rooster offered.

"Cat's pajamas?" the toad countered.

"Pig's Eye," Hari groaned. "Why so suddenly magnanimous? What's in it for you?"

"Why, sir, you wound me to the quick," the toad said. "I am a certified necro . . . necrom . . . mage and bound by my oaths to faithfully fulfill all legal contracts." He paused as Hari fixed him with a glare. "And besides, I need the magic of the Orb to restore myself to human form again. Which reminds me, could you please scrape up, very carefully mind you . . ."

". . . what's left of me from that nasty pile on the floor, and put it into some container," the rooster completed.

Hari sighed again. "All right. I can't see that I have a choice. We'll summon the demon again. Let's get on with it."

"Get on with what?" both creatures asked.

Hari groaned.

The next night, Hari stood again in Sanfalor's tower room. The toad and rooster sat on a large table behind him.

Hari checked the tower window. The moon in full round radiance was just edging into view. He raised a vial containing a deep red liquid so that the moonbeam from the window struck it. In his other hand, he juggled a tiny jewel that wouldn't decide if it was blue, green, or a color Hari could not name.

"Now?" he asked.

"Now!" both creatures chorused.

Hari dropped the jewel into the vial. The liquid began to bubble and smoke, and Hari felt the glass growing hot. Just as he thought he would have to drop it from the heat, the reaction slowed and the glass cooled. He lowered it and looked in. A golden powder filled about a third of the vial.

"Hope this is enough," he muttered as he poured the powder over the chalk lines of a pentagram traced on a large clear space on the tower floor. He stepped outside the symbol and looked at where the moonlight now struck the floor.

"Hurry!" the rooster cried. "In another minute, the moonbeam will touch the pentagram. You must begin."

Hari put down the vial and took a deep breath. "Well, here goes nothing." Raising his hands, he began to chant the incantation as he did the necessary finger manipulations. His fingers brushed against something in the empty air. Something gooey, cold, and slimy. He swallowed and continued. Moving his hands required more and more effort, as if a cold tentacle had wrapped around each finger and was pulling against him.

The moonbeam now covered a third of the pentagram. Hari focused on the pattern. The air clouded. A moment later, a yellow-green blob hovered at eye level above the pentagram. Pulsating strands extended from it to each of Hari's fingers. Other strands stretched out into the room.

Hari strained to see where they reached, but they seemed to disappear more than end.

Three red eyes popped open on the blob, followed by an opening that kept changing shape, size, and location on the blob's surface. "Area code, please." A voice, nasal and feminine, came from the opening.

"Uh, excuse me?"

"Which area of the nether regions are you calling, please?"

"Oh, right." Hari checked his shirt cuff for his crib notes. "Uh, Purgatory 777. Person-to-demon."

"Demon's name, please, and I'll connect you." As it asked this, the blob's mouth curled in a grin around all three eyes. The moonbeam stabbed directly at the heart of the pentagram.

Hari swallowed, cleared his throat, and took a very deep breath. "I summon . . . Lewee-thorbruster-tenfi- . . ." The blob creature began to fade. ". . . makaluster-indockondingy-loinclutcher-prewsatar-tintinganalong-quionverbat . . ." A smoky orb formed in the middle of the pentagram. ". . . rah-TAY-toe . . ." Hari glared at the toad and rooster. ". . . -mal-feasiator-do-do-do . . ." The orb twisted and grew to a spiraling column of blackness. Hari was almost out of breath. ". . . dah-dah-dah-dah-helfion-zarfbuket-squidprokwo-hamnjeez-ohnrie-dupplcapa- . . ." Two legs appeared, then flippers, and a large horned head. Hari finished, gasping out the last syllable. ". . . joenz." He looked up.

This time, the demon resembled a blue dolphin with a bull's head and legs. Red eyes locked on Hari. It lumbered forward.

"Oh, shit," Hari yelped.

"We're frog's legs!" the toad cried.

"Fried chicken!" the rooster wailed.

The demon touched a line of the pentagram and a wall of

sparks erupted. It stepped back again. "Damn it! Oh, well."
It grinned and exploded.

A spray of something showered Hari, accompanied by a
wonderful aroma of cooked fish and beef, tantalizing until
he remembered it came from splattered demon parts. The
demon stood in the pentagram wearing the same human
form as the last time. "A little surf and turf for you, thief."

"I did it! I did it!" Hari cried, wiping off his tunic and
beaming triumph. The demon shrugged and smiled back.

"*We* did it!" the toad said. The rooster crowed.

"Sanfalor?" The demon eyed the toad and sniffed the air.
"Yep, it is you, you old charlatan. So you've finally found a
brain suited to your ability."

"Two brains. I am Sanfalor, too!" the rooster cried.

The demon shrugged. "Waste of a good chicken dinner."

Both toad and rooster started to mouth their protests, but
Hari silenced them with a look. He frowned at the demon.
"Why are you so pleased? You're bound. You have to do
my bidding."

The demon waved a hand, and a chair appeared beside
him. He settled into it. "Yeah, this time. But to get the Pig's
Eye, you'll need to summon me more than once. And *one*
of those times, you'll mess up." He grinned and crossed his
legs.

Hari grinned back. "I believe I have a way around that."

The demon's smile melted away. "What do you mean?"

Hari pulled up a chair too, straddling it backward. The
toad hopped nearer to him, as the rooster flapped over to
land on his shoulder. "Well, as you so rightly pointed out,
the problem is the name. It's got some tricky parts to it . . ."

The demon beamed. "Thank you."

". . . and it's so-o-o-o long!"

"Oh, please! You'll make me blush!" the demon cried.

Hari felt puzzled. "Am I missing something?"

The demon stood and threw out its chest. "In the nether regions, the length of a male demon's name is synonymous with—how can I put this delicately?" It spread its hands apart. "Well, the length is indicative of your, uh, virility."

"You're kidding, right?"

"Nope. It's the name, man. Chicks dig the name. I've got one of the longest around."

"Names?"

"Whatever." The demon grinned.

Hari looked at the toad. It was quivering all over and making little croaks. Hari had never seen a toad laugh before. "Well, then this is going to be interesting," Hari said.

The demon's eyes narrowed. "What do you mean?"

Hari grinned. "You're bound, right? You must faithfully execute one command from me, right?"

The demon nodded, eyeing the toad and rooster. "So?"

Hari grinned and the toad shook with even more violent mirth. "So I'm going to ask you to . . ." The rooster crowed. ". . . change your name!" Hari finished.

The demon blinked. "What did you say?"

"We're going to give you a new name," the toad said.

"You can't do that!" the demon roared. It exploded, and in its place was a large vulture with flippers instead of wings.

"Yes, we can," Hari replied.

"Yes, we can," the toad and rooster echoed.

"Yes, you can," the demon groaned. "But I like my name. I've had it all my lives. It's so . . . me."

"You're right. Giving you an entirely new name wouldn't be fair," Hari said. The demon brightened and Hari continued. "So we'll just take the one you have . . . and shorten it."

"SHORTEN IT!" the demon screamed, clutching at his groin with his flippers.

Hari looked up at the ceiling, hand on his chin. The toad mimicked him. "Something easy to remember, easy to pronounce."

"And short," the toad said.

"SHORT!" the demon screamed again, still clutching himself.

"Let's see. How does yours start? Oh, yeah, I've got it. Lewee! Yep, that's it." Hari faced the demon. "Sir demon, *I order you to change your name to . . . Louie.*"

The demon slumped to the floor. "Louie?" His voice was a whisper. "That's all? Just . . . Louie?"

Hari nodded. The demon groaned, then brightened. "How about Louie-doo-doo-doo . . ."

Hari shook his head. "Nope. Just Louie." Louie whimpered and covered his beak with a flipper. "Now, Louie, we've got some planning to do if I'm going to get the Pig's Eye by Midsummer's Eve." He rubbed his hands together. "I'll soon be free of the curse and back to being the greatest thief Taryaryo has ever seen."

"And I'll be Sanfalor again," the toad and rooster cried.

"And I'll be . . . Louie," the demon whined.

Hari ignored him. "You know, Louie, this could be the start of a beautiful friendship." Louie growled and exploded. In his place was a foul-smelling, steaming greenbrown mass. Hari sniffed and wrinkled his nose. He looked at the rooster and toad. "Then again . . ."

". . . maybe not," they chorused.

Rena 733

by Lisa Silverthorne

There wasn't much left of #733. Hardly enough to bury, much less autopsy. I snapped on my rubber gloves, hating this job, and peeled back the body bag flaps.

I never called the soldiers by anything other than their tag numbers, but this one was so young, barely more than a child. The name Rena popped into my head. Rena 733. Her one eye, green, stared strangely content past me as I sloshed her remains onto the chrome table. Stale blood scent mixed with germicide. I scanned the reclamation orders on the side of the bag with a light pen: recover one microfeed and one MRC. A memory replacement chip. My hands began to shake.

I shifted Rena 733's body toward the small image-capture scanner at the edge of the table. The red light winked on and encircled her head, gathering streams of data from the MRC. Sometimes, MRCs were damaged by the extraction, so this prescan was a failsafe. The HQ suits had to have their data. The scanner hummed, converting the raw data into an enhanced viewable format, a third-person video effect of the stored memories. In a few moments, a summary scan of the chip, only the last forty-eight hours of this soldier's life, would be played back on the screen above my head.

The autopsy-room door slid open, and Deanna Fitzsimmons entered the chamber. Her bobbed blond hair lay flat against her pale cheeks and thin face. This was Deanna's first week at the station as a medtech student, and already she reminded me a lot of myself back in medical school. It had been more than a year since I last worked with a partner. Deanna's face contorted when she glanced at the body on the table.

"Another one?" She inhaled sharply. "That's the fifteenth casualty since lunch. Don't you get tired of this, Doctor?"

I leaned against the table, studying Deanna's tired blue eyes and the fine lines beginning around her nose and mouth. She wasn't much older than Rena 733. I hated throwing so many cases at her in her first week, but she'd have to get used to it.

"I don't think I can look at another one today," I admitted, surprised by the weariness in my voice. I knew Deanna couldn't handle doing another autopsy like this one today. "Why don't you take log duty this time?"

Deanna smiled, relieved by my suggestion. She turned away from the table and picked up the datapad that hung on the far wall. "Ready whenever you are, Dr. Kingston."

"Good," I said. "We'll begin as soon as the data capture is complete."

"When do you match tags with names?" she asked, as if trying to take both our minds off what was to come.

"I don't. They handle that back on Earth," I answered. And for that, I was thankful.

I glanced up, seeing the blank screen that indicated a finished capture, then flicked on the autopsy laser. Deanna flinched at the sound. The chrome fixtures cast the scanner's red sheen against the shiny gray, tiled walls and floor. Deanna walked over to the space station portal as I cut open Rena 733's cranium.

Voices echoed through the chamber and I looked up to see desert stretching into velvet, umber hills on the viewscreen, the horizon a mixture of creams and rust. The barrel of Rena 733's Stupor plasma rifle, slung over one shoulder, bobbed at the edge of the viewscreen.

A child, barely twenty, if that. I cringed, gazing from Rena 733's burned face to Deanna's pale profile. I remembered being twenty once. Before medical school. Before the Antaris War. Before retroviruses crippled the nets and we lost most of our private technology to the government. I sighed. Before MRCs.

I reached up to shut off the output. I didn't want to know any more than I had to—it just made my job harder.

"What are you doing?" Deanna asked.

"Shutting off the MRC's output."

Deanna frowned. "Don't you want to know who she was?"

I shook my head and looked away from the screen.

"But why? She's out there protecting our world. She should be given more respect than a number."

I set down the laser. "Do you really understand what an MRC is?" I asked, knowing at best she'd only read about them.

"It records—"

I shook my head. "No, Deanna, it—parses—. It selectively parses out memories and feeds back only the ones that pass the algorithm. Anything that causes adverse emotional reactions to the job is quickly and permanently parsed out."

Deanna's face whitened. "God. How horrible."

"The parsed-out memories remain on the chip, so HQ can access them. But she can't. I don't want to invade her privacy."

Reaching up to the screen, I laid my hand against the

shutoff switch, but something made me stop. "Are you sure you want to see this? I don't."

She had that passerby look on her face, that mixture of revulsion and unblinking curiosity that people display at the scene of a tragedy. Finally, she nodded. "In case she had a last request or something," Deanna said in a small voice.

I pulled my hand away, dreading the playback. Only once had I allowed myself to watch one of these.

On the screen, another soldier crouched beside Rena 733, his sandy hair tousled and his face sweaty. He examined clawlike footprints, dipping a gloved hand into the fine, gold sand. "No sign of them, Gates," said the man. "Continue tracking or return to camp?"

"Are we seeing through her eyes?" Deanna asked, fascinated.

"Sort of. The many layers of images and points of view are brought together so we see this soldier as well as what she saw and felt."

"Her name's Gates," said Deanna.

I sighed. Yes, she was right. Rena 733 had a real name, but in her present state, I found that fact too painful.

"They can't be far, Ryan," Gates answered in a smooth, alto voice. "The colonel wants a position report before 19:00."

"Until we find our patrol's insides strung out like streamers, those Antaran bastards won't show themselves."

"Shut up, Ryan," Gates said and squinted at the horizon. Her thoughts whispered through the speakers, the tone softer and echoing because of the computer enhancement of her thoughts.

I tried not to watch the screen, but I couldn't help myself.

What if we do find them? What then? I'm not afraid, and I should be. Why do I want so desperately to go after the Antarans like this? I even dream about it. I want to come out here and fight . . . except when I'm here. What's the matter with me? Gates rubbed her face and gripped the rifle tighter.

"She doesn't know," I said in a half whisper, my mouth falling open. "My God, they put those things in her head and didn't even tell her."

Ryan stood up, brushing the sand off his beige uniform. "Gates? Do you ever— No, forget it," he said, waving her off.

She frowned and turned toward him. "What? Do I ever what?"

He gazed down at the ground, parting the sand into a semicircle with the toe of his boot. "Do you ever . . . well, fear these encounters?"

"Sometimes. Do you?"

He nodded. "I feel like pissing my pants right now."

Why aren't I that scared? She pointed toward a bluff in the distance. "We'll hike out to there and go back to base if we turn up nothing."

"Agreed," said Ryan, who shoved his rifle back over his shoulder.

Gates moved in front of him, her boots whisking across the sand, but Ryan's scream forced her to turn—too late. Talons blurred. A spiky appendage burst up from the sand, piercing Ryan's body. He screamed again. Sliding the plasma rifle into her hands, Gates squeezed off a volley of blasts into the sand until something screeched. The appendage splattered into an inky puddle beside Ryan's crumpled body.

She collapsed beside him and pulled him up from the ground, one arm balancing the plasma rifle that quivered at the edge of the viewscreen. He wheezed, blood dripping from his nose and mouth, intestines dangling from his torso. He grabbed her sleeve.

Oh, God. Don't die on me! Please don't die! "Hang on, Ryan—I got you!"

"Gates, I—Gates—" His hand fell away from her sleeve.

"Sssh, don't talk now." _Why Ryan? Why! We went through boot camp together._ Her hushed voice reverberated again. _Oh, God, he's dying._

I turned away when Gates began to sob, the rawness in her voice grating.

"My God," said Deanna. "Her best friend just got killed!" She let the datapad fall onto a countertop and she looked away from the screen.

"They're both at peace now," I offered.

"At peace? He was ripped apart, and she was blown to pieces!"

I studied Deanna's reddening face, the tears rimming her eyes. "Death is a part of life and we have to accept that. You have to accept that if you're going to be a front-line tech."

The anger twisting her features surprised me. She didn't even know these people.

"And you need to understand that when you open those bags, there are people inside—not numbers!" Deanna shouted.

"That's why this job never gets easier." I turned toward Rena 733 and picked up the tissue-resin separator from the instrument tray.

My stomach ached when I sifted through the remains of Rena 733's cerebrum and midbrain for the microfeed. The nanoprocessor-controlled microfeed was activated by combat and controlled aggression and its effects—adrenaline rushes, endorphin releases. I shook my head. Poor kid was addicted to battle. Kept her out there fighting just to feel good. Craving the kill like some psychopath. This was the

third soldier I had seen beta-testing these new combat en-
hancements.

"Make a note on the chart that Rena 733 is another combat technology beta-tester, Fitzsimmons."

"All this technology, and yet this war goes on forever,"
said Deanna, not diverting her gaze from the viewscreen.
She didn't even look at the datapad as she typed.

She was right. Too many people were dying and with
every territory we gained, we lost one somewhere else. It
was a stalemate at best. When I was a first year, I had
Deanna's idealism. I remember standing at the armed
forces' recruitment desk, fresh out of med school on a mission of mercy. I wanted to go to the front and save lives.
Back then, like Gates, I didn't know the cost. Didn't even
understand it. Not sure I did now.

Busying myself with the extractions, I shut out the
viewscreen's sounds of shifting sand as Gates carried Ryan
back to camp. I found the ATP-driven microfeed lodged in
Rena's brain stem. It had been surgically implanted high
into her brain's third ventricle, but whatever explosive she
had stepped on must have caused the microfeed to dislodge
and pierce the brain stem.

As I probed deeper, I found that some bastard surgeon
had removed her amygdalae so she couldn't develop a fear
of the enemy. Even the hippocampus had been altered, an
MRC attached to it. I shuddered at the sight of the tiny,
black chip containing all her memories. It hijacked her ability to form new ones, storing all of them into the chip and
then selectively parsing out everything but the harmless
memories for transmission. Working with the tissue-resin
separator, I carefully dislodged the microfeed.

I watched as Gates entered her base camp and then her
barracks. Abruptly, the screen went dark, the computer
parsing out sleep and dream sequences. I sighed. Gates had

only twenty-four hours left. Twenty years old with twenty-four hours to live.

The screen suddenly blurred to daylight, Gates fumbling out of her barracks in full field gear. One of the other soldiers approached.

"Sorry to hear about Ryan, Heather," said the soldier, shaking her head. "Tough break. I know how close you two were."

"What are you talking about?" Gates asked.

"I heard about the ambush yesterday. I'm really sorry."

What's she talking about? I didn't hear about any ambush. There was a Ryan in boot camp, but not out here. She's been offworld too long. "Right—thanks," Gates mumbled. "When do we frag the Antaris camp?"

I gripped the edge of the table. That bastard chip had even parsed out Ryan's existence. It didn't even leave her a memory of her best friend.

The other soldier checked her watch. "T minus six hours. We have to wait for an orbit window. Can't go in with those satellites firing at us and our shuttle cover."

I extracted the memory replacement chip and mumbled through my own personal damage assessment, accounting for lost limbs, obliterated organs, and cause of death. Too bad "blown to bits" wasn't anywhere on my medical ROMs. Her legs and half her chest were gone. The only real thing left of Rena 733, the only thing that contained anything that was once her, was the memory replacement chip. It contained Rena 733's entire career as a soldier—and her last days. To the government, it was only beta-test data and now the suits would see it all, whether she had wanted them to or not.

"Open computer log. Autopsy #733, Dr. Jeannette Kingston presiding, Deanna Fitzsimmons assisting."

For the computer log, I rolled off a string of observations, "Enhancement of reticular formation still intact, limbic system remained functional at time of death . . ." For the government report that would be coredumped into some net info tomb.

"So, when you going home, Gates?" asked a voice from the viewscreen. I turned around again, seeing Gates marching beside a weather-beaten soldier with haggard gray eyes.

"End of the month they tell me. Guess my tour's up. I'll miss it." _And that scares me. I miss Mom and Dad. Haven't even seen my new niece yet, but leaving the troop scares the hell out of me. Makes me feel sick. What will I do?_

My eyes misted. That new niece was probably in school now, but she didn't know that. More memories stolen, parsed away by the MRC. It was all stored in the chip, but she couldn't access it. My hands began to shake again. They didn't even let her remember her best friend beyond boot camp. Couldn't let a soldier form attachments. When one died, that memory was parsed into the bit bucket. Soldiers couldn't care about anything out here. Neither could doctors. What had they done to this girl? Gates was hard around the edges, addicted to combat and unafraid of an enemy that had shredded her to ribbons. The suits had made her into some animal with its instinct removed. How many soldiers had they done this to? But this soldier was different now; she had a name, emotions—a family. She didn't know—but I did.

I set down the tissue-resin separator, the distant memory of a little girl brought into emergency once when I was in residency. She had drowned in a swimming pool when her father had left her alone in the backyard. They had revived her en route, but she died before I could even tube her. Where had that memory come from? I hadn't thought about that in years. My eyes filled with tears. In medical school, one of my professors had warned me that there'd be a handful of cases that would stay with me. I guess this was one of those cases.

Biting my lip, I tried not to look at Rena 733's face, but I couldn't stop myself. In the remains of her face, I saw that child's desperate, pleading green eyes suddenly turn dull, the monitor flat-lining with a screech. I had just stood there, the endotracheal tube dangling from my hand. Dammit, it wasn't supposed to be this way here. That's why they all had numbers, and no names. It was too hard when they had names—and pasts. I looked away from Rena 733's half face, and, with shaking hands, I picked up the tissue-resin separator again. Why couldn't I stop shaking?

Suddenly, I felt Rena 733's blood on my gloves. Hopes and dreams ran through it. Anger and tears. Twenty years' worth. Like Deanna. Rena 733 was more than bone to cut through or blood needed for typing and DNA extraction. She was more than autopsy #733.

Carefully, I laid the memory replacement chip in a tray beside the microfeed. Moving to the processing equipment to the right of the table, I sent the chip through. The instrument whirred and groaned, converting all the information into its final enhanced viewable format. All the suits required now was a viewer, and they could access all Gates's memories.

On the viewscreen, Heather Gates screamed as the ground exploded beneath her, throwing her several meters across the sand. For an instant, she survived the blast. Her gaze traveled up to the sky. "Mom, I need you," she gurgled, but in a moment, the viewscreen winked out and the processing unit stopped. The summary scan had concluded. Heather Gates's life was over.

"They'll see it all, won't they?" Deanna asked in a small voice. "And she never even knew about it. It isn't fair."

I picked up the chip from the tray. Gates's entire soldier-ing career lay on this chip; private moments, personal feel-ings belonging only to Heather Gates. And so much of it had been cut off, cheated away from her by this MRC.

"You're right, Deanna," I said. "It isn't fair."

I dropped the little memory prison onto the table. Part of Gates's life had been in my hands, like that little girl's had been and all those soldiers on the front line. Case numbers blurred with blood types and bar codes as I picked up a wide-handled clamp. Those soldiers had lives before they came to me. Heather Gates did, too, and so did I once.

"Computer, pause autopsy record #733."

Slamming the clamp handle against the MRC, I pounded it and pounded it until it was shards of resin and silicon. The crunching of the silicon filled the silence, and I cher-ished the sound. It wasn't bone splitting or a body bag unzipping. It was my anger, and there was nothing the gov-ernment could do about it. Deanna stood frozen beside the table, her mouth gaping.

"Computer, resume autopsy record #733. Note: MRC did not survive the blast. Only shards detected throughout the cortex and cerebrum. Fragments will follow under separate cover. End record. End report." I motioned toward Deanna. "Send the report, please."

While Deanna uploaded the report, I gathered the MRC fragments into a small container. Heather Gates's memories would stay her own—for how ever long she had them. It was the only shred of dignity I could offer her now.

I bar-coded the cause-of-death information into a label that I printed and attached to the body bag. I didn't need to see a viewscreen to know how she died. After microsutur-ing the remains of Gates back together, I laid her to rest in the body bag.

I zipped up the body bag, then laid a hand against my

neck, knowing that tomorrow I would't remember Heather Gates or my conversation with Deanna. Heather Gates would be #733 again.

"Doctor Kingston," said Deanna, her voice soft. "I've been wanting to ask—why did you call her Rena?"

"Computer, scan KingstonJL."

I closed my eyes as the white scan light slid across me.

"Why are you doing that?" Deanna asked.

"Display report on screen." I pointed to the computer viewscreen. "Read it, Deanna."

"Why?" she asked, shaking her head.

"Just read it."

Her gaze flitted across the data, and I read it with her. Every day, it was new to me, too. Finally, she gasped and her gaze jerked toward me. Tears welled in my eyes.

"You've got an MRC."

I nodded. "This job required it. I used to write myself notes when I got out of the hospital, so I wouldn't forget anything. Now, I just append them into my login scripts."

"Why didn't you turn down the job?" Her eyes were wide.

"Turn it down?" I laughed bitterly. "I volunteered for it!"

"You volunteered?"

"I thought it would be better than dying inside every time a soldier died." Or a child. I leaned against the table. "Better than crying my heart out for months and months after a child died in my arms. I thought working with numbers would be easier. That way I wouldn't die inside. I didn't know the MRC was just another way to die." And I didn't know the government would take away memories they had no right to take.

The silence was palpable, and I wanted to reach out and shove it aside. Deanna could only stare at me, a tear funneling down her cheek.

"I'm so sorry," she finally whispered.

"Every morning, when I log into the system, I play back a history file that I create every night. But it isn't enough. Words on a screen meant for someone else. I'm living in the third person, Deanna."

I laid my hand on the body bag, wanting to exchange places with Heather Gates.

Deanna walked over to me and squeezed my arm. "It's all right, Doctor. You don't have to answer my question."

I felt the sobs ache through me, my knees trembling with weakness. "Rena was the name of my daughter, Rena Diane Kingston. She would have been twenty-one this month." I sucked in a deep breath. "She drowned when she was two. When I finished my residency, the government thought it best to parse out her memory—without my consent. When I took this job, I didn't know they would take away my daughter's memory."

"How . . . did you find out?"

I picked up a shard of the MRC left behind on the examination table. "Their algorithm cleaned my memories of Rena, but their chip couldn't totally parse my child from my thoughts. It only pushed her back until she became a nameless child in ER. It was the best the bastards could do. But they missed one thing."

Deanna stared at me for a moment. "What was that?" she said finally in a soft voice.

"My ex-husband. I lost track of him when he joined the Service until—" I sighed. "Until he came through here. And it was all there in his MRC, my daughter, the accident, the divorce—everything."

Deanna shook her head. "But your memory would have been—"

"Parsed out? Most of it, maybe, but not out of my login

script. What happened to her and who she was will always be there—every time I log in."

Pressing against the MRC shard, I snapped it between my fingers and let the pieces fall to the floor. I would re-member and mourn my daughter, whether they let me or not.

Chalk Circle

by Greg McElhatton

I draw the circle on the ground, counterclockwise. Flecks of chalk break off onto either side—I must be certain to remove them before I am finished. I remember Mother telling her students that there must be nothing to break the circle, nothing to twist or bend the perfect shape.

Mother's midwives were not so careful when I was born. *Two,* the farseers proclaimed, *you bear two children. The man will be strong, and in his hands will be the instruments of war. The woman will be crafty, will be devilish, will be intelligent beyond her years. The two will go to battle and victory and defeat will be in their hands.*

Mother gave birth to me inside a chalk circle. People of the village whisper that the circle was accidentally broken by a young midwife, that it let the spirits and demons through so they were able to steal my sister. Mother had already named us both; Ayocuan and Xochitl. The midwives prayed and wailed for hours after I was born, but Xochitl never came forth.

Mother first told me of this when I was five, after she had drank deeply from a gourd of burning-water. She talked to the Gods that night, begged and pleaded to have her Xochitl returned to her. The Gods slapped her for her impudence, and I spent days scrubbing the blood and vomit out of the stone floor. I would still be scrubbing if Father had not removed me, calling it an unworthy task for a warrior son.

I draw a second circle around the first. There is space between the two; there I will write the secret names.

When I was of eight years Father brought me to the school for warriors. He kissed me once, roughly, on the cheek and said good-bye. I would not see my parents again until my years had doubled in size.

Our teacher, Ahuitzol, had heard of me, heard of what the farseers said. He proclaimed that he would be the mentor to the greatest warrior of our tribe. The other children were not so pleased.

At the end of my first week, three of them attacked me while I was resting near the Temple of the Feathered Serpent. *Behind you,* a voice whispered to me. I whirled around and was barely able to block the first macana. I let it hit my left arm—a sacrifice, so that my head and right arm could still defend me.

I rolled across the plaza, grabbing my own macana. That day taught me not to leave my weapon anywhere but by my side. I would have died then, if not that the Gods wished my attackers to learn a lesson as well.

The first of the three boys fell quickly, a blow to the forehead. It was the first time I had vanquished a foe. The second swung at me but I danced away, praising the Feathered Serpent, whose shadow I fought in, for granting me speed and agility. The second boy was downed soon afterward, clutching his shattered knee. The third begged for mercy, sobbing and pleading. *Kill him,* a voice said in the back of my head. I thought better of it and made Paynal my servant in all but name.

Heading back to the school, word had already spread of the failed ambush. Ahuitzol was proud and triumphantly told the students it was a sign that I was, indeed, going to be a great warrior. Only this time instead of hatred I found myself surrounded with respect and admiration.

I write the first name, that of the devourer. The second name is more difficult to write, and it is only with great reluctance that I put Xochitl's name inside the two chalk circles.

Walking into my parents' home after so many years was a strange experience. It was smaller than I remembered, more cluttered and messy.

My mother was sitting at the table, staring at me. I smiled at her. "I have returned," I said. "I am a warrior now."

She sat at the table, silent.

I stared at her. "Are you not proud of your son?"

Mother stood up and spat onto the ground. "Proud?" she snorted. "Why should I be proud of a son who could not defend his own sister?"

"A son who was able to keep himself from being taken by demons," I angrily replied. "Provided there even *was* a sister. The farseers may have lied."

She stalked across the room toward me. "You gave Xochitl to the demons to save yourself!" she snapped. "You sacrificed my baby girl!" She slapped me across the face.

I staggered back a step—not from the impact, but out of surprise. My cheek tingled where she had slapped it.

"Xochitl! My baby, eaten by demons!" she sobbed.

The tingling spread from my cheek into the base of my

skull. I could feel the pressure building, getting tighter and stronger.

It was then that the table flipped upside down.

Surprised, we both looked at the table—just as a clay pot toppled off a shelf. Instead of falling to the ground, it swooped through the air and shattered as it struck my mother's head.

The pieces of clay then began to swoop around the room, darting back and forth past me before whistling through my mother's long black hair. Dirt I had tracked in began to fly around as well, followed by pebbles and twigs from outside.

Mother screamed as she was assaulted on all sides, her house and home rising up to strike her. Through it all I remained untouched.

Mother, a voice said disdainfully in the back of my head. *Breed-stock, no more.*

"Can you not hear her?" I said.

Mother stared at me, uncomprehending.

"Xochitl runs with demons now." I laughed. "Perhaps your beloved *daughter* is one of them!"

I watched as Mother ran out of her own home, screaming and wailing. No sooner did she leave than the tempest swirled to a halt, the debris settling onto the ground.

"Xochitl," I whispered, but there was no response. "Oh, Xochitl, we shall go far together."

Xochitl's name now rests between the two circles. It hurts to do this, to condemn her. Once, I remind myself, the two of us watched out for each other, protected each other. And those who spoke ill of us . . .

Paynal and I were walking through the marketplace, he three steps behind me. There was talk of our going to war against the tribes to the south, and most who saw us treated us with respect. We had almost finished for the day when an old man approached me, pointing directly at my chest. I smiled at him, expecting yet another voice of praise.

"Soul-Eater!" the man screamed. "Soul-Eater!"

"You are old and senile," I said. "I am Ayocuan. My hands will hold the instruments of war for our tribe."

"Soul-Eater," he said again. "You cannot fool me. You devoured your sister at birth, and in her anger she will take a horrible revenge and devour the rest of the tribe." He threw a handful of ash at me, and I coughed and choked in surprise.

"Soul-Eater," he said one final time, "your sister shall use you to devour us for failing her. And when she is done, she will devour you."

The old man's grandson ran up to him. "You must rest," he said, glaring at me as if it were my fault he was so riled up. "Here, eat," he urged the old man, pressing a strip of dried meat into his hand.

As I walked away, Paynal right behind me, I felt something *twist* in the back of my head. Almost instantly I heard loud coughing, then choking. The young boy cried out in fear, and people around me turned in curiosity, several of them running past me.

I walked away, not turning back.

For a brief moment, I stop. Should I be doing this? Is it really necessary? Then I remember Rosita and Paynal, and my resolve strengthens.

I am told that I walked with my head high all that week, and with good reason—I had led our people against the tribes to the south and vanquished them. Many said that the Gods themselves had helped us, raining down the side of the mountain on top of our enemies. Only I had seen Xochitl's hand in the victory. And now, most importantly, I was to be married to Rosita in two days' time.

Rosita and I had met months earlier, our eyes catching across the marketplace. I made Paynal find her name for me, discover who she was and of what family. From there it was only a matter of time. Her father was overjoyed that a war hero was interested in his daughter. Rosita and I met and began to learn more about each other.

Rosita was not enthralled with war, did not care for what her potential-husband did. I found myself intrigued by her and her beliefs; I found myself wanting to know more about her.

Rosita talked of peace among the tribes, of uniting them into one kingdom not through conquest, but through mediation and understanding. As she explained this to me, I could see in my mind's eye a tribal nation united under one figure—me.

In the back of my head I could feel Xochitl stir. Fool that I was, I mistook her anger for joy.

That evening, I sent Paynal to bring Rosita to me at my—soon to be our—home. We would sup together and walk under the stars, making our plans for uniting the tribes into one cohesive unit.

Walking to the window, I could see the Temple of the Feathered Serpent in the evening sky, its considerable bulk blocking out the stars. How long ago was it that I fought under its shadow and Xochitl first made her presence known? It seemed like a thousand years.

Xochitl? I thought. *Are you happy with our arrangement?*

Silence greeted me. I rarely heard my sister's voice, but its absence unsettled me.

Xochitl? I tried again, and then spoke out loud. "Xochitl? Sister?"

The air was still now, and while I could not explain it I knew something was wrong.

I found myself racing frantically toward Rosita's home. As I grew closer, I could hear people—lots of people—and from their voices I knew that something terrible had happened.

Finally I reached Rosita's family home. Ten times ten people were gathered outside, and many of the women were weeping. Ahuitzol, my old teacher, tried to pull me back, but I pushed my way past him and entered the dwelling.

Rosita and Paynal were both dead.

There were bruises all about Rosita's neck, and her face was a dark blue, deeper than the waters of the ocean. As for Paynal . . . if I had not known what he was wearing, I would not have known it was him. Someone had split his head open with a macana, the bloody obsidian-edged club now thrown into a corner.

Blackness overtook me, and I am told that my screams could be heard for miles.

When I came to, Ahuitzol was there with me. He explained how Paynal was found choking Rosita, screaming over and over, "No, you won't have her!" Rosita's father had struck Paynal down, but by then Rosita was already gone, her spirit in Iluicatl. Paynal must have been jealous, everyone said, and all grieved with my loss.

All save Xochitl.

I could not understand why Xochitl had not prevented this from happening, protected me in this as she had for so many other things.

Later, I would understand.

* * *

I step into the circle, making sure not to touch the chalk. I close my eyes and focus on the darkness, the darkness into which Xochitl would lead our tribe. Darkness and blood.

Rosita had now been dead for three months, but our dream of a unified tribal nation had not faded. Itzcoatl, the head of the tribes immediately to our east, had reluctantly agreed to meet with me. This was unheard of among our tribes, and I wondered if Itzcoatl had agreed to meet only out of curiosity, or if he was truly interested in what I had to say.

As I left our city, I could hear tlapitzalli and teponaztli being played, the high whistling and beats lifting my spirits. This could happen. It would.

Before long my escorts and I arrived at the meeting place—a stone circle that had once been used as a primitive temple. Itzcoatl and his five-man escort were already there, waiting impatiently.

As we had agreed, my men and I placed all of our weapons outside of the stone circle and then entered. On the far side of the circle, I could see Itzcoatl's tribe's weapons piled up as well.

"May the Feathered Serpent smile upon you," I said, giving a half bow to Itzcoatl as I crossed the stone boundary. In the back of my head, I could feel Xochitl stir.

"May his wings bear you," Itzcoatl replied, his face stern. He took a step toward me, his hand outstretched. "When I first planned on coming, I never—" A sudden look of surprise came over Itzcoatl, and he stopped in his tracks, only a pace away from me.

"Itzcoatl?" I said, puzzled. I turned around and followed

his gaze—and saw an obsidian knife hovering up above my tribesmen's pile of weapons.

XOCHI—

The knife sank into Itzcoatl's chest, and he staggered back, his eyes rolling up into his head.

The stone circle exploded as warriors grabbed for their macanas and chimallis, and I found myself grabbing my own club and shield.

The struggle was brief but bloody, ending only when the last of Itzcoatl's men ran, evading my own men's pursuit.

The walk back was a solemn one, the only noise Xochitl's laughter in my head.

That night I spent hours thinking about Xochitl's betrayal, and the more I thought about it, the more clear it became.

Every time she had helped me, it had always been to further my path as a warrior; killing armies, wounding my attackers, silencing my accusers.

Xochitl was violence.

Xochitl had moved Paynal's hands around Rosita's throat while he screamed that Xochitl would not take her.

Xochitl had perhaps just plunged my people into war with Itzcoatl's.

When I woke up in the morning, I understood what had to be done. There was, perhaps, still a way to save our people. But to do that, I would have to betray my own sister.

Then again, she had never been afraid to betray me.

YOU HAVE CALLED ME, I hear the demon say. Instinctively I look down at the inner chalk circle, then the outer one. They are both still whole.

"Yes," I say. "I call you and I bind you, just as I call my

sister Xochitl, she whom demons took from my family at her birth."

The demon laughs, and I press on.

"I have a need for you," I say.

A NEED? the demon says. WHY SHOULD I CARE WHAT YOU NEED?

"Because my sister escaped your clutches," I reply. "My need is for you to take Xochitl back."

There is a pause. IF YOUR SISTER IS INSIDE OF YOU, the demon finally says, THEN I WILL NEED TO ENTER YOUR BODY TO TAKE HER.

I swallow in surprise. The words come to my tongue almost unbidden, my mind working quickly.

"You may enter my body so long as you swear to do to Xochitl what you have done to her before. Once you have taken Xochitl, you must swear to leave."

I AGREE, the demon's voice echoes around me.

Reluctantly, I close my eyes and extend my hand into the darkness.

You are so stupid, brother.

I look around. The world is dark now, blacker than the purest obsidian. "Xochitl?" I say.

Yes, she replies. *Thank you for doing what I wished.*

"What you wished?" I laugh. "Were you so eager to be dragged away by demons?"

I hear Xochitl laugh back at me, and it is a dark, chilling sound. *You have played into my hands, brother.* There is a momentary pause. *You should have listened to the old man, you know. He was right all along . . . Soul-Eater.*

I am puzzled by Xochitl's mirth. "Soul-Eater?" I numbly repeat.

Demons never took me, Xochitl patiently explains. **You** *did. You devoured my soul before we were born. Oh,* *demons have come to me—but only to offer advice. Advice on how to give you false memories of Mother summoning inside circles. Mother was a fool, she never could have done this. No, I taught you . . . as they taught me.*

They gave me plenty of ideas. And most importantly, they told me what I should plant in the back of your head. You told the demon that he must do what he has done to me before. And so he has—given me advice on how we shall conquer the world. And he swore he would leave once he had taken me . . . and dear brother, that will not be for quite some time.

"No," I whisper. I struggle, trying to move in this darkness, but find myself immobile. "I have a destiny to fulfill."

THE MAN WILL BE STRONG, AND IN HIS HANDS WILL BE THE INSTRUMENTS OF WAR, the demon's voice echoes.

The woman will be crafty, will be devilish, will be intelligent beyond her years, Xochitl continues. *The two will go to battle and victory and defeat will be in their hands. And so it all comes to pass, dear brother.*

While I cannot see, I can somehow feel my body moving, stepping across the chalk circle, one foot deliberately, tauntingly dragging itself across the marks.

WE HAVE SO MUCH TO DO, the demon says to Xochitl.

Indeed we do, she replies. *And now we can begin, all thanks to my treacherous brother.*

In the darkness, I pray that this will soon end. But I know that it is only the beginning.

True Love in the Day After Tomorrow

by Scott Edelman

You didn't believe him at first when he said he was from the future. Now he's dead, belief is all you have, and there doesn't seem to *be* any future.

You buried Alonso yesterday, planting the coffee can of his ashes beneath his favorite tree in the backyard you shared for so many years. You insisted on doing it alone, even though in your life together you had gathered around yourselves many loving friends who would have liked to have been a part of the private ceremony. But after this long and blissful marriage which you never expected to have, the happiness of which you were never allowed to explain fully, you wanted to approach the empty future alone. You did not want to be surrounded by even the most well-meaning of sympathizers while your mourning mind still reeled from the story you could not share. So you slowly filled in the hole, and then, dropping the trowel by the door, retreated into the house with a desire never to step from it again.

You have spent the hours since, stumbling from room to room, bumping into the furniture as if Alonso's leaving had rearranged it all. A deep sadness has settled on you like fine dust, clogging your pores with grief. You know that grief has twisted your perceptions, and yet, you feel that no one

has ever felt the sense of love and loss you feel today, no
one save Alonso. You saw it in his eyes the first time you
met him, which was . . . how strange, twenty years ago to
you, and last month to him.

You were a secretary then, for a storefront insurance
company, and though you had at times thought of daring to
be more, life had not been kind to your attempts. It was
Alonso who later had taught you how to make those attempts succeed. You were looked upon by the men you
worked for as a machine that typed. A meat machine, never
allowed to know for sure whether you'd been hired for the
speed of your fingers or the look of your legs.

How stifled you felt then, and how fulfilled you've been
since. You can remember that first moment perfectly.
Stretched out now in your useless king-size bed, with a box
of tissues by your side, a bag of potato chips tucked in your
elbow, and crumbs nestling in the folds of your bathrobe,
you close your eyes and relive it. That's all that's left of
him now, you think. Memory.

You had been rereading a memo one of your bosses had
wanted retyped. It was the fifth time he'd asked for
changes, and this made you angry. Wasn't it possible to satisfy *anyone*? You bit down so hard on your pencil you left
marks.

You suddenly felt yourself being watched. People often
paused before the storefront insurance agency to study
those inside, and you had long ago made yourself get used
to it. But this felt different, piercing your urban shell. You
removed the pencil from between your teeth and slowly
lifted your head.

The eyes of the stranger who was standing by the window were clamped shut that first instant in which you saw
him. He was no longer watching you. The tracks of his
tears sparkled in the sun. You were not afraid of him; his

was not a look that inspired fear. You studied him in the freedom his tear-crumpled face gave you.

His forehead was flattened against the glass and he looked in great pain, as if mourning a greater loss than anyone else had ever had to experience, as if mourning the loss of an entire universe. No other man had ever stood before you like this, his skin so transparent that his emotions burned your eyes. Because of that, it took you a few moments to begin to notice the details of his physical features rather than just the manner in which they were contorted; all you were aware of at first was that this was the saddest person you had ever seen.

But then you noticed the hair that was starting to go gray, the broken nose, the few extra pounds that hitting forty had started to fill in on his jowls. He had been a handsome man once, you'd decided, and you could see that it was only time and the hard life he had lived that had downgraded what would have been threatening handsomeness into the harmlessness of solid good-looking.

He opened his eyes. He caught you watching him, and you saw those eyes become pools of fear. He jerked back from the window, his forehead leaving a greasy spot where it had rested. His lips moved, and though you could not hear him, you could read the word he mouthed.

"No."

He pressed the back of one hand to his lips, and then ran off.

You jumped up as he did so and raced immediately to the door, but the street was clear in both directions. You stood puzzled in the doorway, and one of your bosses shouted at you to get the hell inside and finish the damned memo, which you did, restoring the pencil firmly to your lips to prevent the curse words from coming out that would have cost you your job.

You'd thought of the stranger as you worked, wondering at the odd attention which he had given you. How peculiar was his expression at first, when he did not know you were watching! Love and loss, triumph and depression, desire and sadness, all had fought for dominance of his features. It was only that last horrified expression, snapping into focus when he suddenly opened his eyes to you, that was stable.

Fear.

No one had ever looked at you with such fear before. Or, actually, any fear at all. You tried to imagine why anyone would be terrorized by you. When both of your bosses were out to lunch, you phoned a girlfriend to tell her what had happened, and she was no help. She took it as simply another one of the big city's weirdo stories, and told you to make sure those sleazy bosses of yours didn't make you lock up. You did have to work late that night, so you didn't have much time to think about the encounter again until you were on the subway, heading home. You started to feel paranoid then, continually wondering if there was a crying man watching you from a far corner of the train. Each time you looked up, you saw nothing but other harried commuters.

You arrived home with your dinner warm in your hands, a pint of fried rice from the Chinese restaurant on the corner. You opened a diet soda and plopped down in front of the television set and began searching for a show that would make you feel a little less alone. Barely had you stuck your chopsticks into the carton when you heard footsteps behind you. You dropped to the floor and rolled quickly to one side, trying to recall what you had seen other people do in movies. Rising up, there he was before you, the stranger from that afternoon, one hand on the doorknob.

He was on tiptoes, his shoes in his hands, trying to get out the door.

He started to speak, but you tackled him without thinking.

"You son of a bitch!" you'd shouted. Your toughness shocked you then, and it still shocks you now. You laugh now, thinking about yourself, leaping across the room, instant anger having overpowered any fear. A potato chip catches in your throat, and you find yourself laughing and crying and choking all at the same time.

He did not move once you'd brought him down. There was a touch of blood at his temple, but he was still breathing. You nervously clapped your hands together while you wondered what you were supposed to do next. You backed to the kitchen, not taking your eyes off him. You found a length of rope in a cabinet there which you used to tie his hands together around the pipe that connected the ancient radiator in your apartment to the floor. You watched him carefully as you dialed the police emergency number. You were halfway through the number before the strange appearance of the clothes he was wearing sank in. His suit was of a shimmering, opalescent fabric you had never before seen, its futuristic tone made even odder by being cut in a style twenty years out of date. The aesthetic tug of war between cloth and cut meant that no one could have been wearing a suit exactly like that.

Intrigued, you put down the phone and moved a few steps closer. Dangling from the man's collar were two narrow ties, both of the same design, or perhaps it was only one, sliced lengthwise by a razor. He wore his hair in a short ponytail, held together by a jeweled barrette. You had never seen an older man who allowed himself to be that ostentatious.

His eccentric dress swept thoughts of the police from your mind, and you searched him for identification. Your fingers patted where pockets should be, and though you found a rectangular bulge by his right hip, you could not get the cloth to part. Your frustration built as you tugged uselessly at the fabric. You looked for an ID bracelet, hoping maybe that would give his name, and instead found that his wristwatch had no face. The metal of its band was fused to his wrist. You went back to groping at the unseen wallet. He opened his eyes as you pulled, and looked at you dazed and lovesick, as if Cupid had decided to expend every last arrow.

"Jude," he whispered. You were shocked to hear him call you the loving nickname only your mother used for you rather than the full Judy the world knew. With that one syllable of your name, you felt his love through your fear. You remember shivering from the full force of that love.

You shiver now.

He had looked down at his captured wrists.

"Oh, no," he whispered, hypnotized by the rope that bound him. "Oh, no."

Maybe it was wrong, but you could not help but smile at your intruder's helplessness. You had never been allowed such a position of power before. It felt good.

He tugged at the rope, but though the metal pipe creaked, he was held fast. He sighed, and you could see the message sinking in that he would be going nowhere unless you chose to let him.

"Ah, Jude, you really got me this time," he said, settling back calmly. He spoke to you as if he'd known you for years, and you'd just caught him at some particularly impish act that he knew he should have known better than to pull. His calmness angered you more than the breaking and entering itself.

"You looked plenty scared before, Mister," you'd screamed at him. Where were these words coming from? You'd never yelled at anyone before except your own damn self. "Why the fuck don't you look scared now? I called the police, and they're already on their way to lock you up."

"No, they're not," he'd said.

"How do you know? You were knocked out when I did it."

"If you'd called the police, you'd have already told me about it."

"I've never even met you before," you said angrily.

"Ah, Jude," he said, putting on a sad smile, "but I've met *you*."

You found yourself taking a step back from him at the mention of your name.

"How do you know to call me Jude?"

"All right, then," he said. *"Judy."* He struggled with your second syllable as if it took him a great conscious effort to remain so formal.

"Judy," he repeated, then took a deep breath. "I'll try to call you whatever you want. At first. I was hoping to slip away, but now that you've caught me, I can imagine how hard this is going to be for you."

You took a step closer, close enough to kick him. "Don't think a potential rapist can score points by being polite. Life doesn't work that way."

His smug demeanor angered you, but you knew not to be surprised by his politeness. That's what the rapists usually looked and acted like. The nice ones. The polite ones. The boy-next-door type, not the drooling, unshaven, trench-coated monsters of myth. His patronizing coolness made you snatch up the phone again.

"Wait!" he shouted.

You paused, holding the phone tight. "Give me a reason."

"Because that's the way it must have happened," he said. "Because you already *have* waited."

He licked his lips, and you watched his tongue nervously.

"I never expected this," he said. "They told me it couldn't happen. That it would create a paradox. I thought that the most I could do was just look at you one last time. That's why I was so afraid this morning when I accidentally let you see me. I figured I *couldn't* meet you because you'd never told me you'd met me. See? Because you can't change the past. And yet you saw me. I was scared to death that would erase all that is to come. I just hope that instead you managed to keep this a secret for a long time."

"What the hell are you talking about?"

"I'm from the future, Jude," he said. His eyes were moist as if from memory. "*Your* future. We've been married for years. Hell, married's not the right word. We're still more lovers than married. We've joked about that for years."

"Mister, you are full of shit."

You punched the magic number that would rescue you from this mad talk. The stranger squirmed as you listened to the ringing.

"Look in my pocket," he pleaded. "Then you'll believe me."

"I tried that. Your pockets are sewn shut."

"Not really. That's just the way pockets will come to be. Come here."

You set down the still-ringing phone, and that time, when your fingers touched where the wallet lay, the cloth parted.

"How did you do that?" you asked. "Before, it seemed as if I'd have needed a knife . . ."

He shrugged. Your fingers trembled as you slid out the wallet. Inside, you saw a picture of you and this stranger, your arms resting comfortably around each other. The man in the picture looked similar to the one before you, as if it were taken recently, but the you . . . it was not the you you were. You could tell that. Your face there had filled out, and you seemed unafraid of anything. But at the moment, you *were* afraid, and your heart thudded wildly. You listened to the man's words as he talked, but you continued to look only into your own eyes.

"Tomorrow," he said softly, "you will make a visit to the county library. You will meet a man there. More a boy, really. Me."

"I don't go to the library."

"You will. And you will meet a gangly boy named Alonso, the boy who will eventually become the man you see before you. I love you, Jude. And you, eventually you'll love me."

"This is too much . . ."

"I know. That's why I hadn't planned on being seen. I just wanted to look at you once more. To see the woman with whom I fell in love. I wanted to see this place again, too, this apartment where we first made love."

He began crying, and you were mad at yourself, because you could not deny that you wanted very much to wipe away his tears. You were proud that you held yourself back.

"I'm dying, Jude. With death so near, this is all too, too silly, I guess. But you never know what can become important as the time dwindles down. And you, Jude, you are the most important thing in my life. I have a close friend who's a scientist. Once, when he was drunk, he let the secret of his work slip out, and later, after he'd sobered up, I was able to convince him to let me do this thing as his last favor to me. If he'd dreamed this could have happened, that we could have actually met, he would never have let me go. I've just blown his theory about paradoxes. But thank God for that. You don't know what it's like to be able to see you again."

"They have time travel in the future?" you'd asked. Your

throat was dry, and you could barely recognize your own voice.

He thrust his wrist up toward you as best as he could, showing you his odd watch.

"Not that everyone knows. But they're starting to. They have many things in the future. Most importantly, they have our love in the future."

You were finally able to pull your stare away from your photo. You looked from his flat eyes to the real ones there, and the promise that they held. Here was a man who loved you truly, or at least thought he did, you could see that. But you'd always said that you were not ever going to be taken in by the lies of true love.

That was the day it all began to change. . . .

You dumped the contents of the wallet on the couch and spread them wide with a sudden sweep of your arm. There was his driver's license, with a photo that painted him far more solemn than it appeared he ever allowed himself to be with you. The expiration date would not arrive for at least another twenty years. There were membership cards to museums and video stores, receipts for dry cleaners and supermarkets, all with dates far in the future. The money, too, all had late dates, and there were no singles, only two-dollar bills, bearing the portrait of a president you did not recognize. The checks were from a joint account bearing both of your names.

"Okay," you said, mostly to yourself, surprised at the readiness with which you were willing to start accepting all this. And then, to him: "If you're really from the future, then tell me . . ."

He smiled, which made you grow quiet.

"All the little details of how life turns out? The results of wars and elections and horse races? I wish I could. But look." He stretched his restrained wrist as close to you as he could reach. "The same contraption that helped send me here and will bring me back also keeps me from talking about anything but me. Funny. I think that's the only reason I've been able to get away with talking about us—that the two of us are so entwined that you *are* me."

"Try," you'd said.

"For you, Jude," he said. He looked at you as if you'd asked him for a cup of his blood, but that he'd willingly provide it. "For you."

He thought a moment, and as he started to open his mouth again to speak, his entire body was captured by a seizure. You saw the bloodshot whites of his eyes as his every muscle shuddered. You fell to his side and shoved open his lips to stuff part of your shirt between his teeth.

"Enough!" you'd shouted. "I don't need to know. Enough!"

The tension in his body slowly faded. You felt guilty for torturing him so. He looked up at you and sighed.

"I don't like to fail you," he said. "I love you, Jude."

And you found yourself stroking the hair of this crazy man you had netted yourself. You nestled his head in your lap, and then listened as he told you all of your deepest secrets, things you had never confessed before anywhere but in the pages of your diary.

"How did you know?" you'd asked. You could barely state the question.

"These are all things you told me, Jude. We had no secrets."

He recited you a list of all the people who had hurt you, and all the things of which you were ashamed. All those embarrassments which you thought another would have had to turn from in disgust had you spoken of them were instead handed back to you as tokens of love. He even calmly mentioned the one thing you'd sworn that you'd never be able to tell anyone but the man you loved. This was his final gift to you, he said. Maybe by telling you back all the things you had revealed to him with such difficulty in your future and his past, you would know peace a little earlier.

By the time he finished speaking, you were massaging his wrists, the rope that had bound him on the floor between you.

From the look in his eyes, you thought he might kiss you. Instead, he slowly stood.

"I have to go now," he said, reassembling the contents of his wallet. "My friend will be expecting me. If I don't go back soon, they will come after me. I don't think either of us would want that. Thank you for this last moment, Jude. I will speak of it to no one. I will simply tell them that I watched you from afar, and that you were as beautiful as I'd remembered."

He opened the door slowly, and too soon. Full with this unexpected love and belief, you did not want him to leave you.

"When will I see you again?" you'd asked.

"Tomorrow," he'd answered, and you'd had a strange faith that it would be true. "Go to the library tomorrow. And promise me that you will not speak of this night at all to anyone else ever. Not even me. In my past, you have not, and I don't want to change the world in any way. Who knows? The wrong word could tear us apart. Good-bye, Jude."

"Don't go yet!"

He moved through the door and you followed him out into the hallway. His hand lightly touched the instrument at his wrist, and he turned and shouted for you to cover your eyes. There was a bright flash of light, and then he was gone, and you were left with only the afterimage of his form dancing on your retinas. That, and memories of your future. You went back inside your apartment. Mixed with your sadness at having seen him go was a strange hope, one which you had never before allowed yourself to feel.

The next morning you phoned in sick for work from a pay phone in the county-library lobby. As you rattled off your lie of being stricken by the flu, you kept staring at the front entrance, not wanting to miss Alonso. But you couldn't miss him, you realized, could you? After all, if you didn't meet here, he couldn't have come back to see you the previous day. Even though you'd never taken a sick day before, your bosses didn't understand. You'd have thought that just this once they'd have been cooperative, or at least been able to feign, if not feel, sympathy. Balanced on the edge of a new life, you'd almost quit right there over the phone, but then your habitual lack of confidence in the future resurfaced, and you promised to arrive at work early the next morning.

You chose a table near the main doors and piled dozens of textbooks around you to look as if you were studying. You occasionally stared down at them, but most of the time you maintained an unfocused glance off into a distance that allowed you to take in the whole of the library. You tried to ignore the passage of time. Eventually, your bladder began to hurt, but you refused to move. You sat with your knees pressed tightly together. You could bear any burden if it meant recapturing the comfortable feelings of the night before. Even if there was such a thing as fate, you weren't going to let it handle this itself.

It wasn't until almost closing time that you thought you saw him. He was younger, slimmer, and with a nose not yet broken. He had shorter hair, and was no longer wearing an eccentric potpourri of clothing, but dressed in the style of the moment. He'd paused in the doorway, and looked down to read a worn scrap of paper. He turned his head slowly to scan the entire library, and his eyes tracked over you without stopping. As he walked briskly to the reference desk, you tried to imagine the details of the guaranteed instant in which you would meet.

You watched him through the crenelated stacks of your books, and waited as patiently as desperation made possible for him to make his move. With his back to you he asked the reference librarian a question you could not hear. She answered him, and you could imagine him giving her a warm smile as her reward. You were jealous that she was the first to hear that voice and see that smile. You held on tightly to the books before you to stop yourself from waving at him. The woman led him to a battered set of encyclopedia, where he knelt and took notes. Your eyes did not leave him. He sometimes frowned at the words on the page, and you wondered what worried him so. You wanted to relieve that worry, as his visit yesterday had apparently relieved yours. He slammed shut the book, and you jerked erect. You looked down and saw that you had torn a page you had been holding too tightly.

You began to sweat. You expected him to bring the book to your table, to sit down across from you until he could pierce the barrier of your separateness with some innocuous question, unaware of his place at an historic nexus of your lives. Instead, armed with innocence, he slid the book back neatly into its place. He folded the worn slip of paper into a pocket with an air of finality as he twisted his head toward the door. You saw a face possessed by thoughts of lunch that should have been possessed by thoughts of you. Your heart thudded as he passed you on his way to the exit. You scooped up an armful of books and dashed after him, your head down. Bumping into him as if it were an accident, you dropped the load of books at his feet. He spun, apologizing, and his concerned face made you feel good, reminding you that you were doing the right thing.

You stopped trembling. He gathered up all your books and held the stack toward you. You were shocked at first when you saw that he did not recognize you; he was truly seeing you for the first time. His eyes were wide, absorbing you as if this would be their only chance. You had spent most of the day waiting for him, and were embarrassed that you could not think of what to say to keep him, and yet the future promised that he be kept. Your mouth grew dry. He looked from your face to the books which you were too frozen to accept, then back up at you, then towards the spines of the books again.

"Ah," he said, smiling, and you noticed his voice had grown higher-pitched, no, you corrected yourself, *would* grow deeper. "So you're into modern art, too? Where are you going to school?"

You smiled at him in a sickly way which you'd hoped he would take as sheepish. You'd put in all those hours with your heart fluttering over the pages, and you didn't know *what* the books said. You'd simply picked up a large enough pile to justify your space by keeping you looking busy throughout the day. You took back the books and mumbled something about not being in school. You were flustered, and whatever it was you said next you no longer remember, only that it worked, for he insisted on apologizing for bumping into you by inviting you out for coffee. He helped you reshelve your books, and you marvelled at him as he spoke. You followed him to a coffee shop, where he told you his name was Alonso.

You tried to act as if you'd never before met anyone with that name.

You looked at his face through the steam of the coffee he'd bought you. It had been a long time since you'd let anyone buy you coffee. His perfect nose. How would that be broken? Would it be shattered after a future romantic evening when he leapt to your defense on some dark street? You longed to tell him the hints of what you knew, but you were sure he would not believe, not without showing him all the evidence that you had been shown, evidence which his older self had taken back into the future. The afternoon turned effortlessly into night. You found yourself wandering an art museum with him, listening as he led you by his favorite paintings. You didn't mind that he did most of the talking.

And then, the two of you were back at your place. You were surprised to find yourself there, and yet at the same time not. You peeked carefully through the doorway first, momentarily fearful that Alonso would run into his tomorrow form. You took his hand, and led him inside. It felt proper, this surrendering to the inevitable. You sat on the sofa, your arms entwined with his, and told him all the things that had ever pained you, each solitary scar that twenty years into his future he would come back to repeat to you in your yesterday.

You ended up spending that night together, huddled safe in the sanctuary of his embrace, that night and every night since.

Only now, your sanctuary has crumbled to a fine gray dust entombed in a coffee can.

You leap up, scattering potato chip crumbs across the rug. You pace the house thinking of all the unexpected happiness that has passed between long ago then and too close now. Your sobbing echoes in the empty rooms which had once seemed so full.

Alonso had officially moved in with you one week after you'd met, instead of going home each morning for a change of clothes.

Your love grew, just as you expected it would. And as the years went by, you did not tell Alonso any of what had occurred the day before you met, afraid to jinx the transformed life you had been given.

You chose not to ask many questions of this life. You had chosen to become a person who did not need answers. All you wanted was for life's happiness to continue. You knew that someday he would die, he had told you himself that he was dying, but before then he would meet a friend who would send him back to encounter your yesterday self. So you waited, watching for the subtle changes that told you that that time was approaching, that the gift you'd been given would end.

That changed the day he came home from work with his nose bandaged. Someone at his office had tossed him a paperweight, he'd said, and he'd fumbled the catch. There was blood on the front of his short. You cried far beyond the weight of what you beheld at this immediate instant. You crumpled in his arms, and wailed not only for his pain, but also for the swiftly approaching pain you saw for yourself, the injury a sign of his eventual leaving having moved closer. Alonso comforted you, and you managed to avoid having to explain the reasons behind your apparent overreaction.

From that instant forward, you tried to avoid thinking about the blackness ahead, but instead to think only of the blackness you had escaped behind you. You stopped looking for the signs that he was growing into the man who had stepped into your life the many years before. You no longer mirrored the Alonso you knew over the one that had made that first visit. You did not want to know how fast he was gaining on the man he would be when he died. You practiced acceptance. You tried to remain aware that you had achieved a state of grace. You loved this man, and worked at existing in a state of being beloved, both by Alonso, and the universe.

And now, so soon, he was gone.

You don't understand how it could possibly have been so soon.

You go to his dresser and open the top drawer. You close your eyes and inhale. You can smell him there in the room with you, but when you open your eyes again, all you can see are his shorts and socks. You pick up a pair of each and dab your damp eyes with them. You position them on the bed in the places they would be were he lying there. You imagine him filling them out, resting as he often did with his hands cupped behind his head. You decide to get one of his suits from the closet, and to place it over the shorts and socks, and then you will climb onto the bed and press yourself against them, and remember.

You are glad that there will be no one to see you. You feel as if it will be silly. You feel as if it will be holy.

You go to the closet and begin sliding the suit hangers across their metal rod. The scrape of metal against metal makes you cringe. You move the suits first to the right, then back to the left, then to the right again, picking up speed as you do so. You feel yourself growing angry, as you search for one particular suit. You cannot remember exactly which suit. The metallic squeaking is getting on your nerves. You are crying, and you grasp the rod tightly and pull it toward you, wrenching it from its moorings. Alonso's suits fall about your feet. You still do not see the right one. You are angry. You know that it is from more than Alonso's death, but you cannot say from *what* more.

You bend to pick up his suits and see a square of plywood attached to the rear wall of the closet, near the floor. The board is painted so as to be almost indistinguishable from the wall that surrounds it. Two screws hold it in place.

You go back to Alonso's dresser, where you find his nail clippers underneath his handkerchiefs. You use the nail file to remove the screws.

Behind the board is a small alcove, one you never knew existed. Inside is a small carton the size one would get from a liquor store. The box is wrapped in brown paper which has been made very soft by age. You hold your breath while you pull the box closer. The paper is bare of any writing, as if the person who'd wrapped it had been unsure of to whom it should be addressed. Your fingers tremble as you shred the paper easily, and soon you are tearing at the corrugated walls of the box itself.

A suit sleeve tumbles from a split in the torn cardboard. You reflexively reach out to catch it, but then your fingers freeze in mid-reach. You recognize that fabric. It belongs to a suit you have seen but once.

You rip into the package, grunting, and the whole of the suit bursts forth. You recognize what follows. There is a tie, split lengthwise in two. A short ponytail, two hairpins piercing the fake hair where it would join the base of the skull. Wrapped in plastic were a few doughy balls the color of flesh, a skin tone you'd lived with every day. The hip pocket of the suit pants, its lining containing a confusing array of wires that ran up to the waistband, contains a wallet, its leather dry and cracked. You nod as you look through the wallet. It is filled with IDs for companies you've never heard of, with licenses in styles that never came. There is a photograph of you and Alonso, apparently caught in a loving moment. You linger over this photo, a photo that had never been taken.

You study the print carefully, more carefully than you had twenty years before. And though the photo looks real, you know that these were not the forms the two of you came to embody.

No, you had not asked questions of this happy life. As you paw through the contents of the box, you realize you should have. At the bottom of the box is a sealed envelope. You open the clasp, and slide out dozens of pages within, all written in your hand. You begin to read, and see that it is a photocopy of one of your old diaries. You riffle through the pages. The last entry was written just days before Alonso's travel through time.

You shake the box, but nothing more falls out, no easy answers. You were hoping to find meaning inside, but at the same time afraid to find out what that meaning might be. You wonder what it would feel like to have a nervous breakdown. No one could ever have loved you more. Perhaps his going had shattered your mind. That's it, you think. That makes far more sense than this.

You pick up the jacket once more, and try to pinpoint exactly when you had stopped thinking about it, but you cannot. How silly you were to think anyone could ever wear anything so ridiculous, no matter how far in the future. How silly. How terribly, terribly silly . . .

You hug the shimmering jacket to you. You sob, rocking back and forth, your head banging against the closet door.

All these years you felt guilty about not telling him what you knew about his future, about how you had come to meet. Goddamned secrets. You hated secrets.

And now this. You wished the house and all its contents had burned to a fine ash along with Alonso. Now it's too late for that. It's too late for so many things.

Eventually, you stop moaning. You are not sure how long it has taken to cry yourself out, but you are now sitting in a dark room. You carry the box to the front door and peer out. The stars are blinding with their brilliance. When you are sure that no one is watching, you step quickly to a trash can, and throw the box in. You rush inside again, and slam the door harder than you need.

Once in the bedroom, you spread your favorite coat of his out on the bed that is now yours alone. You settle yourself on top of it, and wrap the sleeves tight about your waist. You try to remember. And to forget.

The love was real, you think. If nothing else, goddamn it . . . the *love* was real.

The Divi

by Irene Radford

"**Y**ou are accused of treason, Mary Gray, for murdering our beloved governor, Eloise Abernathy. We have physical evidence, but we need your memories of the event to convict you." Stefan Marble, the police lieutenant in charge of the investigation, read from a pre-printed form in a monotone that betrayed none of his true emotions. The white badge on his crisp yellow uniform proclaimed his name to the world in letters two inches high. Mary couldn't read anything else about him. Yet. He sat back in his chair and signaled the two psychics in the room to take over.

"Tell me, Mary. How do you 'know' when an object has been handmade?" Lily's voice dropped into a musical lilt, as lovely as an undamned creek chuckling through the woods. She stared directly into Mary's eyes and never glanced aside at her fellow psychic or the police officer who shared the interrogation room.

Mary stared at the police psychic, knowing she had to answer the question. Lily had locked on to her mind and would pull the information from her memory even if she resisted.

"When I'm near a genuine antique, I sense . . . I don't know. My hands get clammy and my heart races. It's like my brain gets washed clean with cold water and the only thing left is a compulsion to touch the object." Her fingers arched and reached. The instinctive gesture relayed to Lily and Julian, the other psychic, her need to break free of the talent-damping iron handcuffs that bound her to the uncomfortable wooden chair. The absence of her signet, a plain garnet representing the nonprecious level of her psi talent, on her left index finger left her feeling naked and alone.

Stefan Marble clenched his fists until his knuckles blanched. Mary didn't have to be psychic to know he hated working with psychics. His posture, his hastily averted eyes, and his uneasy fists broadcast his mistrust of his trained minions as well as of Mary.

Mary swallowed a small smile of triumph. She could use his mistrust. He didn't have enough hard physical evidence to convict her.

"Mary is a registered psychic, Lily," Stefan Marble said. He almost spat the words. "I can order a dose of Mental Transmission Equalizer so you can finish your Readings." He grimaced as he made the offer.

Bare white walls without windows absorbed his words without a trace of an echo. Only a few pieces of ugly utilitarian furniture were present to capture the emotions of the four people present. Mary almost screamed at the lack of readable vibrations. She had only their words to help her understand what they wanted of her, words that chilled her to the bone.

She huddled into herself. The MTE drugs would do more than force her to tell the truth. Too frequently, they stripped the psi synapses in the brain. Sometimes MTEs stripped the brain entirely.

"Not yet." Julian smiled so that his long eyeteeth extended menacingly over his lower lip.

Mary had seen police psychics work before. They always came in pairs of complementary talents; one sympathetic, the other hostile. Julian's and Lily's one hundred percent arrest and conviction rate was well-known in Mary's circle of antique dealers. None of them talked about what happened to the innocents who came under their interrogation. Best not to tempt fate by discussing the growing number of blithering idiots now on the Subsistence Rolls.

Mary shuddered again. Maybe she shouldn't have registered with the Bureau of Psychic Assistants. It wasn't as if her abilities were truly useful to society. Not like Lily the TruthReader and Julian the TelePath, both of whom worked full-time for the Portland State Constabulary. But Mary's talent was socially acceptable and earned her a decent living. In this world of make-a-fast-buck-and-leave-before-you-get-caught, fakes and reproductions flooded the jewelry and antique markets. Mary could literally sense a real antique from a block away.

The BPA listed her as a psychometric. Other psis contemptuously called her a divi. No capitals.

"I have three witnesses and a good set of fingerprints on the murder weapon," Stefan Marble replied, as if Mary wasn't sitting less than two yards away. "She has no alibi." He kept looking at a spread of papers on his desk rather than at her.

He accused her of murder and treason. Why wouldn't he meet her eyes?

He looked like a thousand other cops. Uniform height, weight, coloring, and lack of personality seemed to be the major qualifications to become a member of Portland's finest these days. Probably so they wouldn't have to order more than one size uniform. His neutral skin tone, sand-colored hair, and light brown eyes gave no evidence of his ethnic background. If he couldn't be linked to any one group, he couldn't offend a member of another and possibly lose an arrest on grounds of prejudice.

"She has no memory of killing Governor Abernathy. We have no psychic evidence that will stand up in court. Your dependence upon the fingerprints isn't enough either," Julian said to the anxious police lieutenant. His signet ring from the BPA winked in the glare of the single, bare lightbulb in the ceiling.

A diamond for TelePath, platinum setting because he was male—the year of his registration and the level of his powers were engraved on the sides. Mary knew from the cut of the diamond that he'd had the piece custom-made from an older piece of jewelry. She longed to touch it and read the gem cutter's emotions at the time of the crafting.

She felt suddenly empty. She wanted—needed—to take the gem cutter's emotions into herself, adding that craftsman's life and personality to her own. Who was she but the hundreds of artisans she'd accumulated over the years?

"Mary, physical evidence as well as antiques can be faked," Lily said. "The justice system in the State of Portland recognizes that no one can fake psychic evidence. Show me your true memories so Julian and I can set you free. The testimony of two psychics authenticating the weapons, fingerprints, and witnesses is required. The Provinces aren't as enlightened." Her contempt for the region outside Portland dripped from her voice like venom.

The city of Portland had seceded from the old State of Oregon and formed its own state twenty years ago, partly over the relative merits of psychic versus physical evidence. The state and the city-state had more differences of opinion than the use of psychics in court, but that had been the loudest issue at the time of the split.

Lily and most every other psychic proclaimed the police procedures in the majority of the states—the Provinces—as barbaric. Only those jurisdictions that allowed psychic evidence were considered humane. Mary wondered about the humanity of MTEs.

Maybe I should have set up shop in Salem, Mary thought. *I could have just run an honest antique and curio shop without hiring out as a divi to make a living.*

The authorities in Oregon forbade drugs during interrogation.

"Her TruthReading shows total neutrality. I can't tell if she's telling the truth or not." Lily continued to scan Mary's face and aura. "In fact I'm not picking up any information from her at all. It's as if she's blending in with the office furniture. If I look with my *Sight,* I can't see her. I have to use my eyes." She rubbed the sapphire in her gold signet ring. Mary sensed the stone had been manufactured rather than mined. But if she managed to touch the stone while the iron handcuffs bound her to the chair Lily would know from her aura that iron didn't really dampen a talent unless the psychic thought it would.

"We'll have to resort to drugs, Mary, if you don't lower your shields and let us *Read* you," Julian coaxed in a voice Mary thought was supposed to be soothing. "How in the hell does she have shields with the handcuffs on?"

"Unconscious shields aren't unheard of," Lily replied.

Mary's heart raced in panic.

"I hate to resort to MTEs," Julian said to the policeman. "Any talent she has will be destroyed forever. She'll be useless in her job and have to go on state subsistence after her rehab. Will you take responsibility for creating *another* ward of the state, Steve?"

"I want a murder one and treason conviction. This woman killed our governor." Steve Marble pounded the desk with his fist. The force of his blow set up a shock wave of emotions that the desk had absorbed from him.

Mary drank them in and understood some of Steve Marble's thought processes.

She understood the desk as well; 1954, machine-made, walnut, no veneer, standard institutional issue. Rare and moderately valuable now because of its age and solid wood. Dozens of policemen had used the desk; their personalities were buried deeper in the wood grain than Steve Marble's. She'd have to work at rooting them out.

But she couldn't lose herself in the desk. She needed to respond to the threat in front of her.

"I didn't kill anyone!" Mary protested, fighting the iron handcuffs that bound her to the chair. She knew the chair was an original mate to the desk. A set. Her assessment of their value doubled. Was Steve Marble's chair also part of the set? Damn the handcuffs that kept her in place.

"If you didn't kill Governor Abernathy, then you can show me the truth in your mind," Julian said. "Show me how you spent the hours between 11 A.M. and 1 P.M. today. Let down your shields, Mary." He used psychic compulsion in his words again. He placed his hands on the arms of her chair, well away from the iron handcuffs, and leaned closer to her, pinning her in place with his eyes.

Something started to slip in Mary's mind. She relived the first two hours of her day in sparkling detail. Then, like cellophane, wrapping air out and freshness in, she drove away all other memories.

"Damn!" Julian exploded away from Mary's chair and began pacing the little interrogation room. The walls seemed to grow closer with each pass he made in front of Mary. "She either has the strongest controls I've ever seen in a registered psychic or no controls at all and her own fear is shutting her down."

"Where did you learn to control your shields while under interrogation by a Level 6 TelePath and while in iron bonds?" Lily asked. "That kind of control is unprecedented. Under your oath as a member of the Bureau of Psychic Assistants, you are required to reveal all new techniques and where you learned them." Her eyes crossed slightly, a signal that she was going into a trance. Mary would have a very difficult time hiding anything from a trance-induced aura Reading.

"I have no formal training. I just 'know' when an item is handmade or machine-made." Mary tried to make herself invisible again. Physically and psychically. She didn't trust Lily to report an accurate aura Reading.

She had to prove she hadn't murdered Governor Abernathy before they manufactured evidence to gain a conviction. How else did Julian and Lily have a one hundred percent conviction rate?

As a judge, Eloise Abernathy accepted psychic testimony in her courtroom. As a legislator she helped set up the BPA and made psychic operations outside the organization illegal. As governor, she set up training facilities and tuition grants for psychics. No true member of the BPA would wish to harm a hair on her head.

The psychics of the world idolized her. They'd want her murderer tried, convicted, and executed immediately. Publicly. Brutally.

Steve Marble moved away from his desk and stood over Mary. His knees almost touched hers. If he came just two inches closer, she'd know what drove him—whether he truly loved Governor Abernathy or was pursuing this investigation strictly under orders.

"What happens when you actually touch the antique?" Lieutenant Stefan Marble leaned forward as he spoke. His eyes crossed, too. But he wasn't a psychic. Policemen weren't allowed to be psychics, only employ them.

Mary studied him warily. "The person who makes an object by hand," she replied, choosing her words and her emotions carefully, "that person puts a lot of love and care into the making. Especially artifacts made long ago when craftsmanship was a thing of pride. Their emotions become embedded in the object. When I touch it, I relive the act of creation with that person." Mary closed her eyes. Some of her most compelling visions of the past flashed across her memory. The memories and personalities of those long-dead artisans lived on inside her. Through them she could be artistic, too.

Maybe she could use their presence as a defense if Julian and Lily managed to concoct evidence to the contrary.

She sensed Julian trying to share her memories. She let him. The blacksmith who had made a truly unique wrought-iron fence jumped to mind. He had led a particularly violent life.

Julian retreated to a corner, a look of puzzled alarm on his face.

"That part of her story is the truth," Lily said. "I think we can settle this matter without drugs. Steve, bring in the murder weapon. The violence of the murder should have impregnated the metal."

Mary grew cold. She would relive the murder.

She shrank within the bonds, hoping to pull free. But they'd been designed by a psychic to trap a psychic. Once set by a TeleKinetic, they could only be opened by the same TeleKinetic or one of the same rating who knew the working methods of the first.

Mary pushed the violent blacksmith away from the front of her mind. He'd relish reliving the murder whether she had wielded the weapon or not. She brought forward the memories of a lacemaker who cringed at the thought of blood marring her beautiful white threadwork.

"We'll have to open the cuffs and free her talent," Julian

said. He sat down in a straight-backed chair in the corner, a smug grin replacing his previous alarm.

Mary thought about the chair: 1982, machine-made, walnut veneer over pine. More institutional furniture, no value at all, except as firewood.

"That's okay, we'll have a med-tech standing by with an injection of MTE in case she gets out of hand or tries to bolt." Steve Marble stepped away from Mary and rubbed his left hand across the back of his neck. Something in his eyes—weariness? desperation? maybe pity? compelled Mary to watch him as he exited the room. He slammed the door behind him. The thin walls vibrated in response.

Silence hung around the room like an unwelcome ghost.

Moments later, Steve reentered the windowless room, letting in a wisp of fresher air. Mary gulped it. She hoped she'd have the strength to control the coming ordeal.

Steve slapped his open palm with one end of a titanium-alloy crowbar. Mary couldn't sense any trace of iron in the common tool. Specialty stores sold a number of similar items that had been manufactured especially for iron-sensitive psychics who still needed strong, resilient tools.

Behind Steve stood the TeleKinetic and the med-tech.

Julian stood behind Mary, hands on her shoulders. His strong fingers dug into her flesh, preventing her from rising from her chair.

The TeleKinetic waved his left hand with its signet ring of emerald. He blinked his eyes. Mary's left cuff sprang open. He blinked again and the right cuff released her. The TeleKinetic removed the offensive restraints with tongs, then took up a position beside Steve Marble's desk, ready to confine Mary in the cuffs again if necessary.

She breathed deeply. She chafed feeling back into the raw skin that circled her arms like bracelets. Julian and Lily would believe the injuries metal burns. Mary continued the illusion.

Before she could think, or move, Steve dropped the crowbar into her lap. Instinctively she grabbed it to keep it from falling to the floor.

The room spun. Her mind jerked. Suddenly she found herself standing at the edge of a small crowd. Governor Abernathy, short, trim, neatly dressed in a woman's professional suit in bright purple, descended the ten marble steps from the State House. The governor extended her hands to greet her adoring public. Children shoved flowers and balloons at her. Mothers held babies for the governor to kiss and admire. Men thrust their hands out for Eloise Abernathy to shake.

But not every person in the crowd loved the governor. A figure, concealed within the depths of a too-large overcoat of indiscriminate gray and a floppy gray-wool hat, edged through the throng of well-wishers. It could have been a man or a woman, no way to tell with the very effective hat and coat masking face and form.

Mary watched helplessly as the unknown person pulled the long crowbar out from the concealing folds of the coat. Before Mary could cry out, the crowbar descended upon the back of Governor Abernathy's head. Once, twice, three times. Bright red blood spilled over Eloise Abernathy's gray-blond hair onto the lovely purple suit.

People screamed. A man rushed to block the fourth blow and received it on his own head. A second man tried to wrestle the assassin to the ground. A woman emerged from the coat and hat, like a butterfly bursting free of a cocoon. The would-be captor clasped only the coat. The floppy hat lay at his feet.

Mary watched the woman run and dodge among the crowd. At the first wail of an ambulance siren she turned and looked directly at Mary, wearing Mary's face and clothes.

In the stuffy interrogation room, Mary dropped the crowbar. The room spun around her again. She was back in her own body. She wilted in the chair, covering her face in her hands.

"But I didn't do it. I know I didn't kill anyone," she cried.

"Your memories just revealed that you did murder our governor, with malice aforethought." Lily's voice and eyes took on a cold edge. She beckoned the med-tech forward with his cursed syringe of MTE.

"She didn't do it," Julian said, still clasping Mary's shoulders.

"What do you mean? I watched her memories through your mind, Julian," Lily protested.

"Perspective. She watched the murder, she didn't participate. I sensed no anger, malice, or revenge, none of the emotions required for such a violent encounter. Only horror at what she saw as the scene unfolded. She was there, but she didn't do it."

"Then why did she see the murderer wearing her own face?" Lily sat down, hard, in the chair recently occupied by Julian. It wobbled.

"I don't know why she saw her own face." Julian rubbed his eyes and temples with his fingers as if clearing his mind of the memories he'd just viewed.

"If what you say is true, then someone must be manipulating her memories. That's illegal," Steve said.

"And impossible. Memories can't be altered; neither can dreams." Lily rubbed her eyes in imitation of Julian. Mary saw their weariness, knew they'd have to stop the interrogation soon.

"What do you think is the basis of rehab?" Julian looked

at Lily, one corner of his mouth twisted up in a contemptuous sneer. "It takes a Level 8 TelePath to do it, but they alter a person's thought patterns and memories to reflect the happy, useful person society needs. The dream center is also adjusted to reflect the new personality. That's what strips the criminal of any psychic ability, latent or active."

"Then I guess we need to look for a rogue psychic who also altered the vision of all the witnesses." Lily shook her head resignedly.

"Or a twin. Do you have a twin sister or very close cousin?" Julian leaned down excited by the possibility.

"I don't know. I was adopted." Mary looked up, allowing a glimmer of hope to shine in her tears. "I searched and searched for my birth mother, but the records were psychically sealed. I couldn't get the authorization or afford to have them broken."

"I've got the authority and the power to break them," Julian said. "We'll look there first, Lily. Maybe we won't have to alert the entire BPA of a new rogue talent." Julian and Lily nearly ran out of the room. The med-tech and TeleKinetic followed.

"Does that mean, I'm free to go?" Mary raised hopeful eyes to Steve Marble.

"Without the corroboration of two licensed psychics, I can't detain you any longer." He continued to look at her with a fascinated stare. "The desk sergeant will get your coat, purse, and signet ring for you, but first, there's something I need to know."

"I've already told you everything I know about the assassination."

"Not everything."

Mary stared at him, cocking her head in question.

"How'd you do it?"

"What? Julian and Lily just proved I didn't do it."

"I know what they said. I want to know how you led a Level 6 TelePath and a Level 4 TruthReader down the primrose path with your false memories. Oh, you can answer with impunity now. There is no way I can get a conviction after the Reading they did. How did you do it?"

"Trade secret." Mary smiled, suddenly liking this nondescript man for his intelligence and perception.

"I need to know how you committed the perfect murder."

"How did you know I did it?"

"I have unregistered psychic talents, too."

"Like fading into the wallpaper because you have no distinguishing characteristics?"

"All policemen have that talent these days. I also read fingerprints like you read antiques. One look at a blowup of the print and I *know* who they belong to and that person's whole life history. I *know* you murdered our governor, but I can't prove it without registering my talent and losing a job I feel is important. If you won't tell me how you changed your memories, then tell me why."

"My father was Walter Gray. The first man to be convicted based on the testimony of a psychic. Eloise Abernathy as good as murdered him when she convinced the jury to ignore his perfectly good defense in favor of psychic Readings. The jury as good as gave Dad the death penalty. I know of no greater treachery than what Eloise Abernathy did to my father."

"I didn't read that in your fingerprints."

Mary smiled. "If I can alter my memories under a psychic scan while bound by iron handcuffs, what makes you think I can't disguise my fingerprints as well?"

Confusion clouded Steve Marble's eyes. "You just confessed to a murder and told me your motivation. Now you're throwing smoke screens around my physical evidence. Next thing I know, you'll have me thinking I committed the murder."

"And when you tell the world what I can do, psychics won't be so well respected. You and I aren't the only unregistered psychics. If I can corrupt a Reading, others can, too. You, Stefan Marble, will begin the downfall of psychics in the State of Portland. Eloise Abernathy won't be a saint anymore. She'll revert to being just another victim, like the rest of us."

"Why? From what I remember, Walter Gray wasn't that great a father. He left your mother frequently, let you nearly starve on state subsistence, and slapped you around as much as he claimed his parents did to him."

"I don't just share the emotions of the people who hand-crafted tools, furniture, and art, I absorb their personalities. Walter Gray was the first personality I added to my own. I know how much he loved me and my mother. He left us because he was afraid of hurting us when he lost control of his temper."

"Did Walter Gray adopt you or give you up for adoption?"

"Walter Gray is my blood father. I was the one who psychically sealed my birth and adoption records. In fact I planted them and made up the twin sister Lily and Julian seek. Eloise Abernathy destroyed my father. He was a latent telepath. The MTEs that were supposed to make him a useful citizen, left him a vegetable, kept alive by machines and round-the-clock nursing care. He's as dead as the abolished capital punishment would have left him."

"We'll get the records unsealed one way or another. We'll prove them fake. We'll come after you again."

"But the reliability of psychics is dead. I've broken the power of Eloise Abernathy and her BPA. I will survive as a plain antique dealer somewhere in the Provinces. The other psychics who are responsible for turning thousands of vital human beings into vegetables with their Mental Transmission Equalizers will be out of work and have to go back to being impoverished quacks. Who really committed treason against their own kind, me or the psychics of the BPA?"

Her Fair and Unpolluted Flesh

by K. D. Wentworth

Shafts of thin April sunlight slanted down into the Avignon cathedral from the row of tiny clerestory windows. Below, chill black shadows drowned the ornate tombs of notable locals and clerics that lined the walls on either side. The gleam of a marble cherub's pouting cheek attracted Father Frederick's eye as he trailed his superior, Father Barnardo, through the vast echoing nave. He stifled a yawn, weary from the interminable train trip down from the holy city of Copenhagen.

White under gray flashed just ahead, like the underbelly of a dove. A young ophelia, clad in the traditional long-skirted habit, turned at the hollow echo of their footsteps to stand transfixed in a golden rectangle of sunlight. The older priest ducked between columns and headed toward her.

Frederick followed, the cleansing fires of Lyon bright and terrible in the back of his mind, the agonized screams still echoing. Only last month, Father Barnardo had condemned ten of the worst heretics in that city as an example, although he declared all the sisters guilty, to a greater or lesser degree. Sweat broke out on Frederick's forehead despite the coolness of the stone-insulated cathedral.

Father Barnardo motioned the ophelia to stop. The girl hesitated, then obeyed, bowing her head. He rested his gnarled fingers on her long chestnut hair and spoke in heavily accented French. "Don't be afraid, child. I am Father Barnardo and this is Father Frederick. We're here to preside over the Ceremony of the Blessed Immersion."

The ophelia's pale gray hood was thrown back on her shoulders. Her long chestnut hair spilled down her back in careless ringlets, and on her breast rested the traditional tiny silver sword threaded onto a delicate chain. Her downy cheek gleamed in the sunlight, white as a winter morn's new frost. She was the most perfect thing Frederick had ever seen, fresh and youthful, the quintessential ophelia.

" 'I cannot chose but weep,' " she whispered.

"Yes," Father Barnardo said, "I'm sure you know your scripture impeccably. How are you called?"

She looked up. "Sister Yvette Ophelia."

"I found something disturbing outside." He snapped open his leather satchel, then pulled out a wrinkled, crudely printed handbill. "Have you ever seen one of these before?"

Frederick was puzzled; surely this child was too young to have seriously strayed. Her skin smelled of scented soap, violets mixed with a hint of honey, quite sweet, but appropriate. Her eyes were a hazel that shimmered to sea green in the light, eyes that could set a man adrift, never to return home again. He felt himself dangerously drawn as they flickered downward and focused on the black letters.

When she looked up, she searched the older priest's face, her expression mystified and guileless. "I—do not understand."

The older priest thrust the paper at her. "Examine it very carefully."

The girl averted her head. "We are, of course, forbidden to read. We have no need of it." There was the faintest lisp to her syllables, a hint of childhood not quite left behind. Scarlet bloomed in her maidenly cheeks.

Father Barnardo perched his spectacles on his nose. "It's quite ill phrased, but, in essence, relates the theory that all women have souls, not just those who have taken vows and Gone Ahead, or those who take vows, but remain behind to serve, but even those outside the church altogether."

"That's wicked!" Tears brimmed in the ophelia's green eyes and she dropped convulsively to the chill marble floor. Her gray-and-white skirt pooled around her knees.

"Then there's the nonsense about forgiveness." His mouth twisted. "The ridiculous notion that, through repentance, sin can be canceled out like some sort of bad debt, that justice is not the highest virtue, nor balance of the Eternal Scales the holiest of all states."

The girl's eyes gazed past him into the blue-tinged shadows. Her breast heaved, as though she'd been running.

"It even hints that the Prince's sacrifice pales beside Ophelia's, that His life was merely taken, while hers was freely given." Father Barnardo leaned over the delicate seashell curve of the girl's ear until his wiry gray beard brushed her shoulder. "If you know anything about this, you must tell us where it came from. We have to save these poor creatures from themselves."

" 'There's rosemary, that's for remembrance.' " She bent over her knotted hands, her knuckles shining bone white through the skin.

"Come, come, girl, I know the Blessed Madness when I see it. Your mind is clear enough." Father Barnardo straightened. "How old were you when you came here?"

"Six." Her voice was a whisper.

Father Barnardo cocked his head. "I thought most in this order were given at birth."

The girl's velvet eyelashes brushed her cheeks. "My fleshly father said I was willful and would otherwise surely perish in hellfire."

Voices murmured at the far end of the vast cathedral, then several girls sang a series of thready scales. The sound echoed through the side chapels and the arching galleries overhead like a lost soul seeking salvation.

Father Barnardo sniffed. "He obviously had your best interests at heart."

A tear trickled down her cheek. "Father, please, I've never seen that paper before, and I'm late for kitchen duty."

"Very well." Father Barnardo nodded. "Tell Eldest Sister Otille Ophelia that we are here, then say ten Blessed Vindications and observe strict Silence for the remainder of the day and night."

She curtsied, then fled toward the transept, her footsteps mingling with the sweet childish voices of the choir.

Frederick took the creased paper. "This is identical to the handbill you found in Lyon. Is it circulating here in Avignon as well?"

"It is the same one." The older priest wiped a hand across his forehead and sighed. His face was grim, his coloring pasty. "I find it a waste of time to go rooting around for evidence at each new site. Heresy is everywhere." He took the bill back and returned it to his satchel. "Don't be fooled by a sweet face and a few tears. She recognized those letters and words, read them each and every one. This place reeks of blasphemy, and I'm sure we've only just scratched the surface."

While Father Barnardo met with Eldest Sister Otille, head of the convent bound to the cathedral, Our Lady of the Blessed Brook, Frederick wandered into the comforting precision of the attached vast geometric gardens. The orange-red sun was sinking in the west, fat as a bloated tick. He settled on a bench beneath the spreading branches of an ancient yew tree and folded his hands, trying to compose his overactive mind to pray. All his life, he had dreamed of serving the Church, of being a force, however minor, for the sacred causes of Balance and Justice. He knew Father Barnardo was wise and experienced in the ways of the world; if he thought heresy flourished in this hallowed place, it must be true. Yet the encounter with the ophelia troubled him. How could one so young and lovingly protected in one of the finest convents in the world be already corrupted and therefore damned?

He closed his eyes. The air was bitingly cool against his face, filled with the sharpness of yew and freshly turned earth. Just behind the cathedral, the river murmured to itself in the background like an old man telling stories. "God, the Father." He intoned the old litany under his breath. "God, the Prince, God, the Holy Ghost, hear my prayer. I am naive and blind, and Father Barnardo has seen much more of this wicked, willful world than I have, and yet—"

The ophelia's smooth cheek shone in his mind, those mellow hazel eyes that plainly knew nothing of duplicity and error, the soft, trembling mouth, then he heard the screams in the hard cold dawn at Lyon as he stood with Father Barnardo before the heaps of burning faggots at the massive river's bank, heard the sizzle of crisping charred flesh—

" 'Now cracks a noble heart,' " a husky voice whispered. A hand grazed his shoulder.

He started violently, opened his eyes. Yvette stood before him, her gray hood drawn modestly over her curly hair, her hands clasped demurely at her waist. The sword emblem at her throat caught the sun in a painful burst of silvery fire.

He adjusted his high black collar. A heat moved through him, massive and riverlike in its slow insistence. "Didn't Father Barnardo assign you Silence?"

She pushed her hood back and tipped her face up into the

roseate light of the setting sun. Her nose was straight in
profile, her lips full. A lark burst into song, shrill and oddly
off-key. "I shall be quiet then," she said, "if you wish it."
She stared at him solemnly, not a trace of sense or reason or
fear in those large hazel eyes, the perfect ophelia. She
smiled and cocked her head. "'White his shroud as the
mountain snow.'"

Maybe the Blessed Madness had descended upon her
after all. He had heard of those afflicted at irregular intervals, not as blessed as those who had attained that state permanently, but still holy and to be admired.

She picked at the seam of her long gray skirt. "'There's
pansies, that's for thoughts.'"

She was quite convincing. If he were on the Selection
Committee, he might have recommended her to Go Ahead
himself. He wondered if this order had selected a candidate.
Time was growing short; the first Sunday after the equinox
was only two days away. He had a sudden flash of his
youngest sister's face on that last morning in Dublin. The
sunlight had streamed down, haloing her hair. She had
looked at him in the same way as this ophelia, seemingly
unaware of approaching events, as was meet in such an un-
worldly child. He remembered how she had stood on the
sacred pier, just before she cast herself backwards into the
embrace of the green-brown waters in that most holy of
Sacrifices, her young body clad in the traditional white
robes, almost translucent in the sunlight. She had not quite
finished the first verse of the customary hymn to the Prince
before the swirling waters took her. His throat closed and
he pressed a hand over his eyes.

When he opened them again, Sister Yvette was gone.

He took a seat in the second row at evening vespers and
watched the ophelias file in, the oldest ones in front, the

smaller ones behind, their habits rustling like sparrow wings, their heads covered and bowed. As the choir sang a hymn, he focused on the great silver burnished sword hanging point down above the altar. The artist had suggested the form of a standing man caught within the blade, his arms outstretched in victory to form the crossbar of the hilt. Fat white altar candles flickered as the local priest murmured verses from the sacred text and spread incense.

"Provoke God not to wrath, for His Hand shall always restore the world to Balance, and His great Sword cut down all who stand in His way." Frederick mouthed the words along with him. Once, before he had left the seminary, he had thought to serve in this capacity, too, traveling from church to church in his own district, knowing the people as they progressed through the many joys and tragedies of their lives, but that was before he'd been selected for this less pleasant, but higher duty of rooting out heresy. What would the world be without Justice, he wondered. His present calling was the most important of all, for, as the Book said, for every wrong committed, for every sin, someone must pay. Otherwise, the devil held sway.

"As the Lord once sent Our Prince to redress the usurpation of power, He shall again, whenever the need arise. His Word is the foundation of all law and order, His Sword the instrument of holy vindication. Praise Him above, all ye heavenly hosts."

The familiar words comforted Frederick and eased the knot in his throat. His sister was in Heaven, a Queen of women, most of whom were too weak and simpleminded to assist in God's quest for justice. He opened himself to the quiet joy these services always engendered, the sense of peace created by the knowledge that life was not a random series of events, that there was a reason for everything that happened, and that God's structure underlay the entire universe.

At the end of the service, the ophelias approached the altar, made obeisance, then filed out through the transept into the cloistered walk below the dormitory. He slipped after them to monitor their conversation. Their sandals whispered over the inlaid stones, but their voices remained stubbornly silent. He froze inside one of the brick arches, lingering in the pooled shadows as a group of older girls dropped out and entered the chapter house. The rest swept toward the stairs and sleeping dormitories above.

After the last girl had cleared the covered walkway, Frederick crossed to the inner wall and peered through the window. Gray curtains had been drawn, yet a tiny gap remained where the seams did not quite overlap. A circle of bright and dark-haired heads were bent over an unfinished plank table inside, seemingly gazing down at something or someone. He craned his head. Were they reading? That would be just the sort of evidence Father Barnardo required.

A small soft hand touched his cheek. He whirled, his heart stuttering.

A hooded ophelia stood before him, her eyes invisible in the shadows. She pushed her hood back and he recognized her long chestnut hair. She folded her slim hands at her waist. " 'Oh, sweet prince.' "

"What?" He took a deep breath and tried to slow his heart rate. "What are you doing out here?"

She twined a curl around her forefinger. " 'Do not, as some ungracious pastors do, show me the steep and thorny way to heaven.' "

In this dim light, she looked so like his sister, even sounded like her in those last few months when she had achieved the holy state of Blessed Madness. His heart tightened painfully as the litany rang again in his mind—*"And from her fair and unpolluted flesh may violets spring."* He saw the tiny purple flowers strewn over her limp body after she was pulled dripping from the embrace of the dank green river. He remembered the chill of her skin as he closed her staring eyes and straightened her limbs before they carried her bier to the grave waiting in the muddy red-brown earth.

This ophelia's eyes caught the yellow light seeping through the curtains and seemed suddenly feral as a lynx. "'Pray you, love, remember.'" She grazed his cheek with the backs of her fingers, then ran up the steps toward the dormitories.

His hands shook so that he had to clasp them together. He stared after her, his heart racing, a brooding darkness raging through his soul.

Father Barnardo woke him from a restless, unsatisfying sleep in the thin gray light of dawn. Frederick swung his legs over the edge of his narrow cot and squinted up at the old man's grizzled face. The priest laid a finger across his lips. "Bring your notepad."

He nodded, then struggled into his cassock and followed the older man out of the visitors' dormitory. The light was raw and gray-pink as they padded down the steps, the air sharp as an old maid's tongue. Frederick stumbled after his mentor, his mouth dry. They turned a corner, hurried under the arches, and burst out into the budding gardens.

Nine or ten of the order's older sisters stood around a marble sculpture of the Blessed Ophelia, their hands folded demurely at their waists. Their freshly scrubbed faces were turned to the rising sun and their voices soared through the notes of an unfamiliar song.

"That is not within the approved list of hymns." Father Barnardo fixed them with a stern gaze.

Yvette turned to him and smiled radiantly. " 'We know what we are, but not what we may be.' "

An older woman stepped forward, silver threading her curly black hair. "I taught them the hymn, Father. It's a folk song the Blessed Ophelia herself sang in its original Danish."

"You have no way of knowing that, Otille! Almost nothing is known of Her life outside of that portion described in the *Prince's Book of Decision*. This will not look good on my report."

Otille's lips curved upwards in a gentle, knowing smile. "It's an old secret, handed down through the order for centuries."

Yvette laid a gentle hand on Frederick's sleeve. "Didn't you like it, Father Frederick?"

Her violet scent threaded through his brain. "Why, yes," he answered haltingly, "it was—beautiful."

His face grimly disapproving, Father Barnardo took Frederick's arm and hustled him into the sanctuary, where he halted before the great silver sword of Justice hanging above the altar. The votive candles flickered in the side chapels, reflecting redly on the polished metal. Father Barnardo locked his hands behind his back, staring up silently. " 'The wickedness of women being greater than all other wickedness of the world,' " he quoted from the *Second Book of Inquisition,* " 'avoid them as you would avoid a poisonous serpent, if thou wouldst safeguard thy soul.' " He turned to Frederick. "Never forget it was a woman who first brought Injustice into the world and betrayed our blessed Prince. It will take both great strength of will and purity to root this wickedness out. Do you know why I chose you for this position over more than two hundred other candidates?"

Frederick sank onto the wooden pew. His throat ached. "No, Father."

"It was not because you were the strongest, or the brightest, or even the most spiritually committed. It was because, although you had great talent, I sensed you were flawed, fatally weak at your most vulnerable point and in dire need of tempering, like the steel in Our Lord's Sword." He tilted his head back and closed his eyes. "If you took service with an ordinary parish, you would fall into Injustice, most likely sooner than later. I thought, by taking you under my wing, I could strengthen your ability to serve."

Frederick bowed his head.

"This work is so important. Left unchecked, heresy will destroy the moral fabric of our society." Father Barnardo turned to face him. His shoulders were sunken, his lips, the corners of his eyes, in fact, every line of his face sagged. He was an old man, bowed beneath an unimaginable burden. "Divine Justice and Eternal Balance are the only things holding the savage at bay in all of us."

Frederick slipped onto his knees and made the sign of the Sword on his chest.

"It's not a disgrace to discover that you do not have a true religious vocation." Father Barnardo laid a gentle hand on the crown of his head. "It happens to a number of the young men in seminary. We cannot all afford the luxury of celibacy. If this work is too difficult, you can make a life for yourself of a different sort—marry and raise a pious family, perhaps one day give a daughter to the holy order."

As his sister had been given. The muddy smell of the turbid river resurged, overlaid by violets. Frederick shuddered, then his mouth compressed. His sister ruled in Heaven at the Prince's side, and now it was his job to be worthy of her. He raised wet eyes to the gleaming sword. "Father, I know I can be strong enough."

Father Barnardo sighed, a long slow exhalation combining the dryness of old leaves and the measured venting of a steam engine. "We have only one more day to examine this order before the Blessed Immersion. We must uncover the truth! It would be unthinkable to let a corrupted sister take part."

Frederick raised his head. "Which of the girls has been chosen?"

"You've already met her." The priest's hand descended heavily on Frederick's shoulder. "Sister Yvette."

"It is of her that we must be most certain." Father Barnardo settled the gold-embroidered white stole around his neck, then traced the sign of the Sword on his breast and folded his hands. "The ceremony is blasphemy if her heart is not pure."

"But surely they will be careful because they're being watched." Frederick lit the incense for the ceremony and the spicy scent of sandalwood filtered through the robing room.

"There's always something, my boy, some sign." Father Barnardo picked up the chain of the ornate brass censer. "Just follow my lead."

The cathedral was filled with mellow candlelight and fresh-cut flowers and voices weaving an intricate contrapuntal harmony. The ophelias had already entered through the main doors, splitting into three lines, two lesser columns flowing up the side aisles, while the main body proceeded down the center toward the altar, which had been strewn with the traditional nettles, daisies, and crow-flowers. Yvette floated in the center of the main body, her shining hair loose and her white gown studded with diamonds and rubies.

Frederick stood in the shadows cast by the tall candles, behind Father Barnardo, as the sisters approached. They were faultless, their singing perfect, their faces composed, their white hands folded at their waists. The air was redolent with the hot beeswax of the candles and the lilies garlanded around the immense stone pillars. He thought again of his sister. Her vigil had been kept at a much smaller church. The candlelight had been golden, the air sharp with yew and holly. Her downcast blue eyes had glistened with tears.

Yvette knelt before the snowy altar and bowed her head. In the unsteady candlelight, she looked no more than twelve. Father Barnardo paced the sacred circle around her three times, censing the altar area. His resonant voice rang out. "The Prince stretches out His Hand, daughter. What have you to give?"

"That which is hers alone," the massed ophelias responded in unison.

The parishioners in the back of the church murmured their approval and craned their necks to get a better view.

Father Barnardo bowed his head over the girl's. "When shall you give it?"

"Whenever it is required," the ophelias answered.

The tension in Frederick's shoulders eased. The ceremony seemed to be going well. Perhaps Father Barnardo was mistaken about the presence of heresy here.

The elder priest's eyes closed. "How is it given?"

"Most freely," the ophelias answered.

"So be it." Father Barnardo raised his arms. "Blessed be God, the Father, God, the Prince, and God, the Holy Ghost. Amen."

The watching parishioners echoed the amen, then surged

forward. Yvette remained motionless on her knees, her closed eyes fluttering, as the eager celebrants each cast a single lily, violet, or daisy onto the altar, then touched her shoulder in hushed reverence.

Father Barnardo waited until the last had gone and the sisters were extinguishing the excess candles. "Father Frederick, you will begin the vigil with Sister Yvette. I have a few matters to discuss with Eldest Sister Otille, then I will join you later."

The heaped flowers trailed off the white altar onto the floor, scattered in bright drops of yellow and white and purple around the kneeling girl's alabaster gown. Her hands were clasped before her breast. "Oh, Lord," she whispered in an unending litany, "make me worthy of the honor I am about to receive. Oh, Lord—"

Frederick settled on a bench behind the altar to watch. A sturdy moonfaced sister brought an ornate freestanding candlestick and placed it beside him on the floor. The wax of the candle was the color of beaten gold and smelled like a freshly mowed meadow as it burned. He rested his head against a marble pillar and let the sisters' solemn chant flow over him like a soft, caressing breeze.

A hand cupped his chin, then fingers caressed his cheek. With great difficulty, he dragged his eyelids apart and peered through an amber haze at the face before him. It was only a pale oval with burning green circles for eyes, as though something altogether *other* peered from behind a mask. He reached out to see if it were real, but his hand faltered like an old man's, trembling and weak.

"I am both first and last," the womanly voice said. "Honored and scorned. Maiden, Mother, and Crone." Fingertips trailed warmly down his neck, then tore his collar open, slipped inside his shirt. He shuddered at the shock of her flesh against his.

"In me, savor both fire and ice," the voice whispered hotly into his ear, and firm curves pressed against his hips. Unbelieving, he felt the corresponding fevered jump in his pulse, the ache in his loins as he floundered to free himself. A lake of molten fire awakened in his belly and spread until every nerve was aflame with need and desire. Sweat broke out on his face and he ached for something he had never possessed.

He struggled against it. "No, no, I won't—" Brilliant fountains of red light burst inside his head, like some immense fireworks display, and his eyes would not focus. He sagged as soft lips caressed his ears, his eyes, and it seemed that a bevy of slender arms held him up. Honey-scented breath breathed fire against his neck. His skin burned wherever she touched until, unbidden, his mouth sought hers. His traitorous fingers buried themselves in her silken hair and he was overcome by her violet-scented softness.

He was both freezing and sweltering as the cool cathedral air stirred over his naked skin. Prisms of shattered light whirled around him in time to a song sweeter than any bird had ever framed, and everywhere there was fire, in his mouth, behind his eyes, and, most of all, raging through his brain. The flames raged higher and higher until her naked flesh was consumed along with his and nothing was left but ashes.

Pain. Dull and pounding. Centered behind his eyes. A steady throb that kept reliable time. Frederick turned his head and grimaced as the throb became a lightning flash of pain. He groaned and raised his hands to his eyes.

"Father Frederick?" A hand tugged at his sleeve. "Don't you have to change before the ceremony?"

He pried his eyes open. "What—?"

A short dark-haired ophelia studied him soberly. "You fell asleep during the vigil. You'll have to hurry. Sister Yvette has already gone to be robed."

The cathedral was empty, the candles snuffed. Pale gray light trickled down from the eastern row of clerestory windows and gleamed faintly on the marble tombs. The stone cherubs gazed upon him with disinterested eyes. He passed a trembling hand over his face, trying to remember. There had been a fire of some sort. He remembered *burning.* "No," he said groggily, "I couldn't have fallen asleep—"

"Hurry, Father." The girl braced his elbow. "They expect you at the pier in a few minutes."

"The pier?" he echoed numbly.

"For the Blessed Immersion," she said impatiently.

He stumbled to his feet and wavered there, but his head was rapidly clearing. He supported himself on the pillars and the backs of the pews until he reached a small side door. In between the diminishing jolts of pain, images kept flashing through his mind, the feverish touch of a delicate hand on his neck, a hot demanding mouth that drew him down into burning ecstasy.

His hand fumbled at his collar. All the buttons were in place, neatly fastened, not torn off, but the memories of the silk of naked skin were sharp and clear. He flushed in shame. It had been real. He had done it, given his body that way with reckless abandon. How in the name of God could he have been so irresponsible? Had they drugged him? He remembered the oddly fragrant candle placed at his side just before his memory of the vigil hazed out.

An ache resurged in his loins, the dregs of desire, and he wanted to die. He should have been more wary, should have suspected the moment he detected the unusual fragrance. Now he would be stripped of his priesthood, cast out to live among unbelievers. Never again would he serve behind the altar, nor have any chance to purge Injustice from the world. He was unclean . . . defiled. He shivered.

Father Barnardo waited for him on an iron bench under the cloistered walkway that bordered the gardens. He wore his most formal ivory cassock with the ceremonial embroidered violet stole. His sparse white hair was carefully combed, his hands locked across his waist. "Did the vigil go well?" There was an eagerness in the set of his jaw, an expectant forward thrust of his chin.

Frederick swallowed hard. "You were supposed to come back and stand it with me."

"I told the sisters that I was ill." Father Barnardo smiled thinly. "There have been rumors that this order's rituals are tainted with a particularly virulent heresy, yet there is never any impropriety unless a *young* priest is sent."

Frederick's head reeled. "You—knew." He forced the words out. "Before we came here, you knew what they would do!" The throb resurged in his head, a wild, pulsating presence.

"We must each serve according to our gifts." Barnardo glanced over his shoulder as the procession of the Blessed Immersion began to wind through the gardens. "When I slipped back to check on you, they had locked every door into the sanctuary and covered all the windows, so it is in your hands now. I need your testimony so we can send these harlots to the stake."

Frederick pressed his hands to aching temples. Barnardo had planned this, had picked a foolish young priest straight out of seminary who was flawed and sure to fall into Injustice anyway, one who was expendable.

Barnardo said sternly, "Tell me exactly what happened so I can use my authority as an Inquisitor to stop this farce."

Frederick, furious at having been used, met the older

man's rheumy eyes. "Nothing," he said hoarsely. "Sister
Yvette Ophelia and I stood holy vigil throughout the night
while the sisterhood chanted the verses in their proper
order. I found no fault with word or deed."

Barnardo's eyes narrowed. "The sin is more theirs than
yours. I will speak for you before the See in Copenhagen,
but you must tell the truth!"

The ophelias' high sweet voices floated back through the
gardens, and Father Barnardo's face reddened. "Are you
going to let them get away with this? For every sin, *someone* must pay. We must stop them before they contaminate
more souls! There is not one among them fit to go to Him!"

He turned toward the pier. Frederick thought of what the
sisters would say, once Father Barnardo began to question
them. Pain loosened the tongue with astonishing alacrity
and then his testimony would not even be needed.

He caught the old man's sleeve with anxious, plucking
fingers. "Yes, you're right, Father. Come—inside, and I'll
tell you everything now, while it's fresh in my memory."

Barnardo glanced back at the river, then nodded and allowed Frederick to lead him into the chapter house. As he
crossed the threshold, Frederick shoved him off-balance,
slammed the door, then barricaded it with the heavy iron
bench. A second later, the old priest had rebounded to the
door, pounding with both fists, demanding to be released.

Frederick's heart raced. Now what? His palms were slick
with perspiration. He would have to deal with Father
Barnardo eventually, and he had no idea what to do. For
now, though, the old man only suspected. He had no proof.
If Frederick could convince the sisters to flee before they
could be questioned and proven guilty, he might be able to
think of some way to make up for his mistakes afterward.

Father Barnardo's furious cries faded as he ran to the pier
to stop the ceremony. The flower-entwined rope lay coiled

on the weathered wood, ready to be tied around the Blessed's waist. A basket of fresh-picked violets from the hothouse was close by. Yvette had changed from the gem-encrusted gown into one of the order's gray-and-white habits, which was wrong. She should only be clad in the simplest of white chemises.

"Harlot!" he cried. "This is a mockery! Take yourself away from this holy place and never show your face again! You are not fit to go to Him! God will strike you down in the name of Justice for what you have done!"

"But, of course, you did it too." She smiled, but it was a more feral and sharp-edged expression than he would have thought that lovely young face could manage. Sunlight glinted off her chestnut hair as though the strands were pure gold. "'They bore him barefaced on a bier,'" she said with a trace of amusement.

The traditional bier did stand close by, and he felt a chill at the sight of it.

Eldest Sister Otille stepped forward, her hood pushed back and her face radiant in the rising sun. "Ophelia's sacrifice has been grievously misunderstood through the years. Did you never wonder why she cast herself into the brook that day?"

"To prepare the way," he said angrily. "To redeem herself and give all women the hope of Heaven, as you have none, now."

Her fingers touched his chin and tilted his face to the east, so that the rising sun blinded his eyes. "Have you any sisters?"

He slapped her hand away, blinking. "Yes, if that makes any difference."

"And did they go to school, or learn to read, or do any sort of useful work?"

"No, of course not. My parents were very devout. Two of

my sisters are married, with children of their own, and the other—" The words caught in his throat.

"Yes?"

"She became an ophelia in the Albigensian Order in Dublin and Went Ahead last year."

"'And will a' not come again,'" Otille said softly, her words straight from the sacred text. Her mouth was grim. "Think, boy. Is it possible that Justice is not highest virtue, that the story of Ophelia and her Prince has been maliciously misinterpreted? Don't you see? Ophelia was saying the Virtue of Purity is a lie. Without physical love, life is simply not worth living."

He stepped back, horrified. "That's blasphemy!"

"It's the plain cold truth." Otille put an arm around Yvette. "*He* was a deceiver. *He* sent Her away and thus drove Her to seek Her death in the dark water. *She* was the one who sacrificed."

Yvette unhooked her necklace with its tiny silver sword. Her sea-colored eyes were calm as she walked across the pier and seized Frederick's hand. "'Good night, sweet prince,'" she said softly, then scratched his palm with the sword. "'Flights of angels sing thee to thy rest.'"

Blood welled up like an inrushing tide. He snatched his hand away, his heart pounding. The wound smarted, then burned as though fire was ricocheting through his veins. He stared down at it, unable to think for fear of what she had done. "Father—Barnardo," he forced out, "he'll burn all of you to ashes!"

"But you locked him in the chapter house and ran away," Otille said. "And we, being but fragile women, could not stop you. You were so very wicked last night, saying bold things to poor Yvette throughout the vigil, making coarse suggestions, trying to touch her and steal that which is most precious to all women."

He turned to flee, but his legs wilted. He found himself facedown on weathered planks pungent with mud and fish and rain. She reached down to pick a bit of lint from his shoulder, straighten his collar. "Later, we will release him, but he will not find you, no matter how hard he searches, for someone must lie in the grave we have prepared."

Frederick's hand was numb now as the burning raced up his arm, into his shoulders, his lungs. The sky dimmed, as though a huge black leathery wing had passed overhead.

Otille leaned down and looped the flower-entwined rope about his trembling wrists. "Sister Yvette would have tarried in this life until Father Barnardo was found, to tell him of your wickedness, but the poor sweet child could not wait to Go Ahead and rest safely in her Prince's arms. It was very beautiful, the look in her eyes as she sank beneath the water."

His lips were numb now, and his tongue. He shivered, cold, his flesh like marble. So cold.

The sisters rushed forward to lay hold of his shivering body and lift him onto the flower-strewn bier. Yvette smiled down tremulously at him, smoothed his forelock, unwound the rope, and positioned his hands across his chest. "'Now cracks a noble heart,'" she said. "'Adieu.'"

Her touch brought back the chapel, the soft lips devouring his, the all-consuming *fire* kindled of naked flesh against flesh. He shivered, wanting her still, despite himself. The sky overhead shrank to a faint circle and he strained against the encroaching numbness of his body.

He had sinned in the chapel with Yvette, far more willingly than he'd wanted to admit. He had almost as much to pay for as she and the rest of the sisterhood, but Injustice was still rife in God's world and he ached to put his hand to the fight. He wanted another chance, please, God, just one more chance to be of worth.

Darkness closed over his face, chill and evil-smelling, like stagnant water left too long in shadow. He tried to reach up for the flowery rope that would draw him from the river and give him one more chance to get it right, but it was too late and he was so cold. He felt the Eternal Scales of Justice swing into balance as the cruel hilt of a great sword was fitted into his empty hands, then laid across his heart.

Perfidy
This is a test,
This is only a test

by Dennis L. McKiernan

Satan and שׁהוה sat atop The Mountain. And still the debate raged as it had for slightly less than five thousand nine hundred years, since 9 A.M. of October 23, 4004 B.C. to be exact, for that's how old the world was, give or take seven days.

"Pfaugh. שׁהוה, Your 'Chosen People' are no different from any other people down there; no more saintly, no more sinful, no more faithful."

"As to saints and sinners, I would agree, Fallen One, but as to faith, that is where We depart. My Chosen People stand above all when it comes to hewing unto Me. Is not My First Commandment specific as to the matter of faith?"

"Ah, You gave them the Commandment, and the believers do worship You . . . more or less. But among the faithful, have You truly tested them?"

"Of course I have. Did You not see that which I did unto Abraham? Was he not sorely tested, right to the very end. And what of Jacob? And Samuel and Samson, David, Solomon, Moses, Noah, Jonah . . . did I not test them all? All My prophets, all My kings? And did they not come out from the trials and tribulations I set upon them with their faith intact?

"And did We not make a compact, You and I, Old Serpent, wherein I did allow Your conditions to test Job most severely to see if he would remain true? And did not he remain steadfast unto Me?"

Nodding, Satan mused for a while. "Aye, שהוה, all did keep their faith. You tested the prophets and You tested the kings. Too, You tested the masses with fire and flood and plagues and bondage. And they all kept their faith. And, yes, You even let Me define the test for Job, and though he cried out in dire anguish, still he remained true.

"But were these genuine testings? I think not! For these were tests mainly of Your own devisings, and I cannot but suspect that those were less than could be, for, שהוה, they were tests that would have no chance of failing, for You intervened. Did You not stop the hand of Abraham? Did You not part the waters, and then cause them to fall upon the Pharaoh? You answered Sarah's call, and Samson's, Noah's and Jonah's and Joshua's. You answered all.

"And as to my devisings for the trials of Job, even there You put restrictions upon Me.

"Has there ever been a test in which You did not intercede? And if not, then how could Your Chosen People ever not succeed? And given that You always intercede, is it any wonder that they keep the faith?"

Satan turned His yellow cat-eyes upon שהוה and awaited an answer.

"No matter the test, they would succeed," declared שהוה confidently.

"Then let Me devise a test, שהוה, an unrestricted test, and We shall see . . . We shall truly see."

And so again a pact was made, there upon The Mountain, and Satan came down unto the world and caused the birth of a child . . . a child without a soul.

The year was 1889.

The place was Austria. . . .

*   *   *

And when in the bunker the child slew himself at last
and the holocaust ended, again Satan and שהוה sat atop The
Mountain. And still the debate raged . . . as it now had for
nearly six thousand years, since October 23, 4004 B.C. to be
exact, give or take seven days.

And Satan turned His face unto שהוה, His yellow cat-
eyes glowing. "I would ask You a question, שהוה. When
Your People were spat upon and reviled, when all was
taken from them and they were ripped from their homes,
when they were herded like cattle into rail cars, when husband was rent from wife and parent from child and brother
from sister and driven into the death camps, when they
were shorn and raped and tortured and experimented upon
and starved and shot and gassed and garroted and the living
were buried with the dead, when they asked for succor You
gave them none. By no sign did You let them know that
they were the Chosen Ones, even though they were dying
at the behest of a fiend, even though they were crying out
for mercy, even though men and women and children and
babies fell victim to this slaughter, to this most monstrous
of evils. When Your people wept and asked for Your divine
aid, You did nothing, *nothing,* absolutely nothing, though
You heard their cries and watched it all.

"And now, שהוה, I ask You this: of the two of Us, which
is truly the Devil?"

Silence reigned long, there upon The Mountain, and still
no answer came. And Satan stood at last and walked slowly
down the slopes, His test done.

The Passenger

by Julie E. Czerneda

It was a pilgrimage and he was its goal.

This understanding had taken years, had the passenger the means or desire to measure them; decades to be convinced of any purpose beyond curiosity to the parade outside his walls. In the first months, he had cowered behind the furnishings, terrified almost to insanity by the ceaseless, silent, mass of flesh quivering against one side of his prison.

At any moment, he could slide his eyes that way and make out a hundred bodies, hung with broad-tipped tentacles, moving with a boneless grace as if the atmosphere outside his prison were liquid. It could have been, for all he knew.

A hundred bodies: They could be the same as the hundred before or different. He still couldn't tell any of them apart. Were only those of the same size and shape allowed to see him? They wore and carried nothing. He was fond of the notion that there was some religious or cultural more that said they should come before him as he was, for they had never provided him clothing.

Other things, yes. Every few days, or weeks, or months, a panel on the far wall from his bed would glow. He'd learned to set his fingers properly in the seven slots beside the panel to trigger it to slide open. Behind the panel would be a box.

He would open it, of course, despite what he'd come to expect of its contents. At first, the sight of charred and melted wood and plastic, stained with blood, had provoked him to rage. He had cursed his captors, spat at the transparency keeping him from them, them from him, tried with ingenuity to kill himself with whatever sad relic or trophy they'd provided. They had never reacted, beyond simply causing him to slip into unconsciousness while they repaired what damage he'd managed to inflict on himself.

Eventually, he'd stopped. What was the point? The pilgrimage of watchers never ended. The boxes with their pitiful cargo continued to come. He began to sort their contents carefully. When he slept, anything he hadn't touched or handled would be removed from his prison. He made sure to touch it all. When a new box was due, anything he had left on the floor would also disappear like a dream, so he began to sort out what mattered to him.

There was nothing useful. Bits of fabric—never enough for clothing, even when he tried to hoard some. The smell of burned flesh usually clung to it. Metal and plastic, usually bent or damaged beyond recognition. Once in a while, a package that seemed intact. Another passenger's personal possessions, he assumed, better protected than other things.

While these were the most distressing gifts from his captors, he treated them with care. The opaque walls of his prison were uneven, with plentiful ledges. He filled these with trinkets from the dead. He slept watched over by the images of other men's mothers and wives, and spent hours contemplating the fates of children whose faces were not reflections of his own.

If he slid his eyes that way, to watch his watchers, he knew it would be the same sight as every other minute since he came to be here, but the thought brought the involuntary glance. Tentacles, overlapping either because they wanted to or there was no room to avoid touching, made the same corrugated pattern as always. Each body was topped with seven small red eyes, pupiled in black, rolling in unison to face him, to track him as their owner moved along from one side of the wall to the other.

He looked away. There had been a time when he tried to communicate or at least learn by watching the watchers. After that had been a time of anger and depression, of attempts at self-destruction when nothing in the room could be defaced—attempts that availed him only intimate memories of futility.

Then he had stopped caring. He had remained motionless, waiting to die. They wouldn't allow his body to fail. He would wake to find himself nourished, no matter how hard he resisted sleep. But he could allow his brain to die. And he tried.

And had almost succeeded. But that was when his captors, though they seemed incapable of communicating with him or understanding him, began giving him the boxes of belongings. Every item tore his heart; every one reconnected his humanity.

At last, one gave him a purpose to match the unknown one sending the aliens sliding past his prison day in, day out. It was a child's box of markers. He held them against his cheek when he found them, breathing in a faint scent of corruption as well as the clean promise of color. He cried for the child who had lost them, then, with painful care—he'd never been an artist—used the markers to draw a stick-figure child on the floor.

He expected the vivid lines to be gone when he awoke, fingers cramped around the markers. But his captors had left them. So he added a dog, a ball, a tree, a house, a rabbit, a book! The markers failed him, dry halfway through the shining red of a bicycle. He flung them away, and cried, turning his back to the wall of watchers.

Sleeping, he dreamed for the first time in years of home, a dream that for once didn't spiral into the nightmare of chase, burning, struggle, and capture, a dream that gave him up peacefully to reality.

There he found that his captors had left him something of their own. On the floor was seven-sided sheet of white. There was a tray containing greasy sticks, each about the length of his hand, in a variety of colors. They were awkward to hold, but he grabbed them eagerly and waved them happily at his watchers as if they'd respond. Or as if he'd recognize a response if they did.

Another hundred beings slid past. It took each exactly fifteen heartbeats to glide from one end of his wall to the other. Always.

Sixty-three years had passed since. He knew precisely, because that sheet of white had marked the beginning of his purpose. There were a few years lost in the beforetime. Ten years ago, the sad packages from other passengers had stopped appearing behind the panel. It didn't matter. He no longer remembered his age when he arrived in this place, but he could rely on nature ending his imprisonment in the not-too-distant future, regardless of the devoted attention of his captors.

He surveyed this day's work. The colors were subtle, layered in explanations of light and shadow, refinements he'd begun several pieces ago. The centerpiece, a bridge, swept upward, its luminous archways of stone almost hanging in air. The Legion marching across moved in trained synchrony, save for the eyes of one man looking out as if wary of surprise attack. There were storm clouds on the horizon, and dewdrops on the moss in the foreground.

There were probably errors throughout the scene, he worried, as he always did. But the errors were irrelevant; he'd done his best. This one was ready to go. He rolled it up, the motion inflaming the soreness in his joints, and leaned it against the panel. Like all the others, it would be gone when he awoke.

Boneless grace studded with eyes; could any even see the colors he intended?

He'd learned his art. It was, after all, a way to communicate, and he'd hoped until hope died this medium would be the breakthrough allowing him to reach the intelligence that held him here, that marched in unending ranks just to look at him. But there had been no response beyond the disappearance of finished works, those he rolled up and placed near the panel. He didn't bother wondering anymore if they valued his art or washed off his colors to return the paper to him in some frenzied economy. It was enough he completed each image.

It took three sets of hands to open the roll safely. When it was spread on the seven-sided table specially built for this purpose, they ever-so-gently slid the holding bars over each edge, each bar locking in place with a light snick of contact. Only then did they release their careful grip.

The lights around the table dimmed, isolating the brightness glowing down on colors and shapes. The encircling six didn't speak for a long moment, their faces lost in shadows, their thoughts in reverence. They were a close group, drawn together years before by common interests and goals, held together by a responsibility none could escape. These rooms, the automated equipment, and, most importantly, the wonderful artwork such as the latest supine before them, had been their discovery.

"The Romans," said Dr. Susan Crawley softly, drawing

in a slow breath around the unfamiliar word. "I've read about them. Earth, early thirteenth century, I think. They were conquerors, builders . . . definitely preindustrial."

"Well, this proves what I have been saying all these years," Dr. Tom Letner's voice held its customary fine and precise diction in the dark, as if those lips never slurred into shipslang after a few beers. "He must have been an historian."

Someone keyed the room lights to full brightness again. Bedlam erupted as others vehemently countered the physicist's assertion. The loudest voice belonged to Lt. Tony Shrib. "All it proves is He was well-read. Susan here is an engineer, for star's sake, and she knows about these Remans."

"Romans," Susan corrected under her breath. She ignored the continuing, well-worn arguments. What was new lay before her. Her eyes moved hungrily over the scene on the table, feasting on its complexity; she admired the stonework of the bridge, the odd moisture on a plant whose name she would have to look up in a text. All were images strange and exotic to the shipborn. Of those party to the secret of this art, only Master Electrician Huong Trang could claim to have set foot on the planet glorified by the Artist, and Huong stubbornly refused to discuss what he remembered, as if the memories were sweeter for the hoarding.

Typically, it was Huong who interrupted her pleasure. "My friends," he said in his gentle, clear voice—the voice that had reproached them so many times before. "My colleagues. Is it not time?"

The good-natured bickering faltered and stopped. The others, all officers or senior scientists, found good reasons to look anywhere but at Huong's stern face. He recaptured their attention by placing one blunt-fingered hand firmly on the surface of the art.

Dr. Natalie Emil, a trim woman in her late forties whose love for the art was matched only by her love for her patients in the ship's hospital—and truth be told, for her mother's legacy of Earth chocolate—cried out, "Careful!"

The sacrilegious hand stayed where it was. "Is it not time?" Huong insisted, looking from one to the other in turn. "Has He not suffered long enough?"

The ship's senior psychologist, Dr. Wayne Simmons, shook his mane of heavy gray hair, his eyes troubled behind their thick lenses. "We don't dare release Him from the sim program. You know that, Huong. We can't predict what the effect on His mind would be. We don't have the facilities on this ship to ensure His recovery."

Huong lifted his hand, prompting at least one sigh of relief, then waved it eloquently over the artwork imprisoned on the table. "And we don't want this to stop, do we."

Susan felt the blood draining from her face. She didn't need to glance at her colleagues to know they, too, would be showing signs of shock. How dare Huong accuse them of—of what?

"We cherish the Artist's work," she said involuntarily. "How is that wrong? Despite His weakness, He's valued by all of us." Susan looked pleadingly at her peers, was strengthened by Natalie's nod of support, by Tony's smile. "You've seen for yourself how our shipmates flock to the Gallery to see His images of our heritage. We've arranged school tours. We let anyone order a reproduction for their quarters. We—"

"We imprison Him in His dream of Earth. We ensure He continues to produce what we crave," Huong said heavily. "And we wait for Him to die and release us from our conscience."

"No! How dare you—" Wayne's hand touched hers briefly. Susan calmed herself but refused to back down.

"You've never been comfortable with our decision, Huong. I understand your feelings about it—"

"I don't think you do. I don't think any of you really do." The Master Electrician walked to the side of the room they usually avoided. He activated the sole control on its surface, turning the blank surface into a one-way view of a room, larger than most of the quarters on the colony ship *Pilgrim III.* The room's sole occupant squatted naked and *old* on the floor, colors in those marvelous hands poised to coax shape and texture from the empty page.

Just as the Artist had done each and every day since they had discovered His existence. Almost ten years ago, yet Susan remembered it as if it had been yesterday. They'd searched for the release catches, frantic to rescue the imprisoned stranger, only to be stopped by Wayne and Natalie, their medical experts. It was obviously a sim chamber, like enough to the hundreds on the *Pilgrim III* to be recognizable, if far more elaborate. The planetborn visited the sims regularly, having come on-ship with their private recorded scenes from the verdant world left behind ready to comfort them when the shipworld became too strange to bear.

The shipborn entered the chambers as part of their schooling, a refresher course built from open skies, scented winds, and uneven ground. It was a matter of pride to avoid them as adults, to prefer acclimation to the Ship, though all recognized the coming generations would need the sims and more to prepare for their new home.

But no one lingered in the sims more than a day at a time. Only those who could accept leaving Earth had boarded the Ship; to admit otherwise was to unsettle one's own sanity and disturb those around you. And there was work to be done, the carefully planned busyness designed to occupy minds tempted to hold on to the past. Survival for all meant looking to the future, not dwelling on what was now forever beyond their reach.

The sim chamber hosting the Artist was quite different from those offering education or a harmless moment of blue-skyed nostalgia. It was capable of full life support even if the Ship failed, of remote functions better suited to quarantine facilities. That had been one of their early fears: that He had been a carrier of some disease perilous to the Ship. They'd used the remotes to run tests as He lay unconscious, until they were sure He was nothing more dangerous than a puzzle.

There were recording devices, notes left behind in this secret place. Those had been studied, too, though all they offered was a seemingly endless list of bodily functions, chilling evidence the Artist had indeed been in this chamber every minute since launch.

As vividly, Susan remembered the morning when they'd met, here, to listen with horror as Wayne presented their conclusion: They must do nothing to disturb the Artist within His sim chamber with its automated, if bizarre, treatment. He and Natalie had been utterly convinced and so convincing: releasing the Artist from his dreams of Earth, replacing them with the here and now of the Ship after all this time, would only shatter whatever reality His mind still recognized.

And, unsaid but understood, it would very likely stop His Art.

So they resigned themselves to being His keepers, to hiding the dark secret within the bowels of the Ship, and to sharing the Art with as many as possible. Huong wasn't the only one to have nightmares since. How dare he set himself as their conscience!

Huong's small eyes glittered at Susan, as though he heard her thoughts, or as though he were close to tears. His emotions were becoming embarrassingly public as he aged, perhaps a consequence of outliving most who had walked onto the Ship with him. "I've found out where He came from," he said calmly enough. "I know the truth."

"What?" Tony, the ship's senior stellar cartographer, ran one hand over his close-cropped hair, then down over his face as if to smooth away an expression he'd rather not share. "How? Where?" Susan understood his dismay. Tony had taken the greatest risk of them all, using his clearance and knowledge to search the Ship's records for any clue as to the origin of the Artist on the Ship. He'd found nothing: nothing to explain how the ship's senior psychologist, Dr. Randall Clarke, had been able to requisition then hide the construction of this chamber at the edge of livable gravity inside the immense core of *Pilgrim III*. Nothing to identify the Artist, even when they'd taken advantage of the automatics and obtained DNA samples from His unconscious body.

Nothing to challenge their assumption that the Artist suffered from some delusional state, some flaw Dr. Clarke had been treating him for in this private, hidden place, some condition too severe to allow exposure to the Ship's environment or company.

"Our past is recorded in places other than the Ship's systems, Mr. Bridge Officer," Huong said with deliberate irony.

"Tell us what you've learned," Wayne ordered impatiently.

Huong spoke slowly, methodically, as if to impress each word on them all. "Did Randall mention his wife to any of you?"

They didn't look at Susan, but she felt their focus on her. Everyone knew she and Randall had been lovers until his death. "Is this relevant?" she asked coldly.

"Very."

"Then, no. I didn't know he had ever married."

"Oh yes. In fact, Randall was supposed to board with his wife. Yet Tony's checked the manifest; Ship's records clearly show Randall arriving alone."

"Where did you find this information?" Tom demanded. He'd found the datacube giving directions to this place in Randall's cabin safe—otherwise they might never have discovered it. Sometimes the thought made Susan weak. The beauty and richness of the Artist's work, languishing as dust-covered rolls on the floor where the automatics dumped them. No classes of schoolchildren seeing His work, awed by their own past made manifest. They'd have reached orbit around New Earth 17, moved to the surface, and started their new lives all unaware, while the great seed ship reconstructed itself as an orbital platform, its automatics sweeping up and recycling the dead organics of the Artist and His Art. She shivered.

Their attention was distracted by the Artist as he stretched then scratched one wrinkled buttock absently before settling back to his labors.

"Corridor sale."

Susan blinked, trying to imagine staid, conservative Huong visiting one of the hundreds of junk sales that went on throughout the colonists' section of the ship. They weren't particularly legal, but the Captains had long ago relented, second-gen officers tending to be more practical than those raised and trained Earthside. Besides being a useful diversion for the colonists, the sales redistributed personal goods no longer obtainable from their source.

"I picked up a collection of gossip mags in the last one." Huong paused patiently as Natalie laughed. "It was worth it. I found our late psychologist—and his wife."

"In a gossip mag?" Susan said with disbelief.

"The wife, Charlette d'Ord, was an athlete turned sports broadcaster. A bit of a celebrity in her way. I found several images of them together—the captions refer to Randall only as her husband, but you can see him plainly enough. Here." Huong drew a datacube out of his pocket and tossed it to Susan.

Numbly, she walked over to the nearest reader panel and inserted the 'cube. The rectangular screen produced an image of a group of people at some public event. Randall's thin face with its surprisingly sensual lips was easy enough to recognize despite the passage of years. He had one arm possessively around the shoulders of an incredibly beautiful woman. Susan smoothed the skirt over her ample hips before she could resist the impulse.

"I know that face," Natalie breathed.

So would anyone on the Ship, Susan thought. Those classic features and warm smile were straight from the Artist's most popular work. Almost every cabin had its copy of the angelic figure hovering, arms spread to shield the Earth from the dark of space, the serene loveliness of the perfect yet so-human face a comfort to folk all too aware they were separated from vacuum by only a hull and skills both a generation stale.

"Pull up the faces behind them," Huong ordered, as if this revelation wasn't enough.

Susan did so, watching with the others as three faces from the background became clearer. The centermost, a young man, was plainly not paying attention to the photographer or event. His dark, *familiar,* eyes were fixed on Charlette. Susan turned off the image, inexplicably frightened by the longing captured in that one look.

Huong didn't object, trapping them instead with his slow voice. "Charlette died in a car accident six months before *Pilgrim III* began final assembly. The accident took place over one hundred miles from their home. The car contained her luggage and there was an unconfirmed witness report that someone else had been driving the car. Randall was apparently questioned by police, then released. After all, he was going offworld for the rest of his life. What point in pursuing an investigation?"

Wayne moved closer to the viewscreen covering the opposite wall, his face shadowed and grim as he stared at the Artist. Susan wanted to refuse his vision, to see a patient under sophisticated care, not a victim. Her lips moved numbly: "You're saying the Artist is that young man in the image. You're accusing Randall of murdering his wife and somehow arranging to kidnap and imprison her lover, bringing him on the Ship."

"Randall was on the planning team," Natalie said reluctantly. "He had the access and opportunity to make modifications."

"Why?" Susan breathed. "Why—like this?"

Huong answered. "We can guess. Revenge. Randall could be ruthless. We all knew that about him." No one disagreed. *Pilgrim III* was immense, as colony ships had to be. It would be their children's children who reached humanity's latest new frontier. In the meantime, the Ship was a world unto itself: shelter, workplace, and space for growth. Yet her thousands of inhabitants existed within smaller, insular communities, communities that had to get along or fail to function. The scientific community was one, and Randall had not endeared himself to many in it. Susan was the first to admit that her social standing with her peers had improved after her lover had choked to death on his favorite synthetic sweetmeat.

"Now you know what I believe. The Artist is no madman, cared for in an automated sim to calm his delusions and keep him functioning. He is—or was—as sane as any of us before being tortured by our colleague, a man who perverted his knowledge to harm, not heal. The Artist does not belong in this travesty of a life. And so we agree," Huong said, swiveling to look at each of them, his hand rising slowly as if to lift some curtain. "It is time."

Wayne shook his head, an identical gesture to his first response to Huong's plea, and Susan felt her heart starting to pound for no reason she cared to admit. "No," Wayne replied. "We can't."

"Why?" Huong's eyes blazed. He raised his fists in the air. "In the name of justice! Why not? Don't you believe me?"

Susan answered when no one else spoke. "It doesn't matter. The Artist lives in His own World, at peace. You know that, Huong. And if we free Him now, so close to His end, what are we offering Him in return? Your theory that all He has suffered was to satisfy one man's desire for revenge? That whatever purpose He found to sustain Himself has been a lie?" She paused for emphasis. "That His very world is gone?"

Huong's face was deathly pale. "What do you care about Him?" His finger stabbed the air, first at Natalie, then at Wayne. "You'd keep Him locked away just to hide your mistakes"—his finger stabbed at Tom—"you, for an excuse to break the rules"—then at Tony—"you're terrified of the Captains' judgment. And you." Susan stared at the now-shaking fingertip targeting her. "You want to keep your lover's legacy for yourself, don't you? I know you believe His Art belongs to you."

"Rant all you want, Huong," Natalie countered, her voice a shade too calm. "Whatever you think are our reasons, you've missed the most important one of all: our shipmates. They believe the Art they love is the secret work of someone among us, someone keeping our heritage alive in a way no datacube can. Do you wish to tarnish their feelings for His work, turn His accomplishments into this sordid melodrama? We must not consider this one individual above the good of the Ship."

There was a murmur of agreement; Susan sensed their resolve hardening. So did Huong. "At what cost?" he asked, his passion drained away at last, replaced by disgust. "At what cost," he repeated.

Susan found nothing to say. Huong turned and left the room, his feet dragging with each step.

"Will he go to the Captains?" Tony asked.

It wasn't a meaningless concern. They'd used their privileged ranks to hide what they'd found, to produce the Art as if by some miracle. If Huong told now, they would all become suspect. At the very least, they would lose control of their departments to underlings and have their work scrutinized for the remainder of their lives. In many ways, *Pilgrim III* was not a large ship at all.

"No," Wayne said, going over to gaze down at the image of the Legion captured in time. One Legionnaire looked back at him, as if seeking an unknown enemy. "Huong protests. He goads us to do what he believes is right. But he also knows we have no choice. The Artist will live a year more at best; perhaps only months. Whatever fantasy fills His mind, whatever beloved view of home comforts Him, let Him keep it. Let Him finish His work. When He is gone—then it will be time to tell His story." Wayne sighed. "At least, as much of His story as we choose to tell.

"Thanks to Him, humanity will not forget its past."

There was a blank seven-sided canvas ready underneath. He sat on one corner of it, half his mind already planning, the other half gently engaged watching his watchers sliding past, tentacle upon tentacle, eyes rolling from side to side.

He believed he understood now. Both their purpose, and his.

He picked up an alien crayon, nodded a proud acknowledgment to the race that forced its guilty millions to parade in shame before him, and prepared to record another piece of human history. As long as he lived, Humanity would not be forgotten.

For like that precious bird, kept until death in a glass cage for all to see, wasn't he the last passenger of Earth?

Dennis L. McKiernan

Praise for the *HÈL'S CRUCIBLE* Duology:
"Provocative...appeals to lovers of classic fantasy—the audience for David Eddings and Terry Brooks."—*Booklist*

"Once McKiernan's got you, he never lets you go."
—Jennifer Roberson

"Some of the finest imaginative action...there are no lulls in McKiernan's story."—*Columbus Dispatch*

Book One of the *Hèl's Crucible* Duology
INTO THE FORGE
❑ 0-451-45700-5/$6.99

Book Two of the *Hèl's Crucible* Duology
INTO THE FIRE
❑ 0-451-45732-3/$6.99

<u>Coming Next Month From Roc</u>

S. M. Stirling

On the Oceans of Eternity

Jim Butcher

Storm Front

Book One of the Dresden Files